A VERY PUBLIC SCANDAL

JENNIFER BACIA

ISBN 9781925995541
Published in Australia and New Zealand by
Booktopia Editions, an imprint of Booktopia Group Ltd
Unit E1, 3-29 Birnie Avenue, Lidcombe, NSW 2141, Australia

Printed and bound in Australia by Ligare

The paper this book is printed on is in accordance with the standards of the Forest Stewardship Council®. The FSC® promotes environmentally responsible, socially beneficial and economically viable management of the world's forests.

booktopia.com.au

PRAISE FOR JENNIFER BACIA

"Superbly crafted thrillers ... compelling suspense."

— THE SUNDAY TIMES

"A novelist to rival Sheldon"

— COSMOPOLITAN MAGAZINE

"Jennifer Bacia's thrillers are irresistible. She hooks her readers from the very first page and the twists and turns just keep coming."

— ROMANCE WRITERS MAGAZINE

"Bacia is especially good at the simple but deadly emotional arithmetic of contemporary relationships."

— THE AUSTRALIAN

"Jennifer Bacia's success helped lay the foundation of my very successful stable of popular fiction writers."

— SELWA ANTHONY, AUSTRALIA'S LEADING POPULAR FICTION AGENT.

"Jennifer Bacia pioneered mass market fiction in Australia."

— MATT CONDON, PRIZE-WINNING AUTHOR AND JOURNALIST

In loving memory of my father,
Stanislaw Adam Bacia, who in so little time
gave me so much.

PROLOGUE

Harry Bowman didn't know his life was about to change.

As he made love that evening he was reminded yet again of his good fortune. The woman he held in his arms never failed to arouse him. Not even now as he stared down the barrel of his sixty-third birthday.

But the young woman he had married did more than arouse his lusts. She had brought him back to life.

That was the way Harry saw it anyway.

He knew there were plenty among his colleagues who had laughed behind his back when they found out he'd asked Margaret to marry him. That was almost two years ago and she'd just turned thirty-two.

Jealous of course. Because he'd managed to land himself a young beauty. But then he hadn't let himself go like the rest of them. He was too vain for that. Even in the city he'd swum daily, played tennis at his club and kept himself fit. He was proud too of his head of thick, if greying, hair.

But more than twenty years at the Bar hadn't left Harry Bowman with too many illusions. As one of the country's leading criminal lawyers, his fees matched his legendary reputation and he was now a very rich man.

He'd felt certain that in all probability it was his wealth rather than his acclaim or his sharp and seasoned mind that had encouraged the slim, curly-haired brunette now moaning into his ear to accept his proposal.

But he'd been a pragmatist - and a widower - too long to worry overly about that. He loved showing off his young pretty wife, loved having someone to spoil and indulge, and if his happiness lasted just a short while, well he would accept it on those terms.

It had taken a heart attack six months ago to convince the high-flying lawyer that he had married a woman who genuinely loved him.

With compassion and patience Margaret had nursed him back to health. And then it was she who had insisted they get out of the city, away from the rat race he'd endured for so long.

'Let's be totally unoriginal, darling,' she'd said one night when they were discussing the future. 'Let's head for the sunshine and minimum stress. What do you say?'

She was stroking his scrotum during their first sexual exchange since his attack and Harry felt filled with the heat of passion and conviction.

The transition had been unbelievably easy. Within weeks they were ensconced in a double-story beachside mansion decorated in the colors of the sea and sky and Harry felt as if God had shown him the path to heaven.

Life was as good as it was ever going to get, he thought now, as he dug his fingers into his wife's grinding buttocks: Margaret, the house, the environment, and just the odd interesting case to keep his brain ticking over.

He could feel his climax approaching. His wife's quivering breathing told him she was right there with him. An experienced lover, Harry knew better than to spoil her intense concentration with too frenzied movements. Together, slowly, they climbed the path to dark unconscious bliss.

And then the abruptness of the interruption killed it for both of them. Margaret slumped back from his embrace and swore ferociously under her breath.

'What the hell...' Harry glanced at the bedside alarm as his phone shrilled in the darkness. Five after ten. When he'd been at the peak of his profession late calls invariably meant trouble.

'Shall I answer it?' His wife's voice revealed her annoyance.

'No, leave it to the machine.' Harry felt his erection die. 'Probably a wrong damn number.'

But Harry Bowman was mistaken. As the answering machine clicked on he heard a voice he recognized and a message that brought him instantly alert.

Beside him his wife held her breath and listened too.

'... it's urgent, Harry. You're the only one I can trust. They're charging her with murder.'

With a rush of the old familiar adrenalin Harry Bowman knew it was going to be a long night.

* * *

THE COUNTRY WOKE to the scandal the following morning. The story was headline news. Shock and disbelief were the almost universal reactions.

Eve Taylor.

A devastating combination of brains and beauty. At thirty-three, the country's top-ranking media personality.

A woman who had interviewed presidents and kings, whose ruthless pursuit of the facts invoked fear among prime ministers and corporate fat cats alike. For three years her prime-time program, "Taylor Made", had operated at the nation's cutting edge, dominating the ratings as it broke a cascade of major stories.

And now, in an almost cannibalistic orgy, it was Eve Taylor herself who was being devoured by the media machine she had ruled over for so long.

Her fate, she knew, rested now in the hands of Harry Bowman. 'Try not to worry,' the grey-haired attorney had said quietly when he'd faced her in the windowless detention room of the central city Police Station. 'Bail won't be a problem. It's all a matter of procedure from here.'

But with the lawyer gone, Eve for the first time felt her control begin to waver. Fiercely she bit back her tears. She had tried so hard and in the end she had failed. It was as if history was determined to repeat itself.

* * *

THE SMALL WOODEN cottage was hidden at the end of a long overgrown drive. Fresh, cool air and lush vegetation made the Blue Mountains a popular tourist spot yet residents well-enough off could still buy themselves tranquility and privacy.

In the fragrant shady garden two elderly women sat in what could have passed for companionable silence.

Janet Byrne placed her empty tea cup on the tray beside her. Her arthritic hands were unsteady as she tried to come to terms with the shock of the morning's headlines. The newspaper was now stored safely out of sight despite the fact that not once in their recent years together had the woman she cared for shown any interest in the printed word.

Indeed, Marianne Rolfe showed interest in very little. Incapable of speech, she spent each long day in silent contemplation, her hands occasionally kept busy with the needlework that draped her lap.

In an agony of despair Janet Byrne glanced at the frail grey-haired woman beside her. Marianne Rolfe was in her late sixties but youthful beauty could still be traced in the fine bones and contours of her face.

Despite the years that had passed, Janet had never forgotten her own breathless reaction at first sight of that stunning perfection. But beauty had not saved Marianne Rolfe from tragedy and now the same curse had extended to the next generation. And unlike the scandal of thirty-odd years ago, this time there was nothing Janet could do...

The older woman's heart squeezed in pain. She could only pray that the horror that had overtaken Maryanne's daughter would be forever beyond her comprehension.

But then, she thought pityingly, who knew what went on behind that endless brooding silence.

1

PARIS 1948

There was an expectant hush in the room. Five people surrounded the hospital bed: the surgeon who had carried out the operation, three of his colleagues, and the woman who had made it all possible.

The patient was a girl of about seventeen, slim and fair haired. She looked confused and vulnerable, as if unsure as to why she was the object of such attention.

'You've been very brave, Marianne.' It was the woman who spoke. She was handsome, big boned, in her early thirties. Mamie Howard spoke perfect French but she could never be mistaken for a Frenchwoman. Even apart from her lumpish lack of style there was something about her that was quintessentially English.

Now her dark eyes glowed with intensity as she addressed the girl in the bed. 'The operations have been a success, my dear.' She spoke slowly, watching carefully to see if the girl understood. It was always difficult to know.

'It's been almost two weeks now since the bandages were removed. There will still be a few bruises, a little puffiness, you understand, but I think you will not be displeased.'

One of the medical assistants couldn't suppress a chuckle. The

English and their talent for understatement. His colleagues caught his eye and seemed to share his amusement.

Doctor Pierre Martell, the internationally renowned plastic surgeon, was more reserved as he studied his handiwork. He remembered his first view of the patient. He had truly wondered then just what might be possible.

But the Englishwoman had pleaded with him. 'She is so young, doctor. As long as you can do enough to stop the stares and ugly comments.'

Pierre Martell refused to give false hope. But on closer clinical examination he saw that the bone structure was intact. That was something. Then, as operation followed operation, he could see he was going to achieve much greater success than his initial prognosis had indicated.

Now, as the Englishwoman raised an enquiring eyebrow at him across the bed, Doctor Pierre Martell gave a silent satisfied nod. Yes, he decided, he had excelled himself here. The girl would have every reason to be delighted.

'Are you ready, Marianne?' Barely able to contain her excitement, Mamie Howard asked the question without any expectation of a reply. The girl in the bed never spoke. The trauma, of course. Such a tragedy. But now, at least, the tragedy was lessened...

Mamie opened her voluminous handbag and removed a tortoiseshell hand mirror. Eyes shining in anticipation, she passed it to the young patient.

Slowly the girl in the bed raised the mirror to her face. Her breath caught; her blue eyes widened in disbelief as she absorbed the perfection of the surgeon's art.

The face was an oval of ideal proportion, the nose slim and straight, the jawline and cheekbones once more sharply defined, the skin as fresh and perfect as a newborn baby's. Mesmerized, Marianne Walenksa stared at the reflection.

She was... achingly beautiful. A triumph of art and medicine.

'C'est perfection, mademoiselle. Un miracle, n' est pas?'

It was the irrepressible assistant who broke the spell. Tears of emotion filled his eyes.

And then the second miracle occurred.

Marianne Walenksa found her voice. The voice she hadn't used for over three years.

She screamed.

She howled.

She shrieked out a stream of foul curses, each worse than the one before. And with the terrible force of her anger she hurled the mirror across the room. Shards of glass sprayed over the dumbstruck onlookers as it shattered against the wall.

'You've made me beautiful!' she screamed in wild-eyed fury. *'I will never forgive you! May you all burn in hell forever!'*

* * *

An icy rain was falling the day they returned to England. The girl sat in the First Class carriage, her face turned towards the window, avoiding the eyes of the other occupants. Her fury was no longer evident but it hadn't diminished.

They lied to me, she raged inwardly.

As soon as she'd finished growing they could operate, they'd told her. Merely give her features some semblance of 'normality'. It was for that reason she had endured the pain.

But they had betrayed her.

* * *

MAMIE HOWARD KNEW she had to do something. And soon.

It was three months since their return to England and the girl was barely eating, hated to leave the house, and spent most of her time alone in her room. She spoke, but chiefly in monosyllables. Mamie was worried sick.

James Howard was worried too, but more about the effect the

situation was having on his wife. He loved Mamie dearly. Now that the war was over he wanted their lives to get back to normal. He to his law practice in Oxford, Mamie to her cooking and gardening and books.

But Mamie Howard had seen too much as a Red Cross nurse to be the woman her husband expected to find when he finally received the official discharge from his regiment. For Mamie had been there during the final days in Berlin, had witnessed the liberation of the hells of Dachau and Auschwitz. These were sights she would never forget. Sights that made her sick with guilt at the idea of returning to the ordered existence of her elegant country home with its historic past and expensive antiques, its rambling roses and overgrown orchard.

That was part of the reason she had brought the young Polish girl back to England with her. To try to do something, no matter how small, to atone, to make up for all she was lucky enough to still have while others continued to suffer.

'James, I've got to do something about Marianne.' Mamie spoke her thoughts aloud as they sat on either side of the open fireplace. It was a cold evening, the nip of winter already in the air.

James Howard lowered his newspaper and took in the anxious lines on his wife's face. Her obvious distress made him answer curtly. 'You've done enough, Mamie. Three years the girl's been with us. You've fed her, clothed her, taught her, nursed her. Arranged and paid for the operations. And what've you got in return? Neither gratitude nor warmth.'

His face was stern. 'If *you* haven't had enough, I certainly have. She's not worth it, Mamie. It's playing havoc with our own lives.'

To his surprise his wife nodded in agreement. 'You're right, darling. I thought love and support would be enough. But they're not. Not after what she's been through.' Mamie Howard's face darkened. She remembered piecing together the girl's story. How she had come to have those terrible facial injuries. Mamie knew she couldn't give up.

'I've decided what to do.'

Her husband looked at her enquiringly.

'I'm going to take her to London. There's a top flight psychiatrist I've read about. Phillip Vaughan. He specializes in just this sort of post-war trauma. I'm going to make an appointment for Marianne to see him as soon as possible.'

James Howard saw the determination on his wife's face and knew there was no point in arguing. He murmured a reply and resumed his reading. The war had changed everything, he grumbled inwardly. Women didn't know their place any longer.

* * *

PHILLIP VAUGHAN'S suite of rooms was in the ubiquitous Harley Street. He was a busy man but Mamie Howard was a determined woman; she managed to wheedle an appointment for one morning two weeks later. Only achieving Marianne's cooperation was not quite so easy.

'I do not need to see this man! I have nothing to say to him, can you not understand!' The girl faced her benefactress in a fury of opposition.

It took more than a little gentle persuasion but at last Mamie succeeded. 'As a special favor for me, my dear. Please. I hate to see you suffering like this.'

Marianne turned away, her blue eyes dark with contempt. *Suffering*... How could this woman have any idea what suffering meant?

Somewhere in the dark frozen center of her heart Marianne Walenska knew that Mamie Howard was trying to help her. But the girl also knew the danger in letting others close. For closeness inevitably meant loss. And loss meant searing pain...

* * *

MAMIE WAS IMMEDIATELY IMPRESSED by the short, slight man with the intelligent grey eyes and calm efficient manner. He listened without interrupting as she explained why they were there.

'If only Marianne would speak about what happened, I'm sure it'd help, doctor. I thought I could do it alone, but I've realized she needs a professional. I'm sure with your help she'll be able to work this through.'

The psychiatrist shifted his gaze to the girl. She was dressed in an appalling shapeless dress and her fair hair hung lankly over her face. Almost, he thought with professional interest, as if she were deliberately trying to make herself as unattractive as possible. He noted too that in place of the usual awkwardness of a girl her age there was instead an almost unnatural control, a strangely defensive poise.

Only her darting evasive eyes gave her away. Behind the rigid mask of control festered an agitation it was Phillip Vaughan's task to lay to rest. He wondered what he would find at its root.

During the remainder of that first visit Mamie waited in the reception room flipping through pre-war magazines that did little to distract her.

Just a short informal chat to begin with, the doctor had explained. When, after twenty minutes, Marianne reappeared, Mamie was relieved to note no sign of distress. She likes him, she thought with relief. Phillip Vaughan was going to work the miracle she was praying for.

* * *

THAT SAME NIGHT Marianne Walenska jolted the Howard household awake with her screams of terror.

* * *

BUT SHE AGREED to go again. Yes, she would visit the doctor once more ... but only if she were permitted to go alone. With the train timetable she would manage easily, she assured Mamie.

Uneasy as she felt, the older woman finally gave in. After all, the girl had been to the doctor's suite once already and if she needed to ask directions her English was up to the task. Marianne Walenska had the Slavic gift for languages; as a schoolgirl before the war she had grown proficient in English, French and German.

By mid-afternoon Mamie's anxiety was laid to rest when the girl returned safely and, externally at least, quite calm. It would take time, the older woman told herself, but she was certain the therapy would achieve results.

The morning of her next appointment a week later, Marianne left the house in plenty of time to catch the London train. She refused Mamie's offer to drive her the short distance to the station. 'I will enjoy the walk today, Mrs Howard. But thank you for the offer.'

And to the older woman's surprised delight Marianne Walenska leaned forward and pecked her on the cheek. It was the first demonstration of affection Mamie had ever received from the girl she had dedicated herself to help and her heart swelled with hope. Everything was going to be all right. With Phillip Vaughan's help Marianne was going to get better. Mamie was quite certain of that now.

Eyes bright with expectant happiness she stood waving from the garden gate until the slight figure had disappeared from view.

* * *

MARIANNE ARRIVED at the main Oxford station with time to spare. The small overnight bag was in the left luggage section where she had left it two days previously.

As she purchased her ticket she felt her heart pound with a mixture of excitement and terror. But nothing was going to change her mind. On the journey she went over in her mind the steps she had worked out for herself. Firstly a rented room, then a job. Luckily she had become quite a proficient typist under Mamie Howard's instruction.

As the train drew into London just over an hour later, Marianne fought back a moment of panic. She was alone and close to penniless in a city where she knew no one. It was a frightening thought.

But not as frightening as being forced to confront the past.

* * *

IT WAS a month before Mamie Howard would admit defeat. She spent hours tramping the streets of London but in a city still overflowing with stateless victims of the war, neither her efforts, nor those of the police had found any clue to the whereabouts of the young Polish girl Mamie had tried so hard to help.

'Let it go, darling. You've done everything possible.' James Howard did his best to comfort his distressed wife. 'The girl had problems no one could do anything about. You can't blame yourself.'

But Mamie could find little solace in her husband's words. 'If only I knew she was all right,' she answered, her voice tight with strain. 'That's all.'

There was nothing James Howard could say to that.

2

She was safe. After almost four months she felt sure of that. They wouldn't find her now.

Everything had worked out even easier than Marianne had hoped. She'd found herself a cheap room in a lodging house in Lancaster Gate. It was cramped, and the shared bathroom none too clean, but at least she was free of smothering goodwill and doctors who were going to "cure" her.

She had been lucky with the job, too. As secretary to the manager of the Lancaster Regent Hotel she worked in the centrally heated surroundings of a first-class establishment. Shut away in her office it was easy enough to avoid any curious questions from other members of the staff.

On the whole Marianne was content with her lot. She was happy to settle for warmth, food, a roof over her head. Routine brought her a feeling of security. She enjoyed her work, and her leisure was spent exploring London's parks and landmarks or taking in the occasional film or concert as her budget allowed.

She gave no thought to the future. It was enough to have escaped confrontation with the nightmare of her past. Almost before she realized it a year had passed and nothing seemed likely to alter her routine.

And then Charles Rolfe came into her life.

* * *

THEY MET the evening she was working late shift. It was seven p.m. when the duty manager came looking for her.

'Miss Walenska?' He gave a perfunctory tap at the office door.

'Yes.' Unsmiling, Marianne looked up from her work.

The duty manager, a pale, whippet-thin man in his late thirties, wondered as always why the girl seemed so uninterested in her appearance. Not a scrap of makeup enhanced her features, while the heavy curtain of fair hair lacked any attempt at style. Even the dark hotel uniform seemed deliberately too large, as if to shroud her figure.

Yet for all that, he surmised, Marianne Walenska still had a natural appeal; all she needed was a little fashion sense and know-how to turn her into a real stunner. Not, he thought quickly, that any chap was likely to get past that freezing barricade. Hadn't he read somewhere that the Poles were supposed to be a passionate race? Well, not Miss Marianne Walenska. Cold as an Arctic breeze, that one.

'Got an Australian gentleman in room 343,' he said now, explaining the reason for the interruption. 'A Mr Charles Rolfe. Seems he's just had some urgent correspondence from a firm in Paris and can't understand a word. I told him you'd be able to help ... if you would be so kind.'

'Of course.' Marianne got to her feet. Her ability with languages was one of the reasons she had been offered the job. She followed the manager towards the elevator and they ascended to the third floor without further exchange.

* * *

CHARLES ROLFE WAS a man in his thirties, broad shouldered, with sandy hair and a sprinkle of freckles on his fair complexion. As he opened the door to his suite his agitation was obvious.

The manager made the introductions and said soothingly, I'm sure Miss Walenska will be able to help, Mr Rolfe.'

'You need something translated, sir?' The girl spoke English with a charming accent.

'Yes, yes. I'm organizing some business with the French. It's essential I have this correspondence translated with absolute accuracy as soon as possible. Can you do that for me, Miss... er...'

'Walenska,' Marianne supplied. She put out her hand. 'If I might see...'

'Of course.'

Quickly she skimmed the contents. 'There is no problem. It will take only a few minutes.'

Assured that all was under control, the duty manager excused himself while a relieved Charles Rolfe sat his rescuer at the small antique desk.

Five minutes later Marianne stood up and presented the Australian businessman with the written English translation he required.

Charles Rolfe read it through speedily. 'That's wonderful. This makes all the difference. Thank you so very, very much.'

He looked up, beaming his gratitude and for the first time noticed the girl's wonderful eyes. They were a deep stormy blue, almost violet, ringed with thick dark lashes. He wondered vaguely why she hid them under that unattractive heavy fringe.

'I am only doing my job, sir.' And with a curt goodnight Marianne Walenska left him alone.

* * *

CHARLES ROLFE WAS thirty-two and a member of one of Australia's oldest and wealthiest families. His great-grandfather, Patrick Rolfe, had arrived in the colony of New South Wales in 1811 with a few sovereigns in his pocket and an impulsive yearning for adventure.

His training as an architect soon made him an invaluable addition to the new colony. The recently appointed military governor, Lachlan Macquarie, had been appalled by his first view of the unplanned hotch-potch of hovels that was Sydney Town. He was determined to create a city in the Georgian style he most admired. Accordingly as soon as Patrick Rolfe's skills became known, the young adventurer found himself set the task of designing many of the new colony's important public buildings.

But Patrick Rolfe had other, equally desirable assets. Ruggedly attractive, charming, with a self-deprecating wit, the red-headed native of Lancashire soon found himself a regular guest at Government House. It was at dinner there one summer's evening three years after his arrival in the colony, that Patrick Rolfe was introduced to Bridget Sullivan, the niece of the governor's aide-de-camp.

When they married six months later, Patrick received a government grant of three thousand acres of land and the convict labor to work them. Within a short time, and taking his lead from that other successful businessman, John Macarthur, he had established the breeding stocks of merinos to supply the ever insatiable mills of his birthplace. By the time of his death at the age of sixty-three, Patrick Rolfe was able to pass on to his three sons one of the biggest landholdings in the country.

Over succeeding generations the Rolfe dynasty had made forays into other fields of business but the backbone of the family's wealth remained its fine merino wool. With the war at an end four years previously the textile mills of England, France and Italy were once more hungry for the quality raw material Australia produced in such quantity. It was to re-establish those business contacts that Charles Rolfe had come to Europe.

There was another reason, too. Charles had needed to prove to himself that he was well again, that after four years of almost continuous medical treatment he was fit enough to re-join the real world.

As a squadron leader in the RAAF Charles Rolfe had emerged unscathed from missions that had seen him awarded the DFC and DSO. But then, in the last twelve months of hostilities, his luck had run out. Flying a reconnaissance mission over northern New Guinea, he and his crew had been shot down by a Japanese carrier-borne fighter. Charles, the only survivor, was eventually picked up by an American flying boat patrol responding to his May Day call. Suffering appalling head and internal injuries, only immediate evacuation back to Australia had given him any chance at all.

In Sydney his mother Edwina had half a dozen leading specialists standing by to try to save the life of her elder son. But for three months his survival had hung in precarious balance. No sooner had one medical crisis been resolved than another developed, until even the doctors began to doubt the final outcome of their strenuous efforts.

But Edwina Rolfe refused to give in. In 1943 she had lost Charles's father to a premature and massive coronary. It made her all the more determined to save her son. Day after day she kept her vigil beside his hospital bed, her sharp eyes searching not only for some sign of a breakthrough but ensuring too that the nursing staff were well and truly kept on their toes.

'This is no ordinary patient, you know!' she was reported to have snapped at the sister in charge over some minor irritation. 'This is a Rolfe. We made this country what it is and I don't want you or anyone else who looks after my son to forget it!' Edwina Rolfe was eminently aware of her position in society.

It had taken a long time but at last there were clear signs that Charles was going to make it. Yet that was just the beginning. The rehabilitation had gone on for close to three years. Charles had had to re-learn to walk, to talk, to dance, to drive a car. It was a slow and painful process.

At the belated thirty-second birthday party his mother had thrown for him after his recovery, Charles looked to all outward appearances the same man who had left home to do his duty for his country. A little thinner perhaps, slightly more withdrawn, but essentially, it seemed, Charles Rolfe had survived the war intact.

Only his fiancée, Peggy Dennison, knew the truth.

A vivacious, dark-haired girl from a high-profile political family, Peggy had had to endure not only Charles's absence during the war but also the long frightening months of his slow recovery. Certain at last of his return to health she was unable to suppress any longer her own urgent needs.

Two weeks before the party she had taken him for a mid-week

drive to Palm Beach, the holiday resort of the well-to-do, north of Sydney. As they neared their destination he could sense her agitation.

'I've got the key to the house, Charles.'

The Dennisons, like the Rolfes, owned a large beach house on the Peninsula. Now, in late autumn, it was closed up for the coming winter.

'In this breeze it'll be nicer if we eat our picnic on the terrace than on the beach, don't you think?' There was a slight breathlessness in Peggy's voice as she turned to smile at her fiancé.

Charles knew then what was expected of him.

Less than a month after they had become engaged he and Peggy had made love for the first time. Her passion and lack of inhibition had come as a thrilling surprise. From then until he had joined his squadron they had made love wildly and often. Now her need for him was obvious.

* * *

PEGGY DENNISON's big blue eyes stared up in confused alarm as her fiancé threw back the covers and left her alone in the bed.

'Is … is it me, Charles? Have I …'

'No. No.' Shock made his answer sharper than he intended. His back to the room, he stood by the salt-smeared windows and looked down at the breakers below.

For a long moment he said nothing. Then he forced himself to turn towards the girl on the bed. In an uncharacteristic gesture she lay with the sheets tucked modestly around her chin.

'It's got nothing to do with you, Peg, I promise.' His tongue seemed to be sticking to the roof of his mouth. 'I ... I can't. I just can't. Don't ask me why.'

'Maybe... maybe it'll just take a little time, darling. You've been so ill...' The words were spoken with such soft understanding he felt like vomiting.

'I think we should go.' Charles snatched up his clothes. Suddenly his nakedness seemed to add to his vulnerability and shame.

* * *

EDWINA ROLFE WAS ABLAZE with precious gems. The fortunes of the Rolfe family were reflected in the diamonds and emeralds that adorned her ears, encircled her neck and her bony fingers. And for the first time since the war the harbor side mansion too was ablaze with lights and filled with guests.

With regal grace Edwina circulated among the country's elite, who had come to celebrate her son's birthday and return to health.

It's just like old times, she thought. *Almost as if the war had never been.* Then her dark eyes clouded momentarily. There were a few missing faces, of course. Including poor Douglas. The shock of her husband's premature death had left her dazed for months. Douglas, always so strong, so focused, so proud of his place as a Rolfe in the history of this country...

Edwina lifted her pointed chin a little higher. Well, she was matriarch now and the standards would be maintained. Nothing would ever be allowed to tarnish the Rolfe name. Her children had been raised to respect their heritage and they would never let her down.

And now, Charles's return to health meant they could all get on with their lives. Thank God, she thought that Hugh, her baby, had been too young for the war. Just twenty-one, he was already working alongside Charles in the family firm, while her daughter Caroline too was settled. A first-rate marriage to the heir to a stockbroking fortune had already produced one child and, at twenty-four, Caroline was expecting again. No, Edwina assured herself, as far as her children were concerned she had no reason to complain.

At the far side of the room she saw Charles standing with two of his cousins. Her prayers had been answered when he had finally pulled through. And now there was so much to arrange with his forthcoming marriage. How she was looking forward to that. Peggy Dennison was a perfect choice; as illustrious a family as their own; the joining of two dynasties just as she'd always planned.

A smile touched Edwina Rolfe's lips. It was her steadfast view that the upper classes had a duty to maintain their purity of stock. Her own father, a titled if rather impoverished Englishman, had been happy to welcome a genteel and wealthy Australian son-in-law into the family. The benefits to all had been obvious. Within eight months Edwina had become Mrs Douglas Rolfe.

Charles and Peggy, on the other hand, had been engaged since halfway through the war. Certainly fate had intervened, but now there was surely no need for further delay.

Then her dark brows drew together in a frown. She had tried to persuade Charles that this evening would be the perfect occasion to announce the date of the wedding. But he had been stubbornly reluctant, even in the face of her continued pressure. 'Please, Mother,' he'd protested, 'you must leave the date to us.'

Now, as her son's attractive, dark-haired fiancée stepped inside from the terrace with a group of young friends, Edwina's expression brightened. What Charles needed was a bit of prompting, she decided, that was all. Hadn't she always known what was good for him?

The ten-piece orchestra had begun to play in the adjoining room and, moving to Peggy Dennison's side, Edwina slipped an arm around the girl's slim waist.

'Come, my dear, the engaged couple should start the dancing.'

A high color suddenly flamed in Peggy's cheeks, but Edwina barely noticed as she shepherded the girl towards her son.

'Ladies and gentlemen!' she clapped her hands for attention and the chatter of the surrounding guests died away. 'I hope you have left room on your social calendars for the very imminent wedding of my charming son and his beautiful fiancée. In the meantime I hope you will allow them to lead the way in the first dance of the evening.'

* * *

Charles Rolfe knew it couldn't be put off a moment longer.

Leaving the crowded dance floor he led the way to the dark privacy of the garden. The music floated out on the night air and in the distance there was the sound of a low hoot from some ship on the harbor.

'It's impossible, Peggy, you know that.' He stood beside her under the denser darkness of one of the garden's massive conifers. 'It's not going to get any better.'

On three further occasions his humiliation had been merely reinforced.

'Oh, Charles...' Her voice was a whisper.

'I'm so sorry about the liberty my mother took in there. I tried to tell ...' He bit off the words, feeling his temper rising. His mother's domineering manner had always been difficult to cope with. She had got away with it when he was younger but he was an adult now, had fought for his country and survived a war. He would make his own decisions from now on. No matter how difficult.

'I'm sorry too, Charles... about everything.'

'You'll find someone else, Peggy. Someone who can give you children. There's nothing to regret.'

In the darkness Charles Rolfe's lips tightened in bitterness. *Only my lack of manhood,* he thought. *Only my utter uselessness to any woman.*

* * *

THE ARGUMENT WAS INEVITABLE.

In the library later that night, after the last guests had departed, a stunned Edwina Rolfe was informed of her son's decision.

'*Breaking off the engagement!* But *why*, Charles? Why, for God's sake? The Dennisons are ...'

'Mother, please. I don't wish to discuss it further. This is between Peggy and me.'

But Edwina Rolfe wasn't used to having her well-laid plans thwarted. With difficulty she tried to control her temper. 'No, Charles, this *isn't* just between you and Peggy. The Rolfe name and heritage is at stake here. As your father's heir you have a duty to make a suitable match. And there is no one better qualified to become your wife than Peggy Dennison.' Her voice rose shrilly. 'I insist you speak to her first thing tomorrow and say you've made a terrible mistake.'

His back turned towards her, Charles clenched his hands in his dinner jacket pockets. Why couldn't she just accept his decision? Why did she always need to control?

His silence seemed to increase her rage.

'Do you hear what I'm saying, Charles? I *won't* let you throw your life away like this! You are going to marry Peggy Dennison.'

He turned to face her then, saw the tightened lips and the glittering anger in her dark eyes. His mother was not used to being disobeyed; in the face of her rages his father had always given in. Edwina Rolfe was accustomed to getting her own way.

Only not this time, Charles thought stubbornly.

'Keep out of it, Mother.' There was a firm finality to his quiet words. 'This is something you don't understand.'

Face pale, Edwina Rolfe stared at her son. Never before had Charles openly defied her. For the first time she realized just how much the war had changed him.

But I'll win in the end, she promised, with silent fervor.

3

The manager had called Marianne into his office to explain the situation.

'The Rolfes are regular guests here, Miss Walenska. A fine Australian family, you understand. Third or fourth generation. Wealthy indeed and most respectable. Most respectable.'

A damned nuisance, the whole business, he was thinking as he spoke. Marianne Walenska was an excellent secretary, dependable and efficient. But when someone of Charles Rolfe's caliber asked for a favor, what could one do?

From the other side of the broad cedar desk Marianne wondered where this talk was leading. Why had Mr Arkwright interrupted her work to talk about the Australian whose letter she had translated two nights before?

The next moment her silent query was answered.

'Mr Rolfe has asked me to put a proposal to you, Miss Walenska. He was most impressed with your assistance the other evening and as he now has to spend some time in France – a matter of about ten days in all – he wondered if you would consider accompanying him as his personal assistant. As the gentleman himself put it, he would feel more comfortable with your services than having to rely on an interpreter provided by the other side. Understandable, of course,' the manager murmured.

'But...' Marianne was still confused. 'My job here? What–'

The manager raised a comforting hand. 'Nothing to worry about there, Miss Walenska. Your job will be waiting for you on your return. This is merely a favor on our part for a most prestigious guest – if you agree, of course. As to the matter of remuneration, Mr Rolfe has agreed to pay double the equivalent of your regular salary. And naturally you would be accommodated in first-class establishments wherever it was necessary for you to visit.'

The manager's nostrils pinched together as if reluctant to admit there could be other hotels equal to his own. He raised an enquiring eyebrow at the girl. 'Does the proposal interest you?' He cleared his throat. 'It is, I might add, quite a privilege to receive such a request from so distinguished a guest.'

Marianne was giving the matter her consideration. It was obvious from the manager's remarks that she was expected to agree to Charles Rolfe's request. From the little she had seen of the Australian he had certainly appeared a gentleman. Not that she had any fears on that level. She knew perfectly well how to keep men at a distance. And there was always the possibility that, if she refused, the hotel might see fit to fire her...

The manager was looking at her expectantly.

Marianne nodded. 'I would be very happy to do this favor, Mr Arkwright.'

* * *

'IT WAS VERY KIND OF you to agree to help me this way, Miss Walenska.'

Charles Rolfe felt it only natural to try to make small talk as the train headed towards Dover. After all, he knew little about the young woman opposite. Only that she was nineteen years of age, had a talent for languages, and was Polish by birth. Had she grown up in England? he wondered. Or had she endured the terrible destruction of the war in her native Poland? If so, how had she made her way to Britain? Diplomacy and good manners precluded such enquiries, he decided.

Murmuring a noncommittal reply to his attempt at conversation Marianne Walenska turned her face to the window.

But Charles found himself discomfited by the silent self-possession of the young woman opposite. Good manners prevailing, he ventured once more: 'You studied French at school?'

'Yes.' Those lovely eyes were seemingly fixed on the passing scenery. 'In Krakow.'

So, he had learnt the answer to one of his questions at least.

'A very beautiful city.'

She turned, shooting him a quick enquiring glance. 'You know it?'

He smiled. 'I've never been there, of course, but the history and architecture have always fascinated me.'

Softly, almost as if speaking her thoughts, Marianne Walenska replied, 'My country has a... tragic history.'

At that moment the conductor slid open the carriage door and Charles reached into his coat pocket for their tickets.

'Thank you, sir.' Duly punched, the tickets were handed back with a smile. Alone again, Charles tried to resume the rather stilted conversation.

'Have you been to Paris previously, Miss Walenska?'

Instead of replying, Marianne Walenska pulled a magazine from the plain black leather handbag on her lap. 'Do you mind, sir, if I read? I have little time when I am working.'

The message was unmistakable.

'Of course not.'

* * *

THEY WERE BOOKED into the Hotel Meurice on the rue de Rivoli. Decorated in lavish eighteenth-century style with Flemish and French tapestries, gilt-edged paneled walls and enormous crystal chandeliers, the hotel looked out on the Tuileries Gardens.

'Salvador Dali made this place his Parisian headquarters,' Charles explained to Marianne with a smile as he signed the register.

Marianne's room was on the third floor, the businessman's one floor higher. As they followed the bellboy into the elevator, Charles suggested, 'Why don't you rest and freshen up, Miss Walenska? If we get together around six-thirty, say, we'll have plenty of time to discuss our plans for tomorrow over a pre-dinner drink.'

'Whatever suits you, Mr Rolfe,' came the coolly polite reply.

While Paris still carried the scars of its fight for liberty, the city had quickly resumed its *joie de vivre*. The tourists were back, the restaurants were busy, the cabarets as risqué as ever. As well, the hotels were full of serious-faced businessmen eager to capitalize on the potential of markets too long disrupted by the irritation of war.

Charles Rolfe was no different. He was as keen as the rest to start the wheels of commerce turning quickly again. In England the bombing had done serious damage to much of the industrial heart of the country; until the mills resumed full production, new markets were needed for the wool the Rolfe holdings produced in such quantity. He was determined to negotiate a first-class deal with the local French manufacturers.

Just before six-thirty he telephoned Marianne's room and arranged to meet her in the foyer.

As the elevator doors opened and she made her way through the busy reception area to where he waited, Charles couldn't help thinking it a pity the girl did so little to enhance her youthful good looks. The dress she'd changed into made her appear almost matronly in comparison to the stylish fashions of the other female guests. Still, he told himself, it was none of his concern.

He greeted her with a smile. 'I hope your room is comfortable, Miss Walenska?'

'Yes, thank you. Everything is perfect.'

The Pompadour cocktail lounge was an intimate cocoon of rosy pink lighting and elegant, silk-covered walls. At this time of the evening it was just beginning to get busy.

Charles requested a corner table and they sat side by side on low comfortable chairs. A waiter took their order; a martini for Charles, a fruit juice for Marianne.

For the next hour or so Charles Rolfe outlined his business strategy in detail. He explained to Marianne exactly the terms he wished to negotiate with the French buyers, indicating the areas in which he was prepared to compromise and those where he would not budge.

Occasionally Marianne interrupted him to clarify some point, but Charles was impressed with her quick grasp of the details. He had no doubt he'd made the right decision in asking for her assistance.

It was almost eight by the time he glanced at his watch.

'Would you care for some dinner now, Miss Walenska? I think the French might be persuaded to serve us at this hour.'

She made no reaction to his attempt at a joke. 'I am happy to eat when you are, Mr Rolfe.' The stiff formality had not eased.

'The hotel restaurant has an excellent reputation. I took the liberty earlier of reserving a table, if that suits?'

'Of course.'

He rose and pulled out her seat.

* * *

THE MENU in the Meurice Restaurant gave no evidence of the rationing or restrictions still applying in Britain.

Marianne couldn't remember how long it was since she'd eaten butter instead of margarine. Or seen coquilles, scampi, or such a range of vegetables on a menu.

Her mouth watered as she ordered first the *pate en croute* followed by the *magret de canard*.

The meal was every bit as delicious as she had anticipated. She savored every mouthful and took a glass too of the smooth mellow wine Charles Rolfe had ordered on the maitre d's recommendation. It was many years since she had eaten so well.

And suddenly, before she could fight it, memory swept her back to that last Christmas before the war. As usual her mother had prepared a goose and all the trimmings. Only ten years of age, Marianne had stood on a stool by the kitchen table to shell the crisp young peas. She remembered how she and her mother had laughed when her father came into the room and teased them that he wasn't the slightest bit hungry, that he wasn't going to be able to eat even a morsel of their wonderful feast.

The last happy Christmas, she thought.

'You're tired, Miss Walenska?'

Charles Rolfe's words jolted her back to the present. His dark eyes were looking at her with concern.

'Perhaps a little, yes.'

He called for the check and saw her to her room.

* * *

SHE WOKE to the suffocating darkness, her body rigid with terror.

With wide, panic-stricken eyes she took in the unfamiliar surroundings. Where...?

Then she remembered.

Heart racing, the tears still damp on her cheeks, she reached with shaky fingers for the comforting glow of the bedside lamp.

And, as so often before, she made her silent desperate plea to a God in whom she had long ago ceased to believe.

Let me forget, God, oh please, let me forget.

But the nightmare, she knew, was the price she was forced to pay.

* * *

SHE'S INVALUABLE, thought Charles in secret admiration as Marianne relayed his point in fluent French to the two local businessmen.

The meeting was taking place in the Paris headquarters of a major textile firm off the Boulevard Haussmann. As point after point was haggled over, agreed to, finalized, Charles realized again what an excellent decision it had been to request Marianne Walenska's assistance. He told her as much as they caught a cab to their next appointment. She accepted the compliment with her usual cool reserve.

At the end of an exhausting day they returned to the hotel to freshen up before once more meeting for dinner. This time they ate in an intimate bistro on the Ile St-Louis. The setting was enchanting, almost medieval with its low-beamed ceilings, its flagstone floor overlaid with fringed rugs, its candlelit tables.

'This was my mother's find,' Charles explained as they were seated. 'Whenever we visited Paris before the war we would always eat at least one meal here.' He smiled at Marianne across the starched white tablecloth. 'It's the sort of place the tourists never stumble on and that pleased my mother.'

'Your mother is still alive?'

'Oh, yes. She's only in her fifties. Very fit still. Unfortunately she lost my father halfway through the war.' He caught Marianne's questioning glance. 'A massive heart attack. I was on active duty when it happened. He died peacefully in his sleep, I'm told.'

He was lucky, was Marianne's silent reply.

* * *

AFTERWARDS, even though there was a nip in the October air, they both agreed to walk a little before finding a cab.

'You enjoyed your meal?' Charles enquired as they made their way over the cobblestones towards Notre Dame.

'I wonder how I will ever eat English food again!' It was the first time he had seen any sign of merriment in her and for some strange reason he found it inordinately pleasing.

* * *

TEN MINUTES after he closed his hotel room door behind him, Charles knew that the discomfort he had begun to feel on the way back to the hotel was not imagined. There was a tightness in his chest, his breathing was strained, and his body felt as if he'd been run over by a truck.

I've overdone it, he thought. The stress of the day, coupled perhaps with the dank night air, was taking its toll. He cursed his bad luck and the weakness of a respiratory system exacerbated by his wartime injuries. He couldn't afford to be sick now. Not with the sort of schedule he'd laid down for himself.

But by dawn, as he lay bathed in sweat, Charles knew he was incapable of meeting with anyone that day. His head throbbed so badly he could barely think straight. Much as he hated to lose the business, he faced the fact he'd have to get Marianne Walenska to cancel that day's appointments. There was no question either of rescheduling; his program was too tight for that. His only hope, he knew, lay with the hotel doctor who might be able to give him a shot of something to get him quickly back on his feet.

Then, as the low pink rays of light crept into his room, it occurred to Charles just how those business appointments might yet be kept...

* * *

HE HAD his call put through to her room at the earliest feasible hour.

'Miss Walenska? Please forgive me for disturbing you so early.'

Marianne glanced at the time. It was seven-fifteen.

'I was awake,' she replied. She had been about to draw her bath, looking forward to the luxury of endless hot water and perfumed soap.

Charles Rolfe explained what had happened. 'It's impossible for me to attend any of today's meetings, Miss Walenska, but if you could come to my room as soon as you're dressed I'd like to discuss some alternatives with you.'

A fit of coughing interrupted him. His voice was husky as he apologized.

'Have you called the hotel doctor, Mr Rolfe?'

'He's on duty at eight. I'll live till then, I think.' Ill as he was, he noted the genuine concern in her voice.

Miss Marianne Walenska, he decided as he hung up, was perhaps not quite the cold creature she'd like the world to think.

* * *

SHE TAPPED on the door just ten minutes later.

Charles Rolfe wore a woolen robe and Marianne could see at once how ill he was. His face was pale and sweaty, his sandy hair plastered against his forehead. She hoped the doctor would come without delay.

'Excuse my attire, Miss Walenska, but until the doctor arrives...'

She took the seat he indicated and Charles Rolfe wasted no time in coming to the point.

'Initially I was going to ask you to cancel today's appointments. But then I remembered how very competently you handled the negotiations yesterday. You learnt a lot and very quickly grasped my position. I was most impressed.' He was watching her closely. 'What I'm proposing is that if I run through some of the important points again I can't see any reason why you shouldn't be able to handle things perfectly well on your own today.'

Marianne's big blue eyes stared at him. 'Me? You want me to conduct those meetings? I ...'

He could see her doubt and confusion.

'I know I'm asking an enormous favor, Miss Walenska, but if you manage to finalize just one favorable deal today it could mean a huge difference to my business. I have every faith in your ability.'

Marianne was thinking fast. If she said no, all those deals would surely be lost. If she agreed, there was still a chance of success.

She made up her mind. 'If you think I can do it I will try, Mr Rolfe.'

The gratitude was clearly visible on his pale face.

* * *

MARIANNE STOOD UP, Charles Rolfe's business diary in her hands. There were four appointments that day, the first at nine-thirty.

Charles reached for his wallet and passed her a handful of francs. 'For taxis and lunch,' he explained.

She was about to go when she realized the Australian had something else on his mind. He was looking at her hesitantly and immediately she sensed his discomfort. Had he changed his mind? Did he think she couldn't handle it after all?

Charles cleared his throat. 'Miss Walenska, please don't take my comments the wrong way. I have no wish at all to offend you, I know how difficult it can be for a working girl...'

Marianne frowned. She had no idea what he was getting at.

'It's just... we are dealing with the fashion trade here. And the

French in particular. I ... I wonder if you might allow me to buy you an outfit more suitable for your task today?'

Then Marianne understood. Her cheap, out-of-date dress would certainly not make her task easier with the businessmen she would have to deal with.

'You do understand, don't you?' Charles Rolfe rushed on. 'Style is so important to the French. As it happens I know of a boutique close by in the rue St Honore. My mother was a regular customer of Madame Renee's before the war. I am sure if I telephoned her now, madame would be happy to help you choose something appropriate.'

* * *

MADAME RENEE PRONOUNCED herself delighted to be of assistance. Edwina Rolfe, she recalled, had been an excellent customer. With the war at an end it was important to re-establish her clientele.

Mais oui, she told Charles in heavily accented English, send mademoiselle around at once. And the bill, no problem. She would forward it to the hotel.

The boutique owner was small and sprightly. In her mid-fifties, she was immaculately groomed, her coppery hair swept into an elegant chignon.

As an assistant showed Marianne into the private fitting room, Madame Renee did her best to hide her reaction. *Mon dieu!* That – she could barely bring herself to call it a dress – was more like a dishcloth... It was beyond Madame Renee's understanding that one so young could attire herself in something so ugly.

'*Bonjour,* mademoiselle,' she welcomed the girl with effusive charm, wondering how this one had become a friend of so *distingue* a family as the Rolfes.

'*Alors,*' Madame Renee was chattering on, 'we must choose something to enhance your charm and natural beauty, yes?' For it was obvious to the Frenchwoman's practiced eye that beneath that terrible dress and depressing haircut existed a creature who merely needed Madame Renee's special talents to bring out her natural appeal.

'I require something suitable for business appointments, madame,' Marianne answered stiffly.

Madame Renee might not have heard as she ordered, 'Please, mademoiselle, disrobe. It is necessary I judge your size.' She suppressed a shudder – impossible to tell anything in that horror of a garment.

Marianne did as she was asked and stood in her slip under the proprietress's scrutinizing gaze.

'But you have a superb shape, mademoiselle!' The older woman was noting with admiration the slim long legs, the narrow waist, the small but perfectly formed breasts. Why, she wondered, did the girl hide herself?

Snapping her fingers, she sent her assistant for outfits in the appropriate size.

Within moments the fitting room was adorned with a dozen suits, nearly all with the latest pencil-slim skirts. Madame Renee smiled with pride. 'Any of these creations will show off your lovely figure, mademoiselle.'

Marianne could feel the sweat breaking out between her shoulder blades. 'Madame, I need something appropriate for the business I have to conduct. Please, could you show me something less... frivolous?'

Madame Renee frowned. She held up a silk printed dress with a nipped-in waist. 'Surely mademoiselle can imagine how beautiful she will look in this?'

Marianne's breath quickened; she could taste the familiar bile in her mouth.

None of you understand how much I hate being beautiful! screamed the voice inside her head.

* * *

FINALLY, and in the face of Madame Renee's obvious disappointment, Marianne settled on a severely tailored suit that buttoned to the neck in a tiny roll collar. Expertly cut, it was made of the first-class woolen fabric she was about to attempt to sell.

'I'll wear it now,' she told the salesgirl, who had also brought her high-heeled shoes to match. Time was running out; Marianne knew she would have to go directly to her first appointment.

'Give my regards to Monsieur Rolfe,' Madame Renee offered sourly as she watched the girl leave.

She would have the bill and that disgusting discarded garment delivered to the Meurice as soon as possible.

Not a moment longer than necessary could she bear to have such a travesty on her premises.

* * *

I CAN HANDLE ANYTHING. Nothing will ever frighten me again.

Marianne silently repeated the words as she held her ground with the three brow-beating businessmen.

After what she had endured, she told herself, arrogance and rudeness were nothing.

To begin with Charles Rolfe's absence had convinced the three Frenchmen they were much better placed to win a favorable deal. But the young, elegantly dressed woman sent in the Australian's place wasn't quite the pushover they had expected. They soon found she was capable of driving as hard a bargain as any experienced businessman.

Marianne had learnt quickly how to play the game: intractable on the points that counted, conceding on those less important so the other side might save face.

In the end she was able to finalize terms she felt certain would please her employer.

By the time she arrived back at the Hotel Meurice she felt drained but elated. Two of the four had agreed to a deal! Excited, she took the elevator straight to Charles Rolfe's suite on the fourth floor. Good news, she thought, might help him feel better.

Poised to knock on the gilt-paneled door she was brought up short by the sound of her employer's angry voice. He had someone with him in the suite. But the absence of a response immediately alerted her to the fact that Charles Rolfe was speaking on the phone.

About to move discreetly away she heard something that made her stop dead in her tracks.

'Listen, Mother, do I have to spell it out? I'm *impotent*! Do you know what that means? *I can't make it with a woman*! If Peggy looks like she's found someone else then good luck to her, because she certainly knew she had a dud in me. *Now will you once and for all get off my back*!'

* * *

AFTER A DISCREET interval Marianne returned to her employer's room.

Charles Rolfe's mood was subdued when he answered her knock but he cheered up immediately when she told him of her success.

'But that's *wonderful*! I couldn't have hoped to do better myself!' He was taking in her appearance. Smart, he thought, if rather severe. 'You've done me an enormous favor, Miss Walenska,' he continued. 'I don't –'

A hacking cough interrupted him.

Marianne leaned forward in concern. 'The doctor, he has given you something?'

Charles nodded, reaching for a glass of water as he caught his breath. 'Yes. An injection and this muck.' He indicated the small medicine bottle by his elbow. 'Rest, he told me, but of course that's exactly what I haven't got time to do.'

'Have you eaten today?'

He shook his head. 'Haven't felt like a thing. Although I suppose I should –'

Marianne cut him off. 'Please, Mr Rolfe, let me order you some hot soup. To continue with your schedule it is important you keep up your strength.' She indicated the telephone. 'May I?'

She's genuinely concerned, he thought, touched and surprised at the same time.

'That would be very kind of you, Miss Walenska.'

* * *

BY THE TIME the soup arrived Marianne had plumped up the pillows, settled Charles back into the bed and dampened a washcloth to apply to his burning forehead.

'Don't tell me you're going to be my nurse as well as my business partner!' he joked, quite enjoying the attention. As she lifted the tray of soup from the serving trolley, he saw he had embarrassed her.

'I'm sorry, Miss Walenska. I'm forgetting my manners.'

'I have not found anything to complain about in your manners, Mr Rolfe,' she answered quietly.

She placed the food in front of him and moved away. 'I shall leave you to eat. I hope you have a more restful night and feel recovered by tomorrow.'

'Thank you, Miss Walenska, for everything.'

She turned at the door and gave him a small, rare smile.

At that moment Charles realized that Marianne Walenska was an extremely beautiful young woman. Inside and out.

* * *

HE WOKE WITH A START. The room was lit by the one shaded lamp. Marianne Walenska was bent over the bed and he could feel the fresh coolness of the washcloth against his forehead.

'I'm sorry,' she whispered, 'I didn't mean to disturb you. I asked the bellboy to let me in so I could check you were all right. I'll go now.'

He murmured a sleepy reply before falling back into a dreamless slumber.

4

On her return to London, Marianne felt a restlessness she had not experienced before. The city seemed drabber, the weather colder, the people more depressed than ever after her time in France.

On the surface she quickly settled back into her previous routine, but there were occasions when she caught herself daydreaming of the ten days she had spent with Charles Rolfe.

While not completely recovered, the Australian had managed to complete his scheduled visits to the industrial cities of Lille, Arras and Amiens. But he had continued to rely on Marianne's assistance. On their last evening, back in Paris, he had showed his appreciation as they shared a final meal. 'You've been a great help, Miss Walenska. I don't know how I would have managed without you.' And across the table he had slipped a small gift-wrapped parcel.

Marianne had looked up in surprise. 'For me?'

He smiled. 'With sincere thanks.'

Carefully she unwrapped the tissue to find a bottle of Balenciaga *Eau de Parfum*. It was the most expensive perfume she had ever owned.

She looked up to see him watching her with a smile. 'I hope it is to your taste?'

'Thank you so much, Mr Rolfe. I am sure it will be perfect. Although there was no need for this, you are paying me well enough.'

'You did a first-rate job.'

'I enjoyed it,' Marianne found herself admitting. 'The business world is more stimulating than I realized.'

Charles Rolfe sipped at his glass of Cote-Rotie. Surely, he thought, he could risk a more personal question after the time they had spent together? 'Your father wasn't a businessman then?' He kept his voice casual, but saw at once that he had made a mistake.

The mask came down on Marianne Walenska's face. She lowered her eyes to the plate in front of her.

'No. A teacher.'

That was all. As before, the subject was closed.

* * *

AT VICTORIA STATION he found her a taxi and they said their goodbyes, shaking hands on the pavement. He closed the cab door behind her and leaned in at the window. 'I'll be up north for about a week then back in London until the boat leaves for Australia.'

It seemed to Marianne he was about to say something more, but at that moment the taxi pulled away. When she turned to look, Charles Rolfe was lost among the faceless evening crowds.

She wound up the window against the frigid air.

* * *

HARD AS HE worked on his trip up north, Charles found himself distracted by thoughts of Marianne Walenska.

What was it about the girl? he wondered. She was cool, reserved, unforthcoming but somehow he felt drawn to her. The more he pondered it the more he sensed a vulnerability and inner sadness behind that aloof exterior. His protective instincts were aroused.

He remembered the mask that had come down after his one or two apparently innocuous questions. What wound had he touched upon? What suffering had she endured?

Those thoughts were still in the back of his mind when, business successfully completed, Charles returned to London to await his departure to Australia.

Settled back into his suite at the Lancaster Regent, he found himself wanting to see the young Polish girl again. For twenty-four hours he resisted.

Finally he could fight his instincts no longer. He asked the switchboard operator for Marianne's extension. As he waited, Charles told himself: *Maybe I'm crazy, but perhaps I can do something to help with whatever it is that's troubling her.*

* * *

MARIANNE WAS surprised by the invitation. Yet she agreed to meet him for a farewell drink after she had finished her evening shift.

* * *

HE WANTED to take her somewhere away from the hotel. Neither of them familiar with the city's popular venues, they ended up in a small club in Soho. It was after nine by the time they arrived and a four-piece combo was playing on a raised platform at the far end of the low-ceilinged room. Three or four couples were already swaying together on the tiny dance floor.

Charles ordered a bottle of champagne before realizing that the place had been a bad choice. Already it was beginning to get busy, the noise levels making conversation difficult. As soon as possible, he decided, they'd find somewhere else.

The waiter poured their drinks and Charles touched his glass to hers. 'To the future,' he said lightly. 'Let's hope it brings us both luck.'

He just caught her soft reply. 'You've been very lucky already, Mr Rolfe. You survived the war.'

Charles saw the pain in those dark blue, almost violet eyes. Something had happened. Something terrible. If only she would talk about it.

Instead he found himself telling her about his own experience, about the crash and its aftermath, the long years of treatment and rehabilitation.

'But you are well now?' she asked.

'As well as I'm ever going to be, I guess.' With an effort he bit back his bitterness. How could he admit to her, or any other woman, his uselessness as a man?

He changed the subject. 'Do you like this music?' The combo was playing something slow and sentimental.

'Very much.'

'Would you care to dance? Afterwards we can find somewhere quieter perhaps.'

Her breath quickened. He was going to touch her, put his arms around her... But then she remembered what she had overheard. A man like Charles Rolfe could never present a threat. With him she was safe.

Unlike the other couples on the floor, they kept a formal distance apart but Charles found pleasure in the touch of her slim, soft hand, in the scent that wafted from her hair, the ease and grace with which she followed his lead.

Yet his response only served to bring home his shame, regret and bitterness at the loss of his manhood. With an effort he pushed away his feelings of self-loathing.

The place was beginning to get rowdy as it became more crowded. 'I'm sure we can find somewhere nicer than this,' he commented as they made their way back to their table. 'Shall we go?'

Marianne agreed and, leaving Charles to settle the check, excused herself to visit the powder room.

The incident occurred as she made her way back across the room. Threading her way through the clusters of tables, she felt herself suddenly seized from behind. Strong male hands dragged her backwards; her nostrils were filled with the scent of alcohol and tobacco as her unseen assailant forced her into his embrace.

In an instant the terror returned to engulf her. Instinct became her only weapon. Blind with rage and fear she fought like a madwoman, lashed out in a frenzied rain of blows, screamed hysterically in Polish.

While other patrons stood dumbstruck by the ferocity of her

response, Charles was on his feet shoving aside chairs and other impediments until he reached her side.

'Marianne! It's me, Charles!' He tried to grab her arms, restrain her from her furious attack. Distracted, she swung round, and in those wide staring eyes he saw only panic and utter terror. Then recognition returned, and, with it, reality. She fell against him, allowed herself to be encircled by his arms, her uncontrollable sobs punctuated by incomprehensible and incoherent Polish.

'*Jesus...*' The ruddy-faced youth sounded dazed as he gingerly touched the lacerations on his face. With nervous darting eyes he took in the surrounding crowd. 'I ... I thought she was my girl; honest I did. From the back, I –' With a defiant gesture he bent down and snatched up his hat. 'Bloody mad foreigners. Who needs 'em here anyway?'

With his arms still around the distraught girl, Charles retorted tightly, 'I won't ask you to take that back, my friend, but maybe you'd better get out of here before I really give you something to squeal about.'

'Come on, Jack.' One of his pals touched the ruddy-faced youth on his arm. With a muttered oath and a final dirty glance at Charles the latter allowed himself to be shepherded out of the club.

* * *

He took her back to the address she gave him. In the cramped but tidy room he found a bottle of cheap brandy and poured her a stiff drink. As he placed the glass in her shaky hands Charles wondered again what had happened in Marianne's past to have provoked such a violent reaction. Certainly that young bastard's action had been out of place, but it was also patently clear that something much deeper lay at the heart of Marianne's hysteria.

For the time being, however, he merely held her hand until her tears were exhausted, the trembling finally eased.

At last, very gently, he asked. 'Do you want to speak about it?'

For a long moment Marianne didn't answer. Finally she lifted her head and looked with swollen, red-rimmed eyes into Charles's pale face. What she saw there was pure compassion and concern.

She hesitated, then took a deep breath. Her trembling fingers still clutched tightly in his, she began to speak.

'I will tell you,' she said in a raw whisper, 'why I cannot bear the intimate touch of a man.'

It was the first time she had opened the door to the darkest recess of memory.

* * *

'So, tell me, Marianne, how was school today?'

It was her father who asked the question. Now that grandfather was dead he had taken the seat at the head of the table. On his right sat her mother, pale and quiet, while Marianne had the chair next to her grandmother at her father's left elbow.

They were sitting in the kitchen of her grandmother's home. The room was full of shadows cast by the two oil lamps, but there was just enough light to see the sparse offering that sat atop the lace tablecloth. Their meals varied little – gherkins, black bread, a couple of hard-boiled eggs, and tonight the treat of a tiny block of cheese her mother had bartered for some withered apples from one of the village women. Food was hard to come by in 1944, even in the country.

Marianne pulled a face as she answered her father's question. 'It's dull at this school, *Tatus*. They never teach anything interesting. I wish we could go back to Krakow.'

'Marianne!' her mother's tone was sharp. 'Stop your complaining. I expect better of a young woman of fourteen. You know exactly the reason why we are not returning to Krakow. Now, give your father some peace. You know how hard he works.'

Immediately Marianne felt ashamed of her petulance. Chastened, she lowered her head and murmured, 'I'm sorry, Mama.'

Ula Walenska glanced across the table at her beautiful daughter. The girl was contrite, she could see. At the same time she understood how difficult the situation was for an outgoing fourteen year old. Especially in the winter. Locked up inside with just the adults for company, discouraged from asking even her few friends to visit, time passed slowly.

Yet Ula Walenska had her own reasons for not encouraging visitors...

The spartan meal over, Marianne helped clear the table.

'Do you still miss *Dziadek* so much, even with us here, *Babcia*?' Marianne addressed her grandmother as she boiled water for the dirty dishes.

'Fifty years of marriage is a long time, Marianne. I shall miss your grandfather until the day I die. To tell the truth,' the old woman sighed heavily, 'I pray to die soon so we can be together.'

'*Babcia*!' Marianne swung round and looked at her grandmother in shock. 'You mustn't think like that.'

Barbara Walenska gave a despondent shrug. 'What difference does it make? This war is slowly killing all of us. Did you see how little your poor father had to eat this evening? How is he expected to continue to work when he has no strength?'

Marianne's eyes clouded. She had tried not to notice how thin and pale her father had become in recent months. It made her regret all the more her outburst at the table. *Tatus* must miss Krakow too, she realized. It can't have been easy for him to give up his academic career and return to the land. Yet with *Dziadek* dead there had been no choice. *Babcia* couldn't be left to run the farm alone.

Although saddened by her grandfather's death Marianne had been quite excited at first by the thought of a move to the country. She had happy memories of long summer vacations spent on her grandparents' farm. And there was also the hope that out of the city there would be fewer Germans intruding into their lives.

But on both counts she had been disillusioned. On a long-term basis she had found country life very boring. She missed her school and close friends. As for the Germans, they were still very much in evidence as they roamed the countryside.

When, she wondered anxiously, was the war going to be over and life back to normal again? When would the invaders who were terrorizing her country be finally vanquished?

At the other side of the kitchen Marianne could see her mother wrapping the leftover bread with care. Bread was their most precious commodity now as starvation became an increasingly pressing threat.

It was one of the ways the Germans tried to keep the population submissive.

Their farm was in that part of Poland under the control of Hans Frank, the Nazi governor who maintained his headquarters in Krakow's Wawel Castle. Laws had been passed forcing the local farmers to surrender all but a tiny proportion of their harvest for shipment to Germany. The Poles were permitted to keep only the bare minimum to sustain their strength and the Nazi boss made it brutally clear that anyone found breaking this strict rule and secreting food would be immediately shot.

But Marianne knew it was worse than that. She had overheard the conversations that her parents conducted in an undertone. She knew that not only were violators of the rule killed, but hostages were taken at random. In that way did the Nazis seek to control, by keeping the countryside in a state of constant fear.

'Go and change into your nightdress, Marianne, and then *Tatus* will read a little to us.' Her mother's voice broke into Marianne's sober thoughts.

It was the time of day Marianne loved best. She hurried out of the kitchen and up the stairs to the bedroom she shared with her grandmother. Every evening the four of them would gather around the fire and in his cultured resonant voice her father would read a chapter or two of some wonderful classic. At the present he was halfway through *Madame Bovary*.

The house was chillier upstairs and Marianne quickly threw off her dress. As she slipped the long, warm nightdress over her head she felt able to empathize exactly with Emma Bovary. For like the heroine in Flaubert's story, Marianne too was stuck in the deadly dull countryside; she too longed for prettier things to wear than this plain, ugly nightgown; and like Emma she also missed the fun and parties of the city.

Her mother always promised there would be time for all that after the war. But, Marianne thought miserably, who knew how long the war might last? The Germans were determined to succeed.

Marianne frowned as she caught sight of her reflection in the speckled wardrobe mirror. *I might be so old by the time the war ends that no boy will want me. I'll be left an old spinster.*

It was a frightening thought because she longed to get married some day, to have children and a wonderful handsome husband. Someone as wonderful perhaps as Josef Pentowski...

Her cheeks turned pink as she remembered the kisses they had shared in the park behind her house in Krakow. Josef Pentowski was two grades ahead of her in school. He was tall, dark haired, with flashing white teeth and marvelous laughing eyes.

Josef had called her beautiful. She was surprised and delighted by the compliment; she had never thought much of her looks before that. But Josef had murmured the word over and over again as his lips nibbled her ears, her cheeks and finally covered her mouth. Now, as she daydreamed, Marianne remembered the heady sensation of the tall, handsome boy's probing demanding tongue, the kisses that had left her weak and confused.

Suddenly ashamed of the warmth creeping between her legs, she turned from her reflection and hurried back downstairs.

* * *

THE TILED STOVE in the corner kept the room comfortably warm. In no time at all her grandmother had nodded off in her chair.

But, curled up between her parents, Marianne was wide awake, enthralled by the unfolding adventures of Emma Bovary. When the story reached the part where Emma cut off a lock of her hair to give to the man she loved, Marianne found herself momentarily distracted by the idea of perhaps sending such a sentimental gift to Josef. He might forget me, she worried. Perhaps if I ...

'To bed, young lady. You are tired.' Her mother was smiling down at her while her father marked the page.

Sleepily, Marianne nodded. 'Tomorrow night, again though, *Tatusiu*, yes? Emma Bovary is so very interesting.'

She leaned over and kissed her father goodnight. When they spent an evening like this it was almost possible to believe the war had never happened.

'Sleep tight, my beautiful one.' Adam Walenski held his precious daughter close.

What am I doing to her? he thought fearfully. *How much am I risking*?

* * *

IT WAS the unexpected sound that woke her. Marianne frowned as she blinked awake. Something had disturbed her.

From where she lay under the cozy warmth of the plump eiderdown she could hear her grandmother's soft snoring in the bed beside her.

But that wasn't what had broken into her sleep.

Then it came again. A deep resonant note.

A voice. A male voice. Not her father's...

Pushing back the covers Marianne eased herself quietly out of the bed. Throwing her grandmother's thick, dark shawl around her shoulders she let herself out of the room.

From the top of the stairs she could see the shaft of yellow light from the kitchen. Motionless, she stood and listened. Now she caught the sound of her parents' voices too.

An iciness ran down her spine. No Pole would dare break the curfew; late-night visitors could only be Germans. And that surely meant danger.

Slowly, carefully, she crept down the narrow wooden stairs, willing them not to creak. Tiptoeing across the living room floor she slipped behind the half-open kitchen door.

Picking her moment she finally risked a quick glance into the room. Enough to see a rough-looking stranger sitting at the table beside her father. They were conversing quietly in Polish while her mother – Marianne's eyes widened in astonishment – her mother was packing a torn haversack with several loaves of dark bread.

The blood drained from Marianne's face. She grasped at once what the scenario implied. Her mother had taken the risk of defying German orders and had illegally retained extra grain. Grain that the Germans demanded under pain of death...

And immediately Marianne guessed the identity of the stranger with the shaggy hair and beard. Like so many others, she had heard the rumors of the Resistance, the underground cells that operated from deep in the surrounding forests. With few resources, they continued to do all they could to harass the German occupiers.

And her parents, she realized, were risking their lives, all their lives, to provide the Resistance with food.

And now she too shared their dangerous secret ... yet she didn't dare let them know. Heart thundering, she turned to make her silent retreat. She was halfway across the room when suddenly one of the ancient floorboards betrayed her.

From the kitchen came a muttered oath, the urgent scraping back of chairs. Marianne made a leap for the stairs, but she was too late. As the vice-like grip descended on her shoulder she cried out in fright and pain.

'Marianne!'

Her father spun her round. Behind him, her mother and the stranger had also appeared.

'*Tatus*, I'm sorry!' She stared wide eyed into her father's ashen face. 'I heard a noise. I thought – I thought the Germans...' She began to sob.

Ula Walenska signaled to the two men to retreat to the kitchen. Putting an arm around her frightened daughter she led her slowly back up the stairs.

'Hush, hush, my darling.'

And when the shaking, trembling girl was tucked up once more beneath the warm feather cover, Ula Walenska whispered close to her daughter's ear. '*Never, never must you mention to another living soul what you saw down there tonight.*'

5

But Marianne didn't have to tell anyone.

It was three weeks later. A bitterly cold winter's night. The shouting and the rain of blows on the front door woke them with hammering hearts some time after midnight.

'It's them.' Marianne's grandmother spoke the two words with dispassion. It was as if she had been merely waiting for the enemy to arrive.

Mouth dry with fear, Marianne clambered out of bed. She could hear her father pulling back the locks, heard the Germans burst into the house, their boots heavy on the bare floorboards.

They were screaming out their orders.

'Everyone here! Downstairs! *Schnell*!'

Dazed with fright Marianne realized her mother had entered the bedroom, a robe thrown over her nightclothes. She was helping her mother-in-law to her feet.

'Come, quickly. Do as they say.' Ula Walenska's face was pale but her voice was steady and strong as she hurried them both from the room.

The living room seemed crowded with the five German soldiers. They held their arms at the ready. The one in charge appeared to be in his mid-twenties, a lieutenant Marianne saw from his insignia. He was of medium height, very blond, with a bony angular face and wide-set blue eyes. Those eyes were as hard as stones as he screamed at the three adults and child to stand to attention in front of him.

Legs shaking so hard they would barely support her, Marianne stood between her mother and grandmother. She could hear the soft insistent mutter of her grandmother's prayers.

Over his shoulder the young SS officer barked an order to two of his men. 'Search the house! You know what to look for.'

Then he pointed with his riding crop.

'You are Adam Walenska.' It was a statement, not a question, made in perfect Polish.

'*Tak*, Herr Oberleutnant.' Marianne marveled that her father's voice was as steady as her mother's had been moments before.

'You are a teacher from Krakow?'

'I was, *tak*.'

A sneer twisted the young German's sharp features. 'You saw no reason to join your comrades in uniform?'

'I am forty-five, Herr Oberleutnant. I was born with a weak heart.'

'But not a weak stomach, I hope.' And without warning the riding crop sliced through the air, smiting Ula Walenska's cheek with full force.

As his wife let out a piercing scream Adam Walenski took a step towards the German. His fists were bunched at his sides, his face white with anger.

The oberleutnant sneered. 'So... you are threatening me perhaps? An SS officer? Obviously it is necessary I defend myself from you uncontrollable Polish peasants.' And slipping his revolver from its holster he pointed it at Adam Walenska.

'Now, tell me the names of your late-night visitors.'

Adam Walenska forced himself to remain calm. It was the only way they might have a chance.

'I don't know what you mean, Herr Oberleutnant.'

The young German's expression became ugly. 'You know exactly what I mean, Polish scum! Did you think your midnight parties with the saboteurs would go unnoticed? We know what you are up to. We –'

He was interrupted by the re-entry into the room of the two soldiers. 'We found it, Herr Oberleutnant!'

With a triumphant grin one of the soldiers placed the box with the two round flat stones at his commanding officer's feet. Marianne recognized it as her grandmother's quern, the small hand mill used to grind wheat. For generations the Poles had used such implements to make their rich nutritious bread. But German law had decreed that all such precious mills were to be surrendered – precisely to prevent the withholding of illegal grain.

'There was also half a sack of grain,' the soldier added meaningfully.

The German officer turned back to Adam Walenski, his blue eyes flinty. 'So, you see fit to disobey the orders of the Third Reich! And as well you provide for those who would aid the Motherland's destruction. For that, Polish scum, you must pay the price!' Aiming his revolver he blew away the side of Ula Walenska's brain.

In rapid succession two further shots exploded in the room. The bodies of Adam Walenski and his mother slumped to the floor, their blood flooding over the bare boards.

Marianne's eyes were squeezed tight in terror. The echoes of the shots, the smell of gunpowder, the dying agony of those she loved paralyzed her senses. She braced herself for the final second of her life.

But the shot never came.

Somewhere in the dark pit of nightmare the words reached her. 'No... maybe for the moment we will save this little one. A pity, I think, to waste such beauty so soon.'

She heard footsteps.

'Open your eyes, my little angel.' The touch of metal beneath her chin.

Numb with shock Marianne did as she was ordered. The butt of the revolver, still warm from its task, forced her to look up into the German's smiling face.

'And such beautiful eyes, too,' he murmured.

Her whole body began to shake in delirium. She crumpled into merciful darkness, her hair fanning into her father's warm blood.

* * *

SHE HAD no idea how much time had passed. Or where she was.

Slowly her eyes roamed the spacious room. Paintings and tapestries decorated the walls. The ceiling was high with gilded cornices. Richly woven rugs covered the parquetry floor and an antique desk and chair stood against one wall.

The bed in which she lay was high and broad with a canopied top and as she struggled to sit up Marianne could see that the closed French windows overlooked a garden which had been allowed to grow wild.

As awareness returned so too were the images of the night of terror inexorably projected on her mind. Her breath quickened and a moment later a terrible sound echoed off the walls. Marianne was unaware that the high-pitched wailing came from her own throat.

Within seconds a key rattled in the lock and a skinny grim-faced woman in a dark striped dress hastened into the room. 'So,' she approached the bed, 'you are awake?'

Reaching out, Marianne grasped the woman's arm, and looked at her with feverish eyes. 'Where am I? What am I doing here?' Nothing made any sense.

The woman shrugged off her hold. 'You'll find out in plenty of time.' She directed a scathing look at the girl on the bed. 'Men. They're all the same. Even the filthy Germans. A beautiful face and they forgive anything.'

It was then that Marianne began to understand...

* * *

FOR A BOY FORCED to leave school at sixteen to work in his father's drapery business Max Klauser had come a long way. The Nazi Party had been his stepping stone and he very quickly recognized the value of ingratiating himself with those who counted in the Party hierarchy. Like everything else his marriage too had been a calculated move. Hanna Friedrich, small, slim and reserved, was the only daughter of a high-ranking official and Max Klauser had set about wooing her with consummate flattery and charm.

Such foresight and cunning had reaped the expected rewards. It was his marital connections he was sure, which had seen him appointed to his present post. As deputy to a low-level Gestapo major he was charged with the task of administering a dozen villages in the area of Poland under the overall control of Governor Hans Frank.

At twenty-four Max Klauser was more than satisfied with his lot. His superior, Major Erich Langer, a florid, overweight man in his late fifties, tended to leave day-to-day matters very much in his deputy's hands, setting himself free to engage in his usual pastime of serious drinking. It was only when the governor himself was due to put in an appearance that Erich Langer managed to pull himself together.

Yet while Max Klauser despised his superior's lack of self-discipline, he also delighted in the freedom it allowed him to conduct business in his own particular manner. For despite his steady crawl up the Nazi Party ladder, what no one had yet discovered was that Max Klauser was driven neither by adherence to Party ideology nor by his oft-professed love of the Motherland. Rather, it was the pursuit of power that had always been his obsession.

The only son of a dominant aggressive father, Klauser had learnt very early on how it felt to be both vulnerable and weak. It was Nazi Party membership that had offered an escape.

And now, thanks to his position with the self-indulgent Langer, he had the opportunity to wield real power. The power of life and death, the power to save or to destroy, to change the course of events with a wave of his thin, hairless hands. His reputation for ruthlessness was well earned and he delighted in the fear his presence aroused in those under his command. Fear meant power. And power was the heady sensation he had always dreamed it would be.

As he stepped from the deep porcelain bath, Oberleutnant Klauser felt smugly satisfied with his life. Certainly, he thought contentedly, his surroundings could not be improved.

As district commander, Erich Langer had commandeered the palatial lodge as soon as he'd arrived. Set among acres of gardens it was owned by Countess Sylvia Marcinek, a sixty-eight-year-old widow and an obvious patron of the arts. When they'd first taken up residence Klauser had roamed from room to room, gaping at the priceless works and magnificent antiques that filled the massive chambers. Yet he had no doubt it was the well-stocked wine cellar, rather than the wonderfully appointed rooms which had convinced that philistine Langer to make the lodge his district headquarters. Erich Langer, he felt scornfully certain, wouldn't know a Rubens from a Degas.

But this evening Max Klauser was more than usually grateful for his superior's prandial indulgence in the cellar's dusty bottles of first-rate claret. Drunk and snoring, Erich Langer was not likely to be calling for the services of his deputy.

Klauser felt the warm throb in his loins and smiled at his reflection in the bathroom mirror as he drew the cutthroat razor over his face. He had willed himself to be patient. A week, he told himself, of good food and fine surroundings and she would be more relaxed and responsive. And now that night had finally arrived...

In the bedroom his clothes were laid out across the massive four-poster bed. White shirt and impeccably pressed trousers, not his uniform, of course.

As he dressed, he could feel his excitement growing. Even in the drab, sexless gown that evening, her beauty had been unmistakable. The skin like cream, the hair thick and blonde, the eyes a deep wonderful blue. Perfect Teutonic coloring, he mused happily. There were Poles like that ... where there had been infusions of Scandinavian and Germanic blood over the centuries. He recalled the mother. A blonde too. Yes, definitely a Nordic influence. Marianne Walenska, he assured himself, was totally worthy of his desire.

* * *

It was almost nine by the time he made his way down the broad hallway to the far end of the house. There would be no interruptions. Only Langer and himself were billeted in the lodge. No one knew of his little secret, apart from the local serving woman, and she would keep her mouth shut if she knew what was good for her.

He didn't bother to knock but the sound of the key in the lock alerted her. Her shock of recognition was obvious as he entered.

'*Dobry wieczor*,' he greeted her pleasantly in Polish.

Marianne was incapable of replying. From the bed, she stared transfixed at the monster who had murdered her family in front of her eyes.

'*Du sprichst Deutsch*?'

Marianne nodded. Then, as the German approached the bed, she managed to croak, 'Why - why have you brought me here?'

The German smiled thinly. She was wearing one of the silk gowns he had made it his business to acquire. The low-cut neckline showed the beginning of her creamy young breasts and Max Klauser felt the ache inside him grow more urgent.

He waited until he was perched on the edge of the bed to reply. 'Well, you see, *fraulein*, I like beautiful things.' He reached out and his thin cold fingers stroked Marianne's cheek.

Biting back a cry of repulsion, she cringed from his touch. Her heart was flopping crazily in her chest.

Surely he wasn't...? Surely he...? Her mind refused to contemplate such a horrifying reality.

Beside her, Klauser could almost smell the girl's fear and it only added to his feelings of excitement. With one smooth movement he stretched across the bed and gripped those fragile wrists. 'I think you should understand, *fraulein*, I allowed you to live because objects of beauty are so rare and precious. They exist to be enjoyed.'

Head twisted away, eyes brimming with tears, Marianne could feel his warm breath on her throat. 'Please... leave me alone.'

But Klauser was dragging her closer, pinning her beneath him with his wiry strength. His breathing grew harsher as his hand found her breasts, as his fingers pinched and squeezed the hard bud of her nipple.

'No! No!' In panic and horror Marianne beat at him with her free hand, used every ounce of strength to try to push him away.

The blow caught her stingingly across the cheek. The pain took her breath away.

Spread-eagled above her Klauser spoke softly into her ear. 'No one will hear you. No one except the woman knows you are here. Believe me, it will be better for you if I do not need to use force. To mark such beauty would be a great shame.'

* * *

THAT NIGHT all Max Klauser's fantasies came true. By first light, when he crept back to his own bed, he glowed with sexual gluttony and the knowledge that such ecstasy was at his disposal for as long as he desired it.

* * *

WHEN THE DOOR finally closed behind her violator, Marianne sobbed out her terror and rage. Her body was torn, her virginity lost among the bloodied, twisted sheets. Yet it was her psyche rather than her physical self which had sustained the greater damage. That her defilement had come at the hands of the man responsible for the ruthless killing of those she loved most, drove her to the very edge of sanity.

* * *

THE ROUTINE WAS ESTABLISHED. Max Klauser's nocturnal demands continued undiminished. Marianne had become the prisoner of his desire. Each day became merely mindless hours of dread as the time for her tormentor's visit grew closer. She tried to distract herself with the lodge's library of classics but too often she found herself reading and rereading the one printed page through a veil of tears. As her torture continued Marianne felt as if she were clinging to the last threads of reason.

How much longer? she despaired. *How much longer must I endure this nightmare*?

And then the nightmare grew worse.

* * *

MAX KLAUSER WAS WORRIED.

News of the war was growing more alarming by the week. The Russians had broken through in the East and were pushing their way inexorably westwards. Already battle-worn troops of the retreating Wehrmacht had appeared in their own district. The Soviet penetration, they reported grimly, could not be halted.

With self-preservation ever his guiding principle, he had begun to look for orders from Berlin that would signal their own evacuation. Yet when he pressed Erich Langer to clarify their position to their superiors Langer airily waved away his fears.

'You have too little faith, Klauser.' The major's eyes were bloodshot as usual as he took his place at the breakfast table. 'The Soviets cannot match our glorious troops. You will see, the Wehrmacht will regroup and drive them back again.'

Max Klauser did his best to hide his anger and growing panic. Langer would hang on here to the last moment, he realized. Why should he want to move when there was still a cellar full of alcohol to get through?

Klauser determined to contact his father-in-law himself and see what might be achieved. He had no intention of meekly waiting to be taken by the barbarians from the East.

In the meantime he was kept busy with his usual tasks, determined even at this stage of the war to maintain his reign of terror over the local population. As a German and an officer, discipline must be preserved at all costs.

* * *

IT HAPPENED on one of those rare occasions when Klauser was forced to spend the night away from the lodge. It was the woman who told him afterwards what had occurred, concerned chiefly that no blame might be attached to herself.

Late that afternoon the remnants of a Nazi company retreating westwards had arrived at the lodge. Led only by a sergeant, they were hungry, exhausted, demoralized.

Erich Langer, the woman reported with a sneer, had welcomed

them with enthusiasm. Here at last were some red-blooded compatriots ready to share a bottle or two with him. The rag-tag troops were delighted to oblige. Over the best dinner the lodge was able to provide the drinking began in earnest.

The woman herself had been called in to assist with the serving and had noted at firsthand how the sergeant's initial attempts to maintain some kind of order were very quickly ignored. Langer, she snorted, was impossible as always.

It was afterwards, close to midnight, when the soldiers in a state of total inebriation decided on a tour of their impressive surroundings. In the grand ballroom she had seen two of them urinate on the priceless Oriental carpet while the others looked on and grinned.

Noisily they had moved from room to room. Keeping a discreet distance the woman had followed, fearful, she had emphasized to Klauser, that the drunken visitors might find their way to the far wing of the lodge.

* * *

MARIANNE JOLTED awake as the door was thrown open.

Blinking in fright she tried to collect her wits as bright light and loud aggressive voices filled the room. Several German soldiers, their uniforms in disarray, surrounded the bed. Their laughter was wild and raucous, their eyes glassy and the reek of alcohol unmistakable.

'So! While we heroes risk our necks, these Gestapo bastards play bully boys and keep their dicks warm in pretty sparrows like this,' exclaimed one.

'A beauty... a princess...' another breathed in awe as he stared with fixed drunken eyes at the girl on the bed.

Marianne lay rigid, the sheet pulled tightly around her throat. Hardly daring to breathe she watched the ring of leering faces with wide frightened eyes.

'What are you hiding there, little sparrow? Show Uncle Kurt. Don't be shy.'

Amid loud guffaws the drunken soldier reached down and with one vicious action ripped away the protective sheet. Numb with fear

Marianne curled defensively away but the next moment the fine silk gown was also torn aside.

There was a moment of complete silence as the soldiers' hungry eyes devoured the slim perfection of her figure.

The one named Kurt was the first to speak. His voice was husky as he moved close to the bed. 'Those bastards have excellent taste.' Even as he spoke he was fumbling to undo his trouser buttons.

His penis sprang forth, erect and threatening. He grabbed for Marianne's hand. 'This is for you, my beauty. I am sure you will enjoy it more than some shriveled Gestapo prick.'

'No...' Pale with shock Marianne tried to pull free but there was no escaping the German's iron grip.

'Hold me!' he demanded harshly.

'Do what Uncle Kurt is asking, little sparrow,' chortled one of the others as he moved to pin Marianne to the bed.

She knew she was powerless to disobey. Fighting back nausea she closed her hand around the warm stiff flesh and turned her head away from the sight.

Above her, the soldier groaned and arched his back. Trembling with desire he began to push her hand up and down his tumescent organ. His head was thrown back, his loins bucked in rhythmic motion, sweat gleamed on his forehead. '*Schnell! Schnell!*'

Sobbing aloud, Marianne did as she was ordered, until with an animal cry the man's frenetic action was suddenly arrested. Seconds later the warm stickiness on her fingers made her want to vomit ... but at least it was over.

* * *

BUT THAT WAS JUST the beginning.

Each took her any way he wished. Marianne lost count of how many times she was penetrated. Her flesh burned and tore as one after another swollen penis forced its way inside her. From front and behind.

They ignored her sobs, her screamed pleas for mercy.

* * *

ONCE, through the mists of pain, she thought she heard the woman banging at the locked door. But no one came to her rescue.

Rough unshaven faces stinking of stale liquor buried themselves against her hair, her cheeks, her breasts.

'*Schon... schon...* Beautiful... so beautiful...' The word was gasped at her again and again and again.

It was the word she would hate to hear for the rest of her life.

* * *

CHARLES ROLFE KNEW she had forgotten him.

Though her fingers still clutched his, her blank distant gaze told him that Marianne Walenska was no longer aware of her surroundings, was no longer in the safety of the present. Somewhere in the darkness of memory she was reliving the haunting hell of the past.

I should have let it be, he admonished himself guiltily. *I should never have asked*.

But there was more...

* * *

'THE SOLDIERS HAD LEFT by the time Klauser returned.' Marianne was speaking again, her voice just above a whisper.

'I will never forget his fury when he found out what had happened. He would have shot them all without hesitation, I am certain of that. And afterwards he couldn't bear to come near me, he didn't touch me again.' She gave a terrible parody of a laugh. 'It was a high price to pay to escape his lust.

'But then three weeks later he appeared once more in my room, waking me around midnight. It's beginning again, was my first terrified thought, just when my wounds – the physical ones at least – were beginning to heal. But no; he ordered me to hurry and dress, told me we had to leave the lodge at once.

'He drove the Mercedes himself. The Russians were just hours away, he explained, we had to find our way to German lines. We would drive until the extra petrol we were carrying ran out. Then he revealed why he had decided to take me along too. If we ran out of petrol in enemy territory – Poland, he meant, of course – then he could produce papers to prove we were man and wife. I would be his cover. And naturally he could speak the language too.

'But the German lines were much further westward than he'd reckoned. We were forced to abandon the car long before we reached them. By the time we made it into German territory the chaos was obvious everywhere. Destruction, starvation, disease. It was clear to even the most fanatical believer that for the Third Reich the war was all but over.'

Marianne took a deep breath. 'And then, somewhere in Germany, when I had served my purpose, he abandoned me at last.'

* * *

FOR A LONG MOMENT the silence lay between them. It was Charles who finally broke it. His words came deep from the heart.

'I can see what it has cost you to reveal this, Marianne. To someone who has lost her family, her country, her innocence, I'm sure any words of comfort I might try to offer can only sound trite. Let me merely state that my respect for you is immeasurable.' He raised her hand to his mouth and kissed it, unwittingly aping the Polish formality. 'You must try to sleep now. If I leave you will you be all right?'

She nodded. The trauma of telling her story had left her totally drained. Every emotion seemed wrung from her and she longed to sleep.

Charles Rolfe rose to his feet. 'May I see you tomorrow? Just once more?'

Again she nodded. It was as if she were expecting the invitation.

* * *

BUT SLEEP DID NOT COME EASILY to either of them.

Through the hours of darkness, Charles Rolfe tossed in a fever of restlessness as he rejected again and again the wild idea pounding in his brain. *I'm crazy,* he told himself. *Mad to even contemplate such an impossible thought.*

But the impossible thought would not go away.

* * *

In her narrow bed Marianne Walenska lay rigid, eyes wide and staring.

Why didn't I tell him the whole truth? she asked herself tremulously.

6

They ate at an unpretentious Italian trattoria in Dean Street. Charles could do little more than pick at his meal and Marianne too was subdued. It wasn't until he took her home and accepted her invitation to come in, that any reference was made to the events and revelations of the previous day.

He took the seat she offered in the one uncomfortable high-backed chair and accepted a small tumbler of brandy. Marianne sat opposite on the bed.

Finally, aware he could put off the moment no longer, Charles broke into their inconsequential talk.

'Marianne, yesterday you did me the honor of confiding the details of your very traumatic past. Now, in turn, I too have something to confide. Not perhaps so tragic a story, but one that has certainly changed my own plans for the future.'

And as succinctly as possible he told her about his engagement to Peggy, about her patience as he fought his way back to health, and the shock as they both discovered his incapacity to resume their sexual relationship.

'I've seen a specialist, of course, but he could promise little hope for recovery. Certainly impotence could be related to my physical trauma, but on the whole the condition is still very much a mystery to the medical profession.'

His eyes looked into hers as he spoke, alert for her reaction. But Marianne Walenska's expression was unreadable. With no clear signal to guide him, Charles forced himself to go on.

'What I'm trying to say, Marianne, is that perhaps we are two people who can help each other. I understand the effect your own tragedy has had on your response to men. But you know you have nothing to fear like that from me. As for the rest, I have a great respect for you. I enjoy your company very much. Perhaps there's no need for us both to lead lonely lives.'

She was looking at him in puzzlement now, and the words came tumbling out. 'I'm asking you to marry me, Marianne. To let me offer you the protection you need – and a lot more besides. I'm a wealthy man, you would want for nothing; we could share a very fulfilling life together. And if in the future you decide you wanted out, then I promise ... I wouldn't stand in your way.'

Still she said nothing, but her expression reflected her astonishment and confusion.

He rose and, crouching in front of her, took her hand. 'I know this is very sudden for you, Marianne. I don't expect you to give me an answer now – I'm sure you'll need time to think about it. So you won't have to feel pressured by my presence, I've decided to visit friends in Surrey for a couple of days. Maybe when I return you'll be able to give me an answer.'

Charles stood up. He could feel the shirt sticking to his back. 'We've both shared our secrets now, Marianne. Alone, our lives are sure to be lonely. Together, we could find a companionship that might help ease the burden we are each forced to carry. I hope – I hope you will at least give some serious consideration to my proposal.'

And with a murmured 'goodnight' he let himself out of the room.

* * *

NOTHING ELSE OCCUPIED Marianne's mind for the next forty-eight hours.

Travelling on the crowded tube, working at her desk, eating her solitary meals, it was Charles Rolfe's offer that was always uppermost in her thoughts, distracting her from everything else.

His own revelation had of course come as no surprise, though she could hardly admit to that. Rather, it was his shock proposal of marriage that had caught her so off-guard. Never for one moment had she anticipated that.

In turn, she did her best to analyze her own feelings. Certainly, she decided, there was much to admire about the quietly spoken Australian. Charles Rolfe was a pleasant companion, cultured, refined, thoughtful; a gentleman in every sense. That the idea of 'love' did not figure in her reckonings caused her no problem. The proposal, she saw, was not dependent on that. Instead Charles Rolfe was suggesting a companionable arrangement, the practicality of which might indeed suit them both.

It was with equal practicality that Marianne wrestled with her decision.

Marriage to the well-bred businessman would offer protection, she could see. No man would be able to touch her again. As for Australia, well, she barely knew where the country was – except that it was a long way from Europe and the scene of all she had endured.

In the end Marianne came to the conclusion that there were few enough chances offered for any sort of happiness in this world.

She made up her mind to accept Charles Rolfe's proposal.

* * *

Over the same forty-eight hours Charles too existed in a fever of uncertainty. What would her answer be? Would she see the advantages for both of them in his pragmatic offer?

To Charles, a marriage to Marianne Walenska appeared the answer to many of his problems. Already she had proved her worth as a business partner; as his bride she would be not only a genteel companion but also the buffer he needed against other predatory women.

In the same way too, he would be able to put an end to his

mother's manipulative games. For she had still refused to accept the reality of his condition; still insisted on trying to match him with women she considered 'suitable'.

The more Charles thought the ramifications through the more he prayed that Marianne too would realized the advantages inherent in their match. He would happily protect her, take care of her, do everything he could to make up for the horrors she had been forced to endure. They would be companions, helpmates, shielding each other from loneliness and alienation.

* * *

HE MADE contact the moment he arrived back in London. She was at her desk but promised to come to his room as soon as she could get away. That alone gave Charles hope. Did it mean she didn't care if any of her colleagues knew?

Tense and on edge he welcomed her into his suite, studying her face for some clue to her reply.

In a soft voice she said, 'I have considered your generous proposal very carefully, Charles.' His heart leapt. It was the first time she had used his name. 'If you still want me, I... I will be happy to share your life.'

He took her hand in his. His eyes shone as they held hers. 'I'm so very, very pleased, Marianne. And I promise I will keep to our bargain in every way.'

* * *

THE MANAGER of the Lancaster Regent accepted her resignation in his usual professional manner.

'You won't be easy to replace, Miss Walenska. But I wish you and Mr Rolfe every happiness.'

Scheming, money-hungry little hussy, was what he was thinking.

* * *

In a jubilant mood Charles set about the myriad tasks that now faced him.

Because of the pressures of time it was impossible to set sail on his original date. Instead, he managed to reserve connecting First Class cabins on a vessel departing two weeks later.

Next in order was the matter of the Registry Office. Thank goodness, he thought, he had contacts in London who could be counted on to speed up the official process.

A trousseau for Marianne was also a necessity, but the same reluctance that for so long had kept her from enhancing her natural appeal had to be overcome.

'It's different now, Marianne. I'm here to protect you. There's no danger in making the most of your looks. Men might look at you, admire what they see, but no one can put a finger on you. We made a bargain with this marriage and I intend to keep it.'

But for Marianne the habit born of such psychological devastation was difficult to change. In the end Charles was forced to explain the importance of making a good first impression on his family and friends ... especially his mother.

'You'll understand a bit better when you meet her, Marianne. My mother is very prominent in the Sydney social scene; she's used to being in the limelight; so clothes, style, image, are very important to her. Please understand, when I ask to buy you nice things it's because I want to make sure you're as comfortable as possible with my family.'

Charles had little doubt about his mother's reaction to his marriage. It would be seen, he was certain, as an act of defiance against her own plans for his future. Edwina was bound to be furious at the unheralded match. Which was why Charles had no intention of informing her until the marriage was a fait accompli. After that, no matter how strongly she might protest, Edwina Rolfe would be forced to accept her son's choice.

Yet the situation was one for which he knew he would have to prepare Marianne. He decided that the six weeks at sea would be the time for that. During the voyage he would fill her in on the details of his family, his lifestyle, his country.

It would be one way to keep themselves occupied on their honeymoon.

* * *

'IF I MAY SAY SO, madam looks quite stunning in that shade.'

The saleswoman in the Beauchamp Place salon appraised her customer with a practiced eye. 'Yes,' she was nodding her severe chignon, 'so utterly striking on a blonde.'

In the full-length mirror Marianne nervously studied her reflection. She turned to look at Charles.

'What do you think?' she asked uncertainly.

From where he sat on the stylish, if uncomfortable, spindle-legged chair, Charles nodded his approval. 'It's wonderful on you. You must have it.'

They had spent all morning in some of London's most exclusive shops and Charles had derived a great deal of pleasure from indulging Marianne in an assortment of finery. Though he could still sense her unease.

It will take time, he told himself, but eventually she would learn to accept his wealth and his promise to look after her – in every way.

The saleswoman was quick to discern who was making the decisions here. 'So, madam will take the plum silk, and the two-piece? Excellent choices. I shall have them wrapped at once.' She smiled knowingly. 'And may I recommend our lingerie section? Everything a bride-to-be might require to please her new husband.'

There was an awkward moment of silence. Marianne felt her cheeks heat.

'I'll change and be with you in a moment,' she said, without looking at Charles.

* * *

AFTER A QUICK LUNCH they caught a cab to a shop a few blocks away. The lettering on the window said "Wartski".

'World specialists in Faberge,' Charles told her as they entered the hushed, elegant interior.

'Ah, Mr Rolfe...' They were greeted by a smiling, immaculately dressed gentleman with a head of thick white hair. He was obviously expecting them. 'How lovely to see you again, sir. How is your dear mother?'

Charles answered cheerfully as they were led into a private room at the rear of the establishment. The manager seated them in two comfortable chairs at a gleaming antique table. He took up his position opposite.

'Now, then. Here we are. Perhaps madam will find something to her liking among these.'

"These" were half a dozen velvet-lined trays containing row after row of wedding bands and engagement rings.

Charles turned to Marianne. 'I thought you would prefer to choose something yourself, my dear. That way I'd be sure you liked it.'

Marianne blinked and looked down at the bewildering rows of gold, diamonds, rubies, emeralds.

'I ... I don't know where to start.'

With a respectful cough the manager spoke up. 'May I suggest you make your first choice a wedding band, madam? The other may then be selected to suit.'

Tentatively Marianne followed his advice, slipping a number of the offerings onto the appropriate finger. In the end she opted for a simple, slim band.

'That's settled then,' said Charles. 'Now an engagement ring to match.'

Vigorously Marianne shook her head. 'No, this is all I need. The others are far too expensive, I'm sure.'

She still doesn't understand, thought Charles. *She still doesn't realize I'm in a position to give her anything she wants.*

'You must make a choice, Marianne. My mother would never forgive me if she knew I had brought my bride-to-be to Wartski's and allowed her to come home without an engagement ring.'

The manager smiled dutifully at the joke. But Marianne recognized that while there was amusement in Charles's tone there was something more besides.

His mother again, she thought. *It always seems so important to keep her happy.*

* * *

DESPITE ALL CHARLES'S ASSURANCES, Marianne couldn't help feeling nervous. The dinner that evening would be her first meeting with any of his friends.

'I've known the Pryors for years, Marianne. Alistair and Nancy are a terrific couple. I'm sure you'll get on with both of them.'

As she bathed and dressed in the suite Charles had booked for her at the Savoy Hotel, Marianne prepared herself mentally too for the evening ahead. She was determined not to slip up. She would play her role of the devoted bride-to-be so that not even Charles's closest friends would have the slightest suspicion as to the true nature of their relationship.

* * *

THE DORCHESTER GRILL ROOM was buzzing with conversation and their table was well placed to catch sight of some well-known faces – a cabinet minister, a famous conductor, various aristocrats and socialites.

Not that such people were familiar to Marianne, but Nancy Pryor seemed to recognize – if not actually greet – anyone of note.

The Pryors were English, around Charles's age Marianne guessed maybe a little older. Alistair Pryor's mother had gone to school with Edwina Rolfe and the boys had become friends during Edwina's frequent return visits to England.

Alistair Pryor was a banker. He was tall, with a large beaky nose and fair hair already beginning to thin. His laconic, dry manner was in marked contrast to his wife's effusiveness.

To Marianne it seemed that Nancy Pryor chatted incessantly, her bony fingers flashing with diamonds as she gesticulated with her silver cigarette holder.

While the men caught up on family and business news the Englishwoman told Marianne about their two sons who were both at boarding school, about her charity work and the renovations to their house in Berkshire. Like most of their class, the Pryors divided their time between their London flat and a home in the country.

'Life's so hectic in town,' Nancy Pryor was complaining happily. 'If I didn't have somewhere to escape to I think I'd go mad.' With practiced ease she switched topics. 'I must say I'm delighted about the marriage, my dear. What a romantic way to meet... And Alistair and I are quite, quite honored to be your witnesses. I can't help wondering though, why you're not allowing yourselves the fun of a big do back in Australia.'

Marianne fielded the comment politely. 'Neither Charles nor I want the fuss of a big wedding.'

'Well, knowing Edwina as well as I do I'm surprised she hasn't insisted.'

Charles overhead the remark. 'If we did it my mother's way, Nancy, the wedding would be six months in the planning.' He smiled at Marianne. 'I had no intention of waiting that long.'

Alistair Pryor raised a suggestive eyebrow. 'Well, I envy you a six-week honeymoon at sea, old chap.'

'So you should, Alistair. So you should.' Charles hoped the note of heartiness was just right.

With the ceremony to be held the next morning, the night finished early.

In the foyer Nancy Pryor pecked Marianne on the cheek. 'I'll be at the Savoy around ten, my dear. That'll give us plenty of time to get you to the Registry Office by eleven-thirty.'

'Thank you.' Marianne wasn't looking forward to having the talkative Englishwoman in attendance as she got ready.

Alistair Pryor shook his friend's hand. 'Sleep well while you can, old boy.' There was nothing subtle in the innuendo.

Charles forced a laugh. He couldn't think of a quick reply.

* * *

'WELL... WHAT DID YOU THINK?'

No sooner were they settled in the rear seat of the Rolls than Nancy Pryor fired the question at her husband. 'Oh, I –'

His wife cut across him. 'I couldn't put my finger on it, Alistair, but there's something funny there. I mean she's charming, of course, wonderful looking – although nothing of a background it seems. What Edwina's going to say when she meets the little Polish refugee will be interesting to say the least. No, what I'm getting at is that for a newly-engaged couple there was a surprising lack of – of intimacy between them. Didn't you think? They were so *formal* with each other.'

Her husband nodded. 'Y-e-s, I suppose I –'

Again Nancy Pryor interrupted. 'Did you hear him call her anything but her name? No *darlings* – no nothing. And on top of that he never put a finger on her.'

'Well, they haven't known each other very long, darling, after all.' He turned to his wife. 'You're not suggesting that the girl might be marrying him for his money?'

Nancy Pryor shook her head. 'No, I don't think it's quite as simple as that – after all, Charles is nobody's fool. It's just... there's something about that liaison that doesn't ring quite true, Alistair.'

7

For Marianne the wedding ceremony and the luncheon that followed had the speeded-up quality of a dream. The morning's preparations, the arrival of Nancy Pryor with the lily of the valley bouquet, the trip to the Chelsea Registry Office and then the ceremony itself ... everything happened so quickly that she had no time for doubts.

It wasn't until after the simple celebratory luncheon when she and Charles were saying their goodbyes to the Pryors in the foyer of the Savoy Hotel that the real significance of what had occurred began to sink in.

Their luggage had been sent on ahead and instead of catching a train to Southampton Alistair Pryor had insisted on sending them in his chauffeur-driven Rolls.

As they left London's suburbs behind, Marianne finally had time for reflection on the momentous events of the day.

I am the wife of Charles Rolfe. The man beside me is my husband, she told herself in silent wonderment.

Perhaps sensing her mood, Charles chatted easily as they covered the miles. He spoke largely of Australia and it was clear to Marianne how much he loved his country.

'You wouldn't believe how different it is from here, Marianne. Huge blue canopy of sky, enormous vistas. The minute I smell the eucalypts and catch sight of the harbor I feel instantly at home. And it's the people too – they're friendlier, more relaxed than the English. You'll love the place, I'm sure.'

Charles couldn't hide his jubilant mood. As he'd stood beside Marianne in front of the registrar and repeated the words of his wedding vows he'd felt confident of the future. *We were meant to find each other,* he'd told himself. From here on life would be easier for both of them.

Yet as he sat in the leather comfort of the Rolls he couldn't suppress a momentary feeling of unease. That morning, on the way to the Registry Office, he had sent his mother a telegram, informing her of the marriage.

She would be upset, of that he was certain. Yet there was nothing she could do now but accept his decision.

* * *

AT SOUTHAMPTON the dockside was teeming with travelers and well-wishers. As Marianne caught sight of the huge ocean liner she felt her insides flutter with a mixture of excitement and apprehension.

So much had happened in so short a time. As Mrs Charles Rolfe she was about to start a new life in a new country. For a moment she felt like pinching herself.

The purser greeted them warmly and escorted them personally to their First Class cabin on the uppermost deck.

Marianne's eyes widened in wonder as they entered. For the first time she began to realize the extent of Charles Rolfe's wealth. The suite was large and beautifully appointed. Crystal vases held exotic blooms, there were fresh fruits in silver bowls and a bottle of French champagne sat cooling in an ice bucket.

'I hope everything is to your liking, sir,' the purser purred. 'Staff are on call twenty-four hours if there is anything at all you need.'

Charles gazed around with a smile. 'Everything looks perfect.'

'And of course the Captain is hoping you will be free to dine with him this evening.'

'Thank you. We will be happy to accept his kind invitation.'

The cabin door closed and Charles turned his smile on Marianne. He could sense her tension now they were alone.

'I reserved this stateroom in particular, my dear.'

Beckoning her to follow he crossed the living area and opened an interior door. 'You see ... your own separate bedroom and bathroom. Mine is on the opposite side.'

Marianne hid her relief. At the same time she felt comforted by the evidence of Charles's thoughtfulness. *I wasn't wrong about him,* she thought. *He really does understand.*

She smiled her thanks at the stranger she had married.

* * *

THERE WERE a dozen VIP guests at Captain Willard's table. Nearly all were older than the Rolfes. In expensive, elegant gowns, the women sparkled with jewels while their dinner-jacketed husbands had the sleek confidence endowed by wealth and power.

With her hair upswept and in her bare-shouldered gown Marianne knew she too fitted the image of a rich man's spouse. She would hold her own with these people, she determined. She had no intention of allowing them to intimidate her.

Introductions were made and then the captain stood to propose a toast. 'To the newly-weds,' he proclaimed. 'May their life together be long, full of happiness, and produce some noteworthy additions to the long line of Rolfes.'

Marianne held her fixed smile as Charles made a gracious response.

* * *

AFTER DINNER there was dancing in one of the salons. As Charles led her lightly around the floor Marianne could feel all eyes upon them. She wondered if she would ever be at ease with the attention she had avoided for so long.

As if reading her thoughts Charles whispered close to her ear, 'Don't worry. I'm here now to keep you safe. Always.' He squeezed her hand. 'It's been a long day for both of us. Shall we go?'

She nodded up at him with a tremulous smile.

In the central living room the steward had left on a single lamp. In its soft glow Charles took her hand and said gently, 'I promise you won't regret your decision, my dear.' He looked into her eyes as he raised her fingers to his lips. *How truly beautiful she looks.*

'Goodnight, Marianne. Sleep well.'

They adjourned to their separate sleeping quarters.

* * *

AS THE DAYS PASSED, Marianne found herself relaxing more and more in Charles's company. His good manners and gentle humor made him easy to be with. Widely travelled, cultured, and well read, he introduced her to topics and ideas about which she hungered to know more. In some ways, she thought in surprise, he reminded her of her father.

Their daylight hours were filled with walks on the deck, games of quoits, swimming and reading. At night there were long leisurely dinners followed by an hour or two on the dance floor or by taking in a movie in the ship's theaterette. Few would have noticed how little time the honeymooning couple actually spent alone in their cabin.

As the liner headed inexorably further and further south, the air became warmer, encouraging a torpor among the passengers. Lazing by the swimming pool, Marianne was surprised how quickly the time seemed to pass without the strict routine of work. Perhaps, she thought, it's because Charles is such interesting company. She was never bored.

The only small disturbance to her new-found peace of mind was the prospect of meeting Edwina Rolfe.

A couple of weeks into the voyage Charles had sat beside her on the deck one afternoon and filled her in on his family. There was his sister, Caroline, who at twenty-four was married to a stockbroker. 'A perfect match ... especially in my mother's eyes,' he added with a teasing smile. 'Gerald comes from one of Sydney's best families. Their wedding was one of the social events of the year. They have a little girl just two, and their next baby's due any day.'

Charles's younger brother Hugh was twenty-one and he too worked in the family firm. Unmarried, he still lived with their mother at the Point Piper home.

'You'll love the house,' Charles enthused to Marianne. 'My grandfather built it. It's quite a landmark on the harbor.'

As he spoke he slipped a photograph from his wallet and handed it to her. 'Here it is – and the family too.'

Marianne studied the black and white snapshot. Three people were standing on the broad steps of what looked like a very substantial home. The architecture – low, sprawling, with wide verandahs – was different from anything she had ever seen in Europe.

With a frown she turned to Charles. 'Your mother lives in the city then? I thought the country properties... the sheep...?'

She was interrupted by Charles's hearty laugh. 'Oh, no! The outback's fine for sheep, as far as my mother's concerned. But she won't leave Sydney unless it's absolutely necessary. Now that my father's gone the stations are run entirely by managers.'

As he replaced the photograph the humorous light suddenly faded from his eyes. 'Marianne,' he gave her a sideways look, 'I feel I have to warn you. I'm sure my mother will be upset that we have married so precipitously. She can be difficult sometimes, but given time, and when she gets to know you, I'm positive she'll accept both you and our marriage wholeheartedly. In the meantime I hope you won't find it too difficult to... be patient with her.'

I'm not sure I am going to like Edwina Rolfe, Marianne told herself silently.

* * *

'I DON'T *BELIEVE* IT! I just don't *believe* it!' Spluttering with rage Edwina Rolfe stormed into the breakfast room.

Her younger son looked up startled from his bacon and eggs. 'Read this!' she demanded, red-faced. 'Just read this!'

Hugh Rolfe reached out and took the telegram from his mother's trembling fingers. The message was brief. 'Married this morning. Very happy. Arriving home...' In his surprise the details barely registered.

'Charles has got *married*? But –'

Dark eyes ablaze, Edwina broke in: 'He's taken leave of his senses! How could he do this to me? How dare he? How *dare* he? I'm going to get to the bottom of this, I can assure you!'

Striding out of the room as abruptly as she had entered, Edwina Rolfe left her younger son to contemplate his brother's astonishing news.

While his mother was not noted for her even temperament Hugh couldn't recall the last time he had seen her in such a towering rage. What, he wondered, had inspired Charles to act so impulsively? Especially considering the sudden breaking off of his engagement to Peggy Dennison. Hugh still had the feeling that there was more to that than met the eye...

With a grimace of distaste he pushed away the plate of rapidly congealing food. Well, Charles was certainly going to have to face the music when he finally arrived home.

As he left the table the younger son of Edwina Rolfe was already wondering if there was any way the situation might be turned to his own particular advantage. It had suited him very well being the only 'Mr Rolfe' in the firm while Charles was away.

* * *

EDWINA KNEW EXACTLY whom to call. Nancy Pryor. Charles was bound to have seen her and Alistair while he was in London. If anyone knew anything about this intolerable situation it would be Nancy.

Impatiently she waited while the operator connected her.

It was one of the rare evenings when Nancy and Alistair Pryor were at home.

Five minutes later Edwina Rolfe replaced the receiver. She clenched her fists, her breathing shallow. *A nobody...*

Her son had been beguiled by some absolute nobody! Some penniless Polish refugee...

8

'It's... beautiful.'

Wide eyed with wonder Marianne stood beside her husband on the First Class deck as the liner made its stately way up the magnificent harbor.

Around her she could hear similar exclamations of delight from her fellow passengers.

Charles grinned. 'Impressive, isn't it? It never fails to remind me how much I love this country.'

He glanced sideways. Marianne's fair hair was blowing in the light morning breeze. A light tan had given a soft golden sheen to her skin and it served to emphasize the deep blue of her eyes. She really is exquisite, he thought.

The weeks at sea had removed the last vestiges of tension between them. There was a trust on both sides now, and a growing friendship that had enabled each of them to relax. Their days had been spent in happy companionship and at night they had retired to their separate rooms without embarrassment. In public no one could have thought them anything but what they seemed; a newly married couple madly in love.

'Look, Marianne!' Excited, Charles pointed with an outstretched arm. 'That's Point Piper now.'

Even from a distance Marianne could see how grand and imposing the houses were. Their gardens sloped right to the water's edge. She spotted tennis courts and swimming pools. I can't let him down, she resolved silently. I've got to make sure I'm accepted by his family and friends.

Beside her Charles was wondering about the sort of greeting that awaited them from his mother.

* * *

'Do I look all right?' She turned from the mirror, seeking his approval for the slim white suit and the cherry red straw hat. The cabin was clear of luggage. In just minutes they would be docking at the pier.

'Wonderful, my dear.' Charles could see the hint of nervousness in her manner. No wonder, he thought, after all I've told her about mother. His mouth firmed, he would handle Edwina.

* * *

But Edwina Rolfe had not seen fit to be a part of their welcome.

As they stepped off the gangplank and made their way into the cavernous customs hall, Charles saw it was his younger brother, hat in hand, who was waiting to greet them. Alone.

'Hugh! Great to see you! I reckon you've grown another inch since I left.' Warmly shaking his brother's hand Charles added, 'You got my telegram, of course? May I introduce my wife, Marianne? My brother, Hugh, my dear.'

Hugh Rolfe was staring wide-eyed at the slim, well-dressed blonde who stood close to his brother. Crikey, she was a *knockout*.

He pulled himself together, remembered his manners. 'Uh... how do you do ... Marianne. Welcome to Australia. And congratulations – to both of you.'

With a smile Marianne took his hand in her gloved one. Hugh Rolfe was only in his early twenties she knew, but already he looked more robust than his older brother, with his height, his broad shoulders and strong arresting features. To Marianne the family resemblance was most obvious in his thick sandy hair and wide disarming smile.

'I am so pleased to meet you. Charles has told me a lot about you.'

The accent too... Hugh was entranced.

'Is mother well?' Charles asked the question as the three of them moved through the crowds to the exit. Formalities for First Class passengers had been attended to before disembarking.

'Yes, she –'

'*Hey! Hey, Mr Rolfe! This way!*' As Charles turned in the direction of the shout there was a flash of exploding bulbs. To his annoyance he saw three or four press photographers pushing their way towards them. Damn! Somehow word had already got out.

Hugh echoed his thoughts. 'Looks like someone on board must have opened his big mouth. The car's right outside, the luggage should be there already. Let's get going.'

With a hand on the small of Marianne's back, Charles hurried her towards the exit.

But the press were in hot pursuit.

'That your new wife, Mr Rolfe?'

'*The Women's Weekly* would love a photograph, Mr Rolfe...'

They made it out of the customs hall. In the blazing sunshine a navy blue Daimler waited at the kerb.

'Good to have you home, sir.' The uniformed chauffeur was standing by to open the rear door. He had seen what was happening.

The car pulled away just as the photographers came alongside. There was one more quick blinding flash and then they were left behind.

Recovering from her surprise Marianne realized she had got her first glimpse of the interest Australia had in the rich and famous Rolfe family.

* * *

THEY WERE DRIVEN to Charles's flat in Bellevue Hill. He had moved there as soon as he'd recovered his health, eager to regain his independence. Much as his mother would have preferred it, he was far too old, he decided, to live at home again.

The flat was one of four in an impressive mansion block. It was large, airy, well appointed, but now that Marianne was in his life Charles knew he would prefer the privacy of their own home and garden. Finding a place they both liked would be among his first tasks.

* * *

WHEN THE CHAUFFEUR and the doorman had finished carrying in the luggage Hugh said goodbye to Marianne. 'I'll see you tonight, I hope. Mother is expecting you both to dinner of course.' He couldn't take his eyes off her. 'You'll meet Caroline then too.'

'I will look forward to it.' Marianne could still feel the motion of the sea as she stood at the top of the stairs and smiled her goodbye.

'Of course we'll be there,' answered Charles. He walked his brother to the car, standing for a moment in the hot sunshine to ask quietly, 'How did she take it?'

Hugh shrugged. 'I wouldn't say she was exactly thrilled, old boy. But, if you don't mind a personal opinion, may I say you've got excellent taste.'

With a grin he slid into the car. 'See you tonight. And don't worry, I can't see how Mother could possibly not be charmed by your very – unusual wife. Can't wait to hear exactly how she picked you up.'

Charles frowned as he watched the Daimler pull away. Hugh was too young to be a smart Alec, he thought.

* * *

'WELL? WHAT'S SHE LIKE?'

Caroline threw the question at her younger brother as soon as the butler left the room. It was a hot night and she brushed away a trickle of sweat from her crisp auburn curls. Her increasing bulk made her even more uncomfortable but nothing short of her child's imminent birth could have prevented her being present this evening. Caroline Oliver was burning with curiosity to meet the stranger who so suddenly and unexpectedly had taken on the title of her sister-in-law.

'You all right, darling?' Gerald Oliver noted his wife's discomfort. Of average build, with slicked back dark hair and sharp features, he had the conservative manner and dress of a typical stockbroker. Through rimless spectacles he looked anxiously at his pregnant wife.

'Don't fuss, Gerald. I'm fine.' After only four years of marriage Caroline already exerted the same dominance over her husband as her mother had held over her father. Mother and daughter shared other traits too – both argumentative, abrasive, strong-willed ... yet they seldom clashed. They had too much in common for that.

'Well?' Caroline was still waiting for an answer. The smirk on Hugh's face irritated her.

'Patience, Caroline. They'll be here any minute. Then you can see for yourself.'

'What I still don't understand is why he'd want to break off with a top-notch girl like Peggy just to end up marrying some foreign nobody.'

Edwina Rolfe had listened grim-faced to the exchange. She put down her empty sherry glass, her dark eyes cold. 'I intend to get to the bottom of it all, I can assure you.'

Whatever reply Caroline Oliver was about to make was forestalled by a discreet tap on the door.

'Mr Charles and his wife, madam.' The butler stood aside and Edwina's elder son entered the room. But it was the expensively dressed, fair-haired beauty accompanying him who was the focus of all eyes.

* * *

MARIANNE WAS DOING HER BEST.

Seated between Edwina Rolfe and Gerald Oliver she was making every attempt to find some common ground. But Charles's mother was not making it easy. The sweat trickling between Marianne's shoulder blades was not entirely the result of the evening's sticky heat. She had seen the resentment in Edwina Rolfe's face as soon as their eyes met. Charles's mother was a small, very slim, severely elegant woman with graying upswept hair, a fine pale complexion and cold brown eyes. With her almost regal bearing it was easy for Marianne to see how intimidating she might be.

I will win her over, she asserted to herself, her mind drifting from her conversation with Gerald Oliver. When she sees her son is content then she will accept me.

Edwina Rolfe, talking over the top of her son-in-law, broke into Marianne's thoughts.

'So, let me get this quite straight,' – she couldn't bring herself to use the girl's name – 'you lost your immediate family in the war, you say?'

'Yes...'

'But surely you must have preferred to go back to your own country rather than stay in Britain?'

'I'm afraid it wasn't that simple, Mrs Rolfe.'

Edwina felt a sudden sickening jolt. 'You don't mean to say you're of... the Jewish faith?'

'No. I was brought up Roman Catholic.'

Bad enough, but not quite as socially destroying as the other, Edwina tried to console herself.

From the other side of the table Charles felt it time to take control. 'Marianne and I want to find a house as soon as possible, Mother. Perhaps you'd like to help us search for something suitable?' It was one way he hoped that his mother and wife might spend time together and become better acquainted.

Edwina fixed her son with a frosty look. 'You know how I loathe putting a foot outside the door in this heat, Charles.'

And so the dinner proceeded.

* * *

AFTERWARDS THEY TOOK coffee and port in the cool of the verandah. Yet even here the atmosphere was charged with tension.

Her condition making her feel inelegant and frumpish Caroline Oliver was even less inclined to be welcoming to the slim, beautiful stranger Charles had foisted upon them. The fact that both Hugh and her own husband could barely take their eyes off the girl merely increased her hostility.

Little tramp, she thought, infuriated. Flaunting herself in that bare-shouldered dress. Where in the world had Charles picked her up? What her friends were going to say when they found out there was a "refo" in the family, Caroline didn't dare to think.

Over the top of her coffee cup she took in her mother's stiff face. Mother will fix this, she thought confidently. Nothing's going to allow her to sit back and accept this foreign hussy as a Rolfe.

In the semi-darkness Edwina was busy with her own thoughts. From the first moment she'd set eyes on the girl she'd known exactly what had happened. Charles, like so many gullible men before him, had been mesmerized by a pretty face. Or, in this case, she had to admit, a beautiful one... Bowled over by the girl's stunning looks he had allowed the little gold-digger to rush him into marriage. As simple as that.

As for that other matter regarding his broken engagement to Peggy Dennison, well, Edwina still intended to get to the bottom of *that*.

Abruptly she stood up from the wicker chair. 'Charles, if you wouldn't mind? We haven't yet had a word in private. There are a few – business matters I think we should discuss.' She swept her gaze over the others. 'If you would excuse us for a short while?'

Caroline hid a smirk as her brother followed their mother into the house.

* * *

THE CONVERSATION TOOK place in the library.

'Why did you lie to me, Charles?'

'What do you mean, Mother?'

'About Peggy. About your – *medical* problem?'

Charles's face tightened. 'That wasn't a lie, Mother. Nothing's changed in that regard.'

'Oh, come now, Charles. You're not trying to tell me that young healthy girl out there married a man who can't satisfy her.'

Charles was determined not to let her get under his skin. 'If you don't believe me, Mother, why not ask Doctor Bennett? Perhaps,' his tone became biting, 'he might be persuaded to show you my records.'

Edwina Rolfe's dark eyes flashed. 'If that's so, then Charles, tell me this. What kind of woman will settle for only *half* a man?'

The stinging words hung in the air between them.

Charles made to turn away but his mother grasped his arm. '*Answer* me, Charles. Or should I point out the obvious? That the girl married you for your money and your position, that she's a dirty little gold-digger preying on a vulnerable man!'

Charles shrugged himself free of her thin, jeweled fingers. Struggling now to keep his temper he stated coldly, 'You couldn't be more mistaken, Mother, but I have no intention of explaining to you all the reasons for the marriage. Suffice to say that Marianne knows and accepts my condition. The marriage offers other comforts – to both of us.'

'Really?' Edwina's tone was acid.

Ignoring his mother's skepticism Charles continued, 'Marianne lost everything in the war. She suffered in ways you couldn't begin to understand. I want to make up to her for that. As for myself, surely even you can understand that as a married man I'm saved the embarrassment of having to explain my condition – my *impotence*, Mother – to other women who might decide that Charles Rolfe is a good catch.'

He turned to look into her set, tight-lipped face.

'This is the first and last time I am going to discuss the matter, Mother. Marianne is now my wife and I expect you to treat her accordingly. Do I make myself clear?'

In the darkness of the hallway Hugh Rolfe leaned close to the door and listened in amazement to every word.

9

Over the next few weeks Marianne felt her senses bombarded by the myriad impressions of the strange and exotic country that was to be her home. The stifling summer heat, the glare, the colors and scents of unfamiliar blossoms and trees, the stunning spectacle of Saturday afternoon sails on the harbor – it all intrigued her.

Sydney, too, with its trams and ferries and busy streets, had its own particular charm. While the city might have lacked the sophistication of London, the people, she decided, were among the friendliest on earth – even if the slow, drawling accents of some occasionally eluded her.

Charles, meanwhile, had settled back into his work at the Rolfe company headquarters in Pitt Street but he still made time to accompany her as they searched for their future home.

It didn't take long to find. Marianne knew the moment she entered the rose-encircled gate that their search was at an end. The house was a two-storey mansion opposite Centennial Park, the beautiful natural reserve which was a favorite retreat for city dwellers.

The house, with its ivy-covered stone walls, its leadlight windows and imposing turret, reminded Marianne of some of the more elegant addresses in Krakow. The impression of Europe immediately made her feel at home. Inside were wood-paneled rooms, marble fireplaces and acres of soft carpet, while the garden with its shaded lily pond, its huge old trees and colorful flowerbeds was an added delight.

Charles could tell at once how much Marianne liked the place. Her eyes shone as they completed the tour of inspection with the agent.

Emerging into the sunshine, he smiled at her. 'We'll be happy here, don't you think, my dear?'

As she realized his genuine delight in her pleasure, Marianne began to understand more and more that the man she had married was a very special human being.

'Yes, Charles. I will make us a wonderful home here.'

* * *

AND SHE DID. It didn't take her long to familiarize herself with the city and its stores, and with an open check book at her disposal Marianne had the pleasure of seeking out and being able to afford the best of everything.

Complementing Charles's own collection of paintings and antiques she found exactly what was necessary to furnish each room – a French armoire here, a wonderful mirror there, new curtains in the main reception rooms – until at last the house was complete.

They advertised too for a live-in housekeeper. Charles had insisted. 'This place is far too large for you to handle alone, my dear.'

There were a surprising number of applicants and Marianne finally narrowed her choice to three. Janet Byrne she interviewed last and felt an instant liking for the quietly spoken woman with the dark curly hair and intelligent hazel eyes. Raised in a small country town, Janet Byrne was just a couple of years older than Marianne herself. She had married young, she explained, and moved to Sydney, but her husband had been a casualty of the New Guinea campaign.

'You didn't wish to go back to your home town?' Marianne enquired gently.

For the first time there was a hint of evasiveness in the other woman's manner. 'No, I like Sydney. I'm here to stay.'

Something told Marianne there was more to it than that, but she didn't see that it mattered. She liked Janet Byrne and the fact that she had trained as a nurse also counted strongly in her favor. Charles's wartime injuries had left him prone to colds and flu. It would be reassuring, she decided, to have someone with Janet Byrne's training around the house.

* * *

CHARLES FELT a happiness he had feared would always be denied him. Every evening he couldn't wait to return to Marianne and the comfortable elegant home she had created for them both. As they shared their evening meal at the gleaming dining table that had been in the Rolfe family for more than three generations, he said silent thanks for the good fortune that had brought Marianne Walenska into his life.

Only one thing clouded his happiness. It was something he could never have anticipated and the knowledge made his stomach churn in fear.

He knew it was the biggest threat of all.

* * *

EDWINA ROLFE PAID her first visit to the house not long after they moved in. Ignoring her daughter-in-law, she directed her comments at her son as she inspected the new abode.

'Can't see how you can live without a water view, Charles. Surely you could have found something on the harbor to suit?'

'This is the place we liked best, Mother,' Charles answered evenly. 'The view of the park is almost like living in the country.'

Raising a haughty eyebrow his mother murmured, 'All right for those who like the country, I suppose.'

'Will you stay for afternoon tea, Mrs Rolfe?' Marianne was leading the way towards the sunroom that overlooked the rear garden. 'I've had the housekeeper make–'

'Not today, I'm afraid.' Edwina Rolfe was pulling on her gloves. She kissed Charles, nodded at her daughter-in-law.

'I'd rip up that awful carpet if I were you,' were her parting words as she slid into the rear seat of the car.

* * *

THE NEXT TIME Marianne met with her in-laws was at the christening party for Caroline and Gerald's new baby.

'Do we *have* to ask her, Mother?' It was two months after her son's birth and Caroline was sitting with her mother, making out the guest list.

'For the time being,' came Edwina's cryptic reply.

* * *

ON THE MANICURED lawn that swept down to the waters of the harbor, Sydney's social elite stood sipping their drinks and indulging their penchant for gossip. Most of all they were dying to set eyes on the little Polish "refo" who had pushed her way into the Rolfe clan.

As Charles arrived from the church with Marianne on his arm the stares and whispers were blatant. Sharp female eyes raked over the blonde stranger who had somehow managed to land the heir to the Rolfe fortune. Surprise, then envy, was the general response to the elegantly dressed beauty walking by Charles Rolfe's side. The male guests merely ogled in open admiration.

As they crossed the lawn Charles sensed Marianne's tension. He squeezed her hand. 'I won't leave you alone, my dear. Don't worry.'

But for Marianne the afternoon was an ordeal. She hated being the focus of such intense attention. Yet when Charles introduced her to his friends they did little more than toss her some condescending pleasantry. Their message was clear: it was Charles who mattered, not the nobody he had made his wife.

To all present it must have been clear enough how Edwina Rolfe felt about her new daughter-in-law. For not only had she failed to arrange a formal occasion to introduce her son's new bride to Sydney society, but here, at the christening, she was all but ignoring her. Their relationship was made starkly plain.

Charles displayed a rare temper as he drove them home. 'She deliberately insulted you, Marianne, I won't stand for it! I'm going to tell her exactly–'

Marianne put a hand on his arm and gently cut across him. 'It is still difficult for her, Charles. Please don't upset her. Give it time.'

Still smoldering, her husband reluctantly agreed.

* * *

THAT NIGHT CHARLES found sleep difficult. It was a problem that had begun to plague him with increasing frequency.

Restless, he kicked off the sheet and dressed only in his shorts, threw open the French doors to his small bedroom patio.

A low golden moon hung over the park. The noises of the city were stilled. He leaned against the scrolled patio rail, feeling the cold of the metal against his bare flesh. Panic bubbled in his throat and he experienced the now familiar churning in his belly.

Oh, God, he thought, hands gripped like vices around the railing. *What am I going to do?*

What am I going to do?

* * *

JANET BYRNE WAS ENJOYING her new job. With only two adults to care for, the work was undemanding and the salary much better than she could have earned as a hospital nurse. Even if Marianne Rolfe hadn't been as pleasant as she was, Janet knew she would have done anything to stay in the job. For the money was important. Vitally important.

As the weeks passed she came to know her young employer. On occasion Marianne would join her in the kitchen to make some of the Polish dishes she enjoyed, and gradually the relationship between the two women became less formal.

It occurred to Janet that the young bride might be lonely. With no family of her own, with her husband out of the house all day and her Australian in-laws, it seemed to Janet, disinclined to visit, the new Mrs Rolfe spent a lot of time alone. This impression was strengthened by the scene that met Janet one afternoon after her return from her daily visit to the local shops.

As she opened the front door she could hear the grand piano being played in the living room. Marianne often entertained her husband in the evenings, but then the pieces were lively and cheerful, not the brooding, plaintive melody she was playing today.

In the kitchen Janet put away the groceries and decided there was time before dinner to finish a load of ironing. But as she made her way past the living room door her attention was caught by another sound over the cadence of the keys.

With a frown she stopped in her tracks. Then, quietly approaching the living room door, she peeked inside.

Marianne was bent over the keys, the tears pouring down her beautiful face. Her whole body spoke of some unbearable sadness.

Janet hesitated, moved by her employer's obvious distress, yet at the same time awkward about intruding. But the tender-hearted housekeeper could not deny her instincts.

Moving into the room she came to a standstill by the weeping woman. Tentatively she placed a comforting hand on her slim shoulder. For a moment longer Marianne continued to play – a Chopin etude, Janet noted from the sheet of music in front of her. Then, with a tearing sob, she abruptly lifted her hands from the keys and covered her face.

'Oh, Mrs Rolfe...' Janet's whisper was full of compassion. 'You must miss Poland, and your family... so much.'

Shoulders heaving, Marianne took a long time to reply. At last, fighting for control, she lowered her hands and slowly turned to look up into the housekeeper's sympathetic face.

Janet Byrne was taken aback at the sight of the raw pain in those stricken blue eyes.

She barely caught the younger woman's broken whisper.

'Sometimes... it is better not to think of what one misses.'

* * *

IT WAS ALMOST four weeks before Janet had her first full weekend off and she had been counting the days. The journey across Sydney by bus and then train took up far too much of her precious time so that it was almost noon by the time she arrived at the gates of Cleveland House.

Mrs Maguire gave her a frazzled smile of welcome as she opened the door to her ring. 'Ah, Mrs Byrne, how's yourself then? Keeping well? How's the new job going?'

'Very well, thank you, Mrs Maguire.' She stepped into the dim hallway. 'How – how's Danny?'

The woman shut the door behind her. In the background could be heard the sound of children's voices. 'Oh, you know, no better, no worse. Not fretting for you too much, I think.'

'Mrs Maguire! Mrs Maguire!' The call came from somewhere at the top of the steep staircase. The greyhaired woman looked up. 'Now who'd be wantin' me up there?' She turned back to Janet. 'I can leave you to find your own way, can't I, Mrs Byrne? The second doorway on the right at the end there.'

Janet nodded. She was already on her way. Too much time had been wasted already. 'I remember,' she said over her shoulder.

* * *

HE WAS SITTING PROPPED up among a nest of pillows in a corner of the room. Three other boys, a little older, argued loudly as they knelt over a formation of shabby toy soldiers. But Danny sat quietly. Tongue poked out of the side of his mouth his concentration was on his crayons and paper.

For a moment Janet stood motionless in the doorway.

Danny... oh, my precious little boy...

She bit her lip as she took in the thin, wasted frame, the twisted legs. Her son was five years old but the terrible tragedy of the poliomyelitis virus had left him pale and skeletal.

With her husband dead she'd had no choice but to leave her darling son in the care of others. Doctors, physiotherapy and drugs cost money. She had been forced to find work.

It was Father Michael, her parish priest back home, who had found her a place for Danny at Cleveland House. As children's homes go, the priest had assured her, Cleveland House was among the best. Janet trusted Father Michael's judgment. She had known him all her life. It was Father Michael who had buried both her mother and then her husband.

But while Janet was reassured that Danny was well enough cared for that didn't stop her missing him dreadfully. A devout Catholic, all her prayers begged God for the miracle of her son's return to health.

Now she moved into the room and the little boy looked up.

'Mum! Mum!' His face shone as he dropped the crayons and threw his skinny arms out wide. Kneeling beside him Janet hugged him to her breast. 'Oh, my darling. Mummy's missed you so, so much.' She squeezed her eyes tight. Please, God, she prayed, don't let him see me cry.

* * *

JANET BYRNE WAS both surprised and worried that Marianne Rolfe seemed to sense her change of mood after her return from Cleveland House.

Leaving her child again had almost broken both their hearts. Danny had clung to her, sobbing. 'Don't go, Mum, please don't go.'

Janet had no choice; but how do you explain that to a tearful five year old? she asked herself as she endured the long journey home.

'Is there something wrong, Janet?' Marianne frowned as she noted her housekeeper's strained expression. Rather than appearing relaxed, Janet Byrne seemed strangely subdued after her weekend off.

'No, Mrs Rolfe.' Vigorously Janet shook her head. 'Just ... just a touch of a headache perhaps.'

Pull yourself together, she admonished herself severely. *You can't afford to lose a job like this.*

At the same time Marianne Rolfe was thinking: *I hope she's happy here. I couldn't bear for her to leave.*

After all, apart from Charles, Janet Byrne was the closest she had to a friend.

10

Marianne knew she had to do something – for Charles's sake, if not her own. He wanted so much for Edwina and her to become friends. Therefore, Marianne determined, if her mother-in-law wasn't prepared to take the initiative, it was she who must make the running.

That same evening, as they sat together in the living room, she mooted the idea of a family dinner party. As expected, Charles understood her tactics.

'I think it might be a good starting point, my dear. It certainly can't do any harm.' He sighed and shook his head. 'I'm sorry Mother has continued to be so difficult. I warned you she was stubborn, but I'd have expected her to come round by now.'

Six months, Marianne thought, that was how long they had been in Australia. And in all that time Edwina had made only minimal contact.

'She is a proud woman, Charles. And she had other expectations for you. Her hostility is perhaps understandable. I am sure it is hard for her to accept an outsider like myself.'

Charles threw his wife a glance of silent admiration.

* * *

EDWINA EXPRESSED herself delighted at the invitation. The date, however, required some lengthy discussion.

'When I look at my diary, I just seem to have so much on.'

There was a pause at the other end of the line. Marianne waited.

Edwina Rolfe gave an audible sigh. 'Well, I'm sure if I do a little maneuvering I can manage to fit you in.' Her tone indicated that that wouldn't be easy. 'Did you say Caroline and Gerald, and Hugh as well?'

'Of course. I'd like it to be a family occasion. Charles hasn't seen much of you all since he's been home and I would very much like to have the chance to know you better too.'

You won't be around long enough for that, you pushy little upstart, the older woman promised as she hung up the receiver.

* * *

EDWINA ROLFE WAS DETERMINED to break the woman her son had married. Nothing could change her mind that Charles had fallen for the sly wiles of a female whose only interest was his money and his name. Now she was determined to save Charles from himself. And the way to do that, she decided, was to make things so unpleasant for the conniving little bitch that she would voluntarily walk out on Charles and the sham of a marriage.

Why didn't he come to me? Edwina asked herself in frustration. If it was a marriage of convenience he was after, she could have fixed it easily enough. There were women of his own class who would have had no objections to entering such an arrangement. Women who would have fitted readily into their society – not, she thought fiercely, some gold-digging, foreign nobody.

* * *

SHE RANG Caroline and told her about the invitation.

'You *accepted,* Mother? I would have thought - '

Edwina interrupted irritably. 'Caroline, listen to me...'

* * *

JANET COULD SEE how important the forthcoming evening was to her employer. Together they pored over recipe books, planning the perfect meal. After numerous changes of mind Marianne finally decided on a menu.

Then there was the choice of wines, liqueurs, flowers and table linen. It was clear to Janet Byrne that the success of the dinner party was close to becoming an obsession for the young woman.

'Don't you worry about a thing, Mrs Rolfe. Everything'll run like clockwork,' she promised. Yet the expression of anxiety didn't quite disappear from Marianne Rolfe's beautiful face. Sometimes, Janet thought, she seems so fragile, so brittle. And there was a sadness that never quite disappeared from those striking blue eyes.

The housekeeper couldn't help wondering if the separate sleeping arrangements so early in the marriage had anything to do with her employer's mood.

* * *

THREE DAYS before the planned dinner party Charles relayed the news that an ex-RAAF friend would be in Sydney that same evening. He had rung to ask if there was any chance of their catching up.

As Charles explained to Marianne, he hadn't felt he could refuse. 'Simon's company has posted him to Singapore; he and his wife will be in Sydney the one night only. We went through a lot together, my dear, I really couldn't say no.' He gave her an anxious look. He knew how much effort she was putting into the evening. 'You don't mind too much, do you?'

Marianne was already mentally revising her grocery order. 'Of course not, Charles.' She comforted herself with the thought that with outsiders present the evening might be less tense for everybody.

* * *

'You look ravishing.' Charles caught his breath as Marianne joined him in the living room. The slim-fitting dress of red velvet showed off the paleness of her skin and the rope of fat luminous pearls which had been his recent gift.

'Thank you.' She gave him a soft smile. The pride and admiration in Charles's eyes did not disturb her. She knew she had nothing to fear. Both of them had found their harbor in honoring the bargain they had made with their marriage vows.

'Everything under control, my dear?' They were awaiting the arrival of their guests. Charles, dressed formally, was cradling a scotch. A fire crackled welcomingly in the grate.

'Janet is marvelous. I can relax now and leave the rest up to her.'

'I'm sure everything will be perfect.'

Yet Charles couldn't help but feel tense about the evening ahead. He knew his mother. Knew her sharp tongue and the damage it could inflict. He could only hope that this might be the beginning of a more normal relationship for them all. Surely, he thought to himself, they must see the quality of the woman he had married?

He looked at her now, seated in the wing-backed chair, sipping at her sherry. The perfect profile, the slim pale arch of her neck, the hint of a cleavage at the top of her gown... Suddenly Charles felt himself swamped by an intensity of emotion. A white heat seemed to burn along the length of his body.

With shaking hands he lifted his glass to his lips.

* * *

Simon and Donna Larkin were the first to arrive.

Simon was big, dark-haired, outgoing. He had the sort of booming laugh that filled the room. In contrast his wife was petite and serene; a pretty red-head who seemed happy enough to let her husband hog the limelight.

The men kept the women amused with stories of some of their wartime experiences; it was obvious they enjoyed each other's company.

Simon Larkin is just who I need to help break the ice, Marianne thought happily. Surely even Edwina wouldn't be able to maintain her usual frostiness in his hearty company.

But by their third pre-dinner drink a sense of unease began to envelop her. She had told Edwina eight p.m. It was now eight-forty. Once again she excused herself to visit Janet in the kitchen.

'If they're much later it might be best if I turn off the roast, Mrs Rolfe.' Janet Byrne tried not to show her concern at the thought of overdone beef.

Marianne bit her lip. 'Let's give them till nine.'

* * *

AT A QUARTER past nine Charles rang his mother's house. There was no reply. He got the same result when he tried Caroline and Gerald's number.

'They must be on their way,' he announced with forced cheerfulness as he returned to his guests. He could see the anxiety on Marianne's face.

Damn Mother, he thought angrily. Damn *her cruel games*.

* * *

IT WAS a subdued foursome that finally sat down to eat at close to ten p.m. Whatever had happened it was obvious that the rest of the Rolfe family were not going to turn up that evening.

Charles picked at his food, coldly furious. He could sense Marianne's obvious embarrassment in front of the Larkins. By the end of the meal conversation was almost at a standstill. It was with a sense of relief that Charles finally shut the door behind his friends.

Stony-faced he looked at Marianne. 'Don't worry, I won't let her get away with this. I promise you.'

* * *

'BUT *DARLING*,' Edwina protested over the line, 'she said the *eighth*, I'm sure she did. Look, there was so much discussion about dates ... the poor girl probably got herself confused. Perhaps her English...' A smile played around Edwina's lips as she listened to Charles's angry response. '... Caroline and Gerald? Well, you see, they came too ... it was the sort of concert they'd hate to miss. We were all there. Oh, Charles ... darling ... you don't really think I would *deliberately* not turn up? How intolerably rude! Yes, yes, I'm so *very* sorry. Do apologize to Marianne for me, won't you?'

She hung up.

* * *

THAT WAS the beginning of the undeclared war by the matriarch of the Rolfe family against the woman she considered an upstart and interloper. The next shot in the battle was fired just two weeks later.

Following the fiasco of the dinner party Marianne was gratified to receive a follow-up telephone call from Edwina herself. '... an innocent mix-up, of course, but I feel I must make it up to you.'

As far as Marianne could tell Edwina Rolfe's apology carried the ring of sincerity. How could she think otherwise when her mother-in-law was now extending an invitation of her own? 'A very casual affair, my dear. Just an informal luncheon here for some close friends. All women. No need to dress up.'

Marianne took her at her word. On arrival she was mortified to find herself the only hatless, informally attired guest among six other immaculately groomed matrons. Suffering their disapproving looks was bad enough, but Edwina Rolfe wasn't about to let it go at that. Across the luncheon table she announced loudly. 'Perhaps, my dear Marianne, the word *casual* has a different meaning in Polish?' Her dark eyes, bright with condescending amusement, swept the table, inviting the others to share in her little joke.

* * *

THAT EVENING, as she welcomed her husband home, Marianne had no intention of revealing what had occurred. But Charles sensed at once that something was wrong. He knew of his mother's invitation and something in his wife's mood alerted his suspicions.

'What happened today, Marianne? What did she do to upset you?'

Much as Marianne tried to avoid the topic, in the end Charles managed to drag out the details of her humiliation.

He was tight-lipped with anger. 'You'll never have to endure that again, my dear. I promise. I'm finished with my mother. She's not going to have another opportunity to interfere in our lives.'

'Oh, no, Charles, please. She's your mother. You mustn't stop seeing her on my behalf. I'd feel –'

But Charles was adamant. 'No. I mean it, Marianne. She's never going to get the chance to put you in such a position again. If she can't treat my wife with respect then my relationship with her is over ... I'll make that patently clear.'

* * *

IT TOOK Marianne just twenty-four hours to decide.

I've failed him, she thought in despair. *I've let him down*.

She had finally faced the fact that she was never going to win acceptance into the Rolfe family and social circles. Edwina Rolfe hated her; the woman would never forgive her for marrying Charles. And now Marianne was driving a wedge between mother and son.

There was only one option left to her.

* * *

SHE KNEW Charles hadn't as yet had a chance to talk to Edwina. Late the next evening Marianne forced herself to confront him as they were about to retire.

'Charles, I have to speak to you.'

He was in his study, filing away some business papers he'd been working on after dinner.

'Come in, my dear.' He tried to ignore how sensually the full-length robe wrapped around her figure.

She took the seat he offered.

'What is it, Marianne?' He could see something was troubling her.

And the words came out in a breathless rush.

She couldn't keep their bargain, she proclaimed; she couldn't make him happy. Instead it was obvious she was coming between him and his family.

'I never wanted to cause you such problems, Charles. Now I think it is better that I go before I make things even more difficult for you.' Her head was bowed, her blue despairing eyes avoided his.

There was a long moment of silence. Then Charles was crouching in front of her. Tenderly he cupped her chin with his fingers, lifted her head so she was forced to look at him.

His voice was full of soft intensity. 'How can I tell you how wrong you are? You've given me more – much more – than I ever expected to receive. Just having you in my life has made me happier than I believed possible. What I'm saying is, I can't live without you, Marianne.'

They stared into each other's eyes. At that moment both realized something fundamental in their relationship had changed.

* * *

THE AFTERNOON SUN filtered through the Venetian blinds of the surgery and cast stripes of light across Charles Rolfe's worried expression.

'Is it normal for my feelings to be so intense when I – when I can do so little about them, Doctor?'

Dr Ian Bennett laced his fingers together on the desk in front of him. 'Impotency doesn't have to mean the loss of desire, Charles, as I tried to explain when you first saw me about this problem. The fact is that a male can feel normal sexual urges, can sustain an erection even, yet performance may still be impossible.'

He looked at the man opposite. 'I've seen the press photographs of your wife, Charles. She's a very beautiful, sensual woman. Perhaps in time...' The doctor spread his palms suggestively.

Charles felt sick as he left the doctor's rooms. Of course Ian Bennett was trying to reassure him, give him hope about the sexual stirrings which were becoming so torturous.

But he doesn't understand, Charles thought desperately. Nothing was as it seemed.

For how could he ever explain that the chance of regaining his potency would be the one sure way of destroying his marriage?

* * *

HUGH ROLFE DIDN'T BOTHER KNOCKING as he entered his brother's office. He knew that such peremptory action irritated Charles, and it was one small way to assert his status.

It was a status that had been eroded after Charles's return to health. During his brother's touch-and-go convalescence Hugh's own ascendancy in the firm had been accelerated despite his youth. Edwina, worried that her elder son's demise might lead to grasping uncles or cousins making their own grab for control, had backed Hugh all the way.

But in the end Charles had pulled through, assuming his late father's place at the helm of the company and Hugh couldn't help resenting his own displacement.

Now he addressed Charles. 'I've got the figures for the Strathland project here.' He was holding a manila folder.

'Fine.' Charles hid his annoyance at the uninvited interruption. He was in the middle of drafting some important correspondence. 'Just leave them there. I'll find a moment to go through it all later.'

But Hugh ignored the dismissal in his brother's tone.

'How's Marianne?'

'She's well.'

Hugh grinned. 'If it was me, I don't know how I'd manage to drag myself away to work.'

His reward was the sudden change of expression in Charles's eyes.

He smiled inwardly. *Touched a sore point, there, didn't I, old boy?*

Hugh Rolfe found himself fantasizing more and more about his beautiful and sensual sister-in-law. He couldn't help wondering how she was managing to cope with her own sexual frustrations.

11

Janet Byrne was frantic. In her distress she left the house as soon as possible after serving dinner and took a bus into town. At Martin Place post office she waited anxiously while the operator connected her to the only person who might be able to help.

'Father Michael?' With relief she heard the lilting Irish accent. 'Father, it's Janet, Janet Byrne.' She felt herself dangerously close to tears.

'Janet? What is it? Has something happened to Danny?'

And biting back her distress she managed to tell him. About the letter she had received that morning from Cleveland House. The letter which informed her in cold official terms that her son's deteriorating condition meant he could no longer be accommodated at the home.

'They ... they say he's at the stage where they can't give him the care he needs, Father. That a hospital...' Her voice broke. 'Oh, Father, I just don't know what I'm going to do. I can't afford–'

At the other end of the line the priest did his best to comfort her. But this time he had no solution.

* * *

MARIANNE WOULD NEVER HAVE FOUND out if, unable to sleep, she hadn't felt the need to make herself a cup of tea.

It was after two in the morning; she saw the strip of light beneath the kitchen door. Janet must have forgotten to turn off the light, she thought.

As the kitchen door swung open, Janet Byrne's head jerked up. Her startled, tear-swollen face looked into Marianne's.

* * *

'WE'VE GOT to do something to help, Charles. It's a terrible situation.'

It was the next morning, a Saturday. Marianne and Charles were strolling arm-in-arm in the park after breakfast. Around them families and cyclists were enjoying the early summer sunshine.

'All this time there was a child; they were separated. Why didn't she ever tell me?' Marianne's voice trembled with emotion and her fingers dug tightly into her husband's arm. 'And now they won't keep the little boy at the home any longer. He needs too much care, they told Janet. Because now it is almost impossible for him to walk. The tendons have shortened and the muscles, they are at ... at ...' She tried to remember the word Janet had used.

'Atrophying?' Charles suggested.

Marianne nodded. 'Yes, that's it. Surgery is his only chance of improvement the doctors have told her. But of course without money that is no option.'

Charles frowned. He liked Janet Byrne. As Marianne had said, it was a sad situation. 'So what do you think we can do to help, my dear?'

She told him.

* * *

JANET BYRNE hardly dared to believe what she was hearing.

'You and Mr Rolfe will pay for Danny's operation? And then my son can come to live *here*?' She stared in wondrous amazement at Marianne.

'You should have let us know earlier, Janet. Mr Rolfe and I would very much like to do this for you and Danny. And of course you must bring him here afterwards. This is a big house; a child will be no problem.'

Janet Byrne felt her throat squeeze tight. I must be dreaming, she thought.

'Oh, Mrs Rolfe, you have no idea what this means to me. And you mustn't worry that my work will suffer. I can assure you –'

Marianne smiled gently. 'That is the least of my fears, Janet.'

With brimming eyes Janet Byrne watched her employer leave the room.

I'll never be able to repay her, she told herself.

* * *

NEVER IN HER wildest dreams could Janet Byrne have imagined how her debt to Marianne Rolfe might finally be met.

* * *

DANNY BYRNE'S courage made a lasting impression on Marianne. However painful the after-effects of his operation she never heard him complain. Bright-eyed and inquisitive, he was a joy to have around. While his mother worked, he sat in his wheelchair in the sunshine, concentrating on the schoolwork he had missed or listened in rapt silence while Marianne read him one of his favorite adventure stories.

'I like the way you speak. It's funny!' he giggled, as Marianne finished yet another chapter.

She smiled as she got to her feet. Bending over she kissed the child's soft dark hair. 'And I like you,' she said gently.

* * *

MARIANNE WAS MORE contented then she had ever expected to feel again.

The problem with Edwina had been solved as best as possible.

Charles saw her alone. Once a week he would drop into the family home after work; now and then he would take his mother to lunch.

And on those rare occasions when it was absolutely necessary for the family to be seen together in public Charles never left his wife's side.

Feeling both protected and assured of Charles's need for her, Marianne allowed herself to accept the situation.

In fact, as the months raced past she scarcely had time to worry much more about the situation with Edwina. Apart from the happy hours she spent with Danny she and Charles now had a weekend retreat in the Blue Mountains.

A couple of hours' drive from Sydney, the area with its beautiful scenery, bushwalks and fashionable hotels, was a popular escape from the city.

The house they had found was a simple but charming weatherboard cottage with open fireplaces in every room and set among an acre of English-style gardens.

'The air is wonderful after Sydney,' Charles enthused. 'It'll do my poor lungs a world of good to recuperate up here.'

Marianne could only agree. There were times when Charles's fragile health worried her. He seemed prone to every cold and flu around.

But Marianne also understood the other unspoken reason for buying the house: a place out of Sydney provided a more tactful excuse for Charles to further keep his family at arm's length. Yet it seemed to Marianne that while her sister-in-law was obviously her mother's ally, Hugh, at least, seemed happy to accept his brother's wife.

Marianne wasn't sure if Edwina knew about the times her younger son called in at the house at Centennial Park. But Marianne was always glad to see him. Hugh was good company, fun and witty. And when, spontaneously, she invited him to join them for a weekend at the Blue Mountains cottage, he had happily accepted.

He had visited again since, and when they were all gathered round the dining table in the evening, Janet and Danny too, Marianne found herself thinking happily: It's as if I have a real family again.

And then came the single shattering event that changed everything.

* * *

IT WAS a weekend they had planned to spend in the mountains but at the last minute business detained Charles unexpectedly in Sydney.

'I'm sorry, my dear. There are still a few more details we have to hammer out before this chap heads back to Queensland on Sunday afternoon. I hope you understand.'

'Of course, Charles. We can go another weekend.'

But he had insisted that Marianne must not spoil her own plans. 'Janet and Danny are looking forward to it too. There's absolutely no reason why you all can't go without me.'

And in the end she had agreed.

* * *

HE HADN'T BEEN able to get her out of his mind. She plagued his thoughts day and night. He visited the Sydney house just to see her, to smell the heavy muskiness of her scent, to admire her sensual grace. Everything about her stirred his passion. His body ached with unrequited desire.

She must be longing for it, he told himself feverishly. She must be aching for relief. She was young, beautiful, sexy ... how could she bear to live with a man who was incapable of satisfying her?

And then the thought occurred to him: there had to be a lover. Or lovers. There must be someone who offered her gratification. Someone who appeased her appetite.

His mind took the next step. Which meant she may be persuaded to accept him too...

* * *

THE WEATHER WAS PERFECT. They ate lunch in the garden, and afterwards Marianne read while Janet cleared away. Beside her on the lawn Danny lay studying insects with the microscope Charles himself had played with as a boy. He had dug it out for Janet's son.

The air was still and warm, even the cicadas had ceased their sibilant chorus. Feeling sleepy Marianne stretched languidly on the full-length cane lounger. Her face was shaded by a wide-brimmed hat but she was wearing shorts in the hope of getting a bit of color on her pale legs.

'Thought this is where I'd find you.'

Startled, she twisted around to see Hugh's smiling face. He was dressed in casual slacks and an open-necked shirt, a newspaper tucked under his arm.

'Hugh! I didn't know you were coming.' She sat up and smiled a welcome as he pulled up one of the chairs beside her.

'Charles rang me. Asked me if I'd mind dropping in and seeing you were all right.'

How like Charles, she thought warmly.

'Looks to me like things are pretty perfect,' Hugh teased. From behind his sunglasses his eyes were devouring her body: the halter top that allowed him the excruciating temptation of a hint of cleavage, the long, bare, perfectly shaped legs ...

'Can I get Janet to fetch you a cup of tea or a cold drink? It's so hot, isn't it? I really should get out of this sun.'

At that moment Janet appeared from the house. She smiled as she crossed the lawn carrying a tray with glasses and a jug.

'Hello, Mr Rolfe. I saw you arrive. Thought you might like a cold drink. Are you staying for dinner?'

With an effort Hugh forced his eyes away from Marianne. He tried to steady his breathing. 'Well, if you'll have me, that sounds a marvelous idea.'

'Oh, that's wonderful, Hugh!' Marianne was genuinely pleased. With Hugh she felt relaxed, at ease. It was good to know that at least one member of the Rolfe family accepted her unreservedly. She knew how much Charles appreciated his brother's support.

Hugh helped Marianne drag the lounger into the partial shade and for the next hour or so the three of them talked fitfully. Beside them Danny lay asleep on the grass.

'Well...' Finally Marianne pushed herself up from her seat. 'I'm going in for a shower. I feel so sticky.'

Janet followed her lead. 'I think I'll take Danny in for a bath too. Then I'll do something about dinner.'

'Let me help you.' Hugh was on his feet, picking up the tray as Janet gently woke the sleeping boy.

'That's very kind of you, Mr Rolfe.'

'Not at all.' Hugh's eyes were on Marianne's retreating figure as he followed her into the house.

What a waste, he told himself, the blood heating in his veins. *What a bloody waste.*

* * *

HE MADE certain Janet Byrne was out of the way. Bathing the child should keep her busy for a while he was sure.

The main bathroom lay at the end of the hallway. Hugh could hear the sound of running water as he approached. The door was slightly ajar and he was able to see into the room. The glass doors of the shower cabinet gave him an uninterrupted view and he felt his belly clench with excitement ... the small but beautifully shaped breasts, the nipples rosy and protrudent, the erotic curve of pale hips, the slim, firm legs...

Desire spiraled through him. How in hell, he wondered, could Charles fail to be aroused by that?

She had turned off the taps, was squeezing the water from her hair. A hot ache seemed to clamp off Hugh's throat. As Marianne stepped from the shower he reached out and pushed open the door.

Her eyes opened wide. 'Hugh! What is it?' Grabbing for the nearest towel she wrapped it quickly around her.

'Don't hide yourself. You're too beautiful for that.' His feverish eyes devoured the sight.

'Hugh.' Her face had lost all color.

'I know about Charles, Marianne. I know he can't give you what you need. But, believe me,' he gave a brittle, nervous laugh, 'it's not a problem that runs in the family.'

'Hugh, please, get away from me...'

She cringed backwards as he moved closer and ran a hand down her bare damp arm.

The contact made him inhale sharply. He felt his urgency grow. 'Come on, sweetheart... you don't have to play games with me.' His voice was husky. 'You can't tell me that a healthy, red-blooded young woman isn't missing it. Don't tell me you're not aching to feel a man inside you.'

Marianne froze as the full significance of her brother-in-law's words sank into her dazed mind. He was staring at her like a cobra stares at its victim.

'No...' she breathed. 'No...'

Hugh Rolfe's lips curved in a derisive smile. 'No? Oh, come on, Marianne. It's one thing to marry for money but surely you're getting the rest of it somewhere? Who's giving it to you? Who's keeping you from going crazy?'

He was so close now she could hear his erratic breathing.

'Whoever it is I promise I'll make it so much better. I want you, Marianne.' His tone thickened. 'Oh, God, I've wanted you for so long...' And with one violent movement he reached out and snatched away her final protection. Then he was backing her against the bathroom wall, his mouth desperately seeking hers as his hands closed over the soft delight of her breasts.

At once the din of nightmare exploded in her mind.

'*NIE! NIE!*' Eyes glazed with horror, Marianne clawed and lashed out at her attacker, fought with superhuman strength.

No man was ever going to touch her again!

It was her agonized screams and the stream of hysterical Polish that brought a shocked Janet Byrne rushing to her aid.

12

It was the first time in his life that Charles felt he might have been capable of murder.

Marianne's appearance when she arrived back in Sydney that Sunday evening told him something dreadful had happened.

He'd come out of the house to greet her, his smile of welcome instantly wiped away at the sight of her wild, fixed stare, her grey, sagging face.

'Darling...?' He was barely aware of using the endearment. 'What's happened? What's wrong?' Shocked, he put his arm around her and led her into the house.

Her agitation and confusion made it difficult to elicit the details of what had taken such a toll. However, little by little, with gentle encouragement, Charles managed to piece together the essence of what had taken place.

Only after he had seen Marianne safely to bed did he seek out Janet Byrne for further confirmation.

The housekeeper was obviously embarrassed as well as upset.

'Please,' Charles said grimly, 'don't hold anything back, Janet. Just tell me exactly what you saw.'

Janet Byrne blinked nervously as she recalled the scene. 'I was heading for the kitchen when I heard screams. I rushed to the bathroom...' She bit her lip and looked away. 'Mr Rolfe was there with her. She was naked. The towel was on the floor at her feet, I remember, and Mr Rolfe seemed – seemed to be trying to quiet her, to calm her down.'

'Thank you, Janet.' Charles looked at his watch. It was not yet eight. He got to his feet. 'I've got to go out for a short while. Will you keep a close eye on Mrs Rolfe for me, please?'

His voice was controlled, but the expression on Charles Rolfe's face made Janet Byrne understand how anyone might be capable of murder.

* * *

EDWINA ROLFE FACED HER SON, her dark eyes blazing.

'And you *believe* her? You'd take that woman's word over your own *brother's*?'

Charles's face was mottled with anger, his hands were bunched into angry fists. He had come here to confront Hugh, only to be told that his brother had not yet returned home. If his mother could be believed.

'You're talking about my *wife*, Mother! I–'

'Don't you *see*, Charles?' Ignoring him, Edwina spat out the words. 'Don't you see what she's trying to do with these scurrilous accusations against Hugh? This is her way of trying to break up our family! She's lying to make sure you have nothing more to do with any of us. The woman's evil! Twisted! Get rid of her before she destroys us all!'

Charles stared at his mother. He could see the flecks of saliva gathered at the corner of her lips. His voice was unsteady as he replied. 'I believe every word she told me, and nothing will ever make me give her up. You're a strong woman, Mother, and I've let you manipulate me and try to run my life for far too long. From now on I want no further contact with you or anyone else in this family. Tell Hugh as from tomorrow he's appointed to the Newcastle office ... also make very sure he knows that if I ever catch sight of him in this town I won't be responsible for my actions.'

Spinning on his heel, Charles strode out of the room.

Edwina didn't move. As she heard the angry slam of the car door she realized for the first time the extent of the hold the woman she hated had over her son.

* * *

HE TRIED in every way possible to make it up to her. Gifts, holidays, trips abroad.

Charles's heart broke when he saw the damage Hugh's attempt at seduction had caused. The fearfulness had returned, the nervousness and reserve. Marianne had drawn back into her protective shell.

And, he realized, there was something else too – a brittleness, an edgy fragility that made him fearful for her psychological well-being. There were occasions as the months passed and her condition seemed to worsen rather than improve, when it was on the tip of his tongue to suggest she might care to see a doctor. But somehow he could never bring himself to say the words. He guessed that even to hint at her fragility might serve further to undermine her confidence.

* * *

JANET BYRNE SAW the changes too and some sixth sense told her there was more to the situation than met the eye. Her heart went out to this troubled, complex woman who had shown nothing but understanding and kindness to her and her son. *I've got to help her*, she told herself. *I've got to do anything I can.*

* * *

HER DREAMS HAUNTED her once more. Marianne dreaded the long black hours of night. So often she woke, trembling, the images of the past etched as deeply as ever on her mind.

She lost interest in her usual pursuits ... the house, the garden, her music. More and more, her days were passed sitting on the verandah or in the garden, lost in thought. Only Janet's soft offers of lunch or afternoon tea jerked her back to reality.

As time went on, Charles noted Marianne's continuing melancholy with increasing anxiety. He expressed his worry to Janet who had more and more become a friend rather than an employee. Anyway, he asked himself wryly, who else did he have to turn to? His estrangement from his family was absolute.

* * *

To begin with his mother had tried telephoning the office, but his persistent refusal to accept her calls finally convinced her that he meant exactly what he'd said. Charles was determined. He blamed Edwina's continuing hostility and unyielding attitude every bit as much as his brother's barbarous act for Marianne's present state.

They rejected her, he thought bitterly, without ever trying to know her. They never once gave her a chance.

* * *

The social coterie of Sydney soon learnt of the total rift that now existed between Charles Rolfe and the rest of his family. And they made their own judgment about where to lay the blame.

Even those who might have wished to continue their friendship with Charles were too afraid of crossing Edwina. To get on the wrong side of someone with Edwina Rolfe's unquestionable status and clout would certainly mean automatic social death, exclusion from every worthwhile occasion on the social calendar. There were few willing to take that sort of risk.

Such pointed social exile mattered little to Charles. He continued to appear with Marianne at the opera, the ballet, colorful race days at Randwick. With his beautiful wife by his side none of the snubs gave him a moment's concern. And on the inevitable occasions when he and other members of his family might have crossed paths he simply took evasive action, averted his eyes, altered his course. This is the way his mother wanted it, he thought stubbornly, so let her live with it. He knew now that Marianne was all he needed to make him happy.

Charles only wished he could restore his wife's happiness as readily. He did everything possible. They spent a month in London, took a car tour through France, holidayed with some business friends in Hong Kong. On their fourth anniversary he hoped that the magic of Venice might bring back the woman he had known. But nothing could penetrate the wall she had so firmly rebuilt. Marianne had retreated to some part of herself he found impossible to reach.

* * *

'MUM! Look what I made at school today!'

Danny Byrne came bursting into the kitchen. He was a lively boy of almost ten now. Still small for his age, still prone to bouts of ill-health, but no longer a cripple.

Janet blessed the day she had applied for the position with Charles and Marianne. Not only had her son gained the use of his legs but Janet herself had found a support and kindness she would never have believed possible. Her gratitude to the Rolfes knew no bounds. Which made her pain over the changes in Marianne all the greater.

Like Charles, she had tried her best to find the woman she had known. There's something else there, Janet thought with women's intuition, something in the core of her that's eating her away. If only I could do something to help.

That's when she thought of Father Michael. When she checked with Charles he had no objection. If there is any chance at all let's try it, he said, but without much conviction.

The priest was an old man now, in his seventies but he agreed to make the long train journey to Sydney. In his jacket pocket he carried the letter Charles Rolfe had sent him, detailing what had happened to his wife during the war. A tragic story indeed, he thought. Of course such an experience would leave its mark. But there was a time when one had to learn to let go of the past.

Father Michael sat with Marianne in the quiet of the library. He talked gently, tried to draw her out. Marianne Rolfe listened but offered little in return.

'There's a time when we have to put the past aside, my dear. What's gone is over. We must accept the will of God and look to the future.'

Next moment the priest recoiled in shock as the woman beside him exploded in rage. She jerked to her feet and with blue eyes blazing, stared down at him, her whole body trembling with emotion.

'*Will of God!*' she almost shouted the words at the old man. 'Don't tell me your lies! There is no God! No one knows that better than I! Keep your clichés and your useless comfort for the ignorant who believe such things!'

Before the shaken priest could utter another word the woman he had come to help had rushed from the room.

* * *

DANNY BYRNE WAS RECOVERING from chickenpox. He'd missed a few days of school but at last his fever had come down.

'Another day or so and you'll be back on your feet, love,' Janet announced as she replaced the thermometer in its case. Then she left her son to read while she went about her chores.

By eleven-thirty she had given Danny a light lunch of soup and toast and hoped he might drift back to sleep.

Preparing a sandwich and a pot of tea, she carried the tray through to the living room where Marianne was sitting in one of the comfortable wing-backed chairs. A book lay open on her lap but it didn't seem to be holding her attention.

'I'm off to pick up the butcher order, Mrs Rolfe. Won't be long. Danny's reading, I'm sure he won't disturb you.'

'Is he feeling any better?' Marianne's voice expressed her concern. She missed spending as much time with Danny now he was at school.

'Temperature's come down a bit since breakfast. With a bit of luck he'll be right for school tomorrow.' Janet smiled. 'Need anything special while I'm out?'

'No. Just hurry back and keep me company.' The words were said with a wan smile, as if Marianne had tried to make a joke. But Janet Byrne's brows were drawn together in a frown as she picked up the car keys from their hook by the door.

* * *

THE HOUSE WAS quiet with the hush of noon. Restless, Marianne got to her feet and moved to the open window. A light breeze carried the scent of freshly mown grass from the park opposite.

All at once some memory was awoken in her. Of those long ago summers on her grandparents' farm, of the smell of newly cut hay, of her grandmother's poppy seed cake and her grandfather's homemade fruity wine.

Poland...her homeland...the country she would never see again...

For the first time in many months Marianne found herself drawn to sit at the piano. She opened the lid and softly, with great feeling, began to play a favorite Chopin piece. Emotions long suppressed flowed into the music and, with eyes closed, she absorbed herself in the haunting melody.

And then something told her she was not alone.

Opening her eyes she lifted her fingers from the keys and turned to see Danny watching from the doorway. His pajamas emphasized his frailness and under his rumpled dark hair his face looked paler than usual.

'Don't stop.'

Still affected by the poignancy of the music Marianne said nothing as the boy crossed the room and stood beside her.

'Please, keep playing. I love it when you play.'

'Sit down then, here beside me,' she answered softly.

As the boy joined her on the long polished stool, she began again to play, her hands moving fluidly over the keyboard calling forth the beauty of the music.

When the piece came to an end the boy turned to her with wide admiring eyes. 'Do you think I could ever play like that?'

'I didn't know you were interested in learning the piano, Danny.'

The boy gave a self-deprecating shrug. 'Might be better at the piano than I am at soccer. The other kids hate me on their team. I'm too slow, they reckon.'

She looked at him and a smile gradually curved her lips. Lifting his right hand from his lap she placed it on the keys. 'Let's see what you can do, shall we?'

* * *

AND THAT WAS how Janet found them when she returned, both absorbed, bent over the keys, their occasional laughter punctuating the repetition of simple scales.

Later when Marianne came into the kitchen Janet could see the new animation in her face. 'Danny's got a good ear, you know. It never occurred to me he might want to learn to play. I'm going to enjoy working with him.'

Janet understood then how God was going to allow her to repay Marianne Rolfe's kindness.

* * *

TEACHING Danny Byrne to play the piano was what brought Marianne back to life. The youngster gave her a focus and a renewed sense of purpose. The enthusiasm in her face and voice when she spoke about the child's progress filled Charles with an overwhelming sense of delight and relief.

She's going to be all right now, he told himself. Danny had achieved what the rest of them had failed to do.

13

'You know, Charles, he's so talented, I think when we get back he must have a proper music teacher. He needs more than me now.' Marianne faced her husband eagerly over the breakfast table.

Charles smiled. 'You've achieved so much with him in just twelve months, my dear. Leave it to me, I'll make enquiries and we'll find someone first rate.'

Five minutes later they kissed goodbye. Marianne had a busy day in front of her. In two days' time they were off to Europe ... a whirlwind business trip of two weeks. These days they went by jet so that Charles would not be too long away from the office, and Marianne had a dozen pressing tasks to attend to before they left.

Their journey would include three days in Paris, and Marianne had no doubt the wardrobe she had had designed and made by Beril Jents, one of Australia's best-known couturiers, would be stylish enough to impress even the French. Sometime today she had to find a moment to call in to the salon to pick up a last minute order of a wrap to match one of her new gowns.

It was late morning by the time she and Janet finally called a cab to take them into the city.

They made their way through the traffic and drew up outside the St James building. A glamorous redhead was just stepping into a chauffeur-driven car outside. With the Elizabeth Arden Red Door salon in the same building a regular parade of fashionable, well-known women passed through its doors.

'Keep the taxi, Janet, I'll run in. Beril said she'd have it ready.'

Marianne was halfway across the foyer when she saw them. She faltered and her face paled. Avoiding a confrontation was impossible.

Stepping out of Beril Jents' salon were Edwina and Hugh Rolfe and a very attractive young woman. The latter Marianne recognized as Hugh's fiancée, Louise Austen – she had seen the engagement photographs in the press. The wedding, she recalled, must be any day now. Obviously the society couturier had been appointed to make the girl's wedding gown and trousseau.

The trio spied Marianne at almost the exact same moment. While Hugh Rolfe's face flushed a dark red, Edwina's expression hardened, her dark eyes stared straight ahead; only Louise Austen reacted openly.

'Well, *look,* Hugh, darling. Isn't this the sister-in-law who couldn't keep her hands off you?' The jealousy in the girl's tone was unmistakable. As their paths crossed, her eyes raked over the beautiful older woman. 'Perhaps you should make sure, my sweet that she knows you're well and truly taken now.'

Hugh put a hand on his fiancée's elbow, avoiding Marianne's eyes as they passed. 'Come on, Louise.'

Marianne's heart was beating fast but she didn't slacken her pace. Then behind her, just as she was about to step through the salon door, she heard Edwina Rolfe's ringing voice.

'She stole my son, but one day Charles will see I was right about that ignorant hussy. And that's the day I'll see her hounded clean out of this city!'

Her tone was pure venom.

* * *

JANET GUESSED WHAT HAD HAPPENED. She had seen the Rolfe party emerge and climb into the Daimler which had drawn into the kerb behind her. But a few minutes later when Marianne re-joined her in the rear of the waiting cab she made no reference to crossing paths with her in-laws.

Kept busy with the rest of the day's tasks Marianne put the morning's unpleasant encounter out of her mind. She and Charles led their own lives now; there was no way Edwina or the others were going to be allowed to upset either of them again.

There were, however, occasions when she still felt a sense of guilt at the estrangement between Charles and his family. But Charles always reassured her. He was happier, he promised, than he had ever been in his life. No one, especially not his mother, was going to be allowed to destroy that.

* * *

THEIR FLIGHT LEFT from Kingsford Smith airport on Sunday morning. Janet and Danny came to see them off, the little boy full of excitement about seeing the big silver jets at such close quarters.

As their flight was called, Marianne crouched down beside him. 'I'll miss you, my pet.' She hugged him close; his bony frame was still painfully thin for a boy of almost eleven. 'Be good for Mummy, won't you? And remember, when we get back I'm going to get you the very best piano teacher in Sydney.'

Danny Byrne's eyes were bright with the tears he was trying so manfully to restrain. 'Do you have to go, Marianne?'

Releasing him, she sat back on her heels and stroked a hand over his dark hair. 'I won't be long, pet. There'll be just time for you to learn that Mozart sonata before I'm home again.'

The boy nodded, his lips pressed tightly together. *I'll have it super perfect*, he vowed silently, as he watched her give a last smiling wave and disappear through the Immigration entry.

* * *

THE TWO WEEKS passed in a whirlwind of business meetings and continual travel. As usual in France, it was Marianne who handled the commercial negotiations and she enjoyed being able to help Charles again if even for so short a time.

Busy as they were however, they still found time for a nostalgic visit to the tiny bistro on the Ile St Louis where they had dined together that first time in Paris.

As they faced each other in the rosy glow of the candlelight Charles smiled. 'Hard to believe it was almost seven years ago, isn't it?' His hand reached across the snowy tablecloth to cover hers and he asked softly, 'Any regrets, my dear?'

Marianne shook her head. As she looked into the gentle face of the man who had given her so much, who had never betrayed her trust, the intensity of her emotions took her by surprise.

Maybe, she thought in silent wonder, *this is what love feels like...*

* * *

ON THEIR LAST evening in London they caught up with Alistair and Nancy Pryor. On previous visits to England the Pryors had so often chanced to be out of London that Marianne couldn't help wondering if Edwina's tentacles of control didn't also extend beyond Australia. But at dinner that evening the Pryors seemed no different from how she remembered them: Alistair as laconic, Nancy as animated and talkative as ever.

They dined at one of the currently fashionable restaurants near Covent Garden. The food was surprisingly good and Marianne felt relaxed and happy; it pleased her to see Charles enjoying himself with old friends.

'You look wonderful, Marianne.' Nancy was openly admiring as she lit a cigarette. 'Must be all that divine Australian sunshine and fresh air.'

'Thank you. Yes, Europe is wonderful to visit but Australia really is the only place to live.'

Nancy Pryor raised a skeptical eyebrow at *that*.

* * *

THE JARRING NOTE came just as they were collecting their wraps. Nancy Pryor asked the question that had been on the tip of her tongue all evening.

'You certainly seem taken with this Danny... your housekeeper's child, did you say?' The Englishwoman drew the mink stole around her narrow shoulders. She turned and smilingly patted Charles's cheek. 'Perhaps before this one gets any longer in the tooth you'd better start some baby farming of your own.'

The words hung in the air and Alistair Pryor threw his wife a furious look. But as Charles opened his mouth to speak it was Marianne who said smoothly, 'Sometimes these things aren't always simple, Nancy.'

The Englishwoman had the grace at least to blush.

* * *

THE MESSAGE WAS WAITING for them when they arrived back at the Savoy.

Marianne saw Charles frown as he ripped open the envelope. 'What is it, Charles?'

For a moment he didn't answer. Marked urgent, there was a telephone number and a name it took him a moment to recognize. 'Do we know a Father Michael McCoy?'

Marianne knew at once who it was. And she guessed something terrible had happened.

* * *

HE WAS FRIGHTENED to tell her. His mouth was dry as he replaced the receiver and rose to his feet.

'Charles? Please. What is it?'

She was staring up at him, her hands gripping his arms.

He felt a coldness in his bowels. Oh, God. She loved the boy, truly loved him.

Fearfully he told her. 'It's... Danny. He died this morning. The polio had weakened his chest muscles; he caught a cold and...and choked on his own mucus.'

Distraught, her immediate instinct was to call back straight away, talk to Janet herself. Charles had to explain gently what the priest had told him. 'She's heavily sedated at the moment, my dear. It won't help to disturb her.'

After that all he could do was hold her, rock her in his arms until she could cry no more. Then he tenderly wiped her face, got her a cold drink and opened the door to her connecting suite.

'Will you be all right, my dear?' His face reflected his compassion and concern. 'I could get the duty manager to send for the doctor. Perhaps a sleeping tablet?'

Marianne shook her head. Her expression was dazed, her eyes puffy and red. 'No... no...'

He went to his own room, undressed, washed, but couldn't sleep. What a tragedy, he thought. Poor Janet. And Marianne... He knew how much the child meant to her.

It happened a short time later and at first he thought he was mistaken. Then it came again. A soft tap on his bedroom door. Hurriedly he pushed back the bedclothes.

She was standing there dressed in a flowing ivory colored gown. 'Charles...' Her eyes held his, an indefinable expression on her pale face. She came closer and instinctively he enfolded her in his arms. She whispered the words against his chest. 'Charles, I need you... I need the strength only you can give me. Please... will you hold me tonight?'

He felt his heart kick against his ribs.

Without a word he led her to the bed.

* * *

SHE CLUNG to him as if she would never let go, her body scooped against his own. 'Hold me, darling... hold me...' Brokenly she whispered the words over and over again.

The shock of Danny's death had shaken her to the core. But this time, Marianne knew, she had to fight back from the dangerous precipice of her emotions, that precipice which could only lead once more to the deep black hole of weakness and withdrawal.

I have to stay brave for Janet, she repeated forcefully to herself. It was Janet who needed her now.

And the one person from whom she could draw strength was the man who held her now. The man Marianne would have trusted with her soul.

* * *

AT LAST SHE FELL ASLEEP. But for a long time Charles's dizzied senses allowed him no rest. He could hardly believe that after seven years of separate existence it was she who had come to him. Not with physical passion, but driven by the basic human desire for contact and comfort.

He didn't know what might happen next. He didn't care. As he finally fell asleep Charles's only regret was the tragedy that had made it possible.

* * *

THEY LEFT AS PLANNED the next morning. Even given the circumstances, it was the first flight they could have taken.

Marianne sat in stunned silence willing the airplane back to Sydney. Not that it would change anything, she thought, the tears dry on her cheeks. Beside her, Charles gripped her hand in his. Neither of them made any reference to the night before. This was neither the time nor the place.

He shot a glance at his wife's pale set face and prayed she would be able to cope with the funeral that lay ahead.

First thing that morning Father Michael had spoken to them again via a crackling, fading line. He wanted to make certain they would be in attendance. 'Janet's taken it bad, very bad, Mr Rolfe. It's Mrs Rolfe she needs beside her now. She's really going to need her support.'

Charles felt a sharp stab in his belly. His greatest fear was whether Marianne would be able to cope.

* * *

'Oh, Janet... Janet...' Marianne sat on the edge of the bed and held the weeping woman in her arms. Janet Byrne looked like an old woman. Her face seemed to have fallen in, her skin was grey, her eyes sunken and red-rimmed.

'I never expected...' Her whole body shuddered against Marianne. 'I thought once his legs... but he didn't have the strength to clear his poor choked lungs! Oh, God, I've lost him! I've lost him...' And dissolving in a fresh bout of anguished tears Janet Byrne clung to the woman who had become her friend.

'It's terrible. I know...' Marianne spoke softly, her eyes filled with pain, as she stroked the grieving mother's dark curls.

* * *

The funeral was a wrenching affair. It was held in the country town where Janet had grown up. The cemetery was situated beside the dusty highway ... a patch of burnt grass behind rusty railings. Janet's son was to be buried alongside her husband and her mother.

Father Michael performed the service in front of the small group of local mourners. When the little coffin was finally lowered into the parched earth Janet clutched Marianne's arm and sobbed aloud. 'He's with his father now... Danny's with his daddy...'

Marianne felt as if a knife had been driven through her soul.

14

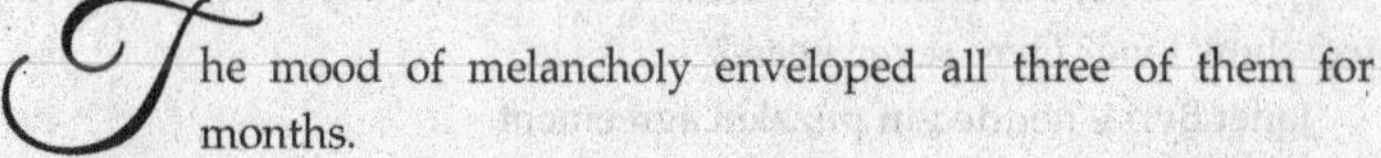

The mood of melancholy enveloped all three of them for months.

Danny's spirit still seemed to pervade the house. So much reminded Marianne of the child whose presence had brought her such joy: when she entered the sunroom where he used to curl up and read, when she caught sight of the rope swing hanging from the gnarled oak in the garden, when she saw the piano closed and quiet. At any moment she expected to see his smiling face.

And if it was so terrible for her she knew how much worse it must be for Janet.

Marianne never wavered from her vow to be her friend's strength and support. She was there whenever Janet needed her ... to listen, to comfort, to hold and soothe. It was as if she and Janet were healing each other.

And each night she renewed her own strength in her husband's arms, found a peace and sense of belonging she could never have imagined possible. Marianne saw how gradually the years had altered the original contract of her marriage. Instead of dreading his touch, she felt comforted and at peace in Charles's embrace. Danny's tragic death had brought an unforeseen consequence into both their lives.

* * *

EIGHT MONTHS after her son's funeral Charles asked to see Janet Byrne alone. It was a bleak, grey Sunday and although it was only early afternoon the lamp was already lit on his study desk. Marianne was upstairs taking a nap.

As Charles indicated one of the comfortable chintz covered seats and took another opposite, Janet couldn't help feel a flicker of nervousness. This was the first time she had ever been asked to see Charles Rolfe alone.

He studied her for a moment, saw how thin she'd become, took in the newly etched lines on her face. As succinctly as possible, he told her what was on his mind.

'Janet, I can only imagine how dreadful these last few months have been for you. Nothing and no one can ease the anguish of such a loss, I know. We all have burdens we must carry alone. But you've been with us ... how long? Over seven years?'

Janet Byrne nodded in puzzled agreement.

'Well, in that time you've been very good to both of us. But especially to Marianne. Things weren't easy for her at the beginning, as I'm sure you have heard. A new husband, a strange and very different environment, and in-laws who did nothing to make her welcome. Your friendship and assistance during all that was a great help; you and Danny helped her to settle in, and she's very fond of you, Janet ... we both are. It's for all those reasons that I'd like to express my gratitude in a practical way.'

And he told her what he proposed.

Janet looked at him in astonishment. 'The cottage, Mr Rolfe? For *me*?'

'Yes. I've discussed it with Marianne. She was in complete agreement of course. We both would like to know you had a house of your own. Danny loved the place; I'm sure it holds happy memories for you. As soon as possible I'll have the documentation seen to by my solicitor.'

Janet Byrne was almost speechless. She stammered out her thanks. 'How can I ever repay you, Mr Rolfe?'

His eyes held hers. 'There's only one thing I ask of you, Janet. Marianne is of course well looked after financially in my will, but apart from ourselves she has little emotional support in her life. I would like to think that I could always count on you to be there for her if anything happens to me.'

'Oh, Mr Rolfe, don't talk like that.' Janet looked upset. 'But, of course, I would do anything ... for either of you. You made those last years such happy ones for Danny and me. I'll never forget your kindness and generosity.'

With a smile and a sense of satisfaction Charles Rolfe rose to his feet and showed her out of the room.

* * *

CHARLES'S PLEASURE and joy in the increased intimacy with his wife was tempered only by his confusion over his growing sexual feeling. When he held her in his arms he couldn't ignore his desire. He loved Marianne deeply yet wondered fearfully if he would ever be able to express that love in a physical act. It was a tormenting question that refused to go away though nothing would have made him break the vow which was the basis of their marriage.

It was a marriage that had now lasted eight years. They celebrated their wedding anniversary quietly with a picnic at sunset on Balmoral Beach. The sheltered arc of sand was a romantic setting and they laughed and chatted easily as they sat on a rug sharing a bottle of Bollinger and a simple meal.

With the skies turning velvet they gathered their things and walked hand-in-hand to the car. Charles was about to turn the key in the ignition when Marianne leaned towards him. Taking his face between her palms she kissed him gently. 'I love you, Charles.' Her voice was a whisper. 'I love you for everything you are ... and all you've done for me.'

His breath caught. In the darkness he could just make out the pale oval of her face. The moment had caught him totally by surprise. 'And I love you ... more than life itself, my darling...'

There, in the front seat of the car, to the accompaniment of the soft murmur of the sea, they kissed with real passion for the first time.

* * *

He didn't dare let himself anticipate anything else. They went to bed as usual and fell asleep in each other's arms.

* * *

To Marianne the dream seemed almost real. She was stroking Charles's hair, running her hands over his chest, whispering for him to kiss her. Her body felt heavy and warm and she sighed in drowsy pleasure.

Awareness came gradually. Drugged with sleep she slowly became conscious of lips on her cheek, her throat, and finally her lips. She stiffened and her eyes flickered open. Charles was smoothing back her hair, kissing her tenderly. His body was pressed tightly against her and she could feel his need. Yet while a flicker of apprehension ran through her she didn't pull away.

Again his mouth covered hers and Marianne felt something stir deep inside her. As his kiss became more urgent, instinctively she opened her mouth. She heard his soft moan of pleasure and felt the shock of his hands against her breasts.

'I love you, Marianne... I love you so...'

Her heart raced. He kissed her again and again until she was left breathless and dizzy. She felt drawn into a dark whirling vortex of emotions she had never before experienced...

Then his hands were slipping the thin gown from her shoulders and she shuddered as their nakedness met. He buried his mouth in the hollows at the base of her neck and a soft moan escaped Marianne's lips.

And at last she was arching towards him, all fear gone, replaced by the undeniable burning ache of passion and love.

Charles lifted his head. Voice raw with desire, he asked huskily, 'Are you sure, my darling?'

Her answer was to draw him on top of her. As her body opened to the man she loved, Marianne felt as if she had emerged from her cage of ice.

We've brought each other back to life, she thought in joyous wonder.

That first night was repeated again and again as they discovered the exquisite joy of complete union. Stunned by the pleasure that resulted from the joining of heart, mind and body Marianne learned to give herself to her husband with passionate abandon.

Charles too was drunk with love and delight. In his arms his wife had finally found release from the nightmare of the past, while his own torment too had been overcome. Marianne had made him whole again, had given him back his manhood and his confidence. The bond between them was complete and he felt blissfully happy, totally alive.

A visit to the specialist had calmed his last nagging fear.

'I told you at the start, Charles, that recovery was unpredictable. I'm delighted it's happened for you. And try not to worry ... if your relationship with your wife is happy and strong I see no need to fear a relapse.'

Those were the words Charles was praying to hear.

* * *

From the moment their marriage was physically consummated Charles and Marianne lived at a new level of intensity. Their happiness was total; their lives complete. They needed nothing else.

For Charles there weren't enough hours in the day to spend with the woman he adored. It made him realized how the pressures of business had been gradually encroaching on their time together. A couple of months after that momentous evening he put his proposal to Marianne.

'I'd like us to get away, darling. Have a proper honeymoon ... say, about six weeks in Europe and North America ... no plans, no business, free to do what we like. Janet's here to look after the house, so why don't we aim at leaving in about a month from now? That'll give me plenty of time to arrange things at the office.'

As they happily discussed the details neither could have guessed how much would change in that short space of time.

15

Marianne was in the garden cutting flowers when the telephone rang. 'I'll get it,' she called to Janet, who was hanging up a load of washing.

Pulling off her stout gardening gloves she hurried into the house. The nearest telephone was in the front hall.

'Marianne Rolfe.'

She listened to the strange, earnest voice. Her knees went weak and a ring of ice seemed to form around her lips.

The taxi sped dangerously through the mid-morning traffic. The two women sat in a tense silence until they reached the front entrance of St Vincent's.

'I'll pay and come and find ...'

But Marianne was already gone, leaping out of the car and running towards the hospital's swinging glass doors.

She found him on the fourth floor. The doctor was waiting for her outside the room, but Marianne barely noticed his somber face or heard his rapid explanation ... '... collapsed...a major coronary... we're doing everything...' ... it was Charles she wanted to see.

She pushed her way into the room and the sight of his grey

sweating face made her stomach clench in panic. An oxygen mask covered his nose, various tubes were attached to his body.

Dropping to her knees beside the bed Marianne grasped her husband's hand. It was icy cold. 'Charles... oh, darling...' She could barely choke out the words. Her heart felt as if it had risen into her throat.

His eyes flickered open. Slowly they moved until they found her.

'Darling,' she fought to keep the panic out of her voice. 'I'm here, I'll stay with you. You'll be all right. I promise you.' Her fingers tightened around his.

He blinked as if to say he understood.

* * *

THE ONLY TIME she left his bedside was when Edwina and the others arrived. This was no occasion for acrimony or confrontation.

She waited with Janet in a small private sitting room on the floor below. 'Janet, please... tell me,' she begged, 'tell me what chance he has.' Her face was the color of paper, she couldn't bear to sit still.

Janet Byrne had been out of her profession for a long time but she still understood the cryptic language of the wards. They had warned her it was best that Marianne Rolfe didn't go home.

'If he makes it through the night he's got a fighting chance,' she offered gently. She could hardly endure the sight of Marianne's stricken face.

* * *

THEY CAME for her just as dawn was breaking.

She knelt by his bedside and stroked his ashen cheeks. His eyes were closed and his tortured breathing told her it was all but over.

'Oh, darling... I love you. I love you so much...' Her tears fell onto the starched stiffness of the sheet, her grip tightened on his hand and she raised his fingers with infinite gentleness to her lips. 'Oh, Charles, I can't live without you... I love you, my darling...'

His eyelashes fluttered. She saw the effort it took him to open his eyes. But he managed.

And in their dying light those eyes told her how much he loved her too.

* * *

NOTHING SEEMED REAL. She felt as if she'd been sucked into a bottomless black void where pain was the only emotion.

'Why now, Janet? Why now just when everything was perfect?' Prostrate with grief Marianne asked the question over and over again.

In the bedroom, with the Venetians closed against the intrusive daylight, Janet held her and murmured useless words of comfort. At forty, Charles Rolfe had been too young to die, but the pressures of a rapidly expanding business coupled with a system weakened by his wartime injuries had exacted their toll.

Janet's heart broke for the woman who had become her friend. The marriage had indeed seemed 'perfect'. It hadn't escaped her notice that in the past year the couple had begun to share a bed. In recent months too she had sensed an added depth of intensity to their relationship. She had made her own guesses as to the reason why.

* * *

EDWINA HAD RUNG the house not long after their return from the hospital. 'The family will be taking care of all funeral arrangements,' she'd announced curtly when Janet took the call. Not a word of sympathy did she relay to her son's widow.

* * *

THE FUNERAL WAS HELD three days later at St Mark's, Darling Point, the accepted place of worship for Sydney's social set.

The church was packed with high-profile mourners. If Charles had been ostracized in life for fear of alienation by Edwina Rolfe, in death he once more gained acceptance. The occasion was made easier by the fact of the widow's absence. It was Edwina, severe in a slim black suit and veiled hat, who presided over the proceedings.

Afterwards, as she stood in the sunshine, accepting the condolences of her peers, she saw the unspoken question in their eyes. 'Of course she's not here,' came the icy response. 'It's obvious ... she got what she wanted from my son. Now he's dead, there's no reason for her to pretend any longer.'

* * *

BUT MARIANNE COULD NEVER HAVE ENDURED the funeral service. Shattered, she teetered on the edge of total collapse, barely aware of the passage of time. She didn't eat, couldn't sleep, felt drained of every last shred of mental and physical strength. Her only consciousness was of unrelenting pain.

If it hadn't been for Janet she would never have got out of bed at all. It was Janet who bathed her, changed her, helped her through the terrors of the night when her anguish seemed even more unendurable.

As the days passed, Janet held grave fears for the state of her friend's health. But it was when the scandalous rumors reached her ears about why Charles Rolfe's widow had failed to appear at the funeral, that Janet finally decided she had to get Marianne out of Sydney. In her present fragile condition such malicious gossip might be all that was needed to push her completely over the edge.

* * *

AS ON PREVIOUS occasions the cottage offered sanctuary. But while Marianne's devastation gradually gave way to a more rational acceptance of her loss, it was her continuing physical symptoms that still worried Janet.

For two weeks Marianne had woken every day to nausea and retching. Finally Janet felt forced to ask the question that hovered frighteningly in her mind.

She waited until after dinner when they were sitting together by the open fireplace.

'Marianne, my dear... do you ... do you think you might be pregnant?'

Covering her face with her hands Marianne Rolfe burst into heart-wrenching sobs.

She confirmed for Janet then what she had done her best to deny since the day Charles died.

She was six weeks pregnant. Charles had known before his death. They had both been delirious with joy.

* * *

IT TOOK that forced admission to shock Marianne out of her despair. As the days passed, the young widow gradually found the strength and courage she needed to face the future.

'This baby was sent for a purpose, Janet,' she declared with new resilience in her voice as they strolled together one afternoon. 'It's going to give me the courage I need to go on. It means Charles will always be part of my life. And there'll be a child in the house again ... for both of us.'

Suddenly she stopped and threw her friend an anxious look. 'You *will* stay, won't you, Janet?' Charles's death had brought the two of them even closer but the thought had just struck her that Janet might not be able to bear tending to another woman's child.

Tears glistened in Janet's eyes. She put her arm around Marianne and hugged her close. 'You won't be on your own, my dear. I promise.'

I promise, she whispered silently again. This time to the dead father of the unborn child.

* * *

IT WAS a month after Charles's death before they returned to Sydney.

The shock came when they tried to re-enter the house. None of the doors opened to their keys. Standing on tiptoe Marianne peered in at the sunroom window. The room was bare. Not a stick of furniture remained.

They booked into a small private hotel at Edgecliff, not far from the city center. Immediately Marianne put through a call to Charles's solicitor.

'I think it would be best, Mrs Rolfe,' the male voice said carefully, 'if we discussed the matter in these offices.'

She made an appointment for first thing the next morning.

* * *

MARIANNE COULD HARDLY TAKE in what she was hearing.

'But it can't be true. My husband would surely have made adequate provision...'

There was sympathy and dismay in Ian Delaney's dark hooded eyes as he looked across his desk at Charles Rolfe's beautiful widow. As a man who prided himself on his own professional integrity and honor he was appalled at the action taken by the Rolfe family's lawyers in the matter of Charles's will.

He cleared his throat awkwardly. 'I'm afraid the matter is rather more complicated than that, Mrs Rolfe. It has to do with the precise nature of the company structure. We acted as your husband's personal solicitors as you know, and in the document we drew up on his behalf there was certainly a most generous provision made for you as his wife. But, you see, control of the company's assets has now passed to the young Mr Rolfe ... and I am sorry to say that the family's solicitors are taking the stand that there is a certain ambivalence about what your husband as a company director was actually entitled to leave you.'

'But the house... ?' Marianne sat rigidly in the uncomfortable wooden chair. She was still trying to come to terms with the shock of the news.

Ian Delaney couldn't hide his discomfort. Lacing his long thin fingers on the desk in front of him he avoided Marianne's gaze. 'I'm afraid, Mrs Rolfe, they are claiming that the house at Centennial Park was also bought under the company aegis.'

Marianne didn't understand the word. What she did understand was that through her immense power and authority Edwina Rolfe had left her penniless.

* * *

'YOU CAN'T LET them get away with it, Marianne! Charles could never have dreamed that this might happen!

They're using their fancy lawyers to cheat you out of what is rightfully yours. You've got to fight them!'

Normally even-tempered, Janet Byrne was enraged at the injustice of what had occurred. The Rolfes were literally throwing Marianne into the street!

The two women were sitting on a park bench at the harbor's edge. It was a clear sunny day, sailing boats and ferries dotted the water but neither of them noticed her surroundings.

Dazed, Marianne shook her head. 'The bank accounts are frozen, I have no home – I have no means of fighting them.'

Janet's voice revealed her frustration. 'But the baby?'

They'll be cheating Charles's child as well.'

Marianne turned and gripped her friend's arm. 'That's what hurts the most, Janet. That his child too is being robbed of its future. Which is why I think I must now tell Edwina about the baby. However much she hates me, I am sure she will want to do everything possible for her son's child.'

16

Edwina was gradually emerging from the subdued colors of mourning. Charles was dead – but she had lost him years before. Her sole aim now was to ensure that the woman who had stolen her son would never get her hands on a penny of the Rolfe fortune.

The lawyers had been hesitant, but Edwina was resolute. However tenuous the grounds for contesting the will she was determined to exploit them to the fullest.

'Let that bitch just try to take me on and she'll find out exactly what she's up against,' she declared to Caroline. 'I'm going to drive her out of this city if it's the last thing I do.'

Caroline believed her.

* * *

EDWINA ASSURED the others she was happy to hold the next meeting at her home. Life went on, she declared; it was time for her to get back into the swim of things.

The Black and White Committee was among the most socially elite of fund-raising charity groups. Their annual ball at the Trocadero ballroom was legendary.

Anyone failing to gain entry at once lost any claim to being part of Sydney's social set. And today the formidable group of society matrons was coming together in Edwina Rolfe's home for their regular committee meeting.

It was a few minutes after eleven when her butler found her in the kitchen checking on the luncheon arrangements. Her guests were to arrive at noon and Edwina was a stickler for perfection.

'You're slicing that meat a little too thickly, Maureen,' she protested to her latest kitchen hand. The middle-aged woman blinked nervously as she attempted to carve the lamb roast to her employer's exacting specifications.

'This just arrived for you, madam,' the butler interrupted. 'Hand delivered. I thought it might be urgent.'

With a frown Edwina took the proffered envelope and carried it through to the living room before tearing it open.

As her dark eyes skimmed the two sheets of expensive notepaper her cheeks grew mottled with rage. The pages trembled in her hands.

The *bitch*! The lying, scheming *bitch*!

With a furious gesture she screwed up the pages and flung them aside. Everything she had thought about that manipulative foreign tart had been proved right!

But a moment later she was snatching up the crumpled sheets from where she'd just thrown them. Her rage and anger were at boiling point. Oh, no, she was going to deal with this right *now*!

The hotel address and telephone number were written on the first page. Edwina glanced at her watch. There was just time before the others arrived. It would be absolutely unbearable to have this eating away at her for the rest of the afternoon!

Eyes blazing, she hurried to the privacy of her bedroom. When at last the number was answered she demanded curtly to be put through to Mrs Rolfe. It made the bile rise in her throat just to utter the name.

'Marianne Rolfe...'

'How dare you! How dare you lie to me, you little tramp!'

In her hotel room, Marianne overcame her surprise to recognize the voice of her mother-in-law. 'Edwina... Mrs Rolfe... please, believe me. It's true. I am almost three months pregnant with Charles's baby. You must understand ...'

'Oh, I understand, all right!' The older woman's tone was scathing. 'I understand that you're exactly what I thought you were ... a gold-digging, lying bitch who determined to manipulate and use my son from the moment you set eyes on him!'

'No! You're wrong! I loved ...'

'Listen to me ... do you think I didn't know Charles was impotent? Do you think he didn't tell me? Until you came along he told me everything. We were as close as any mother and son could be ... and you spoilt it all!' Edwina gave a mocking laugh then her words spewed forth in fury. 'Oh, no, you scheming whore, you can't pull this one on me. I *know* with absolute certainty that you can't be carrying Charles's child. You've been sleeping around, haven't you? Making a fool of my son. And now you expect that your useless little bastard is going to be brought up in the comfort of the Rolfe fortune. Well, you might have fooled my son, you cheap little tramp, but you don't fool me!'

With furious strength she slammed the receiver back into place.

* * *

THE SHOCK STARTED at Marianne's fingertips and moved steadily through her body.

Tramp... whore... liar... The words rang in her head. Edwina didn't believe her. Didn't believe that it was Charles who had fathered her child.

Numbly she lowered herself onto the nearest chair. And now Edwina Rolfe was going to try to deny her child not only its rightful inheritance but also its legitimacy...

No... *Oh no...*

Marianne got to her feet, scrabbled with shaky fingers in her handbag and found the keys to the car. Janet was in her own room further up the hallway but she had to do this alone.

She had to convince Charles's mother of the truth.

* * *

In her distraught state it never occurred to her to wonder about the half a dozen vehicles parked at the front of the house. She was forced however, to leave her own car at the rear access and enter through the kitchen. One of the kitchen staff, busy slicing tomatoes, looked up, startled.

'Can I help you, madam?' The woman took in Marianne's agitated manner, her lack of hat and gloves. Surely this wasn't one of the guests?

Blind and deaf to all but her need to speak with Charles's mother, Marianne pushed past the protesting woman and into the hallway. From the living room she could hear the faint murmur of voices.

Edwina... Marianne hurried on. She had to see Edwina and convince her of the truth. Once she believed this was Charles's child everything would be all right. For no matter how much Edwina might hate her, she would surely welcome her grandchild, ensure its rightful place in its heritage.

Of that Marianne was positive...

Without stopping to knock she pushed open the door. Eight pairs of eyes looked up in surprise. And then, Edwina Rolfe, her face a pale mask of rage, was rising to her feet.

'*What-do-you-want*?' The words cut like a whiplash through the tense silence that had descended on the room.

Marianne stared. She could feel the eyes of the assembled women boring into her. She saw at once that she had chosen the worst possible moment to confront her mother-in-law but, obsessed with the need to convince Edwina of the truth, she couldn't stop now.

'I must speak to you. It's...'

'Get out of here!' Edwina was crossing the room towards her. 'Get out of my house, you little tramp, before I call the police!'

'Please, Edwina, I want you to understand. You must believe me! Charles ... '

Edwina Rolfe extended her arm backwards. Her stinging slap left a bright red mark on the younger woman's cheek.

'Don't you *dare* mention my son's name, you filthy whore!' Her voice was shrill with fury. 'Now get out of my house! Get out of here at once!'

Her strength belying her petite stature, the older woman put her hands to Marianne's shoulders and with full force pushed her backwards through the living room door.

Marianne staggered, almost fell, as Edwina pursued her into the hall, slamming the door closed behind them.

'How dare you come here and make a scene in front of my friends,' she hissed in rage. 'How dare you!' With a steely grip, she was half-pushing, half-dragging Marianne towards the kitchen. 'You lying little slut! I saw exactly what you were the moment I clapped eyes on you!'

And then she was shoving Marianne through the swinging kitchen door, ignoring the gape-mouthed astonishment of the woman busy at the stove.

As she reeled backwards into the room, the sharp metal edge of the table bit into Marianne's thigh making her gasp in pain. The baby, she thought dazedly. Nothing must hurt the baby...

Reaching behind to steady herself, she flinched as her hand touched something cold.

Cold and sharp.

Flecks of spittle were flying from Edwina Rolfe's lips. 'Don't think you're cheating this family out of another penny, you scheming bitch! Get out of here and find some other fool to raise your ugly, useless bastard!'

Marianne swayed, suddenly made giddy by the force of Edwina Rolfe's cacophony of hate. A curtain of red rage seemed to blind her eyes. She felt jolted by the ice in her belly and the burning in her blood.

Charles's child... She was talking about Charles's child. With her lying, filthy words this woman was destroying everything that had been pure and good and perfect between Charles and her...

Eyes full of hate and loathing, Edwina swung around to go. At the same moment Marianne's hand closed around the handle of the long-bladed carving knife.

The room began to echo to the cook's screams of horror.

17

She sat absolutely still. From the second-storey window her violet eyes were fixed unwaveringly on the main entry gates.

And then she saw her, walking up the grassy kerb from the direction of the railway station ... the slim figure, the dark curls, which already held fine streaks of silver, the familiar brown overcoat. The child's face instantly lit up with pleasure. Jumping down from her perch on the sill she hurried out of the room to greet her visitor. Her only visitor.

She was scampering down the last of the broad polished stairs when a stern voice boomed from further down the hallway.

'Eve Taylor! Is that any way for a lady to descend a staircase?'

The eight year old recognized the voice. Sister Lois of all people... She turned as the puckered-mouthed nun approached. 'No, Sister,' she replied, head lowered respectfully.

'Then just you go all the way up again and walk down like a well brought up young lady should.'

Stifling her impatience, Eve retraced her steps. Every moment of delay was agony. Janet's visits were rare enough; she didn't want to waste a precious second.

'Now... the right way.' Sister Lois was glowering up at her from the foot of the cedar staircase.

Carefully, slowly, Eve descended once more, her hand sliding along the curved bannister. The sunshine streaming through the tall stained-glass window on the landing threw colored shadows on the bare stairs and reflected on her soft golden hair.

'That was much better.' Sister Lois nodded her approval, causing her pale jowls to tremble slightly. 'We don't want anyone saying that St Ursula's girls don't know the right way of doing things, now do we?'

'No, Sister.' Eve twitched impatiently. And then to her surprise she felt something pressed into her hand. She looked down. It was a cellophane-wrapped barley sugar.

'Off you go now.' There was a twinkle in the nun's small blue eyes.

Eve smiled in delight. 'Oh, Sister... thank you very much.' And with a swift bobbed curtsey she moved as quickly as she dared towards the reception room where Janet was bound to be waiting.

* * *

As usual, Janet took her for a meal in one of the town's two cafes. There were no other customers in the half-dozen booths that lined one wall, but the empty plates that had held their toasted sandwiches still sat on the formica table, attracting the big bush flies to the crumbs.

Janet glanced over at the girl behind the milk bar counter. The young plump brunette was too busy checking her appearance in the insect-speckled mirrored wall that held the shelves of glasses and sundae containers to worry about her solitary customers.

She turned back to the child sitting opposite.

'So, judging by your last term's report English is still your favorite subject, pet?'

Eve held up her cone and licked at a long trickle of ice cream that threatened to drip from the bottom. She nodded enthusiastically in response to Janet's question. 'I love it. I could write stories all day long. And I love reading too.' She popped the last of the cone into her mouth, swallowed, then threw Janet a quizzical look. 'Do you like reading, Janty?'

'Very much. When I have time.' Janet was working full-time in a small private hospital not too far from the cottage in the mountains where she now lived. Her job, and the fact that Eve's school was in a large country town three hours' travelling time away, made regular visits difficult.

Janet wished there could have been another way. But she knew there wasn't. She needed to earn an income, and St Ursula's was the school where Father Michael had connections. His second cousin was the Mother Superior, and only the three of them knew the true identity of the child known as Eve Taylor.

Janet took a clean lace-trimmed handkerchief from her handbag and handed it to the little girl across the table, studying her as she wiped her hands and mouth. Already the child held promise of her mother's luminous beauty with those wide violet eyes and the broad, high cheekbones with their hint of Slavic ancestry. Her blonde hair hung in two thick plaits past her shoulders, and she seemed taller every time Janet saw her.

What a tragedy, she thought regretfully for the thousandth time. The whole terrible thing. If only she could have had the child with her. But the scandal, and her own connection to the Rolfes, had been too widely publicized for that. The terrible circumstances had kept the story in the newspapers for weeks. All Australia had been agog. Ever tainted by her past, the poor innocent babe wouldn't have had a chance of a normal childhood.

The convent of St Ursula's had been the only viable option. Eve had been taken there just a few weeks after her birth. The other nuns knew only that the mother had been unable in the interim to look after the child and Father Michael had asked his relative to help.

It was virtually the same story that in time had been relayed to Eve herself. And Janet, it was vaguely explained, was a friend of Father Michael; a lady who having lost her own child was happy to take another under her wing. The little girl had accepted the explanation without question.

But Janet shuddered inwardly at the task that awaited her in the future. One day, somehow, she was going to have to tell the child the whole terrible truth. It was a pact she had made with herself, but one she dreaded. In the meantime she would do everything in her power to ensure the daughter of Marianne and Charles Rolfe was educated, healthy and happy. Because she had made that promise to Charles all those years ago. Because Marianne had offered her unlimited kindness and friendship.

Because, Janet thought, she loved the child as if she were her own.

* * *

THE LITTLE GIRL clung to her tearfully when it was time to say goodbye. 'Don't go, please, please don't go.'

Kneeling down beside her Janet's own eyes gleamed with tears. It was the echo of Danny's words of years ago.

'I must, darling. But you know I'll come again.' She tried to keep her voice steady as she gently disengaged the little arms from around her neck. Forcing a smile, she wiped away the tears from those soft cheeks.

'Maybe you won't... maybe you'll go away like my mother did...'

The child had uttered her worst fear. She looked up at Janet and her voice took on a desperate ring. 'When I'm grown up I'm going to find Mummy. I'm going to look everywhere until I find her. You'll help me, won't you, Janty?'

Janet Byrne swallowed hard, nodding as she pulled on her gloves. She didn't trust herself to speak.

* * *

THE RAYS of early morning sunshine streamed in through the rows of stained-glass windows and lit the pews of kneeling girls.

As the priest muttered the Credo and the heavy scent of incense floated from the altar, some of the girls bowed their heads in devotion, others to hide their bored or sleepy faces.

From her place in the very front row Eve turned reverent eyes up to the statue of the Virgin Mary. Silently she recited the same prayer she said every day to the Mother of God.

Please, Mother, let me find her one day... Let me find my mother. And let her love me just as much as you love all of us...

Eve had been taught to look for miracles. There were signs, the nuns had told them. One only had to notice. But the blue painted eyes of the statue never gave any indication that the girl's earnest prayers had been heeded.

Yet that didn't stop Eve from hoping.

* * *

BY THE TIME she was fifteen Eve Taylor was one of the most popular girls in the school. Everyone liked her and no one resented her widespread success.

Eve seemed good at everything. She topped her class, sang in the school choir, got first-rate results in her music examinations, was a good all-round sportswoman and captain of the debating team. From inauspicious beginnings Eve Taylor had made the most of the opportunities offered her.

And to cap it all she had the kind of looks that drove boys crazy. Her cool beauty never went through the plump, spotty stage that other less fortunates had to endure; she was tall, with slender graceful limbs, softly waved strawberry blonde hair and those amazing violet eyes.

But the other girls didn't hate Eve for her looks – they could see she barely noticed the attention paid to her. Eve Taylor was far too concentrated on her studies.

From the nuns she had learnt the important lessons of discipline and determination, and her focus became fixed on acquiring a scholarship to Sydney University.

'I want to study Arts-Law,' she told Mother Margaret during one of their discussions about her future. 'I want to do something positive for the world.'

What she really meant was: *When I find my mother I want her to be proud of me.*

* * *

JANET USUALLY MANAGED to arrange some time off work during Eve's long summer holidays. The two of them would enjoy trips to Sydney to visit the museums, the Art Gallery, theatres and movies. Janet was impressed when Eve stood in front of a painting and talked about the artist, his techniques, his life. It was the same when they took in a concert at the Town Hall. The girl knew so much about the composers and the music. The nuns, Janet was gratified to learn, had indeed given Marianne's daughter a first-rate education.

Over the years Eve had grown close to Janet Byrne. She looked on the woman who had taken her under her wing as the nearest she had to a family. If it hadn't been for the fact that Eve was so totally determined to find her own mother one day, she could easily have accepted Janet in that role. Yet at the same time she sensed that Janet herself was resistant to filling her absent mother's shoes. Maybe, Eve pondered, that was because of Danny.

Janet had told her about the son she had lost so tragically. 'Polio claimed so many children back then,' she had explained. 'It was before immunization and Danny was one of the unlucky ones. It's just something I've had to live with.' She was silent for a moment and the girl saw the pain in her eyes.

In an effort to distract the older woman from her sadness, Eve had prompted, 'And it was after that that your friend Father Michael asked you to visit me?' Eve could only regret that the elderly priest had died before she was old enough to question him about her mother.

A faint flush heated Janet's cheeks and she avoided the girl's gaze. 'It was a couple of years or so after Danny died. I guess he thought it might help both of us.' She hated having to lie.

Eve hugged Janet warmly. 'And he was right, wasn't he, Janty?'

* * *

EVE LOVED the house in the mountains. Even when Janet couldn't be with her all the time she was never lonely. She would read and study on the sun-drenched verandah or potter in the garden under the dappled shade of the broad-limbed oaks. One evening, over dinner, she said to Janet, 'You know, it's strange, but right from the start I've always felt at home in this house. It's almost as if...' she gave a slightly embarrassed laugh at admitting such silly fantasies, 'as if I've been here before.'

The older woman appeared not to hear. Serving spoon poised above the casserole dish she asked, 'Would you like some more shepherd's pie, sweetheart?'

* * *

IT WAS no surprise to anyone when Eve Taylor was made school captain. She was a natural-born leader, a role model who had the respect of her peers. Even the shyest and youngest pupils felt they could approach her with whatever was troubling them and Eve was happy to give something back to the school which had offered her so much.

She sat for her final examinations and felt quietly confident that she had done well. Free of the worry of study she could now enjoy the anticipation of the graduation dance, which was to be held in conjunction with St Dominic's local boys' college.

The day of the dance the senior girls spent the morning transforming the school assembly hall and the early evening transforming themselves as they shed drab school uniforms for the bright colors of their formal dresses.

That night as Eve was swept around the floor by a succession of sweaty-palmed youths over whom she invariably towered, she wondered what it must feel like to fall in love. In her mind's eye she carried a vague, faceless form of the man who might one day make her complete. Recently she had got her hands on a copy of the book that she knew had caused a sensation when it was first released. *The Female Eunuch* had given her much to think about. Yet she had no intention of counting all men as the enemy.

No, Eve decided, deftly side-stepping to avoid the bruising contact of her partner's feet, just because she was determined to have a career didn't mean that she wanted to spend her life alone.

I'm going to have it all, was her confident resolve.

* * *

THE NEXT MORNING dressed in her school uniform for the final time, Eve faced the gathered assembly to give her valedictory address as school captain.

She felt a mixture of emotions. The security of her schoolgirl years was almost behind her; she was on the brink of adult life. The thought both thrilled and frightened her. For a fleeting second she wished she had a crystal ball to get a glimpse of what life might have in store for her.

18

Eve's examination results exceeded even her own expectations. Ranked among the top ten per cent of students in the state, she easily won a scholarship to Sydney University.

It was with a sense of excitement and anticipation that she took up residence in her simply furnished single room in Women's College two days before the start of term. Along with hundreds of other "freshers" she wandered around the sprawling campus, reveling in the sense of tradition and history evoked by the majestic architecture of the university's sandstone buildings.

I'm going to love it here, she breathed to herself, exulting in the heady joy of youth and freedom.

Her thirst for knowledge as keen as ever, Eve enjoyed most of her classes and worked hard on her course assignments. Her marks reflected her industriousness.

While her studies kept her busy she was determined to make the most of the opportunities university life offered. In the little time she had to spare she joined a number of clubs and associations. Debating and music were again top of the list and it was among those who shared these interests that Eve made friends. The women liked her as much as the men, for Eve was no flirt, she made no attempt to use her looks to steal anyone else's boyfriend. In any case, if the adolescent boys were forced to admit it they found themselves slightly intimidated by the intelligent self-assured blonde with the startling violet eyes and lovely face. Few were brave enough to ask her for a date.

Yet Eve was seldom lonely. During her years at St Ursula's she had learned to enjoy her own company. Only occasionally, when she saw one of the other girls turn up at a meeting or function with a new boyfriend, she couldn't help wondering if there was someone out there for her, someone who might make her heart and mind and body catch fire.

Janet made discreet enquiries along those same lines when Eve came home for the long summer vacation at the end of her first year.

'You've done so well, my dear. Absolutely wonderful results ... I'm very proud of you.' They were sitting with their after-dinner coffee in the garden on Eve's first evening home.

Nursing her cup she looked pleased at Janet's reaction. 'I just love being there, Janty. All those brilliant minds to pick, exciting ideas to ponder, and a library I could spend the rest of my life in!'

Janet saw the glow in the girl's face. How lovely she looks, she thought. If only...

She cut off such dangerous musings. 'I hope it's not just a matter of all hard work though, dear. You do have a moment for some fun too ... don't you... ?' She let her voice trail off.

Eve threw her a knowing smile. 'If you mean boys...' She shrugged. 'Well, I guess there are... interested males. But no one really right.' She took a sip of her coffee and thought for a moment. 'You know, none of them seem really serious about why they're at university.'

'What do you mean?' Janet sounded puzzled.

'Oh... just that they seem motivated more by the desire for status and money than by any real interest in knowledge, or in understanding the world around them.'

The light was beginning to fade and Janet turned to look at the pale profile of the girl beside her. She spoke quietly. 'Money's important too, you know.'

'Of course! I understand that. It's just that I see it as secondary to the other. Oh, God,' she laughed and made a dismissive gesture, 'who wants to talk about boys and money...' Putting down her empty cup on the cane table between them Eve pushed herself to her feet and standing behind Janet leaned over to kiss the top of her head.

'Did I ever tell you how grateful I am for all you've done for me, Janty? I really don't know what I did to deserve it ... it's not as if you even knew my mother, yet you still took me under your wing.' She kissed the older woman affectionately again, this time on the cheek. 'Thanks, Janty. Thanks for everything.'

As she reached back and gripped the girl's hand, Janet was glad that the cover of darkness hid the heat in her cheeks. One day soon, she thought fearfully. One day when the time was right she would tell her the truth.

Janet only prayed she would be wise enough to know when that moment arrived.

* * *

THE RECITAL HALL was about three-quarters full. Eve sat three rows from the front, her eyes riveted on the young male pianist playing Schubert's *Impromptu Number 2* with such skill.

Her program informed her that his name was Paul Dawson, twenty-one, a third-year Conservatorium student. His talent was obvious to anyone who understood music.

Sunday afternoon recitals were a common feature of the Sydney Conservatorium calendar. It gave students the chance to play before an audience and today's program featured not only the talented pianist but also two young violinists.

Eve was glad she had allowed friends to persuade her to attend today's recital. She'd finished two long assignments in the last week and realized how much the music was helping her to relax.

At the completion of the program the audience was invited to partake of afternoon tea with the performers and other music students in a small reception room overlooking the neighboring Botanic Gardens. Elderly ladies in pearls and fur stoles, proud parents and casually dressed students all mingled as they sipped their tea and discussed the afternoon's performances.

Eve noticed him the moment he entered the room. Changed now from his formal attire into blue striped shirt and jeans, Paul Dawson was hard to miss. He was tall, broad-shouldered, with thick dark hair curling over his collar, and only an obviously broken nose saved his face from being almost too handsome.

She couldn't help staring. Paul Dawson had presence, and the confidence of someone assured of his own talent. He was bound to go a long way, she decided as she turned back to rejoin the conversation of the group around her.

Five minutes later, Eve was helping herself to another cup of tea when she was suddenly bumped from behind. Hot liquid splashed out of the cup and onto the floor.

'Oh, I'm *so* sorry! Here... let me take that from you.'

Half-turning, she found herself looking into the anxious, apologetic face of Paul Dawson. He took the cup and saucer from her hands and placed them on the table.

'Are you all right? You didn't burn yourself, did you?'

'No... no...' She shook her head. 'I'm fine. Really.'

'I'm a clumsy oaf,' he put out his hand with a smile, 'but I'm also known as Paul Dawson.'

Eve felt her heart kick against her rib cage as their hands met. Up close, the young pianist's good looks were even more striking. 'Eve Taylor,' she responded, and added in a rush, 'at least now I can tell you in person how much I enjoyed your playing. That Schubert piece is one of my favorites. You have real talent.'

Paul Dawson looked genuinely pleased at the compliment. 'Thank you very much. You're... not a student here, are you?' He was taking in the long-lashed eyes, the thick blonde ponytail and fine-boned, sensitive face.

'No, I'm at Sydney Uni. Second year Arts-Law.'

'Paul...'

He turned as a middle-aged woman, her red hair drawn into a tight knot, tapped him on the arm. 'Sorry to interrupt, my sweet, but there are a few people over here who are dying to meet you. Important people... if you know what I mean.' The woman gave him a knowing nod and Paul Dawson understood. The music business was like any other; it was who you knew that helped you get ahead.

'Uh... sure, Mrs Ryan. Just a moment.' But by the time he'd turned back to her Eve Taylor had disappeared.

Paul Dawson couldn't deny his disappointment.

* * *

THREE WEEKS LATER, on another Sunday afternoon, Eve was taking one of the city walks she loved. It was a damp, miserable day and the usual crowds were missing in the Botanic Gardens that edged the harbor. But Eve loved the grey, lowering skies that helped break the monotony of the Australian sunshine. And after studying all morning she'd felt the need to escape the quiet confines of the library.

Paul Dawson saw her first. Hands stuck in the pockets of a long shabby overcoat that covered his jeans and sweatshirt, he was strolling across the lawn from the direction of the Conservatorium.

'Well... hello.'

Her head shot up and he saw her surprise.

'The clumsy oaf... Remember?'

She smiled. The dampness had made her hair curl around her forehead and her violet eyes were as striking as he remembered them.

'Of course. How are you? Not playing this afternoon?'

'Even genius needs a break.' He gave a self deprecating grin as he fell into step beside her. 'Been practising all morning actually. I needed some exercise.'

'Me too. Studying, I mean. I love walking down here. The rain doesn't worry me.' She knew she was talking for talking's sake. Paul Dawson's compelling grey eyes were making her strangely nervous.

'If you're not going anywhere special can I find out how brave you are?'

She gave him a puzzled half-smile.

He grinned. 'I'm trying to ask if you're game enough to join me for a cup of tea.'

* * *

THEY SAT TALKING for three hours. Neither noticed the time.

Eve discovered that Paul had grown up in a town on the north coast, where his father was a pineapple farmer and his mother a high-school teacher. Both parents shared a love of music, which they had passed on to their only son.

'Mum and Dad used to play all the popular classics over dinner. They'd talk about the music, tell my sister and me a little about each composer. I loved it but Julie loathed it. She lived for sport ... swimming, riding, tennis ... while I was hopeless at everything except swimming. My idea of hell was being forced to play cricket at school every summer. Pretty early on I knew I wanted to make music my life.'

'It's so important to follow your dreams,' Eve asserted quietly.

He looked at her across their empty tea cups. Outside it was dark and the rain was falling heavily. Paul was glad. It meant they'd have to sit together longer.

'And what are your dreams?' he asked gently. He was beginning to be intrigued by this girl who had been raised by nuns in some country convent.

Eve lowered her eyes. She didn't want to speak about finding her mother.

At the same time, deep inside her, she could feel the beginnings of another desire. *To have a man like you love me forever.*

He was watching her, waiting for an answer.

'My dreams?' She laughed lightly. 'Just to have it all.'

* * *

SHE COULDN'T GET Paul Dawson out of her mind. He intrigued her. He was attractive without conceit, confident without arrogance, friendly without being bold. When they'd finally parted that wet Sunday night he'd mentioned something about seeing a Woody Allen film together. 'I've heard it's a departure from his usual style. Does it interest you?'

The thought of spending more time with Paul Dawson was what interested her.

* * *

He rang a week later just when she'd despairingly begun to think he wasn't interested.

Exactly on time, he picked her up at Women's College wearing a blue and grey tweedy jacket over his usual jeans and sweatshirt. To Eve's eyes he looked more handsome than ever.

The movie flickered across the screen but almost as soon as it ended Eve would have been hard pressed to repeat the storyline. Her concentration hadn't been on the screen but on the youth beside her.

Whenever he leaned close in the darkness to offer some quickly murmured comment, she had been acutely aware of the faint scent of his aftershave, the soft warmth of his breath, the unexpected brush of his hair against her cheek.

Her emotions were in a turmoil. Was it possible to fall in love with someone you'd met only three times? she wondered later as they sat together in the cheap, student-filled coffee shop in Glebe Point Road.

It was close to midnight when he walked her to the college entrance.

'Thanks for the company, Eve. I really enjoyed myself.'

His profile was just visible where they stood outside the circle of light illuminating the front door.

'Me too.' Oh, God, the triteness of those two words.

What she really meant was – *Please call me again. Soon.*

His face came closer to hers and she felt her heart take a perilous leap. His lips brushed her cheek, moved gently, very gently to her lips. He kissed her with exquisite tenderness at the same time as he ran a finger caressingly down her cheek.

'Can we see each other again?' he whispered.

She nodded, not trusting herself to speak.

* * *

Eve fell madly, crazily in love. Paul Dawson was that faceless soul mate she had dreamed of for so long. The other part of her soul, her link to the fundamental reason for existence.

And the most wonderful, joyous, thrilling part was that the man she loved made it unequivocally clear that he felt exactly the same way about her.

19

In a short space of time Eve and Paul were spending every spare moment together. He introduced her to the two other music students who shared the rundown rented terrace house just off Crown Street. From there it was only a short bike ride to the conservatorium or the city, and the two of them enjoyed the activities Sydney had to offer. They took in films, art galleries and concerts on cheap student tickets; they rode the harbor ferries to surf at Manly, and bought fish and chips to eat on the sand.

They were in love and life was wonderful.

The intensity of their relationship might have had a detrimental effect on their studies but instead it brought each of them a peace and contentment which enabled them to work even harder.

Eve had spoken to Janet about Paul – and now, after two months, she asked if she could invite him to the cottage for the weekend.

When Janet first saw them together she was immediately struck by what a stunning couple they made.

That evening, as they sat chatting over dinner, she was pleased to note the depth too beneath the tall, dark haired young man's external appeal. Paul Dawson was thoughtful, intelligent, well-mannered. Eve had made a good choice, she thought, pleased. And it was obvious that the boy adored her.

After the meal was cleared away they went through to the living room where Paul's eyes, Janet noticed, went immediately to the piano in the corner. It was a stolid upright she had bought second-hand when Eve had started to learn to play. A far cry from the baby grand Marianne Rolfe had owned in the house at Centennial Park.

Janet smiled. 'I suppose you wouldn't like to play something, would you, Paul? Or couldn't you bear to touch that old monster?'

He threw her a smile and slid onto the piano stool. 'Let's see what she sounds like,' he replied, opening the lid.

His fingers trilled over the keys for a moment or two while Eve and Janet sat watching. Then very softly, gently, he began to play a Chopin etude.

Janet stiffened. The piece was one of Marianne's favorites; she had played it often. Now, bent over the keys, Paul Dawson filled the room with the emotional spirit of Chopin's beautiful evocative music.

Janet felt overcome with memory. She glanced at the girl beside her and saw Eve's gaze riveted on the handsome young pianist, her face aglow with love.

If only things had turned out differently, Janet thought painfully. If only Marianne... She clamped down quickly on such distressing thoughts. But she knew the moment of truth was drawing inexorably closer.

* * *

It was on a subsequent visit to the cottage that Paul and Eve became lovers for the first time.

That particular Saturday Janet had to work evening shift at the hospital and they had the place to themselves. Over their months together they had gradually become more intimate, their caresses had grown more eager and unrestrained. Now, as if by silent agreement, they both knew the moment for consummation had arrived.

Despite her convent upbringing Eve had no reservations. Jesus spoke about love. She loved Paul with every shred of her being; by inference, how could what they were doing be wrong?

By the soft light of the one shaded lamp they lay naked together on her single bed. Through the open window the scent of jasmine filled the air as they whispered their love for each other.

Their bodies entwined and their kisses grew more urgent. Eve knew the time was right. Her whole body was alight with desire; she was ready to experience the ultimate bond with the man she loved so deeply.

Paul rolled on the condom he had been carrying with him for weeks now. 'Darling.. Breath quickening he lowered himself onto her, gently probing his way into her ready moistness.

Eve felt no pain as she welcomed him inside her. They were conjoined. As bonded as two human beings can ever be. She let out her breath in a low soft sigh of pleasure.

'I love you, Paul. I love you.'

He was arched above her, his beautiful face contorted with desire. 'Oh, Eve... oh, my darling!'

They began their dance of love; their bodies moving together. Spirals of ecstasy ran up Eve's spine; she felt drugged by the touch, the taste, the scent of her lover. Time became a mirage. Nothing mattered but the moment, and the man who had first made her his.

* * *

THEY WERE ENGAGED IMMEDIATELY Eve finished her final exams. By then they had known each other just over two years and planned to marry within six months.

The future looked exciting. Eve was awarded a first class degree and had already started work as a local researcher for a State parliamentary minister. On his own graduation a few months earlier Paul had been paid the honor of being offered a short-term contract as accompanist with the Australian Opera Company.

It was after rehearsal one afternoon that he was approached by a slim, elegantly attired Englishman who had been listening to the performance. His name was John Venniker and, as he explained to

Paul, he was a music critic whose articles appeared in all the leading British newspapers.

'I was very impressed by your performance today,' the Englishman stated in his rich, rounded accent as they made their way down the corridors towards the Opera House exit. 'You have talent, but it needs careful nurturing. Have you thought about finding yourself a London agent?'

Paul felt a leap of excitement. 'No... I ... I thought it was a bit early perhaps for that.'

'Nonsense, my dear chap! The sooner you get yourself known in this game the better.' He pulled out his expensive monogrammed wallet and handed Paul a card. 'Here. I'll be in Sydney for another two days. I'm staying at the Hilton. Call me if you'd like to talk more about this.'

When Paul relayed the news to her later that evening, Eve's face lit with delight. 'That's fantastic, Paul! He sounds exactly the sort of contact you need. You can't not follow up on this.'

'Okay, let's arrange it for tomorrow.'

* * *

JOHN VENNIKER HAD a suite on the twelfth floor. He opened the door with a smile of welcome and Eve saw a man of average height with a neat goatee beard and perfectly groomed graying hair. He was wearing a white, open-necked shirt and dark wool trousers.

'Come in! Do come in.'

Paul introduced Eve. 'Eve Taylor, my fiancée... Mr Venniker.'

'Oh, please, please ... it's John,' the music critic gripped Eve's outstretched hand in both of his. 'I'm not one of those insufferably pompous English types.'

He showed them into the living room and as they took a seat on the yellow silk-covered sofa John Venniker opened a bottle of French champagne.

'I'm sure this is going to be a relationship to celebrate,' he said warmly as he handed them each a brimming glass.

* * *

And it was. John Venniker seemed to know everyone worth knowing in the music world. His contacts spread far and wide. He felt that Paul should waste no time in coming to London and making himself known to those who could do so much for his career.

'Look, Christmas is almost upon us but why don't you try to find a few days in January when you can fit in a quick trip to London?' he suggested. 'I'll introduce you round, make sure you meet the best agents. Then, when you've finished your contract with the Australian Opera, you should be able to walk into something almost immediately in the UK.'

The music critic's enthusiasm was infectious.

Later, as they discussed their meeting, Eve said, 'You've just *got* to go, Paul. We'll find the money somewhere.'

Paul was excited at the prospect, but he was thinking in the longer term too. 'What if we have to move to Europe for a while, Eve? Have you considered your own career?'

She waved away his concern. 'Look, darling, we always knew this was on the cards sooner or later. I'm prepared to do whatever it takes at this stage to give you your chance.'

Paul took in her shining eyes and a flicker of apprehension ran through him. She always wants what's best for me, he thought.

That next morning he telephoned John Venniker and made arrangements to meet him in London in three weeks' time. With the wedding in early March, he'd be back in plenty of time.

There seemed nothing to cloud their happiness.

'You told your mother didn't you that we weren't having bridesmaids, groomsmen or all that sort of fuss?' asked Eve as she accepted a refill of her drink.

Paul nodded. It was New Year's Eve and they were celebrating at a party in the crowded apartment of mutual friends. But he wasn't in a festive mood. The canker that had been worrying him wouldn't go away. Daily it seemed to gnaw more sharply. There were nights when he woke up after only a couple of hours of brittle troubled sleep ... and unable to rest again, saw the rosy fingers of dawn enter the room.

It can't be true, he told himself now as the revelers started to count down the seconds till midnight and the start of a new year. He refused to accept it.

Then the magic hour struck and Eve was kissing him, holding him close. 'This is going to be the most wonderful year of our lives, darling,' she whispered in his ear.

But the cold churning in the pit of his belly wouldn't go away.

* * *

EVE ENJOYED the slackening of her work pace over the Christmas parliamentary break.

As the locally based research assistant to the State Minister for Industrial Relations she worked on numerous fronts ... among them various employer organizations and the unions. It was inevitable too that she would have close contact with the media as she helped prepare the minister's news releases and press statements. The work was stimulating but Eve very quickly had her illusions shattered about the game of politics.

Idealism, conscience and straight dealing, she discovered, were in depressingly short supply. She never found it easy to handle the dissimulation and obvious power plays which were so deeply entrenched, and at the beginning she had discussed her reservations with Paul.

He hadn't really understood. 'Well, why don't you just toss it in and get something else, darling? You don't have to stay. The money's not all that crash hot.'

But it wasn't money that drove her. Rather she was motivated by a sense of responsibility. It was the nuns at St Ursula's who had encouraged such ideals. Women, they stated forcefully, should play an active role in shaping the future.

Yet now Eve was prepared to make a sacrifice for love; to forgo her own career in the interest of allowing Paul the chance to plant the seeds of international success.

* * *

THE NIGHT before he left for London they made love in Eve's sparsely furnished Elizabeth Bay apartment where they planned to live after their marriage.

'I'm going to miss you, sweetheart,' she whispered as she lay in her lover's strong arms.

'I'll be back almost before you know I'm gone,' he answered lightly.

Eve trailed her fingers across his chest. 'Just don't go falling in love with some gorgeous Brit, okay?' she teased.

He drew her closer and whispered intensely, 'There'll never be another woman in my life, Eve, believe me.'

She did.

* * *

WHILE PAUL WAS GONE Eve and Janet went searching for a wedding dress. The ceremony was to be held in the modest surroundings of Eve's local Catholic Church in Oxford Street with the reception at Beppi's Italian Restaurant. It was where they'd gone on their first formal dinner date and they'd been back as often as their finances allowed.

Eve was determined the wedding would be a small affair, no fuss. Just a dozen or so friends, Paul's parents, whom she'd met now on three separate occasions, and his married sister.

'I can't see the point of all that expense, Janet,' she'd stated firmly as they discussed the arrangements one weekend at the cottage. Then her voice had grown wistful. 'Anyway, it's really a family occasion, isn't it?'

Janet looked at her. She should have opened her mouth then, told her everything at last.

But her courage failed her.

Not now, she thought. *Not when she's so happy.*

There was always an excuse.

* * *

20

Paul's exhaustion was obvious when they met at the airport, and Eve did her best to suppress her eager questions as she drove back into the city.

'Home, sweetheart? Or do you want to stay with me?' It was perfunctory politeness, so his answer surprised her.

'I've got to admit I'm absolutely worn out, Eve. Do you mind if I go straight home? I'll come round once I get some sleep.'

She hid her disappointment. 'Of course, darling. Whatever suits.' But she couldn't help thinking how much more peaceful her own apartment was than the noisy, street-front terrace with its two other occupants.

* * *

He called over in time for a late dinner.

'Did you manage to get some sleep?' She smiled at him as she tossed the salad.

'Hardly any,' Paul replied, leaning his slender hips against the kitchen bench.

Eve wasn't surprised; he still looked completely washed out.

Over dinner he told her what had happened in London. John Venniker was every bit as good as his word; apart from introducing him to a wide cross-section of musical London he'd also arranged for Paul to meet with two leading agents. One had virtually promised to take him on.

'John's going to help me negotiate the details.'

Eve nodded. 'That's great. He's certainly been very kind.' She speared a slice of tomato. 'Look... don't take this the wrong way, darling, but I guess I can't help wondering what's in it for him.'

Paul picked up his glass of wine. 'I think he likes to see himself as a bit of a Svengali, probably.' He shrugged, gave a little laugh. 'A sort of father figure maybe, to the raw talent.'

'Well, whatever, the trip certainly sounds as if it was worthwhile.'

* * *

HE STAYED THE NIGHT, but they didn't make love.

When they went to bed Eve drew close, eager for the feel of Paul's body and the intense physical and emotional pleasure their lovemaking never failed to bring her. But she could soon tell that he wasn't in the mood.

He kissed her on the lips. 'I'm sorry, darling. I guess I'm too dog tired to be much good for you tonight. Would you mind very much if I took a rain check?'

She lay cradled in his arms, smelt the wonderful familiar scent of his body and hair, felt the smooth hardness of his body stretched along her own. It was enough, she told herself in consolation, to have him beside her again.

* * *

SOMETHING WOKE HER. The room was still dark. She reached out for Paul but felt nothing. With a start she sat up. 'Paul... ?'

Then she saw his shadow move as he pushed himself out of the cushioned wicker chair. He crossed to the bed.

'Can't you sleep?' she asked softly as he slipped in beside her. 'Jet lag?'

'Must be,' he replied, staring into the darkness.

* * *

BY THE NEXT morning he couldn't put it off any longer. He forced himself to tell her while they were having a quick breakfast of coffee and toast.

'Eve...' She looked up, a piece of toast halfway to her mouth. 'John wants me to enter the Berlin International Piano competition. He thinks I stand a really strong chance of making the finalists.'

Her eyes opened wide in delight. 'That's wonderful, Paul! Are you going to? When is it?'

His gaze held hers. 'That's just it... it's the first week of March. We'd have to delay the wedding.'

Her smile slipped for just a moment. Then she reached across the table and covered his hand with hers. 'Don't look so worried! It's not such a huge affair we can't change the date. And you've given me plenty of notice.'

She saw the hesitation still on his handsome face. Pushing back her chair she walked round and stood behind him, leaning over to fold him in her arms. 'Do it, Paul. Just do it. Delaying a wedding's not going to change what's really important between us.'

* * *

IN THE COUPLE of months leading up to Paul's departure for Berlin the time they had to spend together was severely limited.

Paul was practising harder than ever and at the same time teaching a few hours a week to earn the money he would need for the trip. Even the weekends allowed him no respite. As a result Eve spent more time with Janet at the cottage. The older woman noted the girl's calm acceptance of the delay to the wedding. 'We've put it back by a month that's all,' Eve announced. 'No problem with either the church or the restaurant.'

How much she loves that boy, Janet thought. Paul and his career always came first.

'You look to me as if you've lost some weight.' Janet gave her a scrutinizing look one afternoon a few weeks later. 'I hope that dress is going to fit.'

'Perhaps I should try it on again.' Eve knew she'd lost weight. She wasn't surprised. Her job rarely allowed her time for lunch, and not seeing Paul so regularly in the evenings now, she often didn't bother cooking a proper meal.

She followed Janet upstairs to the spare bedroom, where the dress hung in the old-fashioned wardrobe in its protective cover. Tossing aside her jeans and shirt Eve slipped the ivory silk gown from its hanger. It was close-fitting, bare shouldered and edged in guipure lace.

Janet helped zip her up and both studied her reflection in the mirror. 'It's a *little* loose, I guess... What do you think, Janty?' She turned to face the older woman.

Janet shook her head. 'Nothing noticeable.'

How absolutely stunning she looks, the older woman marveled silently.

Eve turned back to her reflection. For a long moment she stared at herself in her wedding gown. Then she said with quiet intensity, 'I love him so much. He's everything I dreamed of. I can hardly believe how happy I am.'

Janet would remember those words three short weeks later.

* * *

EVE HATED SAYING goodbye at the airport. Paul too, she saw, was getting emotional. Fighting to keep her voice steady, she wished him the best of luck. 'I wish I could be there, darling.'

But there was no way both of them could have afforded to go and anyway, she consoled herself, Paul would only be gone a short time. After Berlin he was returning via London where he would spend a quick couple of days with John Venniker. It was the competition and its outcome that would determine their future plans.

For the four days leading up to the moment when Paul would face the judges Eve found it hard to concentrate on her usual activities. Her thoughts were totally focused on Paul. On the day of the competition itself she could barely settle to any work. He had promised to call as soon as possible after the announcement of the winners, and that evening she sat on tenterhooks by the phone.

The call came through just before midnight. His joy and excitement were clearly revealed over the line.

'... second place! Can you believe it, Eve! They gave me second place!'

Laughing and shouting with glee, they talked excitedly over the top of each other. The conversation was necessarily brief; Paul promised to answer all her questions the moment he saw her.

* * *

THIS TIME they went straight home to Eve's apartment where they talked for hours; over and over again she made him describe the exact moment of his win and every detail of the competition. At last, overcome with exhaustion, Paul headed for the bedroom, even though it was only early afternoon.

'I'm so very, very proud of you, darling.' She kissed him lovingly as he stretched out on the bed. 'This is going to change everything for us now, isn't it?'

'Yes,' he answered.

Just a simple yes.

* * *

SHE WOKE him at eight and while he took a shower she laid out a light supper. She insisted too on opening a bottle of champagne to toast his success. While they ate she filled him in on the last-minute details of their wedding.

'Your mother wants me to book them a hotel. Inner city somewhere, not too expensive.' Eve grinned. 'After thinking about it, she doesn't feel your father's quite up to enduring even one night with your Aunt Cecily.'

Paul murmured a noncommittal reply.

* * *

SHE NOTICED his yawns as they were clearing the table.

'Sweetheart, I'll finish this.' She took the dirty plates from his hands. 'You get back to bed. I won't be a moment.'

'Okay.' His belly clenched sickeningly.

Twenty minutes later when she slipped into the bed beside him Eve felt a flicker of disappointment. Paul was fast asleep, his body turned away from hers.

She'd been looking forward to making love, to welcoming him home. Her body ached for his touch; it seemed so long since they'd had time to spend together.

Well, she thought, fitting her body round his, she'd just have to be patient until tomorrow. It was a normal working day but Eve had arranged to have it free. They'd have the luxury of a full twenty-four hours together.

Beside her Paul stared fearfully into the darkness. He kept his breathing even, but marveled that the hammering of his heart didn't shake the bed.

Tomorrow, he thought desperately. Whatever happened he couldn't put it off any longer. It was the thought of her agony that filled him with dread. The pain he was about to cause her.

She loved him. She trusted him. They had planned a life together.

He heard her small sigh of pleasure, felt her press her body closer, and in that instant he knew there was no way he could get through the night without confronting the terror of the truth.

'Eve...' Abruptly he rolled over to face her.

'Umm... you're still awake?' Her voice was sleepy but he caught the note of hope. Her arms slid around him; she ran her fingers lightly down his back.

'Eve, I've got to...' His voice choked off. Swallowing, he started again. 'There's something I've got to tell you. I've ... wanted to tell you so often before, but I just...'

His tone alerted her to his seriousness and she opened her eyes.

'Paul? What is it, darling? What's the matter?'

His heart was thundering even harder in his chest.

'Eve, I can't pretend any longer... What you and I had' ... the word, the past tense, hit her like a bullet between the eyes ... 'was wonderful, joyous. No other woman could ever give me what you have.'

She hardly dared to breathe; the agony in his voice was unbearable.

'I loved you, Eve. I'll always love you. But for a long time now I've felt something wasn't quite right. It was gnawing at me but I pushed it away, refused to face it, to accept it. Then... in these last few weeks... I've come to realize that I've been fighting it all my life. I just ...'

She couldn't bear it a moment longer. They were still in each other's arms. 'What are you trying to say to me?' The words came out with exaggerated precision; as if she'd been drugged.

'Oh, *darling*.' With a terrible sob he buried his face against her neck. 'I'm no good for you any longer, no good for *any* woman. Eve, I'm gay... I'm *gay*! I only really come alive when I'm with another man...'

His words froze in her brain. Ice seemed to spread into every organ of her body. She felt as if she would never speak, or move, or breathe again.

* * *

HE NEEDED HER COMFORT ... and her forgiveness. She saw that with painful clarity. His guilt was the heaviest burden of all.

'I never wanted to hurt you, Eve. When we met, what I felt for you was so strong, so real. Physically, mentally, emotionally, you seemed everything I needed. I loved you; I felt sure of our future together. I pushed away those vague disturbing feelings; told myself I'd only been waiting for the right woman.' He stroked her hair, his breath was warm against her cheek. 'But in the end I couldn't run away from it any longer. It was in England that I came face to face with the truth.'

'It was John Venniker, wasn't it?' she said quietly. How obvious it seemed now.

'Yes...' he whispered. 'He ... he recognized it at once. The ambiguity, the guilt, the confusion... He'd been there himself he told me...'

For the rest of the night they held each other, talking their way into a different relationship, retreating to separate sides of the dark unbridgeable chasm that now divided them.

As the numbness of shock gradually wore off, Eve felt as if her heart had been torn out. A sense of utter desolation and despair overwhelmed her. In just a few short hours the future she had been anticipating with such happiness and assurance had irrevocably changed. She would be alone, adrift, unloved.

But nowhere in her heart could she blame Paul. What had happened was beyond judgment or condemnation. There had been no betrayal. From Paul she had learnt the meaning of true love. Something deep and elemental inside her had been touched. What terrified her most was the realization that she might never find the same again...

The morning found them both utterly drained by the emotions of the long night. They dressed quickly, each knowing there was no point in prolonging the agony. At the door of the apartment where they were to have lived as man and wife they hugged each other close for the last time. Then Eve drew back and looked up at him through a blur of tears. 'We're both starting new lives now, Paul. I ... I don't think we should have any further contact.'

His beautiful agonized face stared back into hers. He nodded, squeezed her hand one last time. And was gone.

21

She had to tell Janet, of course. There was the wedding to cancel as a first priority. She rang and, without explaining further, said she would be up to visit the following weekend.

* * *

THE MOMENT JANET saw her she could tell there was something wrong. The girl looked so drawn, purple shadows ringed her lovely eyes and she seemed distracted and remote. This was something more than pre-wedding nerves or the pressures of work, the older woman frowned to herself.

Eve waited until they were sitting on the verandah with cold drinks to tell Janet what had happened. Her voice was strained but steady. '... it was a shock, of course, but quite obviously something beyond Paul's control,' she finished. 'There's no point in laying blame.'

'Oh, my dear...' Janet's hand covered her mouth. She was staring at Eve in shock. 'Oh, my poor pet. And the wedding so close... how you must be feeling.' Never in her wildest dreams could she have imagined this.

'I'm okay.' Eve looked out at the garden. 'I've accepted it. It's just a matter now of getting on with my life.'

Janet marveled at the girl's almost unnatural control. 'Darling, if there's anything I can do, you know ... '

Eve cut across her. With exaggerated formality she said, 'Thank you, Janty. Let's just see to the cancelling of the ...' she was going to say "wedding" but changed it to 'invitations. And the reception arrangements.'

Janet took in the girl's expressionless face. *She's so strong,* she thought in silent wonder.

* * *

Over the following weeks Eve performed her usual tasks. She went to work, came home, paid her bills, did her grocery shopping. There was no point in losing control, she told herself. The years with Paul were over and as she'd stated so firmly to Janet, she had to get on with the rest of her life.

She did everything in her power to forget the body that had once brought her so much pleasure in bed, the laughing handsome face, the walks, the movies, the concerts and picnics. To help fill the dark chasm left in her life she allowed her work to consume her, stayed late at the office and brought more work home. She went nowhere socially.

Janet rang regularly. 'Are you sure you don't want me to come down and stay a while, pet?' The older woman couldn't hide her anxiety. Eve had resisted all her invitations to spend time at the cottage ... as she had resisted Janet's offers to come to Sydney. The calm reply was always the same: 'I'm fine, Janty. I just want to be by myself for a little while.'

* * *

And then, six weeks after the shock of Paul's revelation, Eve woke one morning and began to cry ... deep tearing sobs that tore at her soul, that spilled forth the agony and pain she had suppressed for so long.

She lay helpless among the tangle of sheets, incapable of moving from the bed. She moaned out her grief, her body shivering as if in shock. And somehow, through the piercing torture of her mind and body, she realized she needed help.

It was Janet she called, lifting the receiver from the bedside table with trembling fingers. 'Janty!' Her voice was a whisper of raw pain, 'I need you, Janty. I need you...' and over the line the wrenching, pitiful sobs cut like a knife into Janet Byrne's heart.

* * *

JANET WAS SHOCKED by Eve's appearance. She'd lost a lot of weight, her skin was grey and dry, her eyes dulled with pain. The apartment, covered in dust and stacks of old newspapers, looked as if it hadn't been cleaned for weeks.

She sat on the bed and hugged and stroked the weeping girl, smoothing her damp tangle of hair back from her forehead. 'You're coming back with me, my darling,' she said gently when the heartbroken sobs had finally subsided. 'I'm not leaving you to face this alone.'

* * *

IT WAS Janet who called to arrange things at her work, Janet who packed her case and then washed and dressed her.

By the time they arrived at the cottage it was evening and the older woman wondered if it was too late to call out Doctor Clark for a sedative or a sleeping pill of some sort. But almost as soon as she tucked the girl under the flower-printed bedcover Eve seemed to find some peace. Only she couldn't bear to be alone.

'Stay with me, Janty... don't go away.' She clutched at Janet's hand.

'I'll be right here, my pet.' The older woman sat on the chair beside the bed.

The girl was exhausted. Janet watched as those beautiful violet eyes soon closed in sleep.

It's like a curse, she thought in anguish. *Both mother and daughter unable to find happiness...*

* * *

OVER THE NEXT few days Eve gradually confronted the depth of her grief over the loss of Paul. Janet's role was to listen, comfort, and reassure. With the emotional torment finally released she knew that only now could Eve begin to recover.

As the time passed, the girl no longer wept, but there were still long periods when her distraction was obvious, when she stared off into space, her face shattered, her eyes bewildered and lost.

It was on one of those occasions that Janet said quietly, 'You can't imagine it now, my dear, but there'll be someone else. You're young -'

'*No.*' The word was a flat denial. 'No, Janty. I'll never let myself love anyone else. I couldn't bear to have anyone leave me again.'

There was a long silence, which Janet didn't interrupt. She sensed the girl wanted to say more.

'You know,' Eve finally continued, 'I've been thinking about my mother a lot recently. I believed a mother's love was the one thing in this world you could depend on. I thought it was the strongest bond there was. But she abandoned me ... my own mother walked away and never wanted to see me again.' Eyes brimming with tears she turned to look at Janet. 'Do you know how much it hurts to have to accept that?'

For a long moment Janet held the girl's tormented gaze. Her heart began to race and she knew the time to speak the truth had finally arrived.

Nervously she got to her feet. 'Eve, I always meant to tell you the truth ... when the time was right. I prayed God would let me know when that moment came, and ... and I think it's come now.'

Eve was staring up at her, puzzled. 'I don't understand, Janty...'

Janet licked her lips. 'Eve, I know who your mother is ... and I know where she is.'

She saw the girl's eyes grow wide.

'Yes,' she nodded. 'I've always known. And now it's time I told you everything.'

Eve was staring at her, dumbstruck.

'Your mother's name is Marianne Rolfe. When you were born she was ... she was the inmate of a mental institution. And she's still there.'

Janet heard the girl's sharp intake of breath. Before Eve could gather her wits to speak she added, 'I knew your father too.'

She saw the dazed incomprehension in that lovely face.

'Let me start at the beginning,' she said gently.

* * *

AND JANET TOLD everything she knew about Eve's parents – from the day she had come into their lives. She spoke of Marianne and Charles Rolfe's kindness and generosity towards her and her ailing son, of their obvious love and devotion to each other, of the wealthy establishment family that had rejected Marianne right from the start.

'Your father's in-laws never accepted her, darling. It was common knowledge that Edwina Rolfe, your grandmother, was certain Marianne had married her son only for his money and position. She was very bigoted and narrow-minded, you've got to understand that. A penniless Polish refugee was obviously not who she had in mind for the heir to the Rolfe fortune. Edwina also wielded a great deal of influence and power. After your father died she managed to contest his will so that your mother was left with nothing.'

Eve's head was spinning, 'But... an asylum. How did my mother end up... ?'

Janet spoke without expression. 'She attacked your grandmother with a carving knife. They managed to restrain her, but not before Edwina Rolfe was quite badly slashed.' Janet's voice dropped as she met the girl's shocked gaze. 'Your mother was to be charged with attempted murder. Then psychological assessment judged her unfit to stand trial on the grounds of insanity. Details were never released to the press, but there was a suggestion that her wartime experiences might have played a part in pushing her over the edge.'

Eve had gone very still. 'But ... why? Why did she...?' She choked on the rest of the words.

'I heard the story from your mother's own lips. As soon as I got the news I rushed to Darlinghurst Police Station where they'd taken her. Marianne was utterly distraught but I managed to work out what had happened.' Janet looked away. 'Your mother had gone to see Edwina that afternoon to beg her to provide for her unborn grandchild's future. Remember, she'd been cut right out of your father's will, but it wasn't for herself she wanted anything, only for the baby she was carrying. She told me how Edwina taunted her, insisted that the child couldn't be her son's because she knew he'd been left impotent through wartime injuries. As Marianne relayed it to me, Edwina Rolfe threw all sorts of terrible names at her, absolutely refused to believe that it could be Charles's child. She wouldn't listen when Marianne tried to explain that your father had made a complete recovery. Instead, she accused your mother of having other lovers. It was then something in Marianne obviously snapped. And ... and that's when it happened.'

Eve's mind reeled. It was too much to take in at once. She needed time to come to grips with what Janet was telling her. But there was one further question she had to ask.

'Why didn't you tell me sooner, Janty? Why, when you knew how much I longed to know what had happened to her?'

Janet's lined face reflected her torment. 'I felt it was too big a burden for you when you were younger, Eve. When you were older I hoped you'd accept it better. But each time I wanted to tell you something stopped me. Your own future was important. I didn't want to take the risk of affecting your education, or the happiness you were looking forward to with Paul...' Her eyes filled with tears. She dropped to her knees on the carpet at Eve's feet. 'Oh, my darling, forgive me, please. I thought I was doing what was right for you at the time.'

It was the first time Eve had seen the older woman cry. Janet Byrne's distress was terrible to see.

'Janty... Janty,' her voice was a broken whisper as she drew the other woman close, 'I don't blame you. I just blame myself for ever having been born...'

* * *

THEY TALKED LONG into the night as Eve struggled to piece together her background. One shock seemed to succeed another as she studied the birth certificate Janet had kept hidden for so long.

Her father had been a member of the wealthy, socially prominent Rolfe family. Her mother was Polish. An attempted murderess. Now living out her days in a Sydney psychiatric hospital.

And, from the day she had given birth to Eve, she had never spoken another word.

* * *

'I COULDN'T SEE you taken away by strangers,' explained Janet. 'Even if I hadn't made that promise to your father I had to do something. And that's when I went to see Father Michael, begged him to do something to help.'

'And he did...' breathed Eve.

'Yes. Only he and the Mother Superior of the convent knew your real identity. I couldn't bear to think of you growing up with the sort of gossip and attention you were bound to attract because of what had happened. As it was, the public soon forgot the crazy Polish woman who had involved the Rolfe family in such a scandal.'

Eve was silent for a moment. Then she asked, 'Do ... do you see her now, Janty?'

Janet nodded. She knew what Eve meant.

'I try to visit once a month.'

The girl held the older woman's eyes, and Janet Byrne nodded again. 'I'll take you there tomorrow,' she said gently.

* * *

'[illegible] twice a month.'

She put her hand over [illegible] eyes, and Janet [illegible] 'I'll take you there tomorrow [illegible].'

22

Eve barely spoke on the train and bus journey to the psychiatric hospital in Rozelle. She was completely consumed by her thoughts as she prepared to meet the woman who had given her life.

The hospital consisted of many buildings scattered over sizeable grounds. It looked forbidding. Eve and Janet were checked in and given passes that confirmed their visitor status.

'No one here knows of my connection to Marianne.' Janet spoke in an undertone as they made their way through a series of locked doors down the unadorned corridors. 'They think I'm just a friend. Not,' she added, 'that many of the nursing staff would even remember the scandal I'm sure, after all this time. When it became clear that instead of facing trial Marianne would be committed, Edwina's daughter insisted that she be admitted under her maiden name. Obviously as far as the family were concerned the faster the whole thing was forgotten the better.'

When they finally reached the room, Janet halted outside and turned to Eve. 'I don't know what you're expecting, my dear, but try not to be upset...'

Eve found it impossible to reply.

* * *

THE WOMAN SAT in an uncomfortable looking metal chair in the corner of the room. Her greying hair was tied back in an untidy roll and the institutional garb of a plain, shapeless, button-through shift hung on her too-thin frame. Her blue eyes stared at nothing, while one slim, veined hand plucked relentlessly at the fabric on her dress.

'Marianne... it's me, Janet.' Janet Byrne crossed the comfortless room and placed a gentle kiss on the top of Marianne Rolfe's head. As always, she acted as if her friend understood her every word.

'And this,' she gestured to Eve, 'is someone else who really wanted to visit you today. Her name is Eve.'

Eve stood transfixed, staring at the pitiful figure before her. Remnants of Marianne Rolfe's beauty were evident in the fine, flawless complexion and delicate bone structure, but the dullness of her hair and eyes and the frailty of her body made her appear older than her years.

Eve held her breath as those eyes barely shifted their focus; there was a blankness behind them that was frightening. It was as if, she thought, something, or someone, had stolen her mother's soul.

Tentatively she moved across the room to crouch at Marianne's side. Every nerve in her body felt stretched to the limit. This is my mother, she told herself... this is the woman I thought had abandoned me.

Slowly, the grey-haired woman shifted her gaze. For a long moment she stared at the girl beside her. Then one of those frail, restless hands reached out. Her expression didn't change but she took hold of Eve's hand and gently caressed it with the other.

* * *

THEY STAYED ABOUT HALF AN HOUR. It was Janet who chatted on, speaking about the cottage, the state of the garden, some amusing incidents that had happened at her work.

Eve said little. Sitting beside her mother, she found comfort in the touch of their hands. But there was still so much to comprehend. How could her mother have ended up like this? A discarded stranger dumped in this terrible place.

The room was cheerless. Nothing broke the drabness of the walls. The impersonal stamp of the institution was everywhere: on the furniture, the curtains, the bed linen.

At least, she thought, the side table now held the packets of scented soap, the bag of grapes and peaches and the posy of flowers they had brought with them. They were small enough luxuries but, as Janet had explained, 'My job helps to keep her in her own room at least. I couldn't bear it when I first found her in that terrible ward. Here she has some privacy thank goodness and I bring her what little treats I can.'

Eve was stunned by the realization of just how kind Janet Byrne had been over the years to both her mother and herself. She expressed as much later when they were heading out of the hospital grounds towards the bus stop. The parting from the poor pitiful creature in that soulless, barred room had brought tears to Eve's eyes. But her tight hug and kiss had brought no reaction.

'It was the very least I could do ... for both of you,' Janet answered somberly. 'I've told you how very kind and generous your parents were to me and Danny. And the more I got to know Marianne the more I grew to love her.'

Eve's face still reflected the effect of her visit. 'Do you think she has any chance of recovery, Janty?'

Janet Byrne sighed. It was a question she had been expecting.

'Post-natal psychosis seemed the final burden, pet. Poor Marianne had already endured so much. She never spoke of it, but I got the impression she had suffered badly in the war; she lost her family, as you know. And these days it's an accepted medical fact that people who have suffered physical or emotional trauma as children are more likely to develop mental illness. On top of that, of course, she lost your father, so when the authorities forced her to give up her child as well...' Janet shook her head. 'It's my guess that in there,' she gestured over her shoulder at the hospital, 'she's never really had the support and attention she needs.'

Breaking off, she hesitated. She didn't want to give the girl any reason for false hope.

At last she added slowly, 'All I can say, Eve, is that today, when she took your hand, something happened in that room. I've never seen any reaction like that from her before.'

* * *

ALMOST OVERNIGHT THE focus of Eve's life changed radically – from the pain of Paul's loss to a driving desire to learn everything she could about her parents' past. Especially her mother's.

Her first visit was to the state library archives to search through back copies of the *Sydney Morning Herald*. From these she learned about the Rolfe family background and her father, Charles. It gave her an eerie feeling to look at his press photographs. 'War hero, scion of the well-known Rolfe family,' the caption read. Never in her wildest imagination had Eve dreamt she might be related to such a wealthy establishment family.

Yet one, she reminded herself bitterly, whose members had done everything in their power to destroy her mother...

Then there were the reports of the scandal. The story had made headlines at the time and Eve shivered as she read the details. Long Bay jail... hospital security wing for the criminally insane...

Details of her mother's youthful background, however, were scarce. Her parents' marriage certificate was all she had to go on.

Walenska... Eve wondered if it were a common Polish surname or if it might help her in tracing her mother's origins. For that was what was now uppermost in her mind. The urge to fill in her mother's past was irresistible.

'I'm going to Poland, Janty.' She dropped her bombshell just a couple of weeks later. 'I have to find out more. Maybe it's possible to discover what happened to my mother and her family.'

And when I know that, was Eve's silent thought, *perhaps I'll have the key I need to help in her recovery.*

Eve's sudden resignation surprised everyone at work. Impatiently she worked out her notice as she waited for her visa to come through.

To her relief there were no delays and she was able to arrange her flight to Warsaw via Paris. After a night in France she would have three hours in the capital of Poland before flying south to Krakow.

In the cheap Left Bank hotel where she had booked a room, Eve slept off the effects of the long flight from Australia. With so little time to spend in Paris she was left with only a fleeting impression of the beauty of the city's architecture, its grandeur and sense of history.

There would be other times to explore Paris, she told herself without regret. Now her pressing desire was to arrive in Poland as soon as possible.

Warsaw International Airport was shabby, rundown, dimly lit. A chaotic jumble of travellers stood in departure queues, waiting their turn to squabble with some stony-faced official.

Checking her luggage in to the later Krakow flight, Eve took an ancient taxi into the city proper. When the cab driver discovered that his passenger wanted to see as much of the city as possible in the time available to her he quickly negotiated a price.

'I take only US dollars, *pani*. Okay?' His English wasn't bad, thought Eve. Or maybe he knew just those words and phrases that were important.

But he certainly gave value for money. In her whirlwind tour of the city Eve was shown the beautiful eighteenth-century palace in Lazienki Park. In the summer months she learned, the Chopin memorial in the same beautiful grounds became the venue for outdoor classical concerts.

They drove across a wide square her guide pointed out the Grand Theatre of Opera and Ballet. 'Pity *pani* has so little time', he threw over his shoulder. 'Tomorrow night, opera, *Aida*.'

Then they were travelling down the main shopping street, or so the driver informed her. Taking in her surroundings Eve could see only drab, ill-lit shop fronts, their windows displaying very little merchandise. The socialist system, she observed, obviously gave a low priority to consumer goods.

At another corner there was a long queue waiting patiently as a farmer sold citrus fruit from the back of his truck. 'Very expensive,' the cab driver shook his head. 'Not always can we get such fruits.'

Eve was beginning to realize how much Australians took for granted.

Then they were in the Old Town. In broken English, the driver explained how the Nazis had destroyed seven centuries of history when they left the area in ruins on their retreat in 1944. 'The Deutscher knew they were losing the war, but still they do this to us,' he spat.

Since then, he explained, artisans had painstakingly reconstructed the area modeled on former plans.

Eve looked out in delight at the charming old townhouses, their facades decorated and hand painted in the fashions of centuries past. The effect was enhanced by the plumed horses that trotted past, pulling their tourist passengers in open carriages.

In the broad, cobbled Market Square she asked the driver to let her out and spent some time strolling past the sidewalk artists' stalls. In the window of the Cepelia shop, with its display of folk craft, a hand woven wall-hanging caught her eye and she bought it at a ridiculously cheap price.

But time was running out. Back in the cab she headed for the airport and the city where her real mission would begin.

* * *

It was dark when she finally arrived in Krakow. Checking into her Orbis Hotel room she decided on an early meal and a good night's sleep. Her body still hadn't caught up with the jet lag.

* * *

Early the next morning she began her task.

The public records office was her first stop; she had asked the concierge to explain to the cab driver where she wished to go. As they wheeled away from the kerb Eve prayed that the relevant documentation hadn't been totally destroyed in the war.

The pasty-faced clerk behind the counter didn't need to speak English to understand what she wanted as she proffered the piece of paper inscribed with her mother's name and birthdate.

Eve held her breath as the unsmiling, bespectacled man disappeared into the dusty rows of bound documents. After an agonizing wait he at last reappeared with the birth records for the correct year and silently pointed to a booth where Eve could inspect the entries at leisure.

It took her just ten minutes to find what she was looking for. Her excitement grew as she copied down the names of her mother's parents and the family's former Krakow address. With a grateful smile to the unresponsive clerk, Eve hurried out of the drab building into the crisp May sunshine.

She was getting closer. Surely someone would remember what had happened to the Walenska family? And then, she told herself, she would discover the trauma that lay at the heart of her mother's past.

* * *

THE BEAUTIFUL UNIVERSITY city of Krakow embodied so much of Polish history and culture. The various eras were revealed in the dark brooding cathedrals and the changing facades of the houses ... Gothic, Baroque, Rococo and Renaissance, among others.

The address where the cab driver dropped her was a narrow three-story house with crumbling lintels and fading paintwork on its ancient walls. As she rang the bell, Eve could see in the distance the imposing towers and turrets of the eleventh-century Wawel Castle, around which the town had grown up.

A sharp-faced woman with tired blonde hair answered her ring. '*Tak*?' She looked at Eve suspiciously. The girl's clothes revealed her as a foreigner. To be seen talking to foreigners could mean trouble.

Eve spoke slowly, in the hope that the woman would be able to understand. 'I'm hoping to find some information –'

'No information.' The woman began to close the door.

'No, please!' Eve implored. 'I just want to ask a few questions – about people who used to live here.'

The woman shook her head uncomprehendingly and pushed the door to.

Suddenly, behind her, Eve heard in perfect English: 'May I help you, *pani*?'

Eve swung round to see a youth of about seventeen. He was gangly with fine pale hair, clear blue eyes, and wore a patched sweater and a pair of jeans.

'You speak English!'

'Of course,' the boy replied as if she had said something stupid. 'I am a student.'

The woman had opened the door again. Speaking rapidly in Polish, she addressed the boy. He answered using the word Eve recognized as meaning 'mother'.

'Please,' she pleaded with him. 'My family used to live in this house. I only want to ask a few questions.'

* * *

FIVE MINUTES later she was sitting in a tiny living room, a cup of steaming tea in her hands. The boy, Jan, sat beside her while his wary-eyed mother sat opposite. Eve explained again what she was after.

'I was hoping that maybe someone in the house might know what happened to them. Ula and AdamWalenska. They had a daughter, Marianne. She was – is – my mother.'

Jan quickly translated. The woman looked hard at Eve before replying.

Jan nodded as he listened to her rapid-fire Polish. Then he turned back to Eve. 'My mother has been in this house only since the last ten years, but our neighbor, Irena Malkewicz, is a long-time resident. Perhaps she might know something.'

The boy saw the spark of hope in his visitor's lovely eyes.

'She is an old lady. I will go and fetch her,' he said.

* * *

AND IT WAS the softly spoken, black-clad elderly woman who helped Eve take the next step.

Tak, she informed her, the Walenskas had lived here. The father,

Adam, was a professor at the university. The old woman nodded in memory. Such a very nice man – a gentleman, a scholar but his health was not always good.

Through Jan, Eve put her questions: did Pani Malkewicz have any idea where they might have gone when they left?

The old woman pursed her lined lips and considered a moment. Ah, yes, she recalled now... The family had moved to the country ... some time towards the end of the war it had been. Adam Walenska's parents had owned a farm, and she seemed to remember that old man Walenska had died. The family was going to help run the place.

'A good thing too,' the woman's expression suddenly tightened, 'to get out of Krakow. The Germans did not like intellectuals...'

Eve leaned forward in her chair, her tea forgotten. 'Jan, can you ask her if she remembers where exactly in the country they went? The name of the village or even a town close by?'

As the youth put his question, Irena Malkewicz screwed up her already wrinkled face. Now where... Suddenly her eyes brightened. Her memory wasn't so bad after all.

She told Eve the name of the village.

* * *

THE BOY, Jan, agreed to go with her and act as translator while the promise of payment in US dollars easily persuaded a cab driver to take them the distance.

As they sat together in the rear seat Jan asked about Australia. Despite her distraction Eve did her best to appease his curiosity. She talked of Sydney, the outback, the beautiful beaches.

Jan listened attentively. 'It is my dream one day to see the United States of America,' he responded. 'But maybe now I think Australia is a better country to visit.'

Soon they were bouncing over the rutted streets of a small village. Jan had suggested that they start their enquiries at the local bakery, always a focus of local life.

His suggestion paid off. While the shopkeeper herself wasn't able to help, one of her elderly customers overheard Jan's questions. The grizzled old man shook his head. 'No use in looking for them. All shot. During the war. Only the young daughter escaped. But maybe her fate was even worse.'

'What do you mean, sir?' Jan asked respectfully.

The old man cleared his throat. His rheumy eyes grew bitter. 'The murderers took her away to the lodge at Floranska. Their billet was there. There is little doubt what happened to the girl.'

Eve was waiting in the cab.

As Jan slid in beside her he saw her hopeful expectant expression. 'Any luck?'

Avoiding her eyes he awkwardly passed on what the old man had told him.

Eve sat very still. If the old man was right...

But there was more. Jan hadn't been sure whether to tell her; now he made up his mind.

'I have the name and address of the woman who was caretaker at the lodge, *pani*. Do you wish to speak to her?'

Eve felt her mouth go dry. 'Yes,' she said softly.

* * *

ZOSIA PANKOWSKA DIDN'T LIKE visitors. Especially ones she didn't know. And even more especially when they asked questions about a time she had done her best to forget.

But the boy persisted. 'Please, *pani*, this lady has come a long way to find out the truth. Is it as she suspects? That her mother was used by the Germans?'

Zosia Pankowska suddenly erupted. 'Am I to be blamed for something I was forced to do? Can I be held responsible for what they did to that child?'

'*Pani...*' Jan leaned forward in his uncomfortable chair. The thin, hard-faced woman sat on the narrow bed while Eve was perched on a low stool. Three people made the tiny two-room dwelling seem cramped.

'No one is blaming you, *pani*,' the boy continued. 'The truth is all we want. Was the girl... was she used by the German officers?'

The woman looked away. From between clenched teeth she hissed, 'Not only by the officers.'

* * *

JUST TEN DAYS after she left, Eve was back in Australia. Already the trip seemed like a dream. It was what she had learned that remained the nightmare.

Shocked, Janet blinked back tears as Eve filled her in on what she had discovered.

'Oh, the poor, poor darling...' The older woman reached out and enfolded the girl in her arms. 'And how you must be feeling, my pet, at knowing what happened to her.'

'But I'm glad I went, Janty,' Eve said softly. 'I saw my mother's country; I saw where she grew up...' Her voice trailed off.

Janet drew back and gave the girl a searching look.

'There's something else, my darling. I can see it in your eyes. What is it?'

For a moment Eve didn't answer. Her mind was back in Poland, in the cramped shabby room with the woman who had been the caretaker at the lodge.

Nie, Zosia Pankowska had stated stubbornly, avoiding Eve's eyes, she had no recollection of the name of the officer who had murdered the Walenska family and brought the girl back to use as his own.

The woman was lying. Eve was almost certain of that.

And as she'd followed the youth outside to the car, Eve had been left with one other overwhelming impression.

That there was something else Zosia Pankowska hadn't told her.

23

Eve's discovery of her mother and her past completely changed the vision of her own future.

With a sudden shock of insight she realized how her love for Paul had caused her to lose sight of her earlier goals. Despite the encouragement she had received from the nuns, she'd been happy to live through him, to allow Paul and his career to set her own agenda.

Now she became obsessed with the need to make up to her mother for all the years of suffering and rejection. Marianne Walenska had been sneered at, taunted as a refugee, a nobody. Cruelly and irrationally she had been rejected by the establishment. Her daughter was determined to rescue her from the system that entrapped her.

And then there was the Rolfe family.

They had done everything in their power to destroy an already fragile young woman. In the end they had driven her to the very edge of sanity.

Eve's eyes burned with bitterness. One day, she vowed silently, the Rolfes would be made to pay for the wrong they had done. To achieve her goals Eve knew exactly what she would need.

Money and power.

* * *

IT DIDN'T TAKE her long to see that there were only two areas where a woman could achieve what she had set her sights on: politics or the media. For Eve the choice was simple. The latter seemed to offer a faster track to the top – and for those who made it the financial return was unparalleled.

She got her foot in the door via contacts made in her previous position. The interview with the network's news chief was almost perfunctory. Jack Melloy was after someone for the weekend news journo's spot. Not everyone wanted to ruin their social life chasing ambulances on Saturday night.

He lolled back in his chair and checked out the girl across his desk. Great face, good voice.

'Yeah,' he announced casually, 'we'll give you a go.'

* * *

IT WAS the beginning of a career that would see Eve Taylor shoot to the very top – before a fall that would be every bit as spectacular and rapid.

* * *

'SHE'S ALWAYS HANGIN' around asking questions.' The bearded cameraman nodded to where the young weekend staffer stood in the shadows beyond the studio lights.

His colleague followed his gaze, taking in the tall attractive blonde who was earnestly watching the taping. 'Wouldn't mind a bit of *that*...' he murmured appreciatively.

The cameraman gave a dismissive snort. 'Forget it, pal. Cool and *very* hands-off.'

'Waiting for Mr Right, is she? To rescue her from a life of drudgery?'

The two men laughed as they turned back to their work.

* * *

Yet they couldn't have been more wrong about Eve Taylor. Filled now with steely drive and ambition, Eve had little time for a social life, little time to meet and date men. She was never rude as she deflected their advances but made it clear that for the moment work was her priority.

It hadn't taken her long to understand the cut-throat nature of the industry in which she was determined to make her name. The female of the species was particularly vulnerable. Women too often seemed relegated to mere decorations to the set, to playing second fiddle to the male. But Eve was determined that wasn't going to happen to her.

The way to beat the system, she decided, was to know as much about it as possible and then make her mark. That was why, instead of heading home after her work was done, she would linger around the network offices, watching the editors at work, talking to the various producers and researchers, getting herself known.

Money was important too. It was another reason she was determined to worm a place for herself on the weekday news team.

Her commitment and determination were cemented every second weekend when she and Janet went to the hospital to visit Marianne. It broke Eve's heart to see her mother withering away in that ugly, sterile environment which stank of urine and stale food.

As often as possible she brought small gifts ... flowers, perfume, pretty underwear and night attire. But Eve still burned to be able to do so much more. She dreamed of rescuing Marianne from the prison where she'd been held for over twenty years, of filling her life with the luxuries she'd been denied for so long.

It was a dream she spoke of often to Janet. 'Whatever it takes, I'm going to get her out of there, Janty. Permanently. That's my very first priority.'

Janet saw the absolute resolution on the girl's face. 'It mightn't be as easy as just having the money to do it, pet,' she warned with a frown. 'There are the medical and legal implications to be considered as well.'

'Then I'll get round those too. Because if it takes my last breath I'm going to make sure she has the life they cheated her of.'

Her voice carried total conviction.

* * *

SIX MONTHS after she started work as the weekend all rounder Eve got the break she was looking for. Another female reporter was changing networks and Eve was offered her position on the weekday news team.

Her elation was obvious as she rang Janet to break the news.

'It's just what I've been waiting for, Janty! Besides a fair hike in salary it's going to give me the chance to get my face on screen five nights a week.'

At the other end of the line Janet shared her excitement. 'That's wonderful, darling! Congratulations. Before you know it,' she teased, 'you'll be signing your autograph out there.'

And that, Eve frowned as she replaced the receiver, was the biggest worry.

* * *

JANET WAS BRUSHING cobwebs off the front verandah when she heard the sound of a car approaching down the overgrown drive. Now who could that be? she frowned.

The house was off the beaten tourist track and unexpected callers were rare.

The dark blue vehicle stopped in front of the house and to Janet's surprise and delight it was Eve who slid out from behind the wheel. 'Eve!'

A friend must have loaned her the car. But, no, the car belonged to Eve. And at the ripe old age of fifty-four, the girl told her, smiling, Janet herself was going to have to learn to drive.

* * *

IT WAS the only way she could think of to get around the problem. For as her public exposure increased, Eve knew she would no longer be able to visit the hospital. And to achieve her goals it was vital she keep hidden the link between herself and her mother. There must be no risk to her future and career by any connection to the scandal of the past. As for Marianne – she had suffered enough.

* * *

JANET MANAGED to arrange things at the hospital. 'I'm a qualified nursing sister,' she informed the medical director. 'Marianne Walenska knows and trusts me. I'm sure I'll be able to handle her.'

The bespectacled middle-aged man pressed the tips of his fingers together and looked at the woman at the far side of his desk.

'This is a very kind gesture on your part, Mrs Byrne.' There was an obvious question mark in his tone.

Janet explained. 'I knew the patient years ago, and I'm a widow. It'll be nice to have company on the weekend now and then.'

The doctor gave her a steady look. 'Well, I'll have to consult the board, of course. But if she's kept on her medication, I don't predict there will be any strong objections.'

* * *

THAT FIRST WEEKEND Marianne spent at the cottage was an emotional occasion for both Janet and Eve.

For the older woman there was the bitter-sweet memory of all those years before. Then, as the beautiful, kind-natured wife of Charles Rolfe, it had been Marianne who had been the mistress in her charming mountain home.

Now she sat on the verandah gazing blankly at the garden or very occasionally finding distraction in the needlework that lay on her lap. Janet's heart squeezed. Was there any real justice in the world? she wondered.

Eve too was strongly affected by this opportunity for intimacy with the mother she had never known. It pained her so much to see the remoteness in those still lovely eyes, to recall that in these same surroundings her mother had once been a vibrant young woman with a husband and a future.

Yet she found quiet comfort in the knowledge that for a short time at least Marianne was freed from that other terrible existence.

She couldn't help a wild hope too that the once familiar surroundings might trigger something in her mother. But the weekend appeared to effect no change. She's like a zombie, Eve painfully observed, and considering all the medication, it was probably little wonder.

As they prepared to take Marianne back on the Sunday evening Eve silently reiterated her vow: *Whatever it costs, I've got to get her out of there.*

And somehow she had to manage it without drawing too much attention to the scandalous events of all those years before.

24

'You're a ruthless bitch.'

Jack Melloy grinned and shook his head in admiration as he watched the tape. 'It's great, sweetie. How the hell did you get him to mouth off like that?'

Sitting beside the news director in the editing suite Eve leaned forward in her seat. Her eyes were fixed on the screen. Yes, she thought, pleased, the interview 'grab' was exactly what she was after.

The tape came to an end and Jack Melloy rose to his feet. 'Great work, hon,' he patted her shoulder appreciatively. 'Keep it comin'.'

'Glad you're pleased, Jack.' Eve smiled as her boss left the room.

In her two years on-the-road with the network's news team Eve had established her reputation as a tough, tenacious reporter. She showed she could handle everything from the worst motor accidents to the most gruesome murders. Nothing fazed her cool self-confidence – not even the animosity of her peers, who had come to openly resent her growing success.

Eve could feel their dislike every time she entered the newsroom. But she could live with that if it was the price she had to pay for getting ahead. She shrugged off the fact that she wasn't included in the after-work drinking sessions, the usual social networks of her profession. And on those occasions when the isolation and snubs did manage to get under her skin, she reminded herself that she hadn't entered the media arena to win a popularity contest. Making an impact, impressing those who could influence her career, were her priorities.

* * *

HER GRADUALLY INCREASING salary meant Eve could finally ease the burden Janet had carried alone for so long. The cottage, for instance, was badly in need of repairs. The paint was peeling, the gutters rotting and the front steps close to dangerous. Now they could afford to call in tradesmen and get quotes for the most pressing jobs.

'Let's make it pretty and fresh again, Janty.'

Janet Byrne could almost hear the unspoken coda to those words: *So everything will be perfect when we finally get her home.*

The older woman hid a frown. Her worry was that Eve might be counting too much on something that might never happen.

* * *

THE VIPERS' nest of the television world breeds a particular type of paranoia. Ratings are all that count. Rivals one week can be colleagues the next, depending on the whims of owners and network managers. Contracts aren't worth the paper they're written on, and poaching of the 'talent' is the universal blood sport.

Ty Cameron was executive producer of the top rating news and investigative program, "Scrutiny". A slim, casually elegant Englishman, Cameron had gained his experience with the BBC and was generally acknowledged as the "father" of Australian current affairs programs. It was his skills that had launched many of Australia's most successful formats over the years and now it was "Scrutiny", anchored by the highly respected Greg Nelson, that was top performer in the ratings war.

Ty Cameron had had his eye on Eve Taylor for a while. He'd

watched her skills improve, seen her develop into a first-rate dogged reporter. The cool classy blonde was the perfect combination of professionalism and appealing femininity. The longer he thought about it the more Cameron felt certain Eve Taylor would be the perfect complement to the "Scrutiny" team.

He mentioned his thoughts to Greg Nelson one evening, inviting him for a drink in the boardroom annex after the show. Leather chesterfields, paneled walls and a marble-topped bar that ran the length of the room gave the place the ambience of a traditional men's club.

Ty Cameron poured their drinks and settled himself opposite the forty-two-year-old anchorman.

Having survived the rollercoaster ride of the television business for more than twenty years Greg Nelson was at the peak of his career. He'd fronted "Scrutiny" since its inception six years previously and was keenly aware of his position at the top of the ratings. With a salary and perks that reflected his success, Nelson wasn't going anywhere. The show was working and he was content to sit tight.

'Eve Taylor...' he narrowed his hazel eyes thoughtfully at Ty Cameron's proposal. Greg Nelson didn't exactly have right of veto but he was well aware that management were interested in keeping him happy.

He nodded his head of dark springy hair – not a sign of balding yet, thank God. 'Yeah, you could be right, Ty. What I've seen I like.' The anchorman echoed Cameron's own appraisal. 'Cool, but not cold. Bright and intelligent, yet not condescending or intimidating.' He gave the executive producer an enquiring look. 'D'you think you can bring her on board?'

'I'll sound her out.'

* * *

EVERY SECOND WEEKEND Janet drove to Sydney. Her first stop was the hospital, where she collected Marianne, then it was on to pick up Eve, who still lived in the unpretentious flat in Elizabeth Bay.

When they were all together at the cottage Eve observed her

mother closely looking for any sign that might indicate the effect of her change of environment.

'Do you think she seems a little brighter, Janty?' she questioned hopefully as they prepared lunch together in the newly renovated kitchen. Every penny Eve could spare from her salary was being spent on refurbishing the cottage.

'Might still be too early to tell, pet.' Janet wished she could be more encouraging but in all honesty she felt there had been little change in Marianne.

'Trouble is,' Eve protested, 'they've got her on all those mind-numbing drugs. Maybe if they took her off those she'd ...'

'Eve,' Janet's voice held a gentle note of warning, 'you know they only allow her out because she's on that medication.'

Eve didn't reply. The implication in Janet's words was obvious and it filled her with impotent anger.

Marianne Walenska was still being held in a ward for the criminally insane. A charge of attempted murder was recorded against her name.

* * *

DURING THEIR WEEKENDS together Eve wished so often that her mother was capable of communicating. There were so many questions she wanted to ask her. About her father and the Rolfe family, for instance. How could Charles Rolfe have been so different from the rest of them? Born into an old establishment family of such wealth and influence, where had her father learned his compassion and understanding for those less fortunate than himself? Perhaps, pondered Eve, his wartime experiences had given him an insight missing from the rest of his family.

Janet did her best to answer the girl's puzzled questions.

'Your father was a real gentleman, pet – but no snob,' the older woman shook her head. 'No, never that. And he adored your mother, that was obvious. You could see how much she meant to him. He turned his back on his own family because they wouldn't accept the woman he loved.'

'You know,' Janet added thoughtfully, 'I'm pretty sure he must have known what had happened to Marianne during the war. He was always so protective. It would certainly account for why he never again spoke to his brother after the terrible business with Marianne.'

Eve knew what Janet was referring to; the older woman had told her about the shocking incident with Hugh Rolfe that had occurred in this very house. Her eyes grew dark. The Rolfes too were part of her agenda. She had done her homework; the mother had died a few years before; the sister, widowed young, had remarried to a titled Italian and now lived in Rome. But Hugh Rolfe was still enjoying the prestige and wealth that came with heading the family firm.

Eve promised herself that some day, some way, she would find a means of making one Rolfe, at least, pay for the family's sins...

* * *

THE PHONE CALL caught her completely by surprise. Somehow he had got her private number.

'Forgive me for disturbing you at home, Miss Taylor. But, as you can imagine, discretion is called for in this situation.' Fifteen years in Australia hadn't modified Ty Cameron's BBC accent.

Eve's heart pounded with excitement as she listened to the quickly outlined proposal.

"Scrutiny"! She was being offered a position with the country's highest-rating current affairs program! It was everything she had dreamed of.

'If you're interested we'll need to discuss this further,' the producer ended. 'Face to face would be best.'

If she was interested... Eve knew every reporter in the country would leap at the chance.

They arranged to meet in three days' time.

* * *

THE SMALL COCKTAIL bar of the nondescript North Shore motel was empty at that time of the afternoon. Eve had no doubt that was the reason the producer of "Scrutiny" had chosen it for their rendezvous.

The tall grey-haired man stood up from his table in the far corner of the room and extended his hand.

'Eve... how very nice to meet you.'

'Thank you, Mr Cameron, and you too.'

'Please,' he indicated the chair beside him, 'it's Ty.' He smiled. 'I've been in Australia long enough to be as informal as everyone else. Now, can I offer you anything to drink?'

That relaxed opening set the tone for the rest of their conversation. By the time they said their goodbyes an hour or so later, Eve had agreed to the terms and conditions that would see her join the top-rating "Scrutiny" team.

* * *

WHEN SHE TOLD Jack Melloy he was far from happy, but in the television industry it was the sort of thing that happened all the time. Technically he could have demanded she give him three months' notice, but Melloy knew the pointlessness of that.

'I'm only sorry we couldn't find a spot for you on something bigger here, Eve,' he said regretfully. 'I knew you were too good to hang around on the news team for much longer.' He gave her a rueful smile. 'Guess I'll grind it out between my teeth and say we're the losers and best of luck to you. It's a great opportunity.'

* * *

ONLY WHEN SHE was certain everything was go-ahead did she finally tell Janet.

'*Scrutiny*! Darling, that's absolutely wonderful!' Janet's voice was shrill with delight.

'And to make it even better, Janty, my salary goes up by more than thirty per cent.'

* * *

MONEY AND POWER...

The words echoed in Eve's mind as she hung up the receiver.

25

Eve wasted no time in making her mark on the "Scrutiny" team. Her ability to pick up and follow through on important stories was demonstrated right from the start. During her first six months with the program she followed up leads that resulted in the revelation of fraudulent medical treatments, parliamentary travel rorts, and stand-over practices in a major shopping mall.

They were the sorts of stories that the print media couldn't ignore and which further enhanced Eve's name and credibility.

As she continued to outshine her colleagues she was again confronted with an animosity she had now come to expect ... and accept. It was the price she paid for doing her job well.

Ty Cameron and Greg Nelson, on the other hand, had nothing but praise for their new reporter's efforts. Nelson's own position as anchorman was unassailable and he was fully aware that whatever raised the profile of the program also increased his own. He was "Scrutiny". But dedicated reporters like Eve Taylor were essential to the program's success.

As they worked together Greg Nelson couldn't help being intrigued. The cool blonde fascinated him: her intelligence, her reserve, her total commitment. None of the rest of the team came anywhere near to matching her ability.

After the travel rorts expose, which caused an uproar in parliament as the opposition party took full advantage of the information, Greg Nelson invited his star performer to a congratulatory lunch at one of the city's leading restaurants. Even in that sophisticated arena heads turned as the two high-profile journalists entered the room and were quickly shown to one of the prime tables.

'A great piece of reporting, Eve,' said Greg, raising his glass to hers.

'Thank you.'

'Those pollies won't forget your name in a hurry.'

'And the public won't forget theirs come the next election,' she replied smoothly.

During the course of the meal he tried to probe a little deeper into her background. He knew the basics. She'd never tried to hide the fact of her illegitimacy nor that she'd been abandoned at birth.

'Doesn't it worry you,' he enquired now, 'to have no idea of your parentage, your background?'

Eve shrugged. 'Not really. The nuns were good to me, and I guess I never missed what I'd never had.'

As he watched her perusing the dessert menu Greg Nelson wondered if there were more to it than she was admitting. Maybe it was her lack of background that drove her so hard. To prove something to herself, provide some sort of alternative identity. It made an intriguing theory anyway, he mused.

It seemed too that the beautiful enigmatic blonde needed no one to replace the family she'd never known.

'No, there's no one special,' she'd responded on the one occasion he raised the question of her personal life. But it was the first time he had seen a prickle of unease.

For Eve work was her consuming passion. To find someone she could love as much as Paul would be difficult, she knew, and she wasn't going to settle for second best. So while her colleagues led more or less normal lives with spouses or lovers, family, hobbies, other interests, Eve simply had her work – and the weekends at the cottage with her mother and Janet.

With her increase in income she had also begun to make discreet enquiries, to peruse international medical journals in the hope of finding something relevant to her mother's condition. And then she read about a clinic in Berne, Switzerland, which specialized in the treatment of post-traumatic stress disorder.

Eve was determined to bring about her mother's release from the asylum where she had been captive for so long. Once over that hurdle, she figured, she could explore other avenues that might offer hope of rehabilitation. The clinic in Switzerland, for instance. Twenty-odd years of tranquillizing, mind-numbing drugs would surely have taken their toll, but Eve knew that if there was even a ghost of a chance her mother might be helped then she had to take it.

Slowly, gradually, her plans took shape. And she hadn't forgotten Hugh Rolfe.

* * *

IT WAS the touch of a hand playing with his testicles that awoke Hugh Rolfe.

His eyes flickered open, then squinted against the light. He had forgotten to pull the drapes the evening before and now the harsh glare of the morning sun streamed into his hotel room.

The girl was lying on her side watching him. Lipstick smeared the corners of her mouth and her mascara had left black smudges beneath her dark eyes. In the bright light of day she looked ten years older than she had the night before when he'd picked her up in the bar of the Adelaide Casino.

'Hi...' She smiled as she propped herself up on one elbow, her other hand still stroking his genitals. Her pale breasts drooped heavily against his chest as she leaned forward to kiss him.

Hugh turned his face away, his head throbbing with the scotch he'd laid into the previous evening. As memory returned he felt the sharp tug of fear in his bowels. Christ, he'd done thousands. Thousands he could no longer afford...

The girl – he couldn't remember her name, if he'd ever known it – was persisting in her efforts to arouse him. Did she think, he thought irritably, that she was going to hit him for another hundred this morning?

Shrugging off her touch he rolled away and got shakily to his feet. He was conscious of his nakedness, the unfit body of a man in his fifties.

'I'm going to take a shower.' He crossed the room and spoke without looking at her. 'When I come out I don't want to see you here, okay?'

* * *

HE MADE it to the airport just in time to catch the plane back to Sydney. When the flight attendant offered him a drink he couldn't help himself but the alcohol did nothing to elevate his mood. The thought of his losses frightened the hell out of him. Once, his gambling had been an outlet for relaxation, a way to have some fun and a quick thrill. But in recent years it had become more and more an act of desperation, an attempt to reverse the conditions which daily oppressed him.

If only the wool industry hadn't hit the wall, he told himself; if only his mother were still alive; if only he hadn't tied himself up with a bloody spendthrift of a wife...

As he lifted the glass to his lips with nervous hands Hugh Rolfe blamed his misfortune on various factors. But nothing could distract him from the knowledge that he was facing a major crisis.

The past few years had seen a steady and irrevocable erosion of the family's fortunes: first the downward spiral in wool prices, then a stock market disaster which had devastated the company's secondary investments.

With accountants and various advisers pulling him in different directions Hugh hadn't realized just how much he had counted on his mother's advice and judgment. But Edwina had been dead for almost four years, and there was no way he could look to his free-spending wife for support.

At the thought of Louise his eyes darkened. The marriage which had produced two clones of his self indulgent, sharp-tongued wife had been over years ago. Even before the formal announcement, their split had been an open secret among their friends and acquaintances. But only in the last six months had the two of them taken to living in separate abodes. Now with two households to maintain, Hugh's financial burden was further increased. He was struggling to hold onto the family home as it was. While he had that, he consoled himself, he could save face, could pretend to the world that nothing too serious had happened.

Yet as he swallowed the rest of his drink he wondered again how it could all have come to this. And how in the hell he was going to save himself.

* * *

EVE FOUND Greg Nelson an excellent mentor. She was keen to learn all she could from someone whose years in the industry had given him the experience and skills to get to the top.

The "Scrutiny" anchorman seemed happy to encourage her, handing her the most demanding assignments, at the same time ensuring she had total access to the resources she needed to be properly briefed. Eve was grateful for his unstinting assistance. In the backstabbing world of television Greg Nelson gave his help with a rare generosity.

During her first eighteen months on the program the two had formed an easy relationship. Eve knew Greg was a happily married man, a father of two young teenagers. She had met his wife on a number of occasions. Marie Nelson was an attractive, outgoing woman who held an important position in publishing.

There was nothing suspicious about Eve's relationship with her boss. If Greg asked her for a meal it was always at venues where they were openly exposed to the public eye. Other times they would meet informally in his office for a drink after work. If her colleagues weren't afforded the same privileges quite so often, Eve didn't let it trouble her. Greg Nelson was good company and she looked on their meetings as an opportunity to wind down, to discuss, in less pressured circumstances, where the program was going.

And that was the one area that had begun to worry her. Recently

"Scrutiny" had made certain changes to its direction. The word "infotainment" was being bandied around more and more. There was a very gradual, but definite tendency to intersperse the 'hard' news format with the odd soft feature.

At one of their regular informal sessions she voiced her concern. The anchorman listened, his tall, lanky frame leaning back into the leather swivel chair. 'M-mmm,' he responded doubtfully when she'd finished, 'I know what you're saying, but we've no intention of edging out the hard stuff. The thing is, research shows that viewers are responding to this trend in other programs. We've got to keep our eyes on that.'

'But,' Eve protested, '*Scrutiny* has always filled that different role in the marketplace. That's why our audience stays with us.'

He grinned at her. 'Hey, I love it when you get hot under the collar.' She didn't respond to his teasing and he continued, serious again. 'What we've got to remember is that, good as we are, we can always expand our market.'

But not by dishing up garbage, Eve retorted silently.

As she got up to leave, Greg Nelson walked her to the door. 'Anyway, the subject of content is on the agenda for next month's conference. We can all thrash it around then.'

The two-day mini-conference provided an opportunity for everyone involved with the "Scrutiny" program to exchange ideas and brainstorm new angles. This year the location was at the Mirage Hotel on the Gold Coast, the country's premier tourist resort, just an hour's flight north of Sydney.

The team would arrive Friday and fly home Monday morning.

And Greg Nelson had more than work on his personal agenda.

26

Greg Nelson was a careful man, not given to obsessions. But Eve Taylor had gotten under his skin in a way he could never have predicted. He had had affairs before, quick, discreet flings that had satisfied an urge for sexual variety and meant nothing more. But his feelings towards Eve Taylor were completely different. He was mesmerized in her presence, often unable to keep his mind on the topic being discussed; he was transfixed by both her intellect and her physical appeal and the elemental pull towards her was one he could no longer ignore.

The force of his emotions preoccupied him now as he dressed for dinner in his hotel suite.

He was ready a few minutes early and stepping out onto the balcony he breathed in the humid sea air. Hair ruffling in the wind, he looked south towards the string of concrete towers that edged the sand of the famous Gold Coast strip. Thirty years ago Greg Nelson had spent a summer with his family in the sleepy seaside town of Surfers Paradise. Now it was a booming tourist mecca boasting a casino, five-star hotels and restaurants, a myriad golf courses, shopping malls, and a burgeoning population.

As he watched, rectangles of gold began to appear in the apartment blocks which stretched along the coastline as far as the eye could see. It was time to join the others for dinner. This weekend he planned to make his move. The timing was right, he knew; he had bent over backwards to help her, encourage her. She was in his debt. He felt sure his advances wouldn't be rejected.

Dinner started and ended with drinks in the cocktail lounge. The party of a dozen was in an ebullient mood. Tomorrow they would tackle their busy agenda – tonight was for winding down.

Yet as they toasted another year's success there was a little frisson of concern among the hard-working team. The last six months had seen a small but consistent dip in the program's ratings. It was something they would have to address in the following days' meetings.

Sipping at her glass of chilled white wine, lulled by the background music from the pianist, Eve wished again that Ty Cameron had been able to join them. His input was always invaluable. But the last year had been a difficult one for Cameron with his mother in England facing a long painful death from cancer. The producer had made numerous trips back and forth and at this very moment was in London attending the funeral.

'It's a relief, Eve,' he'd stated pragmatically when she'd offered her sympathies. 'But I'm sorry I have to miss the conference. I feel I've taken my eye off the ball a bit these last few months.'

But arrangements and reservations for the conference had been made far in advance. They'd had no option but to go ahead without the program's producer.

* * *

It was on the last evening that the anchorman made his move. They'd had the usual wind-down drinks in the cocktail lounge after the day's work but by ten thirty most people had headed off to their respective rooms. The flight back to Sydney left early the next morning.

Eve, however, wouldn't be on it. She wasn't needed in front of the cameras until Thursday and thought she might stick around for a couple of extra days. It was her first visit to the Gold Coast and, as she'd said to Greg, the place seemed to offer the potential for a mine of stories.

She was in her room, still dressed, when there was a knock on the door.

Eve frowned. It was almost eleven.

'Yes?' she called as she crossed the room.

'It's me, Eve. Greg.'

She opened the door. He stood there smiling, dressed in the tailored slacks and open-necked shirt he'd worn at dinner. 'Got time for a nightcap?'

'Sure.' She was tired but figured Greg wasn't likely to stay too long with an early morning flight to catch.

He took the seat she offered on the green and aqua print sofa. The drapes were still open and the silvery sheen of moonlight reflected off the ocean just meters away.

'Something to drink? Or should I make coffee?'

'There's a great bottle of champers in the mini-bar,' he suggested with a conspiratorial smile.

Eve had had enough to drink that evening but she figured she could handle a glass to be sociable.

Deftly opening the bottle she poured the wine and handed him a brimming flute. She was about to take a seat in the chair opposite when Greg patted the sofa beside him.

'Hey... why so unfriendly?'

There was a teasing note in his voice and it occurred to her that he might already have had a drink or two too many. What the heck, she thought, settling down beside him. They'd all worked hard over the last two days. Why shouldn't he unwind?

For a few minutes they discussed the program, the input that had come out of the meetings. Then Eve found herself unable to suppress a yawn.

'Tired?'

She nodded, hoping he would take the hint.

Greg held his drink in one hand, the other arm stretched out along the back of the sofa. Now he allowed it to drop easily across her shoulders.

'You know how much I think of you, don't you, Eve?'

She stiffened. Before she could make any response Greg had put down his drink and was leaning close. His lips touched her cheek.

'Greg... I –'

'You must know how I feel.'

But she hadn't. His words and actions had caught her totally by surprise.

'Greg,' she tried to pull away, 'I think perhaps you've had a bit too much to drink...'

Resisting her efforts to escape he pulled her closer. 'Sweetheart, you don't have to play games with me. We don't need excuses. I know you feel the same way... Let's not kid around any longer.'

'Greg, you've got it all wrong... I –' He was kissing her now, his mouth hungry on her neck, her cheeks, searching for her lips.

'I'm crazy about you, Eve. I can't get you out of my mind. Why do you think I offered you so much time, gave you so much help? You don't think I'd do that for just anybody, do you? I knew it must be happening for you too ... both of us just waiting until the time was right.'

With an effort she pulled free and jerked to her feet. As far as she was concerned there was only one way to handle the situation ... with equal directness. 'Look, Greg, I'm sorry. Whatever you imagined, you got it wrong. Completely wrong. As far as I'm concerned we were both just working together for the good of the program. I never wanted anything more from you.'

He was staring up at her, realization dawning as he absorbed her words. The prime time star wasn't used to being rejected. And certainly not when he'd just laid himself wide open. 'Hey... listen, love. I did everything I could to help you. The best stories, the best editors, top contacts. Don't tell me you thought I was doing it out of the pure and utter goodness of my heart. Not in this business.' He shook his head, his bloodshot eyes hardening. 'I don't like to be used, sweetheart.'

Eve couldn't believe what she was hearing. Her voice grew cooler. 'I'm very sorry you think I owe you a favor, Greg. That's not the way I see it. Now, I think you'd better go.'

He was already pushing himself to his feet. His lips had thinned to a tight angry line. 'I won't forget this, Eve. No one uses Greg Nelson and gets away with it.'

'I hope that wasn't a threat, Greg,' she answered quietly, standing by the open front door.

'Take it any way you like!' the anchorman snapped as he swept past her.

* * *

THE NEXT MORNING TO save embarrassment she ordered breakfast in her room.

Greg had been drunk, she told herself. Hopefully by the time she got back to Sydney the confrontation between them would be forgotten. But the scene had left a nasty taste in her mouth.

Eve spent the day roaming the streets of Surfers Paradise. At lunchtime she found an umbrella-shaded table in Orchid Avenue, a street full of up-market shops and eating houses which ran off the famous Cavill Avenue. As she took in the passing parade she also skimmed the local *Gold Coast Bulletin* with a reporter's eye. Surfers Paradise, she realized, was much more than just a tourist resort; it was becoming a major center of population growth. It seemed to Eve that the place called out for a feature by 'Scrutiny'.

That evening she dined at the buffet in the hotel coffee shop. It was a delightful setting – marble floors, greenery and glass walls overlooking a pool that bordered right onto the busy restaurant itself.

Eve didn't mind eating alone. She enjoyed watching her fellow diners and couldn't help noting too the flashes of recognition as people placed her face. "Scrutiny" had done a lot to raise her profile.

She was just about to call for her check when a party of well-dressed women entered the dining room. Leading the way was a leggy, bright-eyed blonde wearing a slim-fitting white dress that showed off her glowing tan. As she approached Eve's table the woman glanced at the solo female diner. Her recognition was obvious. Allowing her friends to continue past, she stopped and smiled down at Eve.

'Hi. It's Eve Taylor, isn't it? Are you on holiday, or is "Scrutiny" doing a story on the Coast?'

The question was forthright and direct, yet at the same time the tall blonde exuded charisma and warmth. She appeared to be in her late thirties and if her features were a little too angular for real beauty her animation and obvious sex appeal made an impact instead.

'Bit of both, really,' Eve returned her smile. 'It's my first visit to the Gold Coast.' Why did she think there was something vaguely familiar about the woman's face?

The friendly stranger's bright blue eyes opened wide. 'You're kidding... What are you up to tomorrow? I'll show you round.'

Eve's expression must have revealed her surprise. 'Uh... I...'

'Oh, God, I'm sorry.' With an apologetic smile, the attractive blonde shook her head and extended a hand. 'I always just expect that everyone around here knows me. I'm Rachel Symons. Leo Symons's daughter.'

Of course. Eve knew now why something had rung a bell. She had seen press photographs of Rachel Symons. Her father was millionaire developer, Leo Symons, a former Czech migrant whose name was synonymous with the development of the Gold Coast. Yet his connections to prime ministers, premiers and various leaders of industry had extended Symons' sphere of influence far beyond the confines of the tourist capital. His was one of the best-known names in Australian business.

'How do you do? I thought I recognized you.' Eve took the slim brown hand in her own. 'And sure, if you really do have the time to show me round I'd be delighted to accept. I'm staying at the hotel.'

Rachel smiled, tossing back her softly waving dark blonde hair.

'Pick you up at ten, that okay?'

* * *

EVE COULDN'T BELIEVE her luck.

Hair flapping in the breeze, she sat in the passenger seat of the open-roofed Mercedes sports coupe while Rachel Symons filled her in on the history and current happenings of the famous tourist strip.

Eve knew she couldn't have found a better guide than the slim blonde in the tight red pants sitting beside her. She was the daughter of Leo Symons, after all.

As she'd got ready that morning Eve had recalled what she could of the background of the man who had done so much to put the Gold Coast on the map.

A Czechoslovak Jew who had fought with the partisans and survived the war, Symons had found himself unable to accept life under the subsequent Communist regime. Escaping with his wife and baby daughter he had eventually made his way to Australia.

'Your father worked on the Snowy project first, didn't he?' she asked Rachel now as they headed south along the beach road.

The woman beside her nodded. Her hair was covered by a Hermes scarf, dark glasses shaded her eyes and Eve couldn't help noticing the enormous diamond and sapphire ring that flashed on her right hand. 'Yes, it was the early fifties, I was just a kid, but my mother told me later how much she hated it. They took the men off all week to work on the dam site while the women were left in the hostel. It was about six miles out of Cowra itself, a place they'd used for the Japanese POWs; freezing in winter and boiling in summer apparently.'

'But your father's a widower now, isn't he?' Eve was trying to fit all the pieces together.

'Has been for years,' Rachel took her eyes off the road to throw a quick grin at Eve. 'Despite all the hard cases around here who'd love to snap him up.'

Eve smiled. She could believe it. 'How old were you when your mother died?'

'Eleven. We'd just arrived on the Coast. I always thought it such a shame my mother didn't live long enough to enjoy my father's real success.'

As they drove Rachel pointed out those high-rise apartments, office blocks and shopping malls which had been built by the Symons group of companies. There were dozens of developments.

'It all started with earth-moving equipment,' she explained. 'While he was laboring on the Snowy hydro project my father saw all this massive stuff that companies had to buy and asked himself why they couldn't just hire what they needed ... it'd certainly save on business costs, he figured. The more he thought about it the better the idea seemed. Especially with the huge explosion in construction that was taking place after the war. So as soon as he'd done his time on the Snowy site he sank every cent he had in establishing an equipment hire firm and never looked back.'

'And then he came up here?'

'Yes. Just for a look-see. But he realized at once the potential of the place. It was my father, you know, who was one of the prime movers for the canal developments.'

With a grin she glanced sideways at Eve. 'And now every ex-Sydneysider who can't afford a place there at the water's edge can have it here – at a tenth of the cost!'

* * *

EVE WAS surprised when instead of dropping her back at the hotel Rachel suggested they have a late lunch at her home.

'I was waiting to see if I liked you.' The older woman softened her forthrightness with a teasing smile. 'I figured I do.'

And Eve liked Rachel too – not least for her directness. It made a change from the two-faced world of the media, she thought dryly, remembering Greg Nelson.

And after a few hours spent in Rachel Symons's company Eve had also come to understand the major role the daughter played in her father's business. Beneath that flippant, rich girl persona she realized, lay a shrewd and knowledgeable businesswoman.

For a split second Eve felt a moment's stab of envy for the blonde beside her. Here was a woman who had 'made it', a woman who, unlike herself, could openly and proudly proclaim her heritage and her past.

* * *

THE HOUSE at Paradise Waters was a sprawling structure of glass and stone. Minimalist in style, the furniture was obviously the product of individual craftsmen as were the modern sculptures and works of art that were the only decoration.

Rachel led the way into a high-ceilinged sitting room with unobstructed views of the river. 'What can I get you to drink?'

'Something soft, thanks.' Eve was still taking in the house, the enormous wealth it represented. There was no doubt about it – Leo Symons and his daughter were the quintessential migrant success stories.

* * *

LUNCH WAS A PLEASANT AFFAIR. The two women had more in common than first met the eye. They both loved music, good books, movies, fashion.

Over coffee the conversation took a surprisingly intimate tone as Rachel made an allusion to her short-lived marriage. 'Peter found it very difficult being married to a powerful woman. I guess I didn't give him what he was looking for in a wife.' She shrugged and gave a dismissive laugh. 'He wanted someone tamer and more domesticated, I'm afraid. We were a total mismatch.' Her blue eyes grew gentle. 'I guess it wasn't until I had Katie that I realized what I might really have wanted was a child, not a husband.'

As if on cue the sound of running feet could be heard through the house. Next moment a child of about ten burst onto the patio. She was dressed in school uniform, her blonde hair hung in two thick plaits and her blue eyes were the exact shade of her mother's.

'Mum! I came *top* in spelling! That's three times in a row!' The little girl's face was bright with pleasure as she threw herself into her mother's arms.

'That's my clever, clever darling.' The love in Rachel Symons's face as she hugged her daughter was unmistakable. 'Now, aren't you going to say good afternoon to Mummy's guest? This is Eve Taylor, darling.'

The girl drew back from her mother's embrace and her wide luminous eyes came to rest on Eve. She put out her small hand and said formally, 'How do you do.'

As she took the child's hand in her own Eve suddenly found another reason to envy Rachel Symons.

She thought of Paul. She thought of her promise to herself to have it all.

* * *

IT WAS JUST as they were reversing the car to go back to Eve's hotel that Leo Symons himself drove up. He parked his gleaming Jaguar on the broad sweep of driveway and came over to address his daughter.

He was not tall but had a surprisingly erect bearing for a man who was probably in his seventies, Eve thought. His hair was grey and close cropped and his jowls sagged onto the collar of his open-necked shirt. But his blue eyes were clear and alert and, like his daughter, he had an air of energy and command about him that belied his age.

'You are going out, darling?' Beneath the accent, Eve sensed a hint of irritation in Leo Symons' tone. As if he expected his daughter to be at his beck and call.

'Yes, Dad.' Rachel looked up from behind the wheel. 'I won't be long.' It was a simple exchange but Eve sensed an undercurrent to the words. She guessed that between two such powerful personalities there was sure to be the occasional battle of wills.

'May I introduce Eve Taylor?' Rachel went on. 'She's a reporter on the ...Scrutiny... program. I've been showing her around.'

'How do you do, Mr Symons,' Eve greeted the businessman formally. 'I've certainly been impressed by your achievements on the Coast.' She felt the intensity of Leo Symons's gaze.

I'll bet he never gives his competitors an inch, she thought.

27

Eve's hope that the situation with Greg Nelson might have blown over by the time she returned to Sydney was very clearly misplaced.

He made no secret of his change in attitude to the woman who had once been the recipient of so much favor. None of the rest of the team could have missed his icy demeanor, the way he all but ignored Eve as they put the show together each day. Rumors flew about the reason for the collapse of the relationship between the anchorman and his former golden girl but Eve refused to be drawn into offering any explanation. It would be awkward working with Greg in this sort of poisonous atmosphere, she thought, but she'd manage.

The shock came soon afterwards when she found that another member of the "Scrutiny" team was being handed the sort of major story she would have expected to get. She rechecked her roster and wondered what was going on.

On her first attempt to put a call through to Greg Nelson his secretary informed her he was 'busy', and that he would 'get back to her'. He didn't. An hour or so later, when she tried a second time to reach him, she was blocked again. On that occasion Eve shrugged the matter off.

When the same situation occurred again a few days later, she realized exactly what was happening. Ignoring the protests of his secretary Eve swept past the girl and angrily confronted Nelson in his office.

'You can't get away with this, Greg! You know I can handle those stories better than anyone else.'

He looked at her coldly. 'Do I? Maybe I was wrong.' He swung his chair away so his back was towards her. 'I told you, sweetheart, no one uses Greg Nelson. Now let's see how far you can get without me making life easy for you.'

Two angry spots of red burned on Eve's cheeks. 'You're letting your personal dislike of me put the quality of the program in jeopardy, Greg. I'm sorry, I thought you were a real professional.'

She spun on her heel and strode out of the room.

* * *

AND THEN, ten days later, something happened that changed the situation in a way she could never have imagined.

On his way to the studio for that night's program Nelson was involved in a collision. It was bad enough to have him admitted to hospital suffering concussion, bruised ribs and facial lacerations. Obviously the anchorman wasn't going to be able to appear on camera that evening or the few evenings to follow.

Ty Cameron didn't hesitate when the hospital rang him with the news. Ten days or so the doctor told him. That was about how long it would take for the facial cuts and bruising to heal enough to be concealed by make-up.

Eve was in her office when the call came through. Cameron quickly explained the situation. And then the magic words: 'I want you to front the show until Greg's better, Eve.'

* * *

THE FLOOR MANAGER was giving the wind-up signal. Eve looked steadily into camera two.

'That's it for another night from *Scrutiny*. Be back with us tomorrow evening when we'll again bring you the stories behind the headlines. I'm Eve Taylor, standing in for Greg Nelson. Get better soon, Greg, and good evening, Australia.'

* * *

THE TREND STARTED THAT EVENING. The calls came in for the next hour. The girl was great... Terrific to see a woman heading up an important program... Let's see more of Eve Taylor...

* * *

'*GET that bitch out of my chair!*'

From his hospital bed Greg Nelson was screaming into the telephone. The effort was making his ribs hurt even more but he didn't care. The same way he didn't give a shit whoever else they got to replace him, as long as it wasn't that manipulative, two-faced ballbreaker.

At the other end of the line Ty Cameron listened to the tirade. When Nelson finally ran out of breath he said quietly, 'Leave it to me, Greg. You just concentrate on getting better.'

The producer of "Scrutiny" had no intention of taking Eve Taylor out of the stand-in anchor role. Especially not after the interview she'd done the previous evening.

In the hot seat was a leading businessman implicated in a case involving bribery and corruption. Initially the man spoke sweepingly of his total innocence. Eve let him go just so far. Then, step by step, her skillful questioning eroded his bluster, made him squirm and fumble for effective answers. By the end of the interview viewers could have been left in little doubt that the man indeed had a case to answer.

The police must have thought so too. The midmorning news had carried the story that the businessman in question was now at police headquarters 'assisting police with their enquiries'.

No, thought Ty Cameron, he wasn't in any rush to get rid of Eve Taylor from behind the "Scrutiny" desk.

* * *

TEN DAYS later when Greg Nelson returned to work the atmosphere between himself and Eve Taylor was palpably hostile. It hadn't taken him long to find out the strength of public response to her stand-in role.

The bitch had tried yet again to scratch her way up on his back; but, he vowed angrily, he'd make it goddamn clear that it was Greg Nelson who was once more in charge.

Eve resisted complaining to Ty Cameron about the anchorman's continuing obstruction of her work. Crews rostered to her were suddenly cancelled at the last moment, the best editors were now almost always unavailable... Nelson was doing his best, Eve knew, to freeze her out. Somehow she was going to have to hang in.

* * *

TY CAMERON LIKED the idea of a story on Rachel Symons.

'Sure, Eve, go with it. Good angle, the father daughter team. Positive, upbeat – should make a pleasant change.'

Rachel wouldn't have been a businesswoman if she'd turned down the opportunity for free publicity offered by the "Scrutiny" program.

'Love to do it, Eve!' Her vibrant personality was undiminished by the telephone line. 'When did you have in mind?'

'As soon as possible.'

'It'll be great to see you again.'

* * *

TWO WEEKS later Rachel Symons was facing Eve in the garden of her riverside mansion while the camera crew recorded the interview.

'From the time I was a teenager I was interested in my father's business. Our partnership just evolved naturally. Now every decision we make is the result of close collaboration.'

Eve's next question was deliberately provocative. 'But perhaps most traditional European fathers would have preferred to see their daughters married rather than heading their business empires?'

Rachel threw back her long slim neck in a laugh. 'Look, my father came to this country as Leo Simek, a penniless Czech refugee, a Jew who had been lucky enough to survive the Holocaust. He was determined to make it. Along the way he very quickly tossed aside the traditions of the old world....'

Neatly sidestepped, Eve silently admired. 'Well, there can certainly be no dispute that Leo Symons has 'made it'. His contribution to the development of the Gold Coast is well documented. But he was just one of many, wasn't he? There were so many European refugees who helped change the face of this nation, wouldn't you agree?'

As Rachel answered the question Eve suddenly found herself wishing she could confide her own background to this sophisticated, self-confident woman. But to reveal that would mean revealing the scandal of the past. And there was no way she could risk that.

* * *

IT WAS a half-day holiday for Rachel Symons' daughter and she was home just in time to see the cameramen packing up. As mother and daughter embraced, Eve once again felt the sharp edge of her emotions. She had missed a childhood with her own mother and now it looked as if there would be no child in her future either.

'Rachel.' An idea had just occurred to her. 'I didn't know Katie was going to be home in time. The guys can spare a couple more minutes, what about we shoot a little footage of the two of you together? It'd make a nice balance to the business side.'

'No!'

Rachel recognized that the sharpness of her reply had taken Eve a little aback. She apologized. 'I'm sorry, Eve, but you just never know these days... I really don't want Katie identified like that.'

'Of course. I totally understand. Please forgive me. If I'd thought about it...'

Eve watched as mother and daughter walked hand-in-hand into the house. Katie was sweet and totally unprecocious for a child raised in such opulent surroundings. It was obvious how seriously Rachel took her responsibilities as a mother.

The rest of the afternoon would be spent filming some of the numerous Symons projects along the coastline before Eve and the crew returned to Sydney the next morning. Rachel, however, was hoping Eve was free for dinner that evening.

'I'd like that,' Eve answered with pleasure. The more she saw of the tall vivacious blonde the more she found to like.

* * *

THEY ATE at a first-rate waterside restaurant and several times their meal was interrupted by locals stopping to greet the well-known businesswoman.

'Sorry,' Rachel offered Eve a smile of apology, 'the Coast is a very small pond. Everybody knows everyone.'

They enjoyed a meal of excellent Queensland seafood, while their conversation ranged widely from politics to fashion. As the evening progressed and the intimacy between the two women grew, it was inevitable that the subject should turn to the opposite sex.

'No,' Eve looked down at her wine glass and shook her head in answer to Rachel's question, 'there's no one special at the moment. Something important broke up a while ago now. I guess I've been too busy since.'

She raised her head. 'What about you?'

'Oh, there's always a few sniffing round.' Rachel gave a short laugh. 'Good for the ego at my age. But someone serious? No.' She took a sip of wine and raised an amused eyebrow. 'Anyway, how can any bright confident woman these days expect to find everything she needs in one simple little male? They're only human, after all!'

She threw back her head and gave a throaty laugh.

* * *

THEY DIDN'T MAKE it too late an evening.

As Rachel pulled up outside Eve's hotel the concierge hurried to open the Mercedes' door.

'Thanks a lot, Rachel. A great evening. And many thanks for the interview too.'

'All in a good cause,' the other woman smiled. 'Keep in touch, Eve. Any time you're up this way let me know.'

Eve could tell it was a genuine invitation. The two of them really had established a rapport.

'Thank you. The same if you're coming to Sydney.'

'Might be down soon actually,' Rachel responded. 'We're trying to line up a big project with Hugh Rolfe.' She turned the key in the ignition. 'You know, the big grazing family? Wool's taken a dive, so Rolfe's looking for other fish to fry.'

With a final wave she drove off, before she could notice the abrupt change of expression on Eve Taylor's face.

28

Over the weeks that followed, Rachel's revelation about Hugh Rolfe's possible involvement in some 'big project' with the Symons stayed in the forefront of Eve's mind.

With the continuing drop in wool prices Rolfe was obviously looking to other areas to hold the family finances together. What sort of deal could he be considering that involved Rachel and her father?

It would take a little discreet enquiry but Eve knew she had to find out more.

Meanwhile the problems with Greg Nelson did not diminish. His animosity made every working day difficult.

And then, a couple of months after she'd done the fill-in job as anchorwoman, Ty Cameron called her into his office. As she took a seat his opening words made her stomach turn over.

'I don't think *Scrutiny* is able to handle both you and Greg, Eve, do you?' The producer gave her a speculative look.

She knew at once what had happened. Nelson had succeeded in getting her fired. 'I ... I'm not sure what you've heard from Greg, Ty, but... yes, things have certainly become difficult between us – if that's what you mean.'

Ty Cameron nodded, looking at her in silence for a moment. Then he said, 'I've been talking to the boss, Eve. He was delighted with the response when you fronted for Greg. What we've been thinking is that there's a place now for a hard-hitting format to be anchored by a woman. How does the idea sound to you?'

* * *

IMMEDIATELY PULLED OFF "SCRUTINY", Eve stayed on full salary as plans went ahead for the development of the new program. In seeking to launch a heavyweight format headed by a woman the network was clearly breaking new ground. Women were supposed to shine on daytime television or play second fiddle to a male compere, not front a prime-time politically oriented format. And when Ty Cameron further underlined his commitment and belief in Eve's talent by naming the new program "Taylor Made", her delight knew no bounds.

Greg Nelson made his fury glaringly obvious when he learned the real reason behind Eve Taylor's withdrawal from "Scrutiny".

'It's crazy! No woman's got the clout to carry that type of program on her own!'

Ty Cameron gave him a cold look. 'You do your job, Greg, and let me do mine.'

Nelson choked back his anger as he stormed out of the room. She's bound to fail, he consoled himself grimly. No woman could make it in Australia fronting prime-time hard news. He'd give her six weeks.

* * *

THE PREPARATIONS FELL SMOOTHLY into place. Publicity for the show began to roll – from stories in *TV Week* to profiles on Eve in leading women's magazines.

In this interim period too there were other plans Eve had to set in motion. Important plans that, in contrast to her professional career had to attract no publicity. And the spectacular terms of her new contract at last gave Eve the financial resources she needed.

* * *

JANET MADE her first approach through the charge nurse. A square-jawed woman with a head of short gray curls, she might have proved a formidable barrier except for Janet's own medical background.

'It's been a long time. I'm sure Marianne Walenska is no longer a threat to anyone, Sister. I've come into some money from a relative's estate and I'm in a position now to care for her full time.'

The charge sister gave her visitor a hard, assessing look. 'This is a matter, of course, for the board and medical director to finally decide. And naturally that decision would rest on an independent psychiatric report.'

'Yes,' Janet nodded. 'I am happy to arrange that.'

Money, at last, was no object.

* * *

RACHEL WAS quick to phone and congratulate her on her new role.

'Terrific, Eve! I'm sure you'll do every bit as good a job as the guys – if not better.'

'Thanks for the vote of confidence. I'm determined to make this work.'

Eve was pleasantly surprised by the other woman's telephone call. It seemed that in Rachel Symons she really had made a friend. But she hadn't felt able to bring up the topic of Hugh Rolfe.

* * *

FOLLOWING two other independent reports it was the respected specialist Doctor Alex Shawn who produced the definitive analysis of the patient, Marianne Walenska. An exemplary inmate, he concluded. And as long as her drug program was maintained there was no evidence to suggest she had any further tendency to violence. He recommended her release into appropriate care.

* * *

EVE HAD a lot to arrange in a short time.

The clinic in Switzerland required medical files and other formal documentation pertaining to her mother's condition. And yes, the authorities responded to Eve's other request, her mother's friend would be found accommodation somewhere close by. For Eve had no intention of sending Marianne away – even into such competent hands – without Janet's support.

Dr Rupert Kraus, the specialist psychiatrist who headed the clinic, had, understandably, been unable to state the duration of treatment without first-hand knowledge of the patient's condition.

I think it would be best, madam, his correspondence stated, *to allow at least six months in the first instance.*

Six months of first-class care in a Swiss clinic, the flights, and Janet's keep on top of that would have been an unthinkable expense for Eve just a few months previously. Now, however she was in a position to afford whatever chance might be offered for her mother's recovery.

The money also finally enabled her to move from the small Elizabeth Bay apartment to a well-appointed townhouse in prestigious Bellevue Hill. The cottage, meanwhile, would be shut up until Janet and her mother's return.

* * *

ON THE DAY the two women left it was impossible for Eve to see them off. Her face had become too widely recognized. And her forthcoming program would lift her profile exponentially. Now, more than ever, she had to keep secret the connection with her past. She shuddered inwardly at the thought of the delight her jealous rivals would take in reactivating the old scandal.

Her 'illegitimacy', her unknown parentage, had never been a burden or drawback. If anything, such 'interesting facts' had given an edge to her PR. But Eve felt sure that her rocketing career would not be able to survive the real story – the fact that the groundbreaking anchorwoman of "Taylor Made" had been born in an asylum to a mother labeled criminally insane, a woman whose violent attack had almost cost the life of the matriarch of the famous Rolfe family.

* * *

JANET HAD a room in the small picturesque village of Bettenhausen just a five-minute bus ride from the clinic. She visited Marianne every day, hoping and praying that the Swiss doctors would be able to work a miracle.

'Nothing happens quickly in psychiatry, madam,' warned Dr Kraus. 'We know very little about the brain – maybe only how one third of it works. The rest is still a mystery. You will understand, I am sure, how much a risk this creates in the administration of drugs. One hundred patients may be affected one way, yet another may have a totally unexpected reaction. It is this we must work our way through, step by step.'

Janet listened carefully to the calmly spoken Swiss expert. Dr Kraus was a man past middle-age, distinguished and refined, his manner quietly reassuring. His reputation in his field was first rate. She would have to trust him.

Now as she sat beside Marianne in the crisp sunshine encircled by the glistening towers of the Alps, Janet wrote one of her regular letters to Eve.

Yet all she could really say with confidence was that her mother was receiving the best of treatment.

* * *

MEANWHILE, back in Australia, Eve continued to hope for the same miracle while she concentrated on ensuring the success of "Taylor Made".

The program had got off to a spectacular start. The advance publicity had been enormous and the ratings for the first six weeks were excellent. The viewing public seemed to have no trouble in accepting a woman in a prime-time anchor role.

By the third month "Taylor Made" had achieved the impossible – it knocked "Scrutiny" off its perch at the top of the ratings.

Greg Nelson couldn't contain his wrath. Eve Taylor was beating him at his own game and rival media were glorying in the competition between them.

'While *Scrutiny* travels more and more along the infotainment track,' sideswiped one reviewer, '*Taylor Made* provides for a thinking audience who want their news, both domestic and international, without frills.'

Then, a few short weeks later came the shock axing of "Scrutiny" itself. The program had been dealt a body blow, firstly by Greg Nelson's insistence that infotainment was the way to go, and secondly by the rocketing popularity of "Taylor Made". The once unassailable anchorman found himself side-lined with the vague promise of "something in the near future".

It was then that Greg Nelson made his savage silent promise: he wasn't going to rest until he'd wiped that bitch and her goddamn program right off the map.

* * *

DURING THIS SAME PERIOD, Rachel visited Sydney on a number of occasions. And with her mother and Janet gone Eve was also able to snatch the odd weekend at Surfers. Rachel insisted that she be her houseguest on these occasions and the closeness between the women grew deeper.

In the same way too, Eve forged a real bond with Rachel's daughter. The little girl made her pleasure obvious whenever her mother's friend came to stay and Rachel was as delighted as Eve herself by the growing fondness between them.

'She misses having aunts and cousins, you know,' Rachel explained as Katie ran off to find her latest painting to show Eve. 'She's always asking when we're going to see you again.'

Eve felt warmed by her friend's words. Her relationship with Katie and Rachel filled the emotional void left by the absence of her mother and Janet. Rachel had become the friend she'd never been able to find in her own highly competitive world. The experience with Greg Nelson still rankled. Rachel, thank God, was someone she could trust.

Yet there was one area where Eve was reluctant to step over the bounds of friendship. She knew that many of the businesswoman's visits to Sydney were taken up with fine-tuning the negotiations for the 'exciting development' that was on the drawing board with Hugh Rolfe. Eve had to bite back her curiosity to probe for further information. It seemed like some sort of betrayal of friendship to use Rachel that way.

And then one evening before she left to return home Rachel divulged the information Eve was hoping for.

They had eaten dinner in Rachel's Sydney apartment; it was high-rise living at its best, offering spectacular views of the city, Opera House and harbor.

Over coffee in the softly lit living room Rachel finally brought up the subject that held so much interest for Eve.

'It's been all very hush-hush until now,' the businesswoman explained, her eyes bright with excitement, 'but things have just about got to the stage where we can let the press in on the project. The sooner we attract the attention of prospective investors the better. Believe me, Eve, this is a totally original concept for the Coast. Forget high rise; we're going for villa-style housing, very expensive and exclusive, built around a tournament-standard golf course and incorporating up-market shopping. It's going to surprise everyone who thought the Symons were only capable of high-rise development.'

'It certainly sounds wonderful – very original.' Eve tried to keep her tone casual. 'And you mentioned Hugh Rolfe. Where does he come into the picture?' She hated even having to say his name aloud.

Rachel leaned forward and placed her empty coffee cup on the low granite-topped table. 'He owns the land. It's brilliantly positioned; close to three hundred hectares just a short drive out of Surfers Paradise. Up till now negotiations have centered on getting a joint venture deal between Rolfe as the landholder, ourselves as the developers, and our outside financiers. It was a matter of working out everyone's slice of the action.'

Irrationally Eve couldn't help resenting that the woman whose friendship she so valued was now helping to increase her enemy's wealth.

'The way I hear it,' she responded, picking her words, 'the Rolfe fortune's taken a bit of a beating these last few years.'

'Exactly. That's why we managed to pull the whole deal together. Rolfe was keen as long as he got what he considered a proper percentage of the profits.'

She gave Eve a knowing smile. 'Wait until you see the media releases – they're really going to drum up excitement.'

The conversation ended there. But ten minutes later, as Eve was taking her leave, Rachel extended an invitation.

'Why don't you try to get up to Surfers again soon and I'll show you exactly where it's all going to happen. You'll love it, I'm sure.' She cocked an appraising eyebrow. 'Might even decide to buy in yourself.'

And put another dollar in the pocket of the family who had robbed her mother of her inheritance? Eve thought she'd rather die first.

But she was curious to take a look. Anything in which Hugh Rolfe had his nose was worthy of her attention. Not that she expected to find any real dirt. Not in a deal involving Leo and Rachel Symons.

29

Eve felt on a high as she let herself in her front door. The evening's program had gone without a hitch. Committed to her aim of keeping "Taylor Made" at the cutting edge of international events her satellite link interviews with both the British Foreign Office and a US State Department spokesperson on the recent momentous events in Eastern Europe had proved scintillating viewing. Further adding to her good mood was the envelope with the Swiss postmark that lay waiting in her letterbox.

Janet wrote regularly, always in a positive vein, but while it seemed Marianne was gradually being weaned off a smorgasbord of drugs there appeared little evidence of improvement in her condition. Still Eve couldn't help hoping as she dropped her briefcase by the study door and walked towards the kitchen, opening the envelope as she went.

Her eyes quickly skimmed the page. It was there, in the second paragraph, in Janet's round clear writing.

I don't know why we were never told of this earlier, but the doctors here assure me there is no question about it.

Bewildered, Eve read and reread the words. *What had happened, she wondered, for her mother to require extensive facial reconstructive surgery*?

* * *

It was almost a month before she found herself able to take up Rachel's invitation. Determined to maintain her program's excellent ratings, her workload was heavier than ever, and it required a deliberate effort to make time for a break.

Her friend was delighted. 'Great!' she responded when Eve rang her with just two days' notice. 'Working too hard'll give you wrinkles, darling. Come on up and I'll find a couple of friendly, handsome boys to take us out for a bit of fun.'

'I hope you're joking!'

'Well... it could be arranged.'

'I'll take a rain check this time, okay?' Eve teased in return. 'All I really want to do is catch up and take it easy.'

'Okay. But I'm going to drag you out to the site. Everything's going great guns ... the earthworks started a week ago. Wasn't the PR great? We've been inundated with enquiries and not a brick's been laid yet!'

Eve didn't doubt it. Heavily publicized, the Paradise Grove project would have been hard to miss as leading daily newspapers and up-market magazines carried glossy brochures of the planned development.

'I'm dying to see it.'

* * *

They took the short drive along the coast the Saturday morning after Eve's arrival.

'The interest has been phenomenal,' Rachel enthused as she sat at the wheel of the Mercedes. 'It can't fail.'

Eve said nothing. In the distance she could see the bare earth crawling with trucks and huge earth-moving equipment.

Rachel explained why, although it was costing them a fortune in weekend rates, no one at Paradise Grove was taking it easy. 'It's a matter at this stage of clearing the land so it'll present as attractively as possible for valuation by our financiers.'

They found some shade in which to leave the car. 'Dad's here, too,'

Rachel nodded at the Jaguar alongside. 'He's even more impatient than I am, can't wait for it all to happen.' And with very good reason too, she thought silently, her features suddenly tight.

But that was something strictly between herself and her father.

* * *

As the two women made their way across the dusty ground, Rachel gestured expansively. 'About here is where the golf links should start. And over there,' she pointed, 'is where they're putting up the first stage of the condos.'

Squinting into the distance she turned to Eve. 'There's Dad – with the architect. Let's go over and I'll show you the detailed plans.'

There were three men standing together beside a demountable building. They were peering over a set of unfurled architectural drawings and, deep in discussion, didn't see the two women approach.

Leo Symons looked up first. He greeted his daughter and nodded in recognition at Eve.

Smiling, Rachel put a hand on Eve's elbow. 'Eve you've met my father, of course, but may I introduce Hugh Rolfe ... and our architect, Keith Fleming.'

She had seen press photos but only at the last moment did Eve recognize the man standing beside Leo Symons. Of medium height, he was paunchy with thinning light hair and dark eyes set in a nest of wrinkles.

It took a supreme effort for her to accept the outstretched hand of her enemy. The man who had done so much to destroy her mother's health and happiness.

* * *

'Are you feeling the heat?'

Rachel threw her an anxious look as they headed back along the highway.

'No, I'm fine.' Eve was still getting over the unpleasant surprise of having met Hugh Rolfe so unexpectedly.

For ten minutes she'd been forced to make idle conversation as the project was discussed. She couldn't wait to get out of the man's presence. But it was impossible to confide to Rachel the reason for her upset.

Rachel let it drop. Her intuition told her something was the matter.

* * *

HUGH ROLFE WAS TRYING HARD NOT to get drunk as he sat on the huge protected patio of Leo Symons' penthouse apartment. The ocean stretched like a ruffled blue scarf to the horizon and far below the sand gleamed like a silver ribbon dotted with the ever-present tourists. For a moment Hugh wondered what the hell was keeping him in a dump like Sydney when he could be living in a paradise like this.

But soon, he reminded himself warmly, taking a sip of scotch, he would at least have a retreat up here. A condo of his own had been part of the deal.

With Leo Symons called inside to the telephone, Hugh sat alone, musing as ever these days on his marvelous good luck. A lazy grin lifted the corners of his mouth. He was all set to dig himself out of the shit, thanks to a few hundred hectares of prime grazing land by the ocean's edge. Land he hadn't even been aware he'd owned.

It was Leo Symons, seeking a perfect location for his vision, who had established through the titles office that ownership was in the name of Charles Rolfe. Only then had Hugh learnt that the land was part of his deceased brother's estate.

And now the deal he'd pulled off with this tough, ugly old shit was going to put his life back together again.

Born lucky. The alcohol buzzed in Hugh's brain.

Saved in the damn nick of time, he chortled inwardly, as the aging developer rejoined him.

* * *

BEFORE RETURNING to Sydney Eve spent Sunday morning at the beach with Rachel and her daughter.

As she lay back on the sand and watched the two of them laughing and splashing at the water's edge, she was reminded again of what she had been robbed of with her own mother. Nothing could ever replace the years they had lost.

Bitter tears suddenly filled her eyes. Even now, having finally been reunited, she couldn't hope to find the closeness with Marianne she so longed for. The latest report from the clinic had dashed her faint hopes.

'... there is something she refuses to unblock,' Dr Kraus had written, 'and this is most certainly inextricably linked with her decision not to talk. Because, assuredly, it is a choice the patient herself has made – there is no physical basis for her muteness. The interpretation is not difficult: to speak would mean a confrontation with the darkness inside her.'

Eve recalled the psychiatrist's caution when she had first written to the clinic about her mother's case. *'We are not miracle workers,'* the doctor had warned in his reply.

And now, despite all her hope and efforts, she had to face the despair of acceptance. After trying all possible avenues the clinic had been unable to achieve success.

Eve remembered the final comment in Dr Kraus's report: *Perhaps now only something we cannot predict will turn the key to finally unlock your mother's psyche.*

The words had mocked her. Eve no longer believed in miracles.

Behind her dark glasses she blinked away her tears as she saw Rachel and Katie running hand-in-hand towards her.

Her mother was coming home. Nothing had changed.

* * *

LEO SYMONS WAS glad the journalist woman had gone. He wasn't happy about the obvious closeness of the relationship between his daughter and Eve Taylor. The press had their place; they were there to be used when required. Beyond that, he didn't trust them. Especially in the present circumstances.

'Why do you see so much of that woman?' He voiced his concern now as he faced his daughter in her living room. It was Sunday evening and he had dropped in to get Rachel's signature on a document relating to the Paradise Grove project.

She looked up in surprise. 'Eve Taylor? I like her. We've become good friends. Isn't that enough?'

'Such a relationship could be dangerous at present. I don't have to explain why.'

Rachel knew her father was referring to the company's current pressing financial problems, but she had never discussed the details of their business with Eve.

'You're worrying about nothing,' she replied crisply, resenting his peremptory tone. She was in charge of her own life now. She enjoyed her power and would make her own decisions.

They were interrupted as Katie came skipping into the room, fresh from her bath and dressed in a pink nightdress, her blonde hair loose and tumbling around her shoulders. Rachel's gaze softened as she looked at her daughter.

'Is Grandpa staying for dinner, Mummy?' She slid onto Leo's knee and put her arm around his neck.

'Not tonight, darling,' Rachel got to her feet. 'You've got school tomorrow – early to bed for you. Say goodnight to Grandpa.'

The child pouted half-heartedly, protested with childish emphasis. 'You never ever let him stay.'

'Don't be silly, Katie.' Rachel's voice was sharper than normal as she held out a hand to her tanned, long-limbed daughter.

* * *

LEO SYMONS WAS in no mood for bed when he arrived back at his penthouse apartment. He poured himself a whisky and walked across the room to stand by the open glass doors. A crescent moon hung low in a silver studded sky and even at this height the warm tang of the ocean assailed his nostrils.

Lost in his own thoughts the businessman barely noticed. Slowly sipping his drink he pondered again the situation that was causing him such concern.

Construction and development had always carried risks, and while there had been other close calls over the years, he had always survived. But this time the risk was much greater. The last few years had seen enormous changes in the country which had given him haven in the world, at large, he reminded himself. Economic deregulation, which at first seemed to promise a goldmine of opportunity, had all too dramatically revealed its accompanying dangers.

Two years previously, with Japanese partners and a forty per cent equity in a major resort development near the New South Wales border, Leo had been happy to accept financing in Japanese yen. The problem had come with the rapid escalation of interest rates and the horrifying fall in the exchange rate of the Australian dollar.

Now, not only was his company struggling to maintain its share of repayments but the project itself seemed destined to be a white elephant. It had failed to attract real interest or investors.

Leo Symons knew he was fighting for his life. If his Japanese partners pushed him and he failed to deliver, it would not only put his other properties at risk but could also cost him his most vital asset.

Credibility.

When that went, banks and other financial institutions would very quickly succumb to nerves and the empire it had taken him a lifetime to build could collapse like a pack of cards.

Which was why, he determined as he swallowed the last of the fiery liquid, Paradise Grove had to work. And work fast. The sooner he was able to unload his equity in the project, the sooner he could shore up his company and his reputation. Nothing must be allowed to stand in the way of its success.

Only Rachel knew the full extent of the danger – and it irked him now to recall her efforts to dissuade him from accepting the Japanese backing. Leo Symons didn't like to be proved wrong. Not even by his daughter. Although it might have appeared otherwise on the surface, he had never aimed to share his control and power and there were still occasions when he resented Rachel's input. But her strength surprised him.

It had taken a while, but gradually Leo had come to recognize that within his daughter there existed the same streak of ruthlessness as in himself.

* * *

EVE HAD to curb her impatience.

Janet and her mother had arrived back in Australia the previous morning and had been driven straight to the cottage in the car Eve had waiting for them. Now, as she followed the twisting road up through the mountains, Eve felt a confusion of emotions. After so long a separation it would be wonderful to have the two women back again. Yet at the same time she felt an overwhelming depression.

I've failed, she thought, as she turned into the dark tunnel of trees that led to the house. The miracle she had prayed for at the clinic hadn't happened. For the thousandth time she wondered if she would ever find the key to the whole truth of her mother's past.

30

It was the day Mark Delaney had been dreading. But finally it had arrived.

Dressed in jeans and T-shirt he'd driven into the city early on Sunday morning. His two loyal secretaries and his partner, Sean Murray, had arrived within minutes of his unlocking the office door.

They'd been preparing for the move for weeks and packing boxes lined the halls of the small three-room office suite. The place had been fine when it was just Mark and his father Ian. Fine too when, after his father's retirement eight years ago, he'd taken on Sean Murray. But now, with business expanding, Mark had just hired a third partner and very clearly larger premises were needed to accommodate them all. Just around the corner in Hunter Street he'd found a bright, second-floor suite – an ideal location.

As he stood among the stack of packing cases the lanky, dark-haired lawyer grinned a welcome at the two young women who worked for him. 'Much better than wasting Sunday on Bondi Beach, don't you think, girls?'

Lucy Shaw, her flame-red hair pulled back in a long ponytail, gave her boss a wry grin as she began to close the lids of the loaded boxes. 'Sure, Mark, sure...'

Angela Roselli, a petite, olive-skinned beauty of twenty-five, smiled as she pulled out drawers in the filing cabinets.

Both secretaries adored their attractive, hardworking employer. Angela was engaged and Lucy already married, so neither had personal designs on him, but over after-work drinks they would often discuss the sort of woman who'd be 'perfect' for Mark Delaney.

'A thirty-five-year-old dish like him still on the loose? What's wrong with the women of this town?' Lucy asked incredulously as she sipped her Chardonnay.

'Works too hard, that's his problem,' replied Angela. 'How's he going to meet anyone when he spends all his time in the office?'

It was true. Mark Delaney put in horrific hours. As inheritor of a family business stretching over three generations, he was determined to maintain his company as a small versatile option to the super firms that had emerged through the rapacious eighties.

Mark's professional ethics rested on the belief that access to the law and justice should exist for all ... not just those who could afford it. He had ignored warnings from colleagues that there was no place today for the small operator ... especially in a central city location. So far he had proved them wrong. And a three-man practice, he assured himself, was hardly 'selling out'.

By late afternoon the removal service had taken most of the paperwork to the new location. There was only the office furniture to go.

But not his father's desk. Mark had decided that the cedar roll-top would go to his terrace house. It was quite a valuable antique and would be out of place in the ultra-modern premises to which they were moving. Even in its present surroundings Mark made no use of the desk. Instead it sat in a corner of the reception area – a monument to another era and a poignant reminder of his father who had passed away just four months after retirement.

He thought of Ian Delaney now as he ran a hand over the highly polished wood. The stress of those last few years had contributed to his early death Mark was certain. Trust fund fraud by a partner was every solicitor's nightmare. When it had happened to Ian Delaney, his business had disappeared almost overnight – although he himself was totally innocent of blame.

Only a few staunch friends and clients had continued to deal with the firm but by openly declaring their loyalty and support they had helped Delaney to survive. As a result, on his retirement he had been able to pass on a once more thriving business to his only son. While the struggle had certainly taken a toll on his health, Ian Delaney had lived long enough to nurture in his son that same idealism and fervor for justice which had colored his own professional life.

Mark was distracted from his musings as the two burly removal men re-entered the reception area.

'Okay, now this bit's goin' to your place, right?' asked one.

'Yes and extra careful okay?' Mark cautioned.

Grunting, the two men carefully hefted up the heavy antique. As they made their way out of the room something slid out from the back of the desk.

'Hey, mate!' one of the laborers called over his shoulder for Mark's attention. 'Somethin's dropped out there.'

Turning, Mark saw a dusty legal envelope on the flattened carpet where the desk had sat. With a frown he moved over and picked it up. Hell, he'd cleaned that desk out years ago; this must have been wedged at the back of one of the drawers. It couldn't have been that important, he figured, or he'd have heard something about it by now.

Taking care, he unstuck the seal and withdrew the contents.

* * *

As soon as he realized the significance of what he had found Mark knew he had to act without delay. He realized too just how traumatic his news would be for all those concerned.

Less than twenty-four hours later he was picking up the phone in the cramped, book-lined study of his home and calling the number for Hugh Rolfe.

* * *

As he took the elevator to the second floor of the Hunter Street address Hugh Rolfe was puzzled. What the hell did this tin-pot lawyer want with him?

The name had struck a vague bell in Hugh's memory when he'd called. And then the man himself had explained. 'I'm the son of Ian Delaney, who handled your late brother's affairs.'

It came back to Hugh then. Charles had gone to school with Delaney. They had remained friends. Even when the family's major business was handled by one of the country's largest firms Hugh recalled that his brother had maintained some personal dealings with his old friend. On Charles's death, however, all pertinent documents had been handed over to the Rolfe family solicitors.

So what could Delaney's son want with him after all this time? he asked himself as he stepped out of the elevator.

He very quickly found out.

* * *

Dumbstruck, Hugh Rolfe faced the young solicitor across his desk.

'I don't believe it!'

But Mark Delaney was nodding his dark head. 'Of course, I've seen all the publicity about the project, Mr Rolfe, and I knew it would come as a shock. But while I must apologize, that doesn't change the situation as it now stands. An injunction will have to be issued against all further work until the necessary legal process–'

'Give me a copy of those documents!' Face flushed, Hugh Rolfe interrupted him. 'I'll be getting independent advice about this. You can't pull this on me!'

A few minutes later he strode furiously out of Mark Delaney's office.

That mad whore wasn't going to get in his way after all these years.

* * *

HE WAS STILL SHAKING ten minutes later as he entered the dimly lit bar of the Hilton Hotel. Ordering a double scotch he carried it to a table in the corner of the room and tried to think the nightmare through.

In sight of salvation and now this. A codicil to Charles's will. A codicil which made Marianne Rolfe the sole inheritor of the land at Paradise Grove.

Or, in the result of her death, Marianne Rolfe's child.

* * *

HUGH WAS DETERMINED to say nothing to Leo Symons until he had explored every possible avenue with his own lawyers. Stressing the urgency of the matter he was given an immediate appointment.

After close perusal of the documents one of the senior partners called Hugh at home and made his position sickeningly clear.

The property in question belonged unequivocally to Marianne Rolfe – and subsequently any heirs she might have produced.

* * *

LEO SYMONS' face was tight with cold rage as he listened to Hugh Rolfe's spluttering over the line.

Just two hours earlier the elderly businessman had received formal communication from a Sydney lawyer, Mark Delaney, outlining the circumstances and advising that an interim injunction against any further work at Paradise Grove had been applied for.

Having received no prior warning from Hugh Rolfe, the news had come like a bolt of lightning to the millionaire developer. The title to the land had been in the name of Charles Rolfe; he had accepted it as part of the dead man's estate which had been legally inherited by Hugh Rolfe.

And now this.

But Leo Symons knew there was a way round most problems. He hadn't achieved business success without having learnt that particular lesson.

Curtly he cut across Hugh Rolfe's whining. 'We must deal with this immediately, before the press or the Japs get any scent of it.'

He told Hugh what they would have to do.

* * *

RACHEL WAS AS SHOCKED as her father had been. 'So Rolfe did a deal with land he had no legal right to?' she asked, appalled. Leo had revealed the news to her in the privacy of his office.

'Unfortunately, yes,' Leo answered dryly. 'According to this recently located document the land was made over to his wife. A completely separate matter from the rest of his estate.'

Rachel frowned. 'And the wife is still alive?'

Leo Symons nodded. 'So it would seem. A psychiatric patient for the last thirty-odd years. If I remember, there was some scandal, hushed up.'

But Rachel's mind was racing ahead. 'Well, if the woman is incapable, wouldn't control of the property–'

'... rest with her offspring?' her father finished. 'Yes. And if indeed there is a child, he or she must be found and persuaded to negotiate with us. Without delay.'

He made no mention to his daughter of what he had suggested to Hugh Rolfe.

* * *

THE STARTING point had been obvious. Mark had quickly tracked down what had happened to Charles Rolfe's widow. She had been committed to Callan Park Psychiatric Hospital under her maiden name, Marianne Walenska.

'I'm sorry, sir, we are not permitted to divulge information to the public.' A starchy female voice answered his telephoned enquiries.

Mark hid his impatience. 'You don't quite understand. I'm a solicitor handling a matter which involves the widow of the late Charles Rolfe. It's important that I meet with the medical director as soon as possible.'

* * *

A TRIFLE guardedly the medical director welcomed Mark into his office. A visit from a solicitor always held the potential for trouble.

Mark slipped his card across the bare desk and explained his mission.

The bureaucrat saw no need to obfuscate. Yes, Marianne Rolfe had indeed been an inmate of the hospital for many years. Not at the present, however... Then he rang for his secretary and a quick perusal of the records revealed that in this very hospital Marianne Rolfe had given birth to a healthy child. A girl. Whereabouts unknown.

'It was long before my time, of course, yet even so there is no record of adoption.' He peered at the lawyer over the top of his spectacles. 'I suggest your best course is to follow up via the woman who took custody of Mrs Rolfe about three years ago.'

Mark took down the particulars. As he stood up to leave he added, 'In this circumstance Marianne Rolfe is officially my client and I am responsible for handling her affairs. Therefore I would be grateful if any further enquiries regarding her whereabouts or anything to do with this particular matter are directed to myself.'

He thanked the man for his time and left.

* * *

HUGH ROLFE WAS dead on time for his appointment. It was less than forty-eight hours since their first meeting.

He cleared his throat as he held the alert dark gaze of the man opposite.

'Look, Mr Delaney. My solicitors are certain I'll eventually be able to lay claim to the property in question.' The lie slid easily off his tongue. 'But time is not on anyone's side. Every day work is delayed means a huge loss to the project. What I am hoping is that between the two of us we could come to some... *arrangement*.'

Tight-lipped, Mark rose to his feet. 'I don't think we have anything further to discuss, Mr Rolfe.'

* * *

Eve spent every weekend possible at the cottage now that Janet and her mother were back in Australia. She made her own observations of her mother's condition.

'You know there is a difference, Janty. I can see it quite clearly,' she stated one evening when she and Janet were sitting together in front of the living room fire. 'She's more peaceful, relaxed; her hands aren't as restless as they were. And she does seem to have a greater awareness of her surroundings.'

Janet nodded as she put down her coffee cup. 'The therapy was intense, darling. She had her own private analyst who talked to her virtually incessantly. Then, of course, weaning her off that terrible cocktail of drugs certainly made a difference to her mood and reactions.' She gave the girl beside her a sympathetic look. 'There's still a chance, pet. Improvement is still possible the doctors said, as long as her equilibrium is not disturbed.'

'I'm not going to give up. I–' Eve's response was interrupted by the ringing of the telephone.

With a glance at the grandfather clock Janet pushed herself to her feet. 'Just gone eight... now who do you reckon that could be?'

* * *

Speaking quickly, Mark Delaney introduced himself and explained the situation as succinctly as possible.

'... so I hope I've made it clear, Mrs Byrne. It's urgent that I get in touch with Marianne Rolfe's daughter. If you have any idea where she is...'

Janet felt too old for these sorts of shocks. She could feel Eve's puzzled eyes upon her as she listened in wonder to the story.

'Mr Delaney,' she managed, when Mark had finally finished, 'this is not really my decision to make. I will get in touch with Marianne Rolfe's daughter and pass on the details. After that it will be up to her to decide what to do.'

As she spoke she could see the growing astonishment of Eve's expression.

'I take it then that you know the woman's whereabouts, Mrs Byrne? You have my number, both at the office and at home. Please ask her to call me at either place day or night.' He hung up.

Slowly Janet replaced the receiver and turned to tell a puzzled Eve the amazing news.

31

Mark was just beginning to think of a Sunday evening snack of leftovers when the telephone rang.

His caller came straight to the point. 'Mr Delaney, I think you are trying to get in touch with me. I'm the daughter of Charles and Marianne Rolfe. Are you free to see me this evening?'

The woman's sense of urgency was unmistakable. They agreed to meet in half an hour at Mark's address. Only after she had rung off did he realized that she hadn't given her name. And why did he think there had been something vaguely familiar about her voice?

* * *

It was difficult to say who might have been the more surprised as Mark Delaney opened the door to his visitor.

Eve Taylor... Jesus...

She was dressed in casual tan slacks, topped with a soft pink pullover, and in person her blonde beauty revealed a more fragile edge than was captured by the camera. Mark was struck by the sheer femininity of her.

For her part Eve found it hard not to stare at the man who was ushering her into his home. Apart from the dark eyes it could be Paul, she breathed. The height, the strong-featured face, the dark thick hair and air of quiet confidence... The resemblance continued to disconcert her as he led her through to the quiet elegance of the living room.

He poured them both a drink and took a seat opposite.

'I can't help being surprised,' Mark Delaney began.

Drink in hand, Eve looked at him seriously. 'You can understand why I have no wish to publicize the facts of my background.' She reached into her handbag and produced her birth certificate for the solicitor.

Mark nodded as he read the proof of Eve Taylor's parentage. 'I understand your reluctance, of course,' he said, folding the document and handing it back. 'I explained the situation quickly on the phone to Janet Byrne. Did she –'

'Yes. But please, tell me again exactly what this is all about.'

And Mark did, finally handing across the documents for her to peruse. 'I'm guessing Dad had no idea what was in the envelope. You'll see it was witnessed by your father's bank manager. Dad must have put the envelope in his desk, meaning to file it later. Only it obviously fell into the space behind the drawer.'

Eve skimmed through the papers then looked up. 'So the land in question is legally mine – in the event that my mother is mentally incapable of dealing with the matter?'

'Exactly. There are various legal principles to deal with, of course, involving transfer and title but, in essence, yes, that property belongs to you.' Mark Delaney felt the intensity of those beautiful violet eyes. 'You may simply wish to validate the present conditions with the current developer. I am aware he is very keen to see the project go ahead and as quickly as possible.'

Eve was still trying to come to terms with that shock too: that the land in question was actually the Paradise Grove site being developed by Rachel and Leo Symons.

The man opposite was speaking again. 'I realized you may need a little time to think about this. Of course, you may even wish your own solicitor to handle it.'

But Eve was recalling something else Mark Delaney had told her. 'You say your father knew mine? They were school friends?'

Mark nodded. 'Yes. And then, years later, your father was one of the few who stood by mine when his partner came close to ruining the firm.' He saw Eve's puzzled frown and quickly explained. 'I know Dad never forgot Charles Rolfe's kindness,' he ended.

Those clear dark eyes were staring into hers and Eve felt her belly twist with a long-forgotten emotion. He's not Paul, she told herself. Don't be crazy...

Then the lawyer produced another smaller envelope from the batch of papers. 'This was in the envelope too. I'm sorry... I had to read it.' He rose to his feet and picked up their empty glasses. 'It's probably best I leave you alone a moment to look at it.'

As he left the room Eve unfolded the single sheet of expensive writing paper. The signature was her father's; the letter was addressed to 'My dearest Marianne'.

As her eyes followed the words Eve was left in no doubt about the depth of love between her parents. In his bold flowing writing Charles Rolfe expressed his utter joy in his marriage and the conception of their child.

... you have given me so much, Marianne, more than I ever dreamed or hoped for. And now there will be a living testimony to our love.

This land is my special legacy to you, my darling, to commemorate the birth of the child who has come to us as such a divine gift. I want it to be a sanctuary where we can share the joys of family life, but most of all a haven where you might at last find that serenity and peace of mind you've been seeking so long...

As she read and reread the words written so long ago by the father she had never known, Eve's eyes brimmed with tears. To have been conceived in so much love, to lose it all before ever having a chance to feel its strength...

When Mark Delaney re-entered the room he could see that as tough as Eve Taylor might be at her job she wasn't without vulnerability. The turmoil of her emotions was reflected openly in her face. He said nothing as he put a fresh drink on the table beside her.

Finally Eve whispered, 'They ... they loved each other very much...'

And then the tears were spilling down her cheeks and she covered her face with her hands.

Immediately the lawyer was on his feet, moving to sit beside her. In a natural gesture of comfort he enfolded her in his arms.

Only then did he realized how much he had wanted to touch Eve Taylor.

* * *

'CAN I OFFER YOU SOME MORE?' He gestured towards the rest of the pizza left in the box.

'No, thank you. That was delicious.' Eve wiped her fingers on the paper napkin and gave the dark-haired man beside her an apologetic smile. 'I guess you didn't expect to be landed with a tearful *and* hungry woman all on the one night?'

'Hey, come on,' Mark teased, 'it's comforting for us modern men to know we still have a role to play in a woman's life.'

Eve couldn't help wondering who the lucky woman was in Mark Delaney's life. He hadn't allowed her to feel any embarrassment about her tears and when she'd recovered her composure he'd suggested sending out for a pizza. After that there had seemed something so natural about eating and chatting together.

Now she looked at her watch. It was getting late.

Mark caught her glance. 'Well, I guess you'll need time to decide what to do about this.'

Face suddenly hardening, Eve shook her head. 'Not at all. I have absolutely no intention of letting that property go. I'd like you to handle everything that needs doing for me, Mark.'

He heard the quiet determination in her voice. 'Of course. If that's your decision I'd be glad to. It'll just be a matter of going through the appropriate steps.' He rose to his feet and walked her down the hall.

At the door she turned to face him. 'And you promise me this can be done without having to reveal my identity?'

'The court will need proof, of course, but that can be withheld from the others concerned. For total security we can even name you as Eve Walenska.'

'Good.'

Eve felt reassured. For so many reasons she needed to keep her identity secret. The media would go to town on the story and she couldn't risk that, either for her own career, or for what it might mean to her mother's state of health.

Then, too, there was the terrible complication of her friendship with Rachel. How might that be affected if it was discovered that it was Eve Taylor who was instrumental in killing off the Symons' dream project?

What really mattered, she thought with a sense of giddy triumph, was that a long delayed justice had finally occurred. The Rolfe family had cheated her mother so many years before and now in turn Hugh Rolfe would be denied the financial salvation he so obviously needed.

Warmed by a feeling of satisfaction, Eve put out her hand to the man with whom she had spent so emotional an evening.

'Goodnight, Mark. I'll leave it in your hands now. And thank you again. For everything.'

As his hand closed around hers their eyes met in a magnetic exchange.

'I'll be in touch,' he said.

* * *

EVE WASTED no time in ringing Janet to tell her the details of her meeting with Mark Delaney. Her voice broke with emotion when she described her father's letter.

'He loved your mother very, very much, my dear,' Janet said gently. 'I always told you that. And he must have been delighted that there was going to be a child.'

At the other end of the line, Eve's fingers tightened around the receiver. 'Nothing will make me part with that land, Janty. When Hugh Rolfe learns that, he'll see that the woman they all tried so hard to destroy achieved a sort of justice after all.'

* * *

HUGH ROLFE SAT DRINKING long into the night. Fear and anger gnawed at his insides. His hope of solving his financial nightmare had been blown apart by the phone call earlier that day from the smart-Alec lawyer.

'... not interested in going through with the negotiations ... wishes to hold onto the property in its present state...'

Hugh Rolfe's mottled face twisted with rage. Whatever bitch Marianne Rolfe had given birth to was refusing to come to the party.

'Who is she? Tell me her name!' he'd demanded. 'I want my lawyers to deal with her direct!'

But Mark Delaney had made it clear. The woman had no wish to be identified. 'My client has indicated that everything be handled through myself,' came the cold reply.

With one swallow Hugh Rolfe finished off his drink and struggled out of his chair to pour himself another. The financial hounds were at his heels ... banks, finance companies, debt collectors. He was barely holding the company together. So far he'd managed to keep the financial press from sniffing out just exactly how bad things were. He'd been betting everything on the deal with Symons getting him off the hook.

And he wasn't about to be beaten by some stubborn nobody.

32

Mamie Howard was excited about her trip. With the weather growing colder it would be good to get out of England.

Apart from a little arthritis in her hip she was in surprisingly good health for a woman of her age and was looking forward to the convention in Sydney.

She had been widowed almost fifteen years and her work for the Red Cross had become an even more important part of her life. Mamie Howard had certainly done her duty by her fellow man.

'Do you think I might need an overcoat that time of year, Julia?' Her dark eyes gleamed in anticipation as she questioned her friend. Julia Reynolds had a daughter living in Sydney. She'd been there three or four times to visit; she'd know exactly what one had to take.

'Oh, I don't think so, dearest. Just a warm cardigan should be enough.' Julia Reynolds quite enjoyed her feeling of superiority at being able to tell Mamie Howard anything.

The two women had been friends for years but Julia had always been a little overawed by Mamie's incredible energy and zest, her tendency to organize everyone and everything.

She meant well, of course, Julia told herself as she helped herself to another scone; she'd baked them fresh for Mamie's visit and as she took a small bite she hated to admit it but Mamie's were usually moister.

Discussion about Australia and the forthcoming Red Cross convention took up the rest of Mamie's visit. As they waited for the arrival of the taxi to take her home, Julia suddenly had a thought. From a shelf in the spare room she produced a pile of brightly colored magazines, which she offered to her friend.

'Take these with you, dearest.' She made a feeble attempt to blow away the dust. 'Anne sends them now and then,' she explained, referring to the daughter who lived in Australia. 'Some of them might be a little out of date but you're bound to get some more information on the place.'

* * *

IT WAS two days later that Mamie Howard was flipping through a rather tattered *Australian Women's Weekly*. Glancing at the date she hated to think when Julia might last have had a clean out. Some of these dated from the fifties, for goodness sakes...

* * *

HUGH WAS DOING his best to placate a very angry Leo Symons.

'Look, Leo, I'm sure there's some way out of this without dragging everything through the courts.'

He had flown to Surfers Paradise to thrash out the problem and make sure Leo Symons wasn't ready to walk away from the project without a fight.

The developer's lips were set in a hard line. 'You don't seriously think we can cover up the delay much longer? The press are already starting to ask questions.' He glared at the man who sat in his living room. 'Believe me, this is more important to me than you could possibly know.'

Hugh Rolfe leaned forward in his chair. His face was so close that the older man caught the whiff of alcohol on his breath. He spoke earnestly. 'You leave it to me, Leo. I'm going to find that bitch. And I'm going to make sure she decides to get right out of the picture...'

Leo Symons could hardly hide his contempt. Did this fool really think he needed his help?

He had already set the wheels in motion.

* * *

IN ATTENDING to the legal processes Mark was in touch with Eve on a regular basis over the next couple of weeks. He had her private home number and was pleasantly surprised to find that she lived just a short distance away.

'There're a couple of papers I have to get you to sign, Eve. Perhaps I could have them delivered to your office?'

At the other end of the line she took a deep breath. 'If it can wait until tomorrow evening perhaps you'd care to drop in here? I could repay the pizza.' Her hand gripped tightly around the receiver as she waited for his reply. I can't let this happen to me, she told herself. Not now. Not at this stage of my life.

Mark Delaney's heart had suddenly started to beat at twice the rate. 'That sounds like a great idea,' he answered with deceptive calm.

But the next morning a disturbing event distracted Mark from his anticipation of the evening ahead. Overnight his office had been broken into and papers and files obviously rifled through.

'Told you we should have changed the locks when we moved in,' Sean Murray reminded him, rather self righteously. He gave his partner an enquiring look. 'Any idea what they could've been after? You got anything big happening?'

Mark shook his head, but there was a worried look in his eyes.

* * *

EVE NEEDED time to get home from the network after the evening's program and Mark arrived a few minutes after nine.

She greeted him at the door, face free of the heavy television make-up, dressed casually in dark leggings and a cream sweater. Some wonderful scent wafted from her as he followed her into a living room that was an eclectic mixture of Asian and modern furnishings.

Besides his leather document file Mark carried a bottle of excellent Shiraz Cabernet. 'For your cellar,' he proffered with a smile.

'Oh... thank you. But why don't we share it now?'

In a few moments they had their wine glasses in front of them and Mark was producing the documents he'd brought with him. 'This just starts the procedure of claim.'

It only took a few minutes to deal with the formalities and then Eve led the way through to an intimate dining area that overlooked a spot-lit, shrub-filled courtyard.

The meal was simple – chicken, rice and salad – and as they chatted and refilled their glasses they both began to relax.

Mark was a good listener and Eve's instincts told her she could trust him. It wasn't long before she found herself willing to speak about things she had never been able to discuss with anyone before.

By the time they retired to the living room again Mark felt he pretty much knew and understood where Eve Taylor had found her drive and determination.

'I've never been able to forgive the Rolfes for what they did to my mother.' Her voice was thick with emotion as they sat close together on the sofa. 'They cost her her future and me my past.'

She turned to look at him. 'I can't pretend, Mark, no matter how it makes you think of me. I know enough about Hugh Rolfe's affairs to realized that the failure of this deal is going to cost him very, very dearly.'

Mark stared at the fierce light in those beautiful violet eyes. 'But there's another reason too for retaining that property, isn't there?' he asked softly.

Eve held his gaze. He understands, she thought in wonder. He really understands.

That there was no way she could sell her father's gift of love.

* * *

IT WAS ALMOST midnight but it took a real effort to bring himself to say goodnight.

As they stood by the open front door Mark said, 'I'll lodge these documents as soon as possible. Don't worry about a thing.'

'I'm not,' she answered simply. 'I trust you, Mark.'

Their glances held through the long moment of hesitation.

Then his arms slid around her and she was turning her face up to his. Their lips met in an eagerness of mutual response, the kiss joining them in a soldering heat. Eve felt jolted by the warm firm strength of Mark's body stretched along her own. Oh, God, how long had it been since she'd felt like this?

She was breathing in the scent of his aftershave, his silky hair, drowning in a sensation of a joy and desire she had never expected to find again.

Breathless, both stunned by the force of their attraction, they reluctantly drew apart.

'I've wanted to do that from the first moment I saw you,' he whispered huskily.

It took every ounce of willpower for them to say goodnight.

* * *

BUT THE NIGHT held another surprise for Mark.

As he went to put the key into his front lock, the door swung open.

They'd been there too.

* * *

'I CAN ONLY THINK that they're not giving up! That they're determined to find out the identity of Marianne Rolfe's child.'

At his desk the fit-looking man watched with alert eyes as Mark Delaney paced around the small, file-crammed office near Central Station. Tony Nugent had known Mark Delaney since they'd played cricket together for Shore's Under Fifteens. Both had studied Law at Sydney University, but while Mark had gone into his father's firm

Tony Nugent had taken a different turn, being recruited into ASIS, the Australian Secret Intelligence Service operating abroad.

Disillusion hadn't taken long to set in – especially when Tony found himself undertaking covert operations which, to his way of looking at things, seemed to be actually working against Australian neutrality.

His resignation had come soon after. But his time with ASIS had instilled a need for more excitement than might be found in the everyday practice of the law. Noting Australia's increasing corporate and criminal connection with the rest of the world, Tony Nugent had made the decision to establish himself as an international investigator and security expert. That had been six years ago and his network of worldwide contacts had ensured a steady growth in business ever since.

Now his old friend was asking for help.

'Look, Tony,' Mark swung round on him, his face creased with anxiety, 'Leo Symons carries a lot of weight in this country; he's got lots of influential friends. I don't want him discovering my client's identity and being in a position to hassle her.'

'You're pretty sure he's behind the break-ins?'

'It's either him or Rolfe but Symons has the resources and probably even more at stake.'

Tony Nugent nodded. 'Leave it with me.'

* * *

Eve was apologetic but she couldn't accept his invitation to dinner on Saturday evening.

'I'm sorry. But I try to get up to the cottage as often as possible on weekends.'

'Well, I guess we'll have to catch up next week some time.'

The disappointment in his voice was unmistakable.

Eve hesitated. She was remembering how it had felt when Mark kissed her, held her. And then she heard herself asking, 'Why don't you come with me, Mark? Can you get away Saturday morning?'

* * *

THEY DROVE up in his BMW, arriving in time for lunch.

Janet had been alerted and the table was set for four on the sun-dappled lawn.

As soon as Eve walked into the house and introduced the tall, dark-haired solicitor who bore such a resemblance to Paul, Janet knew.

She saw it in the new sparkle in the girl's eyes, in the glow and animation in her face. Mark Delaney had been the one to break through those walls of fear and distrust the older woman thought.

When the meal was cleared away Janet took Marianne off for her regular afternoon nap.

'You should show Mark some of the beautiful walking trails around here.'

Eve turned to him with a smile. 'That appeal? D'you feel like walking off lunch?'

'Sounds a great idea.'

* * *

THE PATH WAS BATHED in the late autumn sunlight. It was off the regular tourist track and ended in a little grove of trees. They sat beside each other on the mossy grass and peered through the leaves over the deep valley below.

It was a place where magic could occur.

They stretched out beside each other and Paul's hand cupped her chin. Gently he leaned over to kiss her. As his lips and tongue caressed her, Eve felt jolted by the sheer electricity of his touch. Her breath raced as his mouth pressed more urgently against her own. Then they were helping each other to undress, were enfolded in their nakedness, hands exploring, caressing and stroking.

Mark's soft touch between her thighs and then at the center of her pleasure prepared Eve for that greater excitement. When he could see she couldn't bear to wait a moment longer he finally moved his long, lean body over hers.

And there, among the dying gold-brown colors of autumn, they brought each other alive for the first time.

33

It was the meeting Eve had known would occur sooner or later, but one which filled her with apprehension all the same.

On one of her flying visits to Sydney Rachel had invited her for a meal at her apartment. While not wanting to refuse, Eve knew the evening would be difficult to face.

Now, as she listened to her friend's recounting of recent events, she found herself having to fight back irrational feelings of betrayal and guilt.

'This is taking a real toll on my father, Eve. He doesn't say much but I can tell. Just at the moment the company's financial situation is rather more difficult than I ever told you.'

Rachel seemed unable to sit still. Dressed in jeans and a black knit top she was pacing around the expanse of the living room. Her lovely features looked strained as she confided in her friend.

'Oh God!' Rachel burst out. 'If only that woman could be persuaded to sell. Why in the world does she want to hold onto the place? She could make a packet out of it!'

Eve sat stiffly, her stomach clenched into a hard, cold knot. 'Perhaps,' she ventured quietly, 'she's not interested in money.'

Rachel rounded on her, sweeping her arm in an expansive arc. 'Everyone's interested in money!'

Then she caught the expression on Eve's face. 'Oh God, darling. I'm sorry.' She moved quickly across the room and dropping to the sofa beside her, gripped Eve's hand in apology. 'I didn't mean to attack you like that. Please forgive me. There's no need for me to take my worry out on you.'

'There's nothing to apologize for, Rachel.' But Eve's discomfort was growing and she managed to cut the evening short.

As the elevator doors opened the two women kissed goodbye. 'Come up and see us soon, Eve. Both Katie and I miss you.' Rachel forced a smile. 'And I promise I'll try to be in a better mood.'

But as soon as she was behind the closed door of her apartment Rachel's worried frown returned. Thanks to her father's reliance on Japanese financing the future of their company was on the line. If Paradise Grove was truly stalled it could cost them everything.

But there was no need to saddle Eve with all that.

* * *

'So, I WASN'T IMAGINING THINGS?'

Tony Nugent shook his head. 'No. The telephone lines to your home and office – both bugged. Easiest trick in the book.'

Tony had asked his friend to meet him in the lobby bar of the Sheraton Hotel. It was the safest way to pass on what he'd discovered.

'They're determined, I'll give that to them.' Mark's face was set hard.

Tony Nugent picked up his beer glass and asked, as he raised it to his lips, 'How long's it going to take you to iron out all the legal bits and pieces? Still need a full court hearing?'

'It's just formalities, but another three weeks at least.' Mark gave his friend a tense look. 'You know what really worries me about all this? If anything happens to my client before this matter's finalized that property's going to revert to Hugh Rolfe.'

Tony Nugent didn't need it spelled out.

* * *

Mamie Howard thought Sydney was the most beautiful city in the world. She'd decided that the moment her Qantas flight had given her a first view of the famous Opera House, the bridge and the massive harbor with its numerous coves and bays. The sight below had taken her breath away.

I'm glad I lived long enough to see this, she thought in awe.

And, she added earnestly, to fit together the final pieces of a puzzle she had never resolved.

* * *

The convention was being held at the Masonic Hall in the city and Mamie had been billeted with a local committee member.

Nola Donaldson was a rotund, loud but good natured woman a few years younger than Mamie. She lived alone in a small single-fronted cottage in an inner city suburb that edged the water.

To begin with Mamie had had to overcome jet lag; then she had been absorbed by the various doings of the convention itself. There were quite a few dedicated lifelong members like herself ... widows who were still active in the organization – and they enjoyed exchanging reminiscences. The war years in particular featured heavily.

It was almost a week before the Englishwoman found the right moment to raise the matter that had been on her mind ever since she'd seen the photograph in that out-of-date magazine. Now she brought it out of her purse after she and Nola Donaldson had finished their simple meal of lamb chops, mint sauce and vegetables.

'I never serve kangaroo when I've got visitors!' Her hostess offered the same joke at almost every meal she placed on the table.

'Nola...' Mamie had to force herself into the unfamiliar casual address favored by Australians. 'I wonder if I could show you this?'

She unfolded the piece of paper and handed it across.

'What is it, love?' Nola Donaldson peered shortsightedly and reached for her spectacles. She smoothed out the clipping and read aloud the caption beneath the press photograph. 'Mr and Mrs Charles Rolfe were first-night guests at the Australian Ballet's performance this week of *Giselle*.'

She looked at the date and then over at her new friend. 'Goodness, love. This was a long time ago.'

'I think I recognize the woman, Nola. I was in Europe after the liberation. I met her then, a Polish refugee – if it's the same girl. I'd like to make contact again.'

Her hostess was staring at the photograph. Slowly she shook her head. 'Polish... yes... A terrible business really. It's coming back to me now.'

'What do you mean?' Mamie looked at her curiously.

Nola Donaldson explained.

* * *

THE HOSPITAL WOULD TELL her nothing except the name of some lawyer who was, according to the nasal voice on the phone, 'handling anything to do with Marianne Walenska'.

Just to hear the name sent a shudder down Mamie Howard's spine. She had never forgotten.

* * *

MARK CALLED round to give Eve the startling news. It wasn't something he wanted to take a risk with on the telephone.

'Her name's Mamie Howard.' As they sat on the living room sofa he explained about the Englishwoman and how she had come to see the photograph and recognize Marianne.

'She claims she was with the Red Cross in Europe after the war and it was then she met your mother.

Afterwards she took her back to England; into her own home, it seems. Then one day Marianne just disappeared. Went to London and never came back.

'Apparently Mamie Howard always wondered what had happened to her. She's since heard the story of what took place at this end of course, but she still wanted to get in touch with Marianne. I must say she seems totally genuine. I told her I'd get back to her – though I never mentioned a daughter.'

Eve had listened without interrupting. Slowly a little flicker of excitement lit inside her. Mamie Howard had no reason to lie. The Englishwoman had known her mother as a young girl.

She felt her pulse race. The unexpected visitor from the past might be the one person to hold the key to her mother's recovery.

* * *

MARK SET UP THE MEETING. He arranged to pick up Mamie Howard early on Saturday morning – the day before she was due to return to England.

'Marianne Walenska lives out of Sydney, Mrs Howard. It's possible of course for you to meet, but bear in mind she is incapable of speech or normal reaction.'

'I would very much like to see her, Mr Delaney,' came the crisp reply.

* * *

MARK SPENT the Friday evening at Eve's home. The relationship between them needed no explanation or promises. In so short a time they both instinctively knew that in each other they had found that combination of passion and inner peace which made them whole.

As their bodies entwined they whispered their love, stroked and held and caressed, until the urgency of desire exploded in their veins and left them drowning in each other's consciousness.

'I don't think I existed before I knew you,' he whispered into her hair.

Eve knew exactly what he meant. The same way she knew that the memory of Paul had finally been laid to rest.

* * *

FACE HIDDEN BEHIND DARK GLASSES, Eve waited in the rear seat of the BMW as Mark fetched Mamie Howard from the house.

She watched them approach down the narrow garden path and saw a sturdily built woman with grey curls framing pale skin and a strong determined face.

As Mamie Howard settled herself into the front passenger seat she became aware of the girl sitting in the rear.

Mark made the introductions.

'Mrs Howard, this is Marianne's daughter... Eve.' It probably didn't matter, he decided, but he deliberately avoided offering Eve's surname.

As the car pulled away from the curbside Mamie turned a little stiffly to stare at the girl who had removed her dark glasses.

'Yes,' she smiled, taking in the fair hair and high cheekbones, 'of *course* you are Marianne's daughter...'

* * *

THE JOURNEY PASSED QUICKLY as they talked. Mamie Howard told them everything she knew. Some of it Eve had already discovered for herself on her visit to Poland: the murder of her mother's family, Marianne's sexual abuse at the hands of the Germans...

But it was what happened afterwards that the elderly Englishwoman was able to fill in.

'I found her close to death when our forces entered Berlin – in the basement of a bombed-out building where one kind woman had done her best to keep Marianne alive.

'We got her medical assistance at once but I really didn't expect her to make it.' Mamie gave an involuntary shudder. 'Her face... it was a mess of bloodied jelly, encrusted and already showing signs of infection.'

Leaning forward in her rear seat Eve listened pale-faced to the terrible story. She said tentatively, 'We ... we knew there had been extensive facial surgery. Do you know how her injuries occurred?'

The older woman nodded. Her sad tired eyes stared straight ahead. 'He meant to kill her – after he was finished with her. She talked about it in her delirium and immediately afterwards when she was recovering in hospital.'

'Who? Who tried to kill her?' It was a cool day but Eve could feel the sudden stickiness of her palms.

'The German. The same officer who'd murdered her family and then kept her to rape at will. When the Russians broke through, the beast used her as cover for his own escape.'

Mamie Howard's eyes grew dim with memory. 'And as soon as she'd served his purpose he beat her and left her for dead. Only Marianne recovered – although her face was an indescribable sight. That was why I arranged the operation in Paris; the surgery which gave her back her beauty.'

The elderly woman's voice dropped and she shook her head. 'And how she hated that – having her looks restored, I mean. I thought it would make her happy, but later I understood – her armor was gone. She was terrified that men might find her attractive again...'

Eve's heart was pounding in her chest. Mamie Howard had heard the story from her mother's own lips. The same monster who had violated her, who had cold bloodedly murdered her family, had in turn tried to kill Marianne, too. Biting back her emotions, she asked rawly, 'Did she ever tell you his name? Did she ever speak of the man who did that to her?'

Mamie Howard again turned to look at the young woman who sat behind her. 'Your mother mentioned his name only once. At the very beginning. By the time she recovered enough to return with me to England she had lost her capacity for speech. It was as if she had found the means of keeping the nightmare at bay.'

Eve's flesh prickled in nervous anticipation. The same way her mother had reacted to the nightmare years later...

She could barely form her next question. 'Can ... can you recall the German's name, Mrs Howard?'

Mamie's mouth clamped into a tight, hard line.

'I've never forgotten it.'

* * *

THERE, in the living room of the cottage the meeting between the two women took place. Marianne Walenska and the former Red Cross nurse who had saved her life.

There was a gleam of tears in Mamie Howard's eyes as she kissed Marianne's cheek. 'Oh, Marianne... Oh, my dear...'

Tense and strained, Eve stood back with Mark and Janet. Holding her breath she watched intently for any sign of response in her mother's expression.

Marianne looked into her visitor's face, her features puckering into a tiny frown. For a few brief seconds some sort of struggle seemed to be going on behind those faded blue eyes.

Then – nothing.

Marianne turned away and, moving to a seat in the corner of the room, stared placidly out of the window.

On the journey back to Sydney Eve's heart was heavy with despair. While Mamie Howard had helped put together the missing pieces in her mother's background her presence hadn't managed to trigger the breakthrough Eve had so longed for.

When the car came to a stop the elderly woman turned and patted Eve's hand. 'I know this has been very disappointing for you, my dear. I can only say again how sorry I am that I wasn't able to help in any way.'

But that wasn't quite true.

Mamie Howard had known the name of the man who had left Marianne Walenska to die.

34

As experienced as he was, Tony Nugent hadn't been able to totally hide his surprise as Mark ushered the tall, confident blonde into his office.

Eve Taylor was Mark's very private client. *And* the daughter of Marianne and the late Charles Rolfe... Jesus...

As he offered them both a seat, the investigator decided that the acclaimed television presenter was even more attractive in the flesh than on the small screen. And his instincts told him that Mark obviously thought so too. Something going on there, he thought; he'd take a bet on it.

The three of them made a crowd in the small office and Tony Nugent listened carefully as Eve Taylor explained what she wanted him to do.

'Whatever it takes, however much it costs, I want this murderer tracked down. Even if it's only to assure me he's already dead.'

Nugent leaned back in his cracked leather chair and looked thoughtful. 'And the name is our only starting point?'

Eve nodded and fixed the man opposite with an intense look. 'Mark tells me you used to be with ASIS, Tony. You must have some contacts that might be able to help?'

'Sure,' the investigator sounded positive. 'And the good news is that this sort of search might be a lot easier now that Eastern Europe's opened up.' He scratched his high-domed forehead. 'Is there a time factor in all this? I mean, how quickly are you looking for results?'

'We've waited over forty years too long already,' Eve said with cold ferocity.

* * *

It took enormous discipline to concentrate on anything other than the mission Eve had given to Mark's old friend.

Yet no one watching her nightly would have guessed at her inner turmoil. In front of the cameras she was as competent and coolly articulate as ever.

Thank God for Mark, Eve thought. He would make the waiting endurable as Tony Nugent began his search in Europe for the man named Max Klauser.

Having exhausted all his contacts in Bonn with no result, the Australian investigator turned his attention to the recently accessible files of the former German Democratic Republic.

A few appropriately placed bribes, and full facilities were extended. After that it took Nugent just thirty six hours to find the first clue.

He faxed the information to Mark in Sydney. Max Klauser, it seemed, had been the son-in-law of a high ranking Nazi official. There were fingerprints on file but no photograph. After his escape from Poland, Klauser, like so many others with reason to fear, appeared to have vanished.

'But don't worry, darling,' Mark assured Eve as he passed on the news, 'Tony won't give up.'

* * *

As he walked down Pitt Street to where he had left his car Hugh Rolfe was hyperventilating. He had just had a nightmare meeting with his bankers. Half a dozen grim-faced men in dark suits informing him that his personal debts now stood at $8 million. And this time the bastards were after blood. They were about to put up for sale the enormous merino stud that had been in his family's possession for generations.

It was in the hope of overcoming the ravages of drought and the sharp drop in wool prices – not to mention his gambling debts – that Hugh had borrowed heavily against the property. Artificial insemination of stock was the way to go, he had told the money men. The returns wouldn't come overnight but they would certainly arrive.

Yet the technology had never achieved the profits Hugh had envisaged. His only hope had lain in refinancing on the basis of his joint venture with Leo Symons.

And now some unknown bitch was doing her best to screw that.

He had to find out who she was.

* * *

THE ADDRESS WAS A STARK, shabby-looking block of flats circa fifties Marxist architecture.

Tony Nugent climbed the dirty concrete stairs, searching for number 18. Its occupant should be a man called Hans Lomberg. His search had eventually turned up a name and address for the cousin of Max Klauser's wife.

At last he found it. A grimy blue door and a bell that didn't work.

'*Ja? Wer ist da?*' Through the closed door an aggressive male voice answered his knock.

'*Polizei*' Tony answered curtly. He was gambling that the Wall hadn't been down long enough to remove the populace's magnified respect and fear of the law.

He heard movement and the door was opened by an elderly man leaning on a knobbled walking stick. There was a sour defensive expression on his sunken face.

Tony flashed his German version international ID. It indicated his rank as lieutenant in some non-existent organization.

'You are Hans Albert Lomberg?' he asked in German.

'What of it?' The old man had barely a tooth in his head and was old enough not to try too hard at hiding his belligerence.

'A few questions. It will only take a short time.'

The man's contempt was obvious. Which no doubt, was why he had no compunction in telling his visitor about the man named Max Klauser.

'I told Hanna he was a nothing. An opportunist. But she was determined to marry him. Even her father, my uncle, was taken in by Klauser's smooth talk of ideology and the Party. Nobody would listen to me.'

The old man shook his head. His voice softened as he sat stiffly on the edge of the worn sofa, his gnarled hands planted atop his stick. '...Hanna, I said, you are making a big mistake, don't do this. I begged her to reconsider – not to do anything in haste, but no, she was headstrong. She took no notice.'

So the old boy had lost out to a rival, Tony Nugent concluded.

'And after the war? What happened to them?'

Hans Lomberg shrugged his skinny shoulders. 'Who knows? So many disappeared at that time. I never heard from Hanna again.' Again the note of loss was detectable in his voice.

Another dead end. Tony stood up. '*Dankeschon*.'

He had his hand on the doorknob when the old man, shuffling to his feet, pulled out a drawer on an ugly, stained sideboard. 'Look–' he fumbled through the mess of papers, odds and ends. 'You see?' He produced the photographs triumphantly. They were tied with blue ribbon. Romantic.

As Tony waited, Lomberg moved closer to display with pride the pictures of his love. 'She sent them to me. Wedding photographs,' he snorted, 'but better than nothing.'

The Australian looked down at a grainy black and white photo of Max Klauser and his bride. The German, sharp-featured and unsmiling, was in his SS uniform. The bride, looking very young and blissfully happy, wore a slim-fitting sheath and a garland of flowers in her blonde hair.

It took just twenty American dollars to part Hans Lomberg from one of his mementoes of his lost love. Hard currency was hard currency, after all.

Not that a snapshot taken almost fifty years ago was going to prove much help the Australian thought dismally as he walked away.

* * *

Twenty-four hours after his return to Australia Tony Nugent met with his client and Mark.

Slipping the black and white photograph out of the envelope he handed it to Eve.

'So out of date it's probably worthless,' he commented.

But Eve barely heard him. The cold numbness of shock seeped through her as she stared at the images she held in her hand.

And it wasn't the man named Max Klauser who held her horrified gaze.

35

'Oh, God, Mark... I still can't believe it. It's just so incredible...'

He was holding her tight, feeling the terrible tension in her body. 'I know, I know, darling,' he stroked her hair in an attempt at comfort. 'It's been a shock. Let's just leave it to Tony now. That'll be the final proof.'

They were together in Eve's bed but neither was able to sleep. As he held her close Mark thought back to the morning, remembered the expression on her face as she'd stared at the photograph Tony Nugent had brought back from Berlin.

'Darling?' he'd looked at her in alarm. 'What's the matter? What is it?'

Slowly she'd turned to him, face ashen, eyes wide and staring. Her lips moved but emitted no sound.

'Eve!' Mark was by her side, his arm around her. '*Tell me.* What is it?'

And finally she had found the words.

The woman in the photo was Rachel Symonds' mother.

* * *

As she lay in the comfort of Mark's arms Eve replayed in her mind the exact moment when Rachel had shown her the photograph.

It had been the day of the "Scrutiny" interview. They were talking about the past. From a drawer in her desk Rachel had produced the photograph of her mother taken on her wedding day. It showed the bride, alone, blonde and radiant, posed in a garden setting.

'It's the only one I've got,' Rachel had explained and Eve had heard the wistfulness in her voice. 'I found it among her things after she'd died. I didn't even show Dad. I guess as a kid I wanted to keep it totally for myself.' She gave a sad shrug. 'Everything else was lost in the war, the escape from Czechoslovakia... And unfortunately there were none taken of her out here. According to my father she was just one of those people who hated getting in front of a camera.'

And now Eve knew why.

In escaping his past Max Klauser had taken steps to change his own appearance, yet as long as his wife kept a low profile there had been no reason to alter hers...

Eve had seen the shock on the faces of the two men as she told her story. It was hard for any of them to believe that one of Australia's wealthiest and most powerful businessmen was a former Nazi murderer. Yet even presented with the evidence, Eve looked for some excuse, anything that would dispel the nightmare; that might help to save Rachel and their friendship.

There had been a plea in her voice as she'd asked of Tony Nugent, 'How can we be sure that Hanna Klauser didn't remarry? And that Leo Symons is in fact exactly who he professes to be – the Czech refugee, Leo Simek?'

The investigator had given her a long, steady look. 'Simple. I've got Klauser's fingerprints. To get a passport in Australia up until the early sixties you had to have your prints taken...'

The next afternoon the three of them met again. Accessing contacts from his ASIS days, Tony Nugent had run a fingerprint check in double quick time.

'He's Klauser.'

Eve's fears – and hopes – were confirmed.

* * *

Tony Nugent explained just how someone like Max Klauser might have slipped through the immigration process and into Australia.

'In the fifties, don't forget, the threat of Communism was the bogey of all democratic governments. In Australia the Communist Party was at the peak of its popularity and there was a feeling in some circles that the West had fought the wrong enemy: instead of the Germans it should have been Stalin who was crushed.'

The investigator's voice rose with excitement. 'This is an area I've been interested in probing for a long time. I know from their own records that it wasn't unknown for our intelligence people to turn a blind eye to former Nazis trying to get into Australia. These men, after all, were proven fighters against Communism. And for those few who were permitted to emigrate here there were certainly hundreds of others who managed to erase any connection with their Nazi past and enter the country under the guise of genuine refugees. It would have been easy enough for someone like Klauser to manufacture a completely new identity. No doubt his father-in-law's connections would have helped.'

He looked at Eve. Her face was still white and strained. He guessed what she was thinking.

'You have to go public with this don't you, Eve?'

* * *

It would be a massive expose.

The story would have to be broken on "Taylor Made" as soon as possible and in Tony Nugent, Eve had the perfect helpmate. The program would focus on Leo Symons but would also draw into its net others whose secrets might be discovered in the now-accessible archives and libraries of a liberated Eastern Europe.

They knew they had to work quickly. If ASIO, Symons, or others being investigated, got a whiff of the bombshell about to be dropped immediate cover-up action was bound to be taken. Given warning, big names might be able to pull off anything.

Over the next three weeks Eve and Tony worked at a feverish pace with a small crew sworn to secrecy. Faxes and information flew between the investigator and his network of contacts in Europe, and the deeper they dug the more the story grew. Important people and distinguished careers would be on the line. There could be no delay in putting the story to air. Only then would the resultant public outcry ensure a full investigation of all concerned.

Amid all the desperate work there was one dread Eve kept pushing to the back of her mind. The one aspect of all this she hated to face.

Rachel.

The thought of the pain and hurt and horror she was about to cause the woman who had become her friend filled her with anguish.

But Eve knew that the tragedy of her mother's past and her professional ethics would allow her no alternative.

* * *

TWO DAYS before the program was to go to air Eve faced a nervous Ty Cameron. After drawn-out consultations with the network owner and lawyers he'd been relieved when they were finally given the nod to run with the story. The fact that their own anchorwoman was so personally involved could only add to the enormous impact of the expose.

For more than a week now "Taylor Made" had been running trailers for the 'revelations that were going to stun Australia'. Curiosity and expectation were running high among both the public and the program's rivals. And they were going to get a lot more than they'd bargained for Eve thought with grim satisfaction as she sat in Ty Cameron's office.

As they went over the final details, the producer of "Taylor Made" couldn't help feeling a mixture of excitement and apprehension.

'This is going to explode right in the heart of this country, Eve – business, the stock markets, politics, the intelligence forces – the impact's going to be felt everywhere.' He gave her a long, serious look. 'Are you absolutely sure you want to do it this way?'

She knew what he meant. Leo Symons could be unmasked without her own background coming to light. But Eve was determined to tell the truth about her mother's tragedy. Even if it cost her own career and future.

'There's no going back now, Ty,' she stated quietly.

* * *

AND THERE WASN'T.

Yet as the countdown to the expose began, Eve felt more and more tortured by thoughts of Rachel. Total secrecy about the program had been maintained and the woman she had grown so close to had no hint of the horror to come.

It was late on the evening before the program went to air that Eve knew she couldn't do it.

She had to warn Rachel.

36

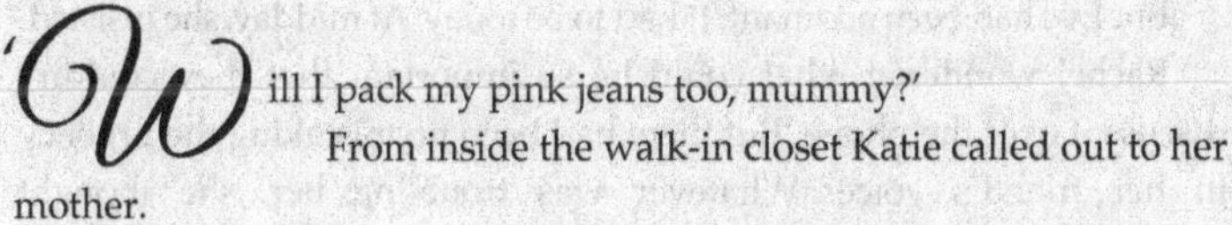

'Will I pack my pink jeans too, mummy?' From inside the walk-in closet Katie called out to her mother.

School had broken up just two days before and she and her mother were going to spend a few days at their house in the hinterland. It was more a cottage really, Katie supposed, compared to their place on the Coast, but she loved it there.

Built on a narrow jutting ledge at the end of a long, mysterious drive through shadowy rainforest, the cottage was small and cosy with rough, wooden beams and a pot belly stove. From almost every room there were wonderful views of the distant ocean.

'Oh, darling, you won't need all *that.*' Walking into the bedroom Rachel exclaimed at the sight of her daughter's overflowing suitcase on the bed.

Katie emerged, protesting, from the wardrobe. 'Yes, I will, Mum. It might get cold – or the Johnsons might ask us over for dinner.'

Rachel hid a smile. So that was it. The Johnsons were their nearest neighbors in the hills. They had a fourteen-year-old son, Michael. Her daughter, it seemed, was growing up.

And her figure was filling out too, she noted, casting an appraising glance at the pouting girl. Any day now she'd have to buy that first bra.

'Come on, now, sweetheart.' Ignoring her daughter's mood she gave an encouraging smile and began to sort through the clothes. 'Let's just take exactly what you'll need. We'll only be gone a week, after all.'

Rachel loved escaping to the hills almost as much as her daughter, but business didn't allow her to be away too long. Even now there were half a dozen things she had to attend to before they left.

Including, she thought, her meeting with Eve.

She frowned now as she zipped up her daughter's suitcase. Eve had sounded so strained on the telephone last night. She was flying up to the Coast and insisted on seeing Rachel around midday today.

'Oh, darling, I wish you'd have let me know sooner. I'm taking Katie up to the mountains tomorrow. What's so important? Can't it wait until I get back?'

But Eve had been adamant. It had to be today. At midday, she insisted.

Rachel wondered what could be so important that they couldn't discuss it over the phone. But there had been no mistaking the urgency in her friend's voice. Whatever was troubling her, she thought anxiously, Eve obviously needed to talk to someone she could trust.

* * *

Eve had barely slept. Her skin felt icy and her stomach churned as she endured the short flight north to the popular tourist strip.

She was dreading the moment that awaited her. Dreading the fact that she should be the one to bring such devastating news. The stark tragedy of the situation made her feel physically ill as she stared with blank unseeing eyes out of the cabin window.

The woman whose friendship she had come to cherish was innocent. But in a few hours' time, when the truth about Leo Symons' past was revealed, in one brutal blow Rachel would lose her father, her business, and every last shred of her respect and status.

And she'll always know that I was the one to destroy her, Eve thought in sick despair.

* * *

Her hire car was standing by when she arrived. She couldn't afford to wait for taxis in either direction. She had timed the meeting precisely. Rachel would be forewarned, but she would have no opportunity to do anything to block the program going to air.

Even so, Eve hadn't told anyone, not even Mark, what she'd intended to do. *They'd say there was a risk*, she told herself. *They'd only try to talk me out of it.*

Nerves stretching tighter with every passing kilometer, she headed up the highway.

* * *

Preoccupied with her fears she barely noticed that the security gates to the beautiful riverside home stood open. She parked the car and made her way to the front door. For a long moment after she rang the bell there was no reply.

She pushed the button again, heard the chime resound through the house. Nothing.

Eve frowned, then finally called, 'Rachel? Are you there?'

Still no reply. And this time, without much expectation, she tried the front door handle.

To her surprise the door was unlocked.

Stepping into the cool of the tiled marble foyer she repeated her call.

But still there was no sign of life in the house – even when she tentatively made her way down the hall and into the spacious all-white kitchen.

Her brows drew together. Surely they couldn't be too far away, she decided, not with the house left open like this? And not when Rachel had known exactly when to expect her.

The thought occurred to her that perhaps there had been some business crisis. Or, her frown suddenly deepened, might something have happened to Katie?

Puzzled, she searched her address book for Rachel's office number and put a call through.

But even that failed to elicit a response.

Glancing at her watch Eve gauged her time. She could afford to wait a short while longer.

* * *

HALF AN HOUR LATER, when Rachel still had not returned and with no response to her repeated attempts to call, Eve knew she couldn't delay any further. Under no circumstances could she take the chance of missing her flight back to Sydney for tonight's vital program.

Heart heavy with a terrible sense of despair and regret, she started the car and made her way back to the airport.

A tragic tattoo beat in her mind. *Forgive me, Rachel... Forgive me, please.*

* * *

AT THE NETWORK there was a palpable sense of tension among those crew in the know. They were on the verge of breaking one of the country's biggest stories and thanks to the continual publicity of the last few days, anticipation among both the public and rival media was at fever pitch.

By the time she arrived at her desk Eve found a pile of telephone messages ... among them a number from Mark. She rang him at once.

'I'll call you back,' he said. Not even at this late date were they taking any chances with the line.

'Where were you, darling?' he asked now. 'I've been trying to contact you all afternoon. Just to say I'm thinking of you and how much I admire your courage.'

Eve's heart quickened. She loved him for his kindness and concern and told him so. Then, as succinctly as possible, she explained about her abortive trip north.

'I just had to, Mark. I hated the thought of her having to find out without any warning at all. But ... I didn't get a chance to see her. She never showed up at the appointed time.'

Mark could hear her despair and misery. 'You tried, darling,' he did his best to comfort her, 'you tried – and maybe in time, when she finds that out, it'll help in some small way.'

And then there was no time for anything else. The countdown until the show went to air had begun.

37

The floor manager held his hand aloft and counted off the seconds. 'Three … two... one.'

Eve fought to control her breathing.

They were on air. She faced the camera.

'Good evening, Australia. Tonight we present a very special edition of *Taylor Made*. The entire program will be taken up with our in-depth report on one of this country's biggest cover-ups. The scandal reaches its tentacles into the very heart of our society and involves leading businessmen, politicians, public servants, and our intelligence forces ...'

Ninety seconds later Eve Taylor was revealing Leo Symons' murderous secret to a stunned nation. And the role he had played in her own past.

Even as she spoke the network switchboard began to pulse with light.

In Surfers Paradise, Tony Nugent and members of the federal police were in the elevator making their way to Leo Symons' penthouse apartment. They carried a warrant for his arrest.

In the nation's capital, telephone lines started to run red hot between public servants and politicians as well as present and former ASIO employees.

In newspaper offices around the country editors were furiously altering their headlines.

* * *

IN THE LIVING room of his family home Hugh Rolfe sat in stupefied shock, his eyes glued to the television set. His whisky-addled brain was struggling to comprehend what he was hearing. Leo Symons... Nazi murderer... clear-cut evidence...

But one thing was numbingly clear.

Eve Taylor was the child who had been born of Marianne Walenska...

* * *

THERE WAS a sense of haven in the hinterland cottage. As Rachel closed the bedroom door, she hoped that Katie would soon be asleep.

Pouring herself a vodka, a strong one, she carried it through to the wood-paneled living room. The house was deathly quiet and she felt the urgent need of some distraction. Crossing the room, she switched on the small portable television set.

"Taylor Made" had just begun.

Moments later Rachel felt herself turn to stone. She barely noticed when the glass dropped from her frozen fingers and shattered into smithereens on the tiled floor.

* * *

EVE WAS TREMBLING. Beneath the heavy television makeup her face was bloodless. But the red camera light had gone off and she knew it was over.

An eerie silence filled the studio. There was none of the usual banter or comment from the crew.

She stood up from her desk and almost fell. Her knees felt as if the bones inside her had melted.

Then, somewhere in the darkness beyond the lights, someone

began to clap softly. Others joined in. Their tribute said they understood what Eve Taylor had just faced.

As she walked across the studio floor all Eve could do was nod her thanks. She didn't trust herself to speak.

And there thank God, pushing his way through the heavy doors, was Mark – accompanied by Ty Cameron. A moment later she was in the comforting embrace of her lover's arms.

'It's all right, darling. It's all right,' Mark whispered as he held her tight.

Ty Cameron was patting her shoulder. 'It's over, Eve. No one in this country can doubt your courage. Go home now.' He threw an enquiring glance at Mark over his anchorwoman's head.

Mark Delaney nodded his response. The producer knew Eve Taylor was in good hands.

* * *

MARK TOOK HER HOME. While Eve put a quick call through to Janet he poured them both a drink. Then they went to bed. Neither sought to make love; it was a moment for comfort against the dark demons of the past.

* * *

EARLY THE NEXT morning Mark bent over the bed and kissed her goodbye. 'I'll call you later, sweetheart.'

Eve blinked awake, her head felt heavy after a restless night. But reaching up she circled Mark's neck with her bare arms. 'Thank you, darling... For everything.'

As he headed into the city Mark was listening to the ABC news.

It was the lead story.

Jesus...

His heart raced as he listened to the details. For a moment he found it almost impossible to believe what he was hearing.

He knew he had to let her know. Before anyone else did.

* * *

'BUT *HOW? WHEN?*'

Eve was jolted instantly awake. Her mind spun as she tried to piece together what Mark was telling her. Pushing back the covers she jerked out of bed and moved agitatedly around the room.

'Some time yesterday. They're still trying to pinpoint it. In Rachel's house.'

'Rachel's...' Her voice was a dry whisper. It had happened in Rachel's home some time yesterday.

Mark was explaining the details. 'Rachel wasn't there when you arrived because she'd already left for the hinterland. It was the housekeeper who found the body – first thing this morning.'

Eve's mind was racing. 'Is there a chance -? I mean, could it have been suicide?' She was wondering if, in spite of all their precautions, Leo Symons might have somehow found out about the program.

'Absolutely not,' Mark answered quickly. 'Stab wounds to chest and face. A "frenzied attack" was how the cops described it.'

He heard her sharp intake of breath. 'Listen, darling,' his voice was suddenly crisp, professional. 'I'm on my way back to you. Don't answer the phone. To anyone.'

It was only Rachel she wanted to talk to. But despite her repeated attempts, in the riverside mansion her call went unanswered.

Eve hung up.

* * *

BY THE TIME she let Mark into the house Eve had seen the report on the television news. Already she'd been forced to take the telephone off the hook.

'Oh, God, Mark...' Her face was a mask of shock as they moved through to the living room.

'Eve, the cops are bound to discover you were at the house yesterday. We mightn't have much time. Tell me again *exactly* what happened.'

* * *

Two hours later, Eve Taylor, accompanied by her lawyer Mark Delaney, was making a statement at Darlinghurst Police Station.

When she emerged the media were waiting. This was the sort of story no one could keep under wraps.

It was impossible for a program like "Taylor Made" to ignore the astonishing aftermath to its previous day's story. As she faced the cameras again that evening Eve found herself in the bizarre position of once more featuring in her own report.

'According to police, who are still trying to pinpoint the exact time of the murder, there is a very real chance that at the time I was present at Rachel Symons's home Leo Symons was already lying dead in the upstairs bedroom.'

Solemnly she faced the camera and signed off.

It was Rachel's anguish she was thinking of as the credits began to roll.

* * *

She was in her dressing room, having her make-up removed, when a white-faced Ty Cameron barged in. He was followed by two close-faced men in suits, and their bulk filled the confined space.

'Eve–' Ty Cameron began on a desperate note.

But one of the men cut across him. 'We have to ask you to come with us, Miss Taylor. We have a warrant for your arrest. For the murder of Leo Symons.'

* * *

Defiantly she faced the cameras and [illegible] on.

* * *

"[illegible]," Cameron began [illegible].

38

Rachel knew that any moment she would wake up.
The nightmare would be over.

But the grim-faced detective sitting opposite only reinforced the fact that nothing would ever be the same again. She felt the strange giddiness that accompanies shock, her limbs were heavy and numb. When she moved or spoke it was as if her body belonged to someone else. The terrifying sequence of events had left her reeling. The horror of her father's death. The shock of the expose. The instant and unequivocal desertion of most of those she had called her "friends".

Staring past the policeman, Rachel fixed her eyes on the blue shimmer of the ocean beyond. She was still trying to come to terms with the knowledge that it was Eve who had broken the story of her father's past. Eve, whose own mother had been one of his tragic victims... To Rachel, the world and everyone in it seemed to have gone crazy.

Escorted back to the coast from her hinterland retreat, she had had the stomach churning task of identifying her father's body.

Never could Rachel have faced returning to the house. Instead, she had sought refuge in one of the company's own high-rise apartments where at least the sensation-hungry media could be kept at bay. Now her daughter, assisted by a light sedative was asleep in a bedroom down the hall while Rachel tried her best to answer the detective's questions.

A terrible pounding began in her head. She felt an overwhelming urge to scream at these three strange men to get out and leave her alone. But they were persisting, assaulting her with the latest horrifying development.

Eve...

Rigid with shock, Rachel listened as the balding officer in his too-tight suit explained that there had been an arrest.

'The evidence is circumstantial at this stage, Ms Symons but it all adds up.' The man cleared his throat. There's little question of a motive. Given what has come to light about her mother's past, Eve Taylor obviously bore a very definite grudge against your father. And she was in the vicinity at the time of his death ... the flight times prove that. As well, there's the fact that she was seen leaving the house ... one of your neighbors has made a sworn statement to that effect.'

The woman opposite offered no comment. The detective wondered how much, in her dazed state, she was actually managing to take in.

* * *

THE ARREST of Eve Taylor for the murder of Leo Symons caused a sensation as it made the late evening headlines. Her former media colleagues turned on one of their own in an almost cannibalistic orgy.

Among the more unrestrained, Greg Nelson, now a mere reporter, led the way.

The bitch's fall tasted very, very sweet.

* * *

HUGH ROLFE WAS EXULTANT. In so short a time his fortunes had reversed. Never in his wildest dreams would he have guessed that the high-profile television personality was his dead brother's child ... and now the stunning news of her arrest filled him with euphoria and new hope.

He knew his enemy now. Knew it was only Eve Taylor who stood between him and the salvation of Paradise Grove.

Patience, he comforted himself. Patience just a little while longer.

Eve Taylor was bound to be convicted. The genetic link was unmistakable. The same mental defect that had inspired Marianne Rolfe's murderous attack on his own mother had now surfaced in her daughter.

Madwomen both of them...

His dark eyes gleamed. In jail, how easily an 'accident' might be arranged. It happened all the time. No one could link anything to him.

And with Eve Taylor out of the way Paradise Grove would be his.

* * *

IN THE WINDOWLESS detention room of Darlinghurst Police Station Harry Bowman faced his famous client.

An acquaintance of the Delaney family all his professional career, he had responded at once to Mark Delaney's call for help. Eve Taylor would have to be extradited for trial. She'd need to be represented by someone who could practise on both sides of the border – and Harry fitted the bill.

It was the sort of case he could never have refused. He'd caught the first available flight south.

'We're working on the bail terms now, Ms Taylor,' he spoke with quiet confidence to the pale-faced woman. 'We'll have you out of here in no time.'

* * *

THE NUMBNESS HAD WORN off and Rachel shivered in shock. Her mind felt as chilled as her body. Wide awake she hugged her sleeping daughter close as the orange fingers of sunlight crept over the dark rim of the Pacific.

Tears slid down her cheeks as she thought of the woman who had done so much to blow her life apart.

She'll get off, she assured herself. They'll never be able to prove it.

* * *

MARK RANG Janet again first thing that morning.

'Harry Bowman managed to get an emergency court date, Janet. He's got her bail.' He injected his voice with as much confidence as he could muster. 'Now I'm going to get her out of sight of the media. They haven't sniffed you out up there yet, have they?'

'No... No.'

Mark heard the strain in Janet Byrne's voice and giving her a final word of encouragement he hung up. There was still so much to attend to.

* * *

SICK AND DAZED Janet walked through to the kitchen to make tea for herself and Marianne. She pulled herself together as she found Marianne already sitting at the breakfast table.

It was important to hide her distress, she told herself. Nothing must be allowed to disturb Marianne's equilibrium.

As she waited for the kettle to boil Janet found herself praying under her breath.

* * *

IT WAS mid-morning when Rachel arrived at Southport Police Station with her lawyer in tow. Her appearance shocked those who were used to seeing her as the elegant, immaculately groomed businesswoman. Devoid of make-up her skin seemed as lifeless as ancient parchment; her once shining eyes were blank and sunken, while her blonde hair hung limply to the collar of her crumpled shirt.

The duty sergeant stared as Rachel Symons and her lawyer were ushered through the reception area and into the interview room. Poor bitch, he thought to himself. What was happening now?

Carl Webber, Rachel's lawyer, nodded to the senior detective across the desk. The Coast was a small pond; everyone in the law knew everybody else.

'G'day, Bob.' He came straight to the point. 'We're here because my client, Rachel Symons, wishes to make a statement.'

The detective frowned. His gaze went to the jeans-clad woman who was sitting motionless, her eyes staring straight ahead.

Before the lawyer could say anything further Rachel Symons spoke up, her words resounding like a thunderclap.

'I'm here to plead guilty to the manslaughter of my father, Leo Symons.'

* * *

PANDEMONIUM BROKE LOOSE.

It seemed as if no other news, international or domestic, existed for the next forty-eight hours as the Australian media reeled from the astonishing, sensational, rapid-fire sequence of events.

Eve Taylor was to be released. Rachel Symons had admitted responsibility for her father's death.

And as the media pressure grew, the motive for the crime was revealed.

The businesswoman had entered her home to find Leo Symons sexually molesting her young daughter ... as once, it shockingly transpired, he had molested her.

As a mother, Rachel Symons response had been instinctive and primitive, born of the rage suppressed for years when her own trust and innocence had been betrayed – by a father whose lust knew no taboos.

It was the sight of that terrible crime being re-enacted with her own innocent child that had driven Rachel to do the unthinkable.

* * *

WIDE-EYED AND SHAKEN, Eve was throwing clothes into an overnight bag in the bedroom of her home.

She had been released from remand just a short time before. As she'd left the central Sydney Police Station she'd been forced to push her way through a forest of reporters, television cameras and microphones. Grim-facedly ignoring the fusillade of questions she'd finally reached the safety of Mark's car.

Now he was with her, waiting to drive her to the airport. Rachel needed her, she told him. Eve was sure of that.

As delicately as possible Mark had tried to warn her.

'She'll be in a highly emotional state, darling. You were responsible for the expose... There's every chance she might hate the sight of you now.'

Eve stopped what she was doing and looked at him with glistening eyes. 'Maybe you're right, Mark. But I can't rest until I let her know I'll do anything to help her and Katie.'

He heard the utter determination in her voice. In the last forty-eight hours she had endured so much. They both had. But nothing would have stopped him loving her.

* * *

As THE BREATH-TAKING events continued to make headlines around the nation, the news of Eve Taylor's unexpected release changed Hugh Rolfe's euphoria into cold hard rage. For a few short hours his future had been bright again. He had felt giddy with the rocketing surge of hope.

Oh no, bitch. His face contorted with anger. *You're not going to stop me now...*

39

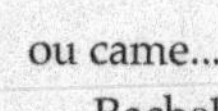
'You came...'

Rachel stared in tremulous wonder as Eve was shown into the detention cell.

'I had to.' Eve tried to hide her shock at Rachel's appearance.

And then they were in each other's arms, clinging in silent elemental need. This was no time for apology, explanation, regret.

Finally, drawing back, Eve looked into her friend's tragic eyes and spoke with quiet confidence. 'You're going to get out of this, darling. No court could convict you in the circumstances. I'm going to stay with Katie until you get bail and then you're both getting out of here with me.'

Rachel drew comfort from the other woman's determination and strength.

'It's Katie I'm so worried about, Eve. After what happened...' A sob caught in her throat. 'I ... I always tried to ensure he was never alone with her. But that morning I got a call; something urgent to see to at the office before we went away. I didn't intend to be out of the house long; I had no idea he was going to drop in. When I got back I found him... on the bed... Katie was naked and he was trying...'

Her voice broke and she covered her face with her hands as her mind replayed the ugliness of the scene. The scene that brought back so vividly her own childhood. When without a mother's protection she too had been at his mercy.

But Rachel still couldn't remember how her hands had found the sharp-pointed scissors...

Eve was hugging her again. 'It's over, Rachel. It's over. He can never hurt Katie or anyone else again. I'll keep her with me until you're out of here.'

Rachel raised her mottled, tear-stained face. 'And he did it to your mother too... all those years ago... Robbed her of her youth – her innocence – her family...'

For a long moment the two women held each other's gaze. The man known as Max Klauser had scarred so many lives.

And then it was time to go. At the door Eve turned to look once more into that tragic face whose loveliness had masked her own secret pain.

* * *

THE CHILD WAS BEING CARED for by a policewoman in the high-rise apartment. She was bewildered, shocked, seemed barely comprehending of the nightmare which had engulfed her.

Crouching down Eve put her hands on the girl's narrow shoulders. 'Katie, darling, this is all going to work out, I promise. Mummy will be home soon but until then I'm going to look after you.'

Katie looked at her with wild, bewildered eyes. 'But will Mummy...'

Eve leaned forward and kissed her. 'Mummy's going to be fine. She'll join us very soon, I promise you.'

* * *

AND SHE DID. By ten the next morning bail was arranged and Rachel was brought by police escort to the apartment.

As she watched her friend hug her weeping daughter Eve knew she had to take them somewhere where they would all be safe.

* * *

THANKS TO MARK'S intervention the authorities at Sydney airport allowed them to slip through without attracting the attention of the media.

He drove them straight to the cottage in the Blue Mountains, where Janet was waiting.

As they walked into the living room the older woman could barely contain her tearful emotions. Her eyes were on the beautiful blonde child.

How could he? How *could* he? The monster. And his own daughter too...

Eve began to make the introductions when suddenly there was a sound from somewhere behind her.

Marianne, disturbed perhaps by the arrival of the car, had woken from her usual afternoon nap. She stood in the doorway and her eyes were riveted on Rachel Symons's daughter.

The expression on her mother's face took Eve's breath away. It was as if she had seen a ghost, she thought in awe.

The others had noticed too. No one moved as they watched Marianne hold out thin, shaky arms to the pretty blonde-haired child.

Slowly Katie Symons moved forward. As she felt herself enfolded in that tender embrace, she began to cry and then tears were also rolling down Marianne's own wrinkled cheeks.

In a way none of them understood, Rachel's daughter had somehow prompted the first evidence of emotional response in Marianne.

* * *

'I'VE TOLD Ty I can do it.'

Eve was talking to Mark as he drove her back to the city. With Rachel and Katie safe at the cottage she was determined to get back to the program.

Mark hadn't been so sure. 'So much has happened in such a short time, Eve. Don't you think you should take a break? At least until–'

'Mark, it's not just me – there's the crew, researchers, a whole team who can't just be put on hold indefinitely. I can't let them – or Ty – down.'

And so, less then twenty-four hours later, they were heading into Sydney.

* * *

IN THE EVENT that any media might still be on watch he dropped her off in a lane which allowed side entrance to the house.

With the engine still running Mark said, 'I've got a meeting down south this evening, darling. Probably be back too late to see you. Will you be okay?'

She leaned over to kiss him. 'Of course. Everything's going to work out, Mark. I'm sure of it.' There was a new note of certainty in her voice.

As she started to slide out of the car Mark reached out and grasped her hand. 'You're an amazing woman, Eve.' His eyes held hers and he spoke with quiet intensity. 'I'm never going to let you go.'

* * *

WHEN EVE TURNED up at the studio that evening the mood among her colleagues was strange mixed relief at having their anchorwoman back, awkwardness at the knowledge of what she had just endured and fear that their winning formula might have been dealt a death blow by the events of the last few days.

But by the time the program came to an end there was nothing but admiration for the woman who had shrugged off her ordeal to face the nation without flinching.

Ty Cameron joined in the congratulations. 'The switchboard's going crazy again, Eve. Ninety-nine per cent of the callers are behind you all the way. They admire your courage and wish you nothing but good luck.'

Eve felt her emotions stirred. Whatever else, she thought with affection, Australians could always be counted on to support the underdog.

Even one who was just a "refo's" daughter.

* * *

The media game had been played out.

With Eve's reappearance on air it suddenly seemed against the rules for her rivals to afford her free publicity. When she arrived back at her home there was no sign of any waiting media.

She pushed the remote on the dashboard of her car and the garage roller door slid slowly upwards.

That was when the man waiting in the dark made his move.

40

Eve caught a flicker of movement as she slid from behind the wheel.

A shadow…slipping into the garage just as the door began to roll closed.

'Who's that? Who's there?' Her voice held a note of exasperation. Surely the media weren't still gunning for her?

And then a prickle of fear ran up her spine. A solitary figure emerged from behind the car.

It was Hugh Rolfe.

'What do you want?' She confronted him in shock. 'How dare you come here!'

'Now I know who you are, you and I have to talk.' By the light of the bare overhead bulb the man she hated moved closer.

'Get out! I have nothing to say to you.' Her fear ebbed as anger took its place.

'I'm your uncle, Eve.' His voice held an ingratiating whine that made her flesh crawl. 'Charles was my brother. We've got to talk this thing through... Paradise Grove. We can be partners. We'll find some other developer. Anyone'd jump at the chance. Both of us can make a packet.' The words were slurred, running into one another, and Eve realized the man was drunk.

'Get out! Before I call the police!'

She swung to move away but he scuttled forward and his hand gripped her shoulder. 'Listen to me! It's my last chance. Paradise Grove is all that can save me.' He was gibbering now, begging. 'Surely you don't want your father's family ruined...'

Eve could hardly believe the man's brazen arrogance, his shameless insolence. She tried to shrug off his hold but his grip was too strong. 'My father wanted nothing to do with any of you – and neither do I. Do you think I don't know exactly what you and your family did to my mother? How dare you imagine I'd want to raise a finger to help you now.'

But the wheedling tone was still there. 'Be reasonable, Eve. Please. Let's just talk about this...'

With an effort she wrenched herself free and rounded on him in cold anger. 'Nothing's going to change my mind! Can't you understand that? As far as I'm concerned you're paying for everything you did to my mother all those years ago! Do you think I don't know about your own particular role? Forcing yourself on her, bringing back the horror she'd already endured... Let me tell you,' Eve spat out the final words, 'I've done nothing but dream of the day I could finally see the death throes of the Rolfe family...'

She turned to go.

He hit her from behind. With all the pent-up rage and frustration of a man who saw his future slipping away.

Caught unawares Eve stumbled, half-turned. Before she could recover her balance Hugh Rolfe's hands were around her neck, squeezing, choking, forcing the life out of the only obstacle that could keep him from what he desired more than anything in the world.

In a ferocious struggle Eve twisted, kicked out, tore at the clamp around her windpipe, but her attacker had weight and strength on his side. Under the relentless squeezing pressure her struggles weakened.

And then blackness flooded her brain.

* * *

Breathing heavily from the unfamiliar physical effort Hugh Rolfe stared at the crumpled form on the garage floor. Trembling, he bent over for a closer inspection and the sweet taste of bile filled his mouth.

Eve Taylor was unconscious – but still breathing.

Panic made his bowels turn to water. Somehow through the buzz of alcohol in his brain he realized what he'd done – and what would happen next.

If she came to, nothing could save him...

Self-preservation his only instinct, he forced himself to touch her again and found the car keys in her pocket. Panting with fear, he fumbled them into the ignition and started the motor.

Her handbag was on the floor and he scooped it up. Assault and robbery ... that's what it would look like, his befuddled brain reasoned. Happening so quickly that she hadn't even had time to turn off the engine...

The garage was small; in no time it'd be over. No one would be able to prove a thing.

Moments later Hugh Rolfe was stumbling away in the darkness to where he had left his own vehicle.

* * *

At the cottage Janet and Rachel were settled in front of the television. One of the late-night news programs, quick to follow up on recent sensational events, had put together a special on survivors of the Holocaust who had settled in Australia.

'Are you sure you want to watch this, my dear?' Janet threw an anxious glance at the woman who sat beside her.

Face strained, Rachel nodded. Without looking at Janet she said in a whisper, 'I have to know... I want to know what he did so I can hate him until the day I die...'

The program began. Neither woman dreamed how it would end.

* * *

MARK WONDERED if it was too late to disturb her. The work that had taken him out of town hadn't kept him nearly as long as he'd expected. He figured he'd be back in Sydney just before ten.

But maybe tonight it would be best to leave her alone. Let her sleep off the trauma of these last incredible days.

* * *

FROM THE CORNER of her eye, Janet slipped a fearful glance at her visitor. How could the poor woman stand it? she wondered fearfully.

Rachel Symons' eyes never left the flickering screen. Arms clasped protectively around her she sat with unnatural stiffness in her chair.

The image of the man who had started life as Max Klauser filled the screen. The ruthless murderer of so many innocents...

The official file photograph of a uniformed Klauser had been reproduced in an underground Jewish newsletter, a copy of which had been retained by one of the survivors. The voice-over was by an eye-witness to one of Klauser's atrocities, and the enduring strength of the man's emotions was obvious.

'1 saw with my own eyes what this murderer did. I was a young teacher in a small country school outside of Krakow, the area within Klauser's jurisdiction. He entered the classroom that day and ordered the children to tell him which ones had fathers in the Resistance. When they refused to talk, or were simply too terrified to find the words to deny his allegations, he pulled out his revolver and shot half a dozen of them where they stood...'

The scream resounded in the small living room. Janet jumped, the hairs on the back of her neck rising in shock.

Marianne was standing in the doorway to the room. Her body shook in the thin, full-length nightdress and her blue eyes were riveted in stark terror on the face on the screen.

Before either woman could reach her she gave a soft moan and slumped to the floor.

* * *

MARK COULD NEVER SAY LATER what made him change his mind.

About to turn into his own street, at the last moment he felt unable to resist his instincts.

I want to see her, hold her, be with her, he told himself.

* * *

THE DOCTOR WAS THERE in less than five minutes. To Mark it seemed like a lifetime as he blew breath into her body, willed her to come back to him.

Oh, my darling, don't leave me. Not when I've waited so long to find you...

* * *

'SHE'LL BE OKAY NOW.' The doctor was reassuring as Mark walked him down the hallway to the front door. 'Another five or so minutes and it might have been touch and go, but you found her in time.' He raised an enquiring eyebrow. 'You're calling the police, of course?' Mark nodded.

Hugh Rolfe...she had managed to tell him that.

* * *

THE COPS WERE TAKING their time, he thought testily as he sat beside the bed. She was murmuring in her sleep and as she moved restlessly against the pillow Mark could see the ring of contusions forming around her neck. Anger twisted inside him. The bastard was going to pay for this...

Nerves already on edge, he jumped as the ringing of the telephone broke the silence.

Who the hell... ? It was almost midnight, for God's sake.

He let it ring. When the answering machine finally cut in it was Janet's voice he heard.

'Eve, I need to talk to you. Urgently. Call me as soon as you possibly can. Something – something remarkable has happened.'

A moment later the police knocked on the door.

* * *

IT WAS ONLY LATER, just as he was about to step into the shower, that he suddenly remembered the telephone message.

* * *

CURIOUS, Eve immediately put a call through to the cottage. She listened in disbelief as Janet quickly explained.

'She's still sleeping, darling. But last night your mother began to talk. Whatever barrier she had inside her was broken when she saw Klauser's photograph on the screen. Over and over again she spoke about the night he burst into her grandparents' house.'

Eve's hand was gripped tightly around the receiver. 'Did ... did she realize that Rachel was Klauser's daughter?'

'Of course not.' The older woman was finding it difficult to hold on to her emotions. 'Eve, darling, I think you should get here as quickly as possible.'

* * *

SHE DRESSED HASTILY, carefully knotting a scarf to hide the marks on her neck. Later she could explain what had happened with Rolfe. Just now Eve wanted nothing more than to be by her mother's side.

Mark made a quick call to his office and they left at once. As they headed out of Sydney, Eve sat in a fever of impatience and excitement.

* * *

JANET ACCOMPANIED her into the bedroom where Marianne was sitting propped up among the pillows, Katie beside her. She looked pale but calm as she held tightly to the little girl's hand. 'Such a lovely child,' she murmured, 'so innocent...'

Eve's heart soared as she heard the magic sound of her mother's voice. This was the moment she had been waiting for, praying for, for so long.

Almost immediately euphoria was followed by confusion. Across the bed she exchanged glances with Janet. How much would Marianne understand? Did she realize that Eve was her daughter? How were they going to help her come to terms with both the present and the past?

But it was Marianne herself who took the initiative. Eyes rarely moving from Katie's face she began haltingly, softly, to talk. At last, and after so many years, she revealed what had really happened with the man named Max Klauser.

* * *

HALF AN HOUR later Eve emerged from her mother's room, her expression incredulous.

Trance-like she moved through the house until she found Mark and Rachel, who were chatting quietly on the verandah.

'Darling?' Mark looked at her expectantly as he rose quickly out of his seat. 'What is it? Something's happened...'

Eve tried to speak. Her lips moved but they made no sound. She had eyes only for Rachel.

'Eve... what's the matter?' Alarmed, Rachel too was on her feet and hurried to put an arm around her friend. 'Darling, what happened in there?'

'Rachel...' Eve swallowed, tried again. 'Rachel, there is every possibility that you and I are half-sisters ...'

* * *

IT WAS IMPORTANT, the psychiatrist made clear, to minimize the shock. The more gradually Marianne came to realize her relationship with Eve, Rachel and Katie, the better.

As they recognized later it was Katie who had turned the first key. The grandchild who looked so much like Marianne herself at the same age. The shock of recognizing Klauser had done the rest.

Over the days that followed, Marianne's mind broke the final barriers to the past until the last pieces of the puzzle were fitted together.

When Klauser had fled with her to Germany he had known she was pregnant with his child. The pregnancy had been confirmed a month before the night the soldiers had so brutally assaulted her.

The baby was born in the tumbledown gardener's cottage in the grounds of Klauser's Berlin home and Hanna Klauser, unable to conceive herself, as Marianne discovered, had had no problem in accepting her husband's child.

The little girl was just a week old when Klauser sent his wife and the child ahead of him to the safety of the Allied zone.

He would "take care" of the mother, he said.

Screaming in anguish Marianne had had her baby daughter torn from her arms. Beaten senseless, her face reduced to a bloodied pulp, she had been left to die while Klauser fled to assume his new identity among the anonymous stateless victims of the war.

Only fate had ensured Marianne's survival.

And fate had brought the two blood sisters face to face.

EPILOGUE

It was the sort of day that made it easy to understand why they called it Paradise: radiant sunshine, sweet, clean air, a sky so blue and expansive it merged seamlessly into the ocean.

There was an air of excitement among the VIPs, official guests and invited media who mingled on the vivid springy lawns that edged the curved lagoon.

Within the hour Charles Park would be officially opened.

Emerging in just over two years from the ill-fated Paradise Grove, the project had been a runaway success. Built around a seven-hectare lagoon and championship golf course, the elegant, tasteful residences avoided flamboyance and ugly excess. Low lying and rarely breaking the tree line, the development blended easily into its bushland setting, earning it accolades as Australia's most environmentally sensitive resort-cum-residential development.

Yet it was the history that lay at the heart of the project that had really captured the public imagination. Few in Australia would have been unaware of the story. It was the sort of tale that had film producers worldwide reaching for their check books – the scandals and tragedies, the hatred and deceit, and finally the reunion decades later of three women who would claim their legacy of love.

* * *

'HOW ARE YOU FEELING?' Eve smiled as she asked the question of her half-sister. They were standing together in the country club foyer, waiting for the official entourage to arrive.

Rachel grinned. 'Same as you, I'd guess. Excited. Nervous. Hardly able to believe we made it to deadline.'

'Hey, come on, darling,' Eve teased, 'the way you used that Polish charm on those contractors they'd have worked twenty-eighty-hour days if you'd asked them.'

Rachel laughed. It was a sound of pure, untainted joy that warmed Eve's heart.

We've all come through it, she told herself. Mother, Rachel, Katie, Janet and myself. We've all survived.

It had taken time and it hadn't been easy. None of them had been able to think too far ahead until Rachel's case had come before the courts.

A suspended sentence... It was what they had all been praying for.

As soon as the verdict was known, Katie's nightmares had become less frequent. And now, thank God, thought Eve, she was a normal happy teenager.

* * *

RACHEL'S HEALING had taken longer. The shock of her father's past continued to haunt her. Especially with the ongoing media pressure for a Royal Commission to investigate how known former Nazis had been allowed access into Australia. The issue dominated the news for months and inevitably several distinguished grey heads looked set to roll.

As Eve saw the physical and emotional toll the tragic events were taking she knew there was only one sure way to get her sister back on track.

She discussed her idea first with Marianne. The sheer joy of being able to communicate with her mother still overcame her.

'I think it is a wonderful proposal, my darling.' Marianne looked at her lovely daughter with soft smiling eyes. 'And I have no doubt that your father would see it that way too.'

And that was how the Charles Park project was born. Rachel would have a chance to move back into the world she knew best. Her energy and drive would return when it had a focus again.

And now Stage One was complete.

It was a triumph of the spirit for them all.

* * *

THE LAST RAYS of the sun lingered on the sea as the small party sat outside on the lawn enjoying pre-dinner drinks. Behind them two rustic residences blended into the trees.

The hard work of the day was over. The opening ceremony had gone without a hitch. Tonight there would be other festivities, but not for the family. They had retreated to their own haven.

These few hectares were a part of the original property they had kept for themselves. Accessible only by water, this private Eden had the added buffer of a broad expanse of environmental parkland which had been an essential feature of the development. Parkland that also included the Marianne Walenska residence for disadvantaged children.

* * *

AS SHE LISTENED to the soft lapping of the water at the edge of the lawn Eve felt sure her father would have approved what had been shaped from his legacy.

She turned, and in the fading light looked at her mother's face. The peace and happiness she saw reflected there told her that Marianne had found her sanctuary at last. Together, she and Janet would be able to live out their lives in this wonderful place.

'Can I get you another drink, Grandma?' Katie, tanned, long-limbed, beautiful, was crouching beside her grandmother.

'No thank you, my darling. But why don't you go inside and play something for us? This time of day seems to call for a little Chopin, don't you think?'

'Not hard rock?' her granddaughter teased.

From where she sat on the grass, head resting back against Tony Nugent's knees, Rachel groaned, 'Katie, you have no sense of the romantic!'

'Okay, okay...' With a grin and roll of her eyes the girl stood up and made her way towards the house.

'You all right, sweetheart? The day didn't tire you out too much?' Mark spoke softly to his wife.

Eve moved a hand to pat her belly. 'No. Junior's taking it all in his stride. Obviously thrives on gala occasions!'

She was five months pregnant. When she'd told her mother she was about to have another grandchild Marianne's eyes had filled with happy tears. 'It seems,' she whispered, 'as if God is trying to make up for everything in the quickest possible time...'

Now, as she sat beside her husband, Eve pondered the immense changes that the last two years had brought. Professionally as well as personally.

She had wanted time for her child and husband, time to be with her mother and Janet in their declining years and time for Rachel and Katie. When her contract for "Taylor Made" came up for renewal she'd put her proposal to Ty. A series of special projects was what she had in mind. And Ty Cameron had agreed. Eve knew she was lucky. She would have the best of all worlds.

Now, as the shadows began to lengthen across the lawn, the lovely melody of the polonaise broke the quiet chatter around her.

Leaning over, Eve reached for her mother's frail hand. As Marianne turned, her daughter saw the faint gleam of tears in those blue eyes which had seen so much.

'And your father is with us too...' Marianne whispered.

Eve nodded, not trusting herself to speak.

The best any of them could hope for, she thought, was that life would stay as good as it was at that very moment.

AUTHOR'S NOTE:

If you enjoyed this story I would appreciate it if you could leave me a review!

Reviews are like gold to authors these days; they help me write better and they help other readers find the books they love!

I would also love to hear from you at author@jenniferbacia.com .

Visit my website http: / / www.jenniferbacia.com for information on my other best-selling suspense thrillers, *Indecent Ambition*, *Whisper Her Name*, *Never Forget Me* and others.

Happy Reading!

Jennifer Bacia.

ABOUT THE AUTHOR

Jennifer Bacia (pronounced 'batcher') has lived in Rome, London and Los Angeles and traveled widely in the Far East and Europe. Her first novel was bought for a record–breaking advance and was an international best-seller. The author of dozens of short stories, she has had her own newspaper and magazine by-line in leading publications, and also written for television.

Apart from suspense thrillers, Jennifer also writes contemporary, fast-paced romantic suspense. Titles include *Everything to Lose, Best Kept Secrets* and *One Door Closes.*

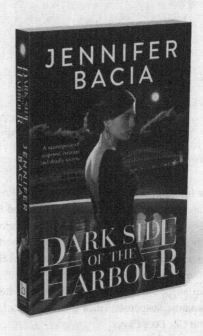

JENNIFER
BACIA
A VERY
PUBLIC
SCANDAL

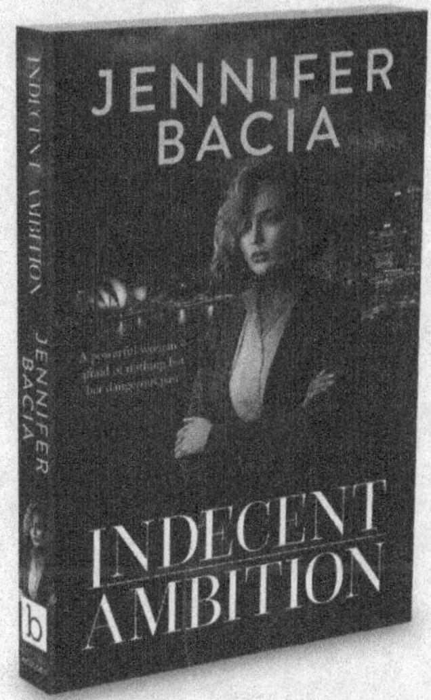
JENNIFER
BACIA
INDECENT
AMBITION

JENNIFER
BACIA
WHISPER
HER NAME

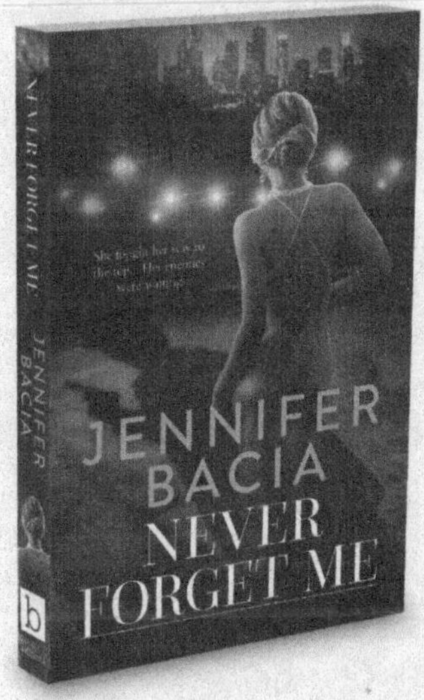
JENNIFER
BACIA
NEVER
FORGET ME

booktopia
editions

Against backdrops of London, Paris, Warsaw and Sydney, Marianne, a beautiful European refugee, marries into a wealthy establishment family. But a mystery lies at the heart of the unusual union.

Haunted by her past, and rejected by a powerful mother-in-law who is determined to destroy this nobody who has 'trapped' her son, Marianne is pushed to the edge. In the scandal that follows, she is forced to pay a shocking price.

Almost three decades later, Marianne's daughter Eve, a high profile media star, is tormented by the mystery of her parents' past. When her search for the truth finds her charged with murder, Eve's only hope lies in betraying the woman who has become her closest confidante.

Jennifer Bacia has lived in Rome, London and Los Angeles. Her first novel was bought for a record-breaking advance and was an international best-seller. Jennifer is the author of 9 novels, including her latest release *Dark Side of the Harbour*, two works of non-fiction and dozens of short stories. She currently lives in Brisbane, Australia.